What Women Want

Fanny Blake was a publisher for many years, editing both fiction and non-fiction before becoming a freelance journalist and writer. She has written various non-fiction titles, acted as ghost writer for a number of celebrities, and is also Books Editor of *Woman & Home* magazine. *What Women Want* is her first novel.

Praise for *What Women Want*:

'Wise, warm, funny and wonderfully observant.'

Cathy Kelly

'Women take heart. Here is a novelist who understands exactly the comedy, absurdities and frustrations of your lives. A delicious read.'

Elizabeth Buchan

'*What Women Want* is like having a long, funny and fascinating conversation with your very best friends and becoming deeply involved in their lives, families and love affairs.'

Penny Vincenzi

'Full of insight with a sharp wit, this is about real women in realistic situations, entertaining and thought provoking. Kept me reading far too late.'

Katie Fforde

'Smart, funny, and uncannily like having your mind read.'

R...ie Thomas

FANNY BLAKE

What Women Want

blue door

Blue Door
An imprint of HarperCollins*Publishers*
77–85 Fulham Palace Road,
Hammersmith, London W6 8JB

www.harpercollins.co.uk

A Paperback Original 2011
1

A catalogue record for this book
is available from the British Library

ISBN: 978-0-00- 735909-7

Set in Minion by Palimpsest Book Production Limited,
Grangemouth, Stirlingshire

Printed and bound in Great Britain by
Clays Ltd, St Ives plc

Peterborough City Council	
60000 0000 21795	
Askews & Holts	May-2011
	£7.99

To Robin, Matt, Nick and Spike

ACKNOWLEDGEMENTS

Huge thanks are due to Clare Alexander, peerless agent and friend; to Patrick Janson-Smith, Laura Deacon, the rest of the fantastic team at HarperCollins, and Hazel Orme, for their enthusiasm and support. Thank you, too, to Lizy Buchan, without whose encouragement I would never have got to the end; to Julie Sharman and Naureen Bhatti, for their advice on things medical (any mistakes are mine alone); to Sue Fletcher, for things culinary; to Jane Turnbull and Dotti Irving for their unfailing support; and to all my women friends, who inspired me and gave me a necessary kick when things got tough.

1

'I'll get out here, thanks.'

Bea cursed as she stepped out of the taxi into the sweltering chaos of Shaftesbury Avenue. July was always hell in central London. She could feel her trousers sticking to the back of her legs. She was already five minutes late and the traffic had slowed to a virtual standstill. If only her meeting had finished on time, she would have reached the restaurant first, just as she'd planned. She wanted to be sitting calmly, waiting, so that she could size up her lunch date as he crossed the restaurant to join her. But Jade, one of the editorial directors, had made such a fuss about which photograph was used on the jacket of an autobiography by another twenty-something D-list loser of whom Bea had never heard that the meeting had overrun by nearly half an hour.

The summer heat was draped over the London streets like a thick blanket. The slight but insistent throb of a headache was an unpleasant reminder that she had drunk too much the night before. Had she? She tested herself by running through the exact route the taxi had taken home from the party. Mmm. Slightly hazy. As she picked her way through the pedestrians, walking as fast as she could without actually running, she could feel a familiar prickling warmth rising from somewhere in her chest and spreading up into her face, around the back of her neck and down into her arms. Not now, please. She had at least to arrive looking like a woman in control. Like a woman who was desirable. Not like a menopausal wreck.

She slowed down, trying to restore her cool. He – she'd been told his name was Mark Carpenter – must have paid £125 for this date too. That was the deal when you signed up to Let's Have Lunch, a discreet dating agency for the over-forties. Having been interviewed by a woman in her twenties who, given her immaculate streaked blonde hair, flawless skin and dazzling if vacuous smile, couldn't have any idea what it was like for someone her mother's age to be looking for love – or even just sex, Bea wasn't choosy – you parted with £750 in return for a pitying glance of appraisal and the guarantee of being 'matched' with six possible partners. Six! Any of us should be so lucky, thought Bea. Yes, he'd wait. Dwelling on the fact that she was about to rendezvous with a man about whom she knew nothing apart from his name, she almost tripped over a knot of American tourists turning their *A—Z*s upside down as they tried to match the streets of Soho with the map.

Cantina Italia was just up Frith Street, past all the cafés overflowing into the street with tables occupied by count-less young men in white sleeveless T-shirts and girls wearing spaghetti-strap tops. If only she still had the body to carry off so few clothes with such aplomb. That was the trouble with being a few (OK, more than a few) pounds overweight.

She still cared about what she looked like so wore clothes to cover up and ended up too hot, unwilling to rid herself of the layers that should be so easy to strip off and reveal all. Oh, where was the 'longer, leaner, looser' her that she'd been promised would begin to emerge after only ten Pilates sessions? So far all she'd managed to do was rick her back when attempting a new exercise on the reformer.

She was aware that the cream linen suit, which had started the day so well, had lost its original snap. As the morning had gone on, her look had deteriorated from the fashionably creased to the unfashionably unironed. But short of taking a forty-five-minute detour up to Oxford Street to buy something new, there was nothing she could do about that now. Remembering all she'd been taught, she pulled in her stomach – skirt would hang better – and held herself upright. 'Imagine a string pulling you up from the top of your head,' echoed the voice of her Pilates teacher, as Bea pushed open the restaurant door, aware that the imaginary string must have melted in the heat.

The restaurant wasn't wide but it stretched back beyond a central table carrying a large arrangement of twirling bamboo, brilliant orange birds-of-paradise and scarlet ginger blossoms. She couldn't see a man sitting alone. Maybe she'd got there first after all. Good. That meant she had time to go to the Ladies and check the make-up she'd jerkily repaired in the back of the cab on the way there (almost stabbing herself in the eye with her mascara) as well as compose herself. There was no point in being nervous, she reassured herself. It was only lunch, not . . .

'Let's have lunch?' The voice came from behind her.

Bea turned to see an effete young man in a loose white shirt of the finest linen, the sleeves rolled up, well-cut dark trousers and expensive shoes. Surely this wasn't him – a more perfect 'match' than she could ever have hoped for. Or was a younger man picking her up before she and Mark Carpenter had even had a chance to sit down?

'I'm sorry?' Say it again, please.

'Let's have lunch?' he repeated, with the slightest of smiles, encouraging her to agree.

She hadn't misheard. Unsure what to say, she tried a rusty attempt at a flirtatious smile. 'Normally I'd love to, but unfortunately I'm meeting someone. Another time, perhaps.'

'No, no, no.' His face spoke volumes. Of course he wouldn't make such an obvious pass at her. She was old enough to be his mother, for God's sake. 'I meant the table booking,' he explained, a little too patiently. 'Is it under Let's Have Lunch?'

She had forgotten that the girl who had rung her about the date had explained that she would book the table for them under the company's name. The entire restaurant staff must know why she was here. Were they all looking at her and whispering, laughing at her mistake? Flushed with embarrassment, but stifling a laugh, she murmured an apology. Hardly hearing his reply, she followed him between the tables of chattering lunchers to the dimmest reaches of the room where her eyes fell on Mark Carpenter for the first time.

He sat with his back to the wall, his head bent as he concentrated on cleaning his fingernails with a toothpick so she had a clear view of the top of his scalp through his

Bea turned to see an effete young man in a loose white shirt of the finest linen, the sleeves rolled up, well-cut dark trousers and expensive shoes. Surely this wasn't him – a more perfect 'match' than she could ever have hoped for. Or was a younger man picking her up before she and Mark Carpenter had even had a chance to sit down?

'I'm sorry?' Say it again, please.

'Let's have lunch?' he repeated, with the slightest of smiles, encouraging her to agree.

She hadn't misheard. Unsure what to say, she tried a rusty attempt at a flirtatious smile. 'Normally I'd love to, but unfortunately I'm meeting someone. Another time, perhaps.'

'No, no, no.' His face spoke volumes. Of course he wouldn't make such an obvious pass at her. She was old enough to be his mother, for God's sake. 'I meant the table ooking,' he explained, a little too patiently. 'Is it under t's Have Lunch?'

he had forgotten that the girl who had rung her about date had explained that she would book the table for under the company's name. The entire restaurant ust know why she was here. Were they all looking nd whispering, laughing at her mistake? Flushed barrassment, but stifling a laugh, she murmured gy. Hardly hearing his reply, she followed him e tables of chattering lunchers to the dimmest he room where her eyes fell on Mark Carpenter time.

h his back to the wall, his head bent as he on cleaning his fingernails with a toothpick ar view of the top of his scalp through his

She still cared about what she looked like so wore clothes to cover up and ended up too hot, unwilling to rid herself of the layers that should be so easy to strip off and reveal all. Oh, where was the 'longer, leaner, looser' her that she'd been promised would begin to emerge after only ten Pilates sessions? So far all she'd managed to do was rick her back when attempting a new exercise on the reformer.

She was aware that the cream linen suit, which had started the day so well, had lost its original snap. As the morning had gone on, her look had deteriorated from the fashion-ably creased to the unfashionably unironed. But short o taking a forty-five-minute detour up to Oxford Stree buy something new, there was nothing she could do that now. Remembering all she'd been taught, sh in her stomach – skirt would hang better – and h upright. 'Imagine a string pulling you up fro your head,' echoed the voice of her Pilates pushed open the restaurant door, aware th string must have melted in the heat.

The restaurant wasn't wide but it s a central table carrying a large ar bamboo, brilliant orange birds ginger blossoms. She couldn't se she'd got there first after all time to go to the Ladies and repaired in the back of stabbing herself in th compose herself. Th reassured herself.

'Let's have lun

b
Le
S
the
them
staff r
at her
with em
an apolo
between t
reaches of
for the first
He sat wi
concentrated
so she had a cl

thinning dark hair. The maître d' pulled back her chair and her lunch-date looked up. A pleasant face – a little on the baggy side, if she had to be critical. She didn't, of course, but she couldn't help herself. As she sat down, still mortified by her initial mistake, Mark attempted to stand although there wasn't enough room to do so without tipping the table towards her. She snatched at a wobbling glass.

'Hallo. I'm Bea,' she said, wondering what on earth had possessed her to sign up for all this. That stripy City shirt with the white collar and the navy pin-striped trousers immediately told her that this was not going to be a match made in heaven. She had been quite specific about her taste in men when filling in the questionnaire – no City types – but the agency had ignored her.

'I know.' He gave a nervous laugh but Bea was concentrating on the sweat beading on his upper lip, telling herself not to be so bloody judgemental. She knew sweat was beading on her forehead too, as another flush swept over her. She could feel the dampness at the nape of her neck and running down the small of her back. She tried willing herself to cool down. No dice.

As Mark sat down again, he reached behind him, whipped out a single red rose and put it in front of her. His smile revealed a mouthful of slightly overlapping teeth that Bea stared at as she tried to take in the significance of his gesture. How ridiculously over-the-top. This is just lunch, she reminded herself, not some full-blown long-term romance. You can leave whenever you want to. But, of course, she couldn't. That would be too rude. Imagine if her date took one look at her and announced he wasn't hungry after all. It would take weeks to recover from the blow to her self-confidence. She couldn't do that. First impressions weren't always everything so she must make the effort.

'Thank you. That's so sweet.' She put the rose deep into her capacious bag where no one could see it, at the same time imagining what her close friends, Ellen and Kate, would say when she told them.

The waiter was standing over them, asking if he could bring drinks. Bea's resolve to stay strictly sober flew out of the window. 'A glass of Pinot Grigio would be lovely. Yes, a large one.' And make it quick, she prayed silently.

'And a sparkling water for me.' A nice voice with the trace of an accent she couldn't place. 'I don't drink,' he added, by way of explanation.

'Oh. Why not?' Bea was wishing she had stuck with her resolve. He'd probably think she was a lush, drinking at lunchtime. Oh, to hell with it. Either he'd like what he'd paid for or he wouldn't. There were always the other five.

'Not during the working week. Need to keep a clear head for the job. You can't play around with other people's money without one.'

'But it's Friday. Surely you can have one to keep me company.'

'No, I don't think so. The markets don't stop trading when I have a drink. I wouldn't risk it.'

'But you drink in the evenings?' Bea was hoping for the reassurance that he was one of her sort, racing to open a bottle of wine as soon as he'd taken the key out of the front door at the end of a hard day.

'Only at weekends. It's a slippery slope otherwise.'

'Oh.' Bea was silenced. Studying the menu, she wondered what was the least she could eat without seeming rude. The sooner she could extricate herself from this disaster, the better. Could she get away with only one course? Just a starter, perhaps? No, she was firm with herself, she couldn't. Come on, Bea, play the game.

'What will you have?' He broke the silence as the waiter returned, pad at the ready.

'I think I'll go for the goat's cheese salad and then the grilled Dover sole.' There. Simple, not too much and lowish on the calorie front.

'I'll have the scallops and pea mash. Thank you.' He sat back, looking, Bea thought, a touch on the smug side.

'But that's just a starter.' Bea couldn't stop herself. 'Won't you have something else?'

'No. That's plenty for me. Got to watch the weight, you know.' He patted his no doubt lean and muscled stomach. She looked at his thick chest hair growing out of the neck of his shirt. What would he be like in bed? she wondered. After all, that was one of the reasons they were meeting – there was no getting away from it. If things went well . . . He looked like one of those men who brought his own tissues and thanked you afterwards. Stopping herself going further, Bea took a swig of wine.

The lunch seemed interminable. Conversation dragged and every time Mark asked her a question, Bea seemed to have a mouthful. She ate her salad, then he picked his way through his four tastefully arranged scallops floating on a pea-green island as Bea filleted her sole with the cack-handedness of a ten-year-old, despite a lifetime of having done it without any difficulty. What was wrong with her? In desperation, she ordered another glass of wine, choosing to ignore Mark's raised eyebrow. They trailed across all the obvious topics, never stopping on one long enough to become too confidential – where they came from (she from London and him from Northumbria); where they lived now (Islington and Clapham); their marital status (both awaiting divorce); children (one to her – Ben, now sixteen; two to him – Bella, thirteen and Stevie, fifteen); where they were going on holiday (hadn't decided because always left it to the last minute; golf and fishing on the Spey with two friends), favourite books (anything by Anne Tyler; *Fever Pitch*) and films (*When Harry Met Sally* – sad but true; anything starring Jackie Chan – even sadder).

The only time Mark became really animated was when he talked about his job as an investment banker. But he did so in such detail, bringing in all his colleagues and the negotiations they'd recently completed, that she soon lost the thread and began to think about the drive she was going to have to make the next morning to see her mother in Kent. What time should she leave to avoid the worst of the traffic out of London? Everybody leaped into their cars the moment the sun came out and drove towards the coast like lemmings. And she was going to join them. Was it all right to leave Ben on his own since he had refused point blank to go with her? Or did that mean she was an irresponsible mother?

Then she drifted on to her own work as publishing director of Coldharbour Press, an imprint of the giant publishing conglomeration Rockfast. Perhaps she should tell Mark more about that, but it would be hard to match his work-related animation. She'd lost her hunger for the business a couple of years ago – although she was anxious to get back to the office after this was over. Something was obviously happening: too many shut doors with senior execs in secret conferences. Someone had started the rumour that an announcement was going to be made this afternoon. That would be typical. Get the announcement off management's chests so they could have a conscience-free weekend while all the workforce would spend theirs worrying about their future with the company.

'Shall we?' His voice suddenly interrupted her train of thought. Oh, God, what on earth had he just said? To ask would only show she hadn't been listening at all.

'Er, yes,' she agreed uncertainly.

'That's wonderful. I'll be in touch then.' He reached across the table and took her hand, oblivious to the alarm that was registering on her face. What on earth had she agreed to? 'I'm so glad we've met. To be honest, I was worried that you might be a proper ball-breaker but I've really enjoyed myself.'

'Gee, thanks. I do my best.' How condescending she sounded. 'No, seriously. I've enjoyed meeting you too. Would you mind if I skipped coffee?' Once she'd got out of here, she need never see him again – whatever it was she'd agreed to.

'Not at all. I have to get back too. I'll just be one moment.' He extricated himself from behind the table and, after pulling a black bag from under his seat, headed for the

Gents. At least they didn't have the awkwardness of establishing who was going to foot the bill. Let's Have Lunch
settled up for them. So they damn well should, given the
little they had to do for their money, mused Bea. Perhaps
Mark wasn't so awful, really. She must try to be less
demanding. He wasn't bad-looking, just a bit humourless.
She imagined he might be quite a considerate lover, if not
very inventive. She was a fine one to talk. What would she
bring to that particular party? She was much more out of
practice than she cared to remember.

'Are you ready?' At the sound of Mark's voice she looked
up to find herself eyeballing a Lycra-covered crotch that
revealed much more than she wanted to know about any
man outside the privacy of the bedroom.

'I should have warned you,' said Mark, looking under-
standably sheepish. 'I must apologise for what isn't the most
attractive look. But cycling is much the easiest way to get
around London.'

'Mmm. Breathing in those traffic fumes must be so good
for you.' Her mother's words rushed into her head: 'Sarcasm
is not the finest form of wit, especially from you, Bea.'

Bea assumed his trousers had been in the bicycle pannier
bag that had been hidden under his seat throughout lunch.
His shirt must be in there now having been replaced by an
old white T-shirt that had long ago lost its shape. On its
front was a washed-out photograph. Bea peered more
closely. Yes, below the words 'The World's Best Dad' was
the near invisible image of Mark with his arms round two
indistinct young children. Bea swallowed. 'Yours?' she asked
unnecessarily.

But Mark didn't hear her. He was already striding out into the street where she could see what must be his bicycle, chained to a lamppost. By the time she had caught up with him, he was ready to go. Bea yanked her eyes from his pale over-muscled and extremely hairy calves to his face, now crowned by a royal blue crash helmet – never the ideal fashion accessory. Mark removed the impenetrably black goggles over his eyes and leaned forward to kiss her cheek, catching the side of her head with the helmet. 'So sorry, Bea. Stupid not to wear it, though.'

'Yes, yes, it would be. Of course it would.' For once in her life Bea was lost for words, torn between hysterical laughter and tears. How could the agency have made such a mismatched pairing? You couldn't have invented it. But wait. Perhaps she should consider, just for a moment, the impression she had given the agency. Perhaps she actually looked like someone who would find this sort of person attractive. Impossible. Much more likely was the dearth of right-aged men on the market. There can't be many who specified they wanted to meet a woman when the shine had rubbed off a bit. Most of them found themselves a younger model within weeks of ending a relationship – or before. She knew that from bitter experience. What was it they said? When a relationship comes to an end, the man finds another woman while the woman finds herself. She wasn't in a position to be picky.

'So, do you have a card? Then I can email you with a when and where.' Suddenly he looked so vulnerable, the hope in his face contrasting with the faded vision of youthful certainty on his chest. She knew then that she couldn't disappoint him. What had she got to lose anyway? Whatever she had agreed to do, it couldn't be that bad. She delved into her bag, scratching her hand on a thorn of the rose, whose existence she'd forgotten, and failed to find her cards in the jumble at the bottom.

'I'll have to scribble my details on this.' She knew she was probably committing herself to more than she wanted. But what the hell? He took the slip of paper then, to her surprise, offered his hand and gave her a vigorous hand-shake and replaced the goggles. Bea prayed that no one from the office had seen them together. In some disbelief she watched the back of what, if Let's Have Lunch had their way, might be her future cycling off towards the City, then turned to look for a cab back to the fray.

2

As Bea tapped in her security code, the plate-glass doors to the editorial and publicity floor clicked open. She walked past the reception desk, where the young temp manning it while Jean was on holiday was busy multi-tasking – nails, book and interrupting her too-loud conversation with her boyfriend to connect outside calls. Impressive as a feat of juggling, maybe, but not exactly what one looked for in a receptionist. Bea made a mental note to mention it to HR. The shelves in the reception area were crowded with Coldharbour's latest books, primed for the bestseller list. In our dreams, she reflected wryly.

All the team knew that whatever the promises made to earnest young novelists or ego-bound celebrities, the reality was that only a few would really get the marketing push they'd been promised and only one or two might, just might, make it to the holy grail of the bestseller list. All the team knew the chances of making it were remote. The ratio of disappointment to expectation in her job was much higher than when she'd been an eager young editor twenty years ago. Back then she could take a punt on an unknown writer and expect to be supported. Calculations were done on the back of envelopes and editors shaped the profile of the publishing list, rather than accountants and salesmen. Was it any wonder that she had her increasing moments of disenchantment?

Only a few steps towards her office and Bea could sense the tension in the air. Something had happened since she'd left for lunch. Unusually, all four assistants in the open-plan area were at their desks, half hidden by piles of manuscripts, boxes of books and the low dividing screens pinned with postcards and notices that made up each workstation. The excited buzz of conversation tailed off as she approached and the girls looked up at her expectant as she walked by. Puzzled, but desperate to take off the new red suede peep-toe shoes that were killing her, she smiled at them and carried on, willing the blister she could feel burning on the side of her right big toe to subside. She was surprised to see that Stuart and Jade, the two editorial directors, were still there. In all the years she'd known them, they'd believed that, whatever the emergency, their weekends began at Friday lunchtime. They were huddled in Stuart's glass-sided goldfish bowl of an office, door shut, intent on their discussion. Stuart looked up as she passed and said something. Jade glanced at her too. Bea ignored them, too anxious to get comfortable.

She reached the sanctum of her office, kicked off the beautiful but offending shoes and hung up her jacket with relief before turning the air-con up a notch as yet another flush threatened. Surrounded by the books that, over the years, she had brought to fruition, whether by acquiring them from American publishers or by gently prising from the authors the best book they could write, she felt at ease. This was where she belonged. Editing, working with authors, was all she wanted to do. If only it didn't come with all the additional admin that she found so trying. Once she had dreamed of being a writer herself but that had retreated into the distance as she'd seen what a precarious existence it could be. As she sat at her fashionably curved desk, which gave her a view across the rooftops of central London, she longed for the days when she'd had a secretary who would tidy her desk whenever she went out to lunch, putting everything in order. No longer allowed such a guardian angel, this afternoon she was faced with God knew how many unread emails and assorted muddled papers – a half-read manuscript, minutes from various meetings, costing forms and the still unopened post.

As consolation, she opened her desk drawer and selected a pink-and-brown-wrapped square ganache chocolate, Earl Grey Tea flavour. Every girl needs a particular passion, she thought, as she popped it into her mouth – and hers was good chocolate. It had begun seventeen years earlier when she was thinking about getting pregnant and needed consolation after she'd cadged her last cigarette (she'd given up buying them months before). But, over time, she'd exchanged the bars of Fruit and Nut for specialist brands, so good they demanded she ate less of them (or so she'd convinced herself). The pocket box of chocolates from Demarquette had been a present from an agent who'd found the most direct way to her heart. As her mouth filled with the divine bitter-sweetness of the chocolate suffused with the delicate citrus undertones of bergamot, she turned to the task in hand.

She tried to live by the maxim 'only touch each piece of paper once'. It had been shared with her by someone much more successful than herself. Since then she had struggled to deal with or delegate each one as she made herself take it from her in-tray but it just didn't work for her. So often she'd be interrupted in the middle of dealing with something and would succumb to the temptation to slip that piece of paper into the pending tray – her desk's graveyard. Once there, nothing ever came out. Of course, there was less paperwork now than there had once been. Welcome to the world of the email. She sighed, noticing that forty more had accumulated during her brief absence. She clicked on the first just as her door opened.

'Bea. What's going on?' Stuart shut the door behind him and, without waiting to be asked, cleared the unsteady pile of manuscripts off the extra chair and sat down. The rich slightly acrid scent of his sweat reached her at the same time as she noticed the damp stains in the armpits of his shirt, which was grubby at the cuff and neck. He was a good-looking guy of about thirty-five, one of the most astute and commercially minded editors she'd come across, but his personal hygiene left something to be desired. His rather brutal haircut and the razor-thin white scar that ran from his right ear to the side of his nose suggested an aggressive streak that she had never, in the three years they'd worked together, come across. If anyone asked him how he'd got the scar, he just smiled and said it was 'one of those things'. As a result he retained a slightly mysterious aura that clearly

16

made him extremely attractive to some, judging from the comments that Bea had overheard in the Ladies.

'Not a clue. Why would I know anyway?' Bea's attention was suddenly caught by an email from Let's Have Lunch and another from Mark that had just pinged their way into her mailbox. Damn. She'd have to open them later.

'Come on. You're always the first to know everything. Stephen's always in and out of here.' Stuart's anxiety to find out whatever was going on was bordering on desperate. He pulled his fingers one after another so they cracked.

'Do you mind not doing that? I honestly don't know what you're talking about. What's happened?' She hated the way everyone assumed that her long-standing friend-ship with the managing director meant she knew everything there was to know. Though she hated it even more when she didn't.

'Piers arrived just after you left, looking like thunder. He came straight up to Stephen's office and they've been in there ever since. They pulled the blinds so they couldn't be seen.' Stuart's voice rose with excitement as he described the unexpected arrival of the chief executive of Rockfast. 'Then all the directors were called in, one after the other, and Jan's been looking for you. They all came out looking absolutely stony and won't talk to anyone.' He leaned forward as if expecting Bea to share whatever secret there was.

'I've no idea what's happening.' Bea hated confessing her ignorance. 'Nobody's said anything to me.' Only because she'd been a bit late getting back from lunch, dammit.

'But Stephen tells you everything,' Stuart sounded outraged that Bea hadn't got the answer.

'Not this time.' But why not? Bea asked herself. She knew that Stephen was talking to the management about retiring early some time next year because he'd decided he wanted to concentrate on his silversmithing. He'd always kept the one thing he was passionate about in second place to his career while his kids were growing up but now they were in their twenties, as he'd told Bea, 'I'm desperate to give it a proper go before it's too late.' Bea had wanted to protest, but she could see he had a point. She had only to glance in the mirror to be reminded that she had her own ticket on time's winged chariot. So that was next year. If there was something to do with the business, she was sure she'd have got wind of it somehow – smoke signals always drifted off the fire in the end.

'Here's Jan now.' Stuart's excitement was almost infectious as Stephen's PA put her head round the door.

'Bea. There you are. Where have you been? Stephen and Piers wanted to see you urgently.' Jan's face was almost hidden by a sheet of blonde hair that she swept back with a perfectly manicured hand to reveal a perfectly beautiful face, and a smile that revealed a set of perfectly even white teeth.

'At lunch, of course,' Bea was immediately on the defensive. 'What was it about anyway?'

'Can't say.' The smile became more like a knowing smirk. 'Anyway, it's too late now. I've been asked to get everyone into the boardroom in ten minutes.'

'What? It's Friday afternoon.' A meeting on Friday afternoon was unheard of. 'I'll go and see them now.' Underneath the desk, Bea's feet felt about for her shoes. The pain in her blistered toe as she stood up was excruciating but her desire to find out what was going on overrode it.

'I think it's too late, Bea.' Another of those slight self-satisfied smiles accompanied Jan's withdrawal.

Irritated both by Jan's cool assumption of control and superior knowledge, and by Stuart's evident disappointment in her ignorance of what was going on, Bea picked up the phone and called Stephen. Engaged. Outside her office, the rest of the staff were moving towards the boardroom in the corner at the far end of the floor. Annoyed that her Let's Have Lunch date had been today of all days – and how pointless it had been – she followed the last of her colleagues into the room.

The long modern table had been pushed up against the floor-to-ceiling windows so there would be enough room for everyone. Some perched on its edge, others occupied the chairs that had been randomly spaced around the periphery of the room while everyone else sat on the stained carpet. Bea took a place in the corner by the door, leaning against the wall so she could take the weight off her painful foot. Even turned up full, the air-conditioning couldn't prevent the room becoming a sauna with that number of people crushed into it. Ties were loosened, jackets were off and pieces of paper flapped as people fanned themselves. Voices rose as speculation mounted. Could Rockfast have sold off the Coldharbour imprint? Surely someone would have heard. Perhaps Rockfast was going under. No, there'd have been word about that too. Perhaps they'd acquired another imprint. Bea stood quietly, as mystified as everyone else, batting away questions as if she knew what was going on but couldn't possibly say while feeling cross that she was the only director in the room excluded from whatever it was.

Eventually Piers and Stephen came in, followed by the financial, sales, marketing, art and publicity directors, all of them looking particularly serious. Bea caught Stephen's eye as he mouthed, 'Sorry.' At that moment, loud alarm bells began to ring in her head, but she still didn't know why. How come Bea was the only one to have gone out that lunchtime? Piers stood. He was the only man in the room wearing a suit, rather a natty Armani, Bea noted, but he still maintained his cucumber cool in the heat. His peachy tie was set off by a lightly striped blue shirt while his dark hair was fashionably short, slicked up and back with just the right amount of gel. Quite the image of an executive who had reached the top and was going to stay there, Bea reflected, as Piers directed a taut smile at the assembled team before beginning to speak. He kept it brief, to the point.

'As you all know, Coldharbour Press has been in trouble for a while. Despite adjustments to the publishing programme, the turnover has fallen again. The board has decided more drastic action is necessary. As a result, I have both good news and bad for you. The good is that Adam Palmer from Pennant Publishing is starting on Monday as the new MD.' The bombshell dropped. The few who knew of Adam Palmer and his reputation for ruthlessness looked stunned – Bea among them. All heads turned to Stephen, who stood with his eyes fixed firmly on his old brown suede shoes unable to look at his staff. 'Stephen will be taking early retirement as of August the thirty-first when he has completed the handover to Adam.' There was a collective gasp. That was less than a month away. Bea couldn't believe her ears. Stephen had never suggested this might happen. But Piers hadn't finished.

'We have also come to an agreement that Louis, your sales director, will be leaving while Sam Spooner will be promoted from his position as sales manager with immediate effect.'

Sam Spooner! He was barely out of nappies. The back-stabbing little toe-rag, thought Bea.

'Obviously this means that there will be a number of changes to get used to over the coming weeks but I know we can rely on you all to do your best to accommodate them. The Rockfast board is convinced that they will be crucial if we're to turn the company around to perform in the way it should. All I can add is that, apart from replacing Stephen and Louis, whom I would like to thank for all they've done for the company, no other changes are envisaged at this time. Thank you. Have a good weekend.' He left the room followed by the directors, with Bea on their tail.

Stunned, the staff left the room in silence, a few holding back tears. Only a few of them knew or cared much about Adam Palmer at that moment. What they cared about was that the close team that had worked together over the last few years was changing. If the results hadn't been everything they might have been, wasn't that because of market forces, rather than specific individuals who had worked so hard for the company? Change was always unsettling but the more so when it was announced as unexpectedly as this. As the staff filtered back to their desks, they began to talk again, wondering what on earth could have happened to prompt this and why the change had been handled in this way.

Bea went back to her office, fending off questions by inventing an urgent call she had to make. She needed a few moments on her own to think. She shut the door, feeling hurt and confused by the announcement. What did it really mean? What were the implications for her, as one of Stephen's appointments? She thought she did a good job as publishing director although, if she were honest, perhaps not quite as good a job as she once had. She was uncomfortably aware that recently she hadn't been responsible for as many sure-fire successes as in earlier days.

She picked up her phone and dialled Stephen. No reply. Had he left the building on Piers's coat-tails? That would be so like him. He always kept a strictly professional distance from his colleagues and would never stop and gossip. That was one of the things everyone respected him for. He knew every member of staff by name and would help or advise any of them at any time, but when the clock struck six, he shut the door on his office and went home. His professional and private lives were kept entirely separate. She tried his mobile. No reply.

She saw Stuart coming towards her office and swiftly picked up the phone again. When he popped his head round the door to invite her to come to the pub for a post-mortem, she signalled she was mid-conversation. 'Hang on a minute,' she said to the dialling tone. 'I've got quite a lot to do, Stu, so I think I'll finish up here first. If you're still there when I leave, I'll join you then.'

It was true. She had got a lot to do but she knew that there wasn't a cat's chance in hell of her doing it now. But she wanted to talk to Stephen if only she could find him. Once she could see the main office was deserted, she went along to his office on the off-chance and knocked quietly on the door.

'Who is it?' He sounded exhausted.

'Stephen, it's me, Bea.' She pushed open the door to see him sitting with his head in his hands, alone at the round table where he held meetings.

'I'm so sorry, Bea.' He looked up and Bea could see he was as tired as he sounded. She hated to think it, but suddenly he looked old.

'But what happened?' She went over to sit with him.

'I wanted to tell you but Piers acted so fast, there was no time. He and the other Rockfast directors have obviously been planning something like this for ages and then Adam suddenly stepped into the frame. Piers knew I was ready to go, and as for Louis – a casualty of war, I'm afraid.' He ran his hand through his thinning grey hair. 'Piers warned me on Monday that they were talking to Adam but I didn't take him seriously. Then he turned up here today and told me the plan. He'd even spoken to Sam and Louis during the week without mentioning it to me, swearing them to silence. I was just the last nail they needed to hammer in. Big pay-off. I couldn't say no.' Bea could see how shocked he was by the way his career had ended so abruptly and, more importantly, out of his control. Deciding to quit when it suited you was one thing. Being sacked according to someone else's agenda was quite different.

'What do you think is going to happen? Is it going to be

the long night of the P45s?' Bea moved over to the desk where she knew Stephen kept some whisky for emergencies in one of the drawers. Pulling the top one open, she took out the bottle and poured them both a large one. She sat down again.

'Well, I'm going to have to play the game and show Adam the ropes but . . . honestly? Adam is bound to have his own ideas about how to run the place. I don't think the changes will end here.'

A penny half dropped. 'Me?' Bea felt a rush of anxiety.

'Maybe. But don't spend the weekend worrying. We'll just have to see what happens next week.' He downed his whisky in one gulp. 'Bea, I'm sorry but I'm going to have to get off. I've got a lot of things to talk about at home.'

'Of course. I've got to get back too.' Bea left Stephen as he took his old blue cord jacket from the back of his chair and picked up his battered leather book-bag.

'Call me if you want to talk about anything over the weekend.'

'Of course. Thanks.'

Back in her office, she sat thinking. Don't spend the weekend worrying. How could she not, for God's sake? On the other hand, nothing she could do would affect what happened next week, so best just to follow Stephen's example and go home. She didn't feel like joining the others at the pub although, by the time she got home, Ben would probably be on his way out for the night. That would give her time to think more carefully about her conversation with Stephen. On the verge of shutting down her computer, she registered the flashing icon that alerted her to new emails.

Of course. She opened her mailbox. Before she went, there were two she wanted to check. First Let's Have Lunch. Their communication was brief.

> Can you make lunch on Tuesday? If yes,
> Tony Castle will be expecting to meet you
> at 1 p.m. at Belushi's in Jordan Street,
> WC2.

Sod it. Why not? Life couldn't be much worse. Fine. I'll be there, she typed.

She opened the one from Mark.

> Enjoyed meeting you very much. I thought
> we might have a drink at the Grape Pip, off
> Regent Street. Friday week any good? All
> best, Mark

What harm could one more meeting do? She'd go for a drink with him and see what happened. Besides, she told herself again, she must try not to judge too quickly. Give the guy a chance. She might at least try to get her full £125 worth.

Great she typed. I enjoyed lunch too. (A small white lie in the interest of good relations.) Let me know what time's best for you.

With that, she shut the screen down, grabbed the manuscript of the novel that she had to finish editing before meeting the author the following week, and walked out.

3

'Come and sit down, Paul. Please.'

Kate lay back on the leg of the white L-shaped sofa, patting the seat beside her. In front of her, Sky News was playing on the wall-mounted TV but with the volume turned right down. Exhaustion gave way to relaxation as her body zinged with the relief of at last being almost horizontal after a hard day's work. She watched her husband busy preparing their supper in the state-of-the-art kitchen area at the centre of their open-plan basement.

Although he was going grey at last, Paul still had the look of the handsome man she had met thirty years ago: tall, athletic and perennially tanned; his strong jaw sagging a bit; deep laugh lines bracketing his wide mouth; wiry eyebrows now out of control; the round wire-framed spectacles that he had always favoured. He had remained slim despite his well-known love of food and drink, so he still looked good in his clothes. This evening he was casual in cream chinos and a loose white linen shirt. When he walked into a room, heads still turned, though perhaps not for quite as long as they once did, and people still flocked to him, wanting to be in his shadow. But, out of everyone, he had chosen Kate. With her petite, dark, retiring appearance and in the definitive way she approached the world, she was almost his polar opposite. It still surprised her that they had ended up together.

'I'll be there in a minute.' He looked up from what he was doing, giving her the oddly attractive asymmetric grin that had never failed to captivate her. 'I've just to get the timing right with this cheese soufflé or I'll ruin the thing.'

'I thought we were having omelettes.' Kate tried to hide her disappointment. All she wanted was something plain and simple, something that didn't demand such attention. She wished she had insisted on her original plan of dragging him out to their local Italian after work. If they were there, at a table for two, they'd be forced to talk to one another over the trademark gluey pasta, to communicate about something other than Paul's culinary efforts. Not that she should complain. The fact that he was a keen cook meant that she rarely had to lift a finger in the kitchen except for the odd bit of dutiful washing-up. Her friends always commented on how lucky she was to have him. Even when he'd had a long day in the City, and often with more work in his briefcase for later, he could still muster the energy to knock up a decent meal. However, his culinary enthusiasm (was there such a thing as culinary obsessive compulsive disorder? she wondered) was something she didn't share. Falling through the door, exhausted after an evening session at the surgery, she was incapable of doing any more than flinging a ready-cooked meal from the freezer into the oven.

She picked up the latest *BMJ* from the top of the small pile of medical journals that served as a constant reminder of how much and how often she should attempt to catch up with the ever-advancing world of medicine. She put it down again. 'You wouldn't believe how late I ran today. I could have spent all morning with the first three patients alone.' A GP who prided herself on her ability and commitment, she was often frustrated by the necessary time restrictions put on her work. 'I kicked off with a guy who claimed he'd collected enough anti-depressants to kill himself, so that was a suicide risk assessment. Then, as he was leaving, he happened to mention that he had a jock itch so I had to look at that, which took ages.'

Paul's full attention was on the window of the oven as he watched and waited for his soufflé to rise, so Kate just carried on, assuming he was listening. 'After him, I had a dear eighty-three-year-old who had nothing wrong with her but who wanted to tell me about everything that was going on in her life. And then I had to refer a woman for a termination, which took ages because she couldn't decide which hospital she wanted me to refer her to. How was I supposed to deal with any of them in ten minutes flat? Paul! Am I boring you?'

He turned in her direction for a second, making a sterling effort to appear interested. 'No, no, darling. Not at all.' His attempt to disguise a yawn was futile. 'Keep going.'

She wasn't fooled. 'No, it's all right. I'll spare you. Just one of those days. How was yours?'

'Same old, same old. Aaah.' Said with the satisfaction of a job successfully executed. 'I think we're ready.'

Triumphant, he made his way to the table by the wide glass door to the garden carrying the perfectly risen soufflé, its smell filling the room. 'Come and sit down.'

Kate dragged herself across the room while Paul examined the interior of the main course as if it was a biological specimen before serving it, then passed her the salad. He was uncharacteristically silent as they ate so she filled the vacuum with more gossip from the surgery while he nodded or shook his head, making the occasional sympathetic sound at the right moments. She could tell by the way his eyes occasionally drifted towards the kitchen that his mind wasn't entirely on what she was saying but she forgave him. Her professional problems must sometimes seem so petty and tedious to him, but she wanted him to understand her irritation when one of the other partners had to go out for a chunk of the morning leaving her and the on-call doctor to share his patients, as well as her impatience with the practice manager who seemed to be having an awful lot of days sick in the run-up to her daughter's wedding. Never mind the frustrations of an appointment system that rationed only ten minutes to everyone, when many needed more time – much more time.

*

Her day had begun to go wrong at 8.15 a.m. when she had turned up at the practice and asked Mrs Yilmaz to come inside before the doors officially opened.

The old woman was leaning against the wall, her stick not enough to support her for the wait until the surgery opened, a warm smell of urine and old age drifting off her. A patterned headscarf covered most of her head and face while an old patched coat hid most of what she was wearing, except for the bottom of a long, shapeless dark skirt, thick stockings and sensible black shoes. Her entire body shook with a guttural graveyard cough as she took Kate's arm, then shuffled beside her to the glass door, coughing again as she waited for her to open it. Kate dug out her keys, aware that she was about to incur the wrath of Sonia, their draconian receptionist, who liked the practice to run the way she thought best. And that meant not having the doctors bringing in the patients to the waiting room, however needy they might be, until the clock struck half past eight on the dot. Not only was Kate about to annoy Sonia but, sensing the pent-up irritation behind her, she'd already alienated most of the remaining queue of patients. Some of them were probably on their way to work, already displeased at being late, while others always felt they had first call on the doctor's attention. Just another Friday morning.

Having settled Mrs Yilmaz into one of the comfier chairs in the waiting room, she greeted Sonia with the cheeriest 'Good morning' she could muster, only to be met with a scowl and a grunt. Their chief receptionist had made herself indispensable to the practice but, all the same, a little compassion wouldn't go amiss, thought Kate, as she walked down the corridor to her room. She was the first of the partners to be in, as usual. She liked it that way, having a bit of time to make the transfer from her life at home to her role at work, to gather herself for the day ahead. She let herself in. The pale blue of the walls at least had a soothing quality as did the view over the small haphazard garden at the back of the building.

She hung her bag on the back of her chair and sat behind her desk, where her computer was already on and a cup of coffee steaming beside it. Thank God for Evangelina, the junior receptionist, who suffered under Sonia's large thumb but remembered the little things that made the partners' lives bearable – a regular supply of hot drinks and occasional biscuits being two of them. Kate flicked to her appointments' screen, her heart sinking as she registered in whose company she would be spending her morning.

With one or two exceptions, it was a question of the same old patients with the same old insoluble problems: people suffering from all manner of aches and pains that were usually merely symptomatic of their circumstances. Unloved, unhappy, lonely, unemployed: the conditions that bred so many minor complaints. All those patients wanted was a reassuring chat or a token prescription and to be sent away feeling someone was taking notice and cared about them. No one else did. She sighed. At least she had the post-natal clinic to look forward to in the afternoon. That was one of the bright spots in her week, where her examinations gave her the perfect excuse to cuddle and play with one cute, unquestioning, doted-upon baby after another.

She glanced at her watch. She had five minutes. Just enough time to check her emails and not enough to do anything else. Having negotiated the rigmarole that got her through to her NHS inbox, she ran her eye down the entries, hoping to see one from her middle son, Sam, who had recently arrived in Ghana on a school-building project. She was disappointed to find nothing.

Dear Sam, the most adventurous of their children, the one who dared to go higher, further and faster than either of his siblings, up for any kind of physical challenge. Always the dreamiest of the three, he had left school and, to her and Paul's dismay, chosen not to follow his friends to university. With no idea what he wanted from life, he had travelled alone to New Zealand where he had found a job in the timber industry. Just when she'd thought he had settled, he was off again, this time to work towards preserving the Canadian wilderness. And now he was building a school in Ghana. She knew rationally that each of their children had to leave home and follow their own path in life. But if only his didn't have to take him quite so far away. They couldn't even pick up the phone for a chat when they felt like it. She missed him terribly.

On her desk, she had a calendar that Sam had given her as a farewell present. Each day displayed a photograph from a different part of the world and each day she tore one off and tossed it into the bin. Today she was saying goodbye to a yellow-and-black-shrouded Japanese monk, his legs in white stockings, his face hidden under the upside-down bowl of a straw hat, begging outside a temple in Kyoto. Taking his place, a small plane flew high through the spray that erupted into the air from a rushing Victoria Falls. In the background, the sky was a cloudless periwinkle blue. Sitting in her purpose-built medical centre off a busy arterial road that took traffic roaring through London, she couldn't have felt more remote from either of them. She stopped herself turning up the corner of Victoria Falls to see what was underneath. Every day she performed this ritual, remembering their son, and hoping that one day when she wasn't so caught up in the politics of her practice and the welfare of her patients, perhaps she and Paul would be able to coincide their busy lives to travel to one or two of these far-flung destinations. One day.

A knock on the door interrupted her thoughts. She glanced at her watch again. Only a couple of minutes until the floodgates opened.

'Come in.'

Pete, the senior partner, entered the room. His wispy beard and sandals gave him the air of a throwback to the sixties. He was thin, slightly round-shouldered and wore a succession of short-sleeved checked shirts that she suspected he bought in bulk from a mail-order catalogue. Kate often wondered why his teacher wife didn't help him in the sartorial stakes. Too preoccupied with her own work, probably. Besides, not everyone was interested in what they wore. They must have higher things on their minds. She straightened her thick woven leather belt, which had swivelled to one side, retucked her coffee-coloured T-shirt into her patterned Hobbs skirt and pulled the front of her long buttonless coral-coloured cardigan together.

'There's bad news. And there's bad news.' Pete pulled up the chair to sit beside her desk. 'Which do you want first?'

'Oh, God. What's happened? Break it gently.'

'There's no easy way to tell you this but Sally's phoned in sick and won't be in today.'

'Again?' She ignored his look of disapproval. Pete never

33

questioned his colleagues' reasons unless they threatened the practice. If the practice manager went sick with no warning there were always difficulties, and today was no exception. 'But the IT people are coming in from the PCT. I suppose I'll have to deal with them. Damn. And?'

'And old Mr Cantor's had a stroke by the sound of it. I'm going to have to go out there. I know, I know,' he said, as Kate put her head into her hands. 'But I'll be as quick as I possibly can. Sonia will divide my patients between you and Jim. Anyone not urgent, you could ask to book to see me tomorrow.'

Out of the corner of her eye, Kate could see the blue light on her computer screen alerting her to her first patient. Sometimes she felt like King Canute trying to hold back the waves and, once again, the waves were beginning to break over her, the swell threatening to increase by the minute. 'All right.' She groaned. 'We'll manage. Let the day begin.'

'Thanks, Kate. I knew you'd understand. I owe you one.' He slipped out of the door.

'Bloody right you do,' Kate shouted after him, before making a final check that her room was in order. She walked down the corridor, past a series of brightly coloured geometric-based prints given to the practice by a grateful patient, and pushed open the door to the waiting room.

'Stewart Bowles? This way.'

*

She looked across the table at Paul. He was staring into the middle distance, as far away as she had just been.

The difference was that she had snapped back to the present and he showed no sign of doing the same. More and more often recently, he had seemed to drift off into a world of his own and she couldn't draw him out of it. Not that he was unpleasant, just increasingly remote. When she tried to talk to him about his day, he would clam up. Unlike her, he'd never really shared his working life, preferring to keep it to the office as much as possible. He had always maintained a strict divide between the two halves of his life, even to the extent that they rarely entertained his colleagues at home. That was what he preferred and she saw no reason for them to change things. Besides, as he said, hedge-fund management wasn't a subject likely to bring much joy to her heart whereas he had always been genuinely interested in the nuts and bolts of her profession. He enjoyed hearing about the lives that came in and out of his wife's practice. But not so much recently. And not tonight, obviously.

'Have you heard from Sam? I wish he'd get in touch.' She knew she was on safe ground here. They never had any trouble talking about any or all of their children. They shared the same sadness that their child-rearing days were over, as well as the excitement and pride in what the children were making of their own lives.

'Nothing yet. Don't worry about him. Let's just assume his silence is a sign that he's too busy having a good time or has a problem getting to the Internet.' He tried to pour her more wine but she put her hand over her glass.

'I've had enough. You finish it.'

'Actually, I'm knackered. I think I'm going to have to go to bed.' He put the bottle down.

'There's nothing wrong, is there?' Kate suddenly had a strange feeling that he was keeping something from her.

'Nothing. Should there be?' He looked up at her, questioning, before starting to gather their plates.

'Don't be silly. You seemed so far away, that's all. I know I drone on about the practice, but if something's worrying you, I'd like to know. If something's not going to plan. Or if there's anything I can help with.'

'There's nothing. Really.' But he sounded far from convincing. 'We're just very busy and we're taking a hammering at the moment so it's all hands on deck. I'm just tired.'

He looked it. Shadows ringed his wide-set eyes and the crow's feet seemed etched more deeply than she had noticed before. She reached across the table for his hand to reassure him of her support. After a second, looking apologetic, he took it away. 'I think I'll just clear up.'

He took the plates over to the dishwasher, loading them far more noisily than necessary, then piling up the things that needed washing up.

'What is it, Paul?' Kate persisted. 'I know there's something you're not telling me.'

'Kate, please. You're not the only one who's had a bad day. Leave it alone.' He banged the soufflé dish onto the draining board, closing the subject. 'I'm going up.'

Kate flinched as if he'd struck her. No 'Goodnight'. No kiss. This was a Paul she hadn't seen for years, not since those awful months when their marriage had almost come to grief long ago – the children had been tiny. She remembered feeling this same distance from him then, as if they were standing on opposite riverbanks, unable to get across. Each was in the other's sight but was unable to hear what the other said above the sound of the rushing water, unable to understand the signals the other was making. When Paul finally admitted to having an affair with a member of his team at work, Kate was surprised by the relief she felt. At least she knew what she was dealing with. He said he wanted to leave her and start a new life with this woman, but Kate refused to accept his decision. In giving her this unwanted knowledge, he had also given her power.

Whatever Paul might believe he felt, she had not been prepared to give up on her family so easily. She had worked so hard in order to show him how loved and wanted he was, not just by their children but by her. She had shown him that despite lavishing so much love on Megan, Sam and Jack she still had enough left for him. She had just got out of the habit of letting him know. She was the one whose attention and support he needed, whose reassurance he wanted, whose love he treasured. When Paul had realised he still had all those things, and more, he gave up his affair, promising never, ever to have another, and Kate came to accept that, in many ways, having a husband was like having another child. Her feminist hackles rose as she tussled with the idea but, in the end, she decided to accept their unspoken pact because the rewards were greater than the cost. Paul made her life so much more than it was without him but, to keep him, she had to make sure all his needs were met. She accepted he was that sort of man and trusted him to keep his side of the bargain in return.

Following him upstairs, she thought about their marriage

now and what would happen when Jack eventually left home. Times had moved on, circumstances had changed, and so had Paul and Kate. They'd weathered the journey so far but were they going to make it together to the end? She recognised the dangers of taking one another for granted, having seen the same thing happen with so many of her patients who had been to, or were heading for, the divorce courts. But with so many things going on in their lives, it was all too easy to let things slip. Were Paul's recent silences nothing more than that or did they have a deeper significance? She didn't like the doubts that were running through her mind. She willed them away, deciding that what sometimes happened to her patients was not going to happen to her.

Paul was still reading what looked like a company report when she came out of the shower. As she climbed into bed, he put it down and turned to her.

'I'm sorry, Katie. Put it down to exhaustion. I'll be OK tomorrow.' He stretched out his arm and she curled into him, inhaling his familiar scent.

'Forget it. Probably my fault.' She ran her hand across his chest and down towards his stomach as she raised herself to kiss him. Sex was the one thing that had always brought them back together after the slightest disagreement. But she sensed him tense and he pulled back from her.

'Not tonight,' he murmured, turning his head and gently pushing her away. 'I've got an early start. Sorry.' He rolled onto his side and reached out to switch off his light.

Within minutes, his breathing had deepened and slowed until he was sound asleep. Kate propped herself against the pillows, unable to concentrate on her book, unable to switch off her thoughts. She looked at Paul, timing her breathing with his. This was the third time he'd pushed her away in as many weeks, each time citing tiredness or stress as his excuse. She couldn't remember a time in their life together when this had happened, not even in those short-lived dark days when they had only wanted to hurt each other. Something between them had changed recently, but what? However often she had heard patients talk about lack of affection or intimacy in their marriages, however often she had listed the possible causes and counselled patience and understanding, she found it almost impossible to apply the theories to her own marriage and follow her own advice. There were any number of possible reasons for Paul's behaviour, and his rejection not only made her question her own worth but, much, much worse than that, it hurt. It hurt deeply. She inched down under the duvet, switched off her own light and turned to lie with her back to Paul's, waiting for sleep to claim her.

4

"Bye, darling. I'll be here when you get back. I'll rustle up something for supper so you needn't worry.' Oliver put both hands on her shoulders and kissed Ellen's forehead.

'That would be lovely.' She leaned into him, relishing his warmth, his solidity, the reassurance she felt when close to him. The long-forgotten feeling of being loved was pushing against the barrier of self-sufficiency and self-control that had protected her for so many years. She remembered Emma, when she was still a little girl, insisting that *Sleeping Beauty* was read to her every night. So, every night Ellen had picked up the illustrated Grimms' *Fairy Tales* with a sigh, turned to the same page and begun reading aloud as her daughter snuggled up to her and drifted off to sleep. For the first time Ellen could almost empathise with Briar Rose, the sleeping princess who was woken with a kiss.

'I love you,' he murmured, as he raised his right hand to the back of her head and, somewhat to her amazement, stroked her wiry grey hair as if she was a woman twenty years younger. 'Come home soon.' He kissed her again, this time lingering on her lips. That's more like it, she thought.

She pulled away, knowing that if she didn't the temptation to go back inside and shut the door on the world for the rest of the weekend would be irresistible. 'I've got to go. The gallery won't open without me and Saturday's my busiest day.'

'I know. I'll be thinking of you as I have another cup of tea, do a bit of weeding for you, read the paper.'

'That's right. Rub it in.' Ellen laughed. As she turned down the front steps, she noticed her next-door neighbour staring at her curiously. 'Morning, Mary. Isn't it a lovely day?'

'For some obviously more so than for others,' growled Mary, as she hurled a bulging black bag into a bin and slammed down the lid before scuttling off down the street. Mary's cage was easily rattled but today Ellen wasn't in the mood to find out why. As her neighbour rounded the corner, Ellen walked down the steps and out of the gate, turning to wave, but Oliver was already inside. She imagined him walking along the corridor, straightening the pictures so they all hung exactly level. Already she knew that he liked things to be just so. Perhaps he would take himself down to the basement, tidy up their breakfast things before he went out to the patio with the paper. If only she could shut the gallery on Saturday mornings and be with him.

Their affair had been so sudden and unexpected. Only four weeks earlier, Ellen had been sitting behind her desk in the front room of the gallery, sorting through the accounts. The light had slanted through the small window behind her, reminding her that yet another summer was going by without her having bought the right blind. The back of her neck felt hot to the touch. Her headache was getting worse. She rustled in the desk drawer for the packet of ibuprofen she kept there. She stood up to get a glass of water from the small kitchenette behind her and felt a familiar prick of pleasure at the pictures that hung around the white walls.

This was the place where Ellen felt most comfortable. The hours she had spent alone here had been hours in which she had time for herself and for the quiet grieving and reflection that she needed to do after Simon's death. Somehow the atmosphere of the gallery gave her an inner calm that she could never find at home with the children. Since her uncle Sidney had willed it to her three years earlier, she had worked hard at building up the business, extending the premises through into the large back room, knocking out one of the cupboards and the dividing wall behind it so a short passage led from the front to the back. Her uncle had taken her on at a moment in her life when she was directionless, kept going only by the need to support her kids. He had the mistaken belief that her art-college training would be qualification enough, but working there with him had taught her everything she needed to know. She had taken on the legacy and turned it into an increasingly vibrant business for him.

At the sound of the bell, she glanced up as the glass door opened and a customer came in. Him again! The same man had been at the latest exhibition opening, had been in twice during the previous week and once already this. Idle speculation had inevitably become Ellen's way of passing the day as people wandered in and out of the gallery. The lean, angular planes of this man's face and his dapper pin-stripe suit said 'City' although his unkempt, boyish, almost black hair suggested something more relaxed, perhaps in the media. He exuded a youthful self-confidence appropriate for someone in what she guessed must be his late thirties. When he'd put his hand on her desk yesterday, as he asked her a question, she had surprised herself slightly by glancing up to notice a pair of cornflower blue eyes edged with long dark lashes – eyes a girl would kill for. For a moment, he held her gaze, then turned to leave.

As she had expected, he walked past her desk, smiling as he wished her good morning. She returned the greeting. He went into the back room where, on the small black-and-white security monitor, she could see him standing in front of the same picture as he had before. Over the last couple of weeks, she had often stood there herself, transported by the richness and power of the colours. Rough semi-circles of neon pink, mustard yellow, Lenten purple and brilliant carmine were juxtaposed with others in shades of apple green, red and aquamarine, all roughly outlined and set against a background of cerulean blue edged by a darker, more mysterious night sky: *Starship* by Caroline Fowler. Caroline was one of the newer artists that Ellen had brought to the gallery, impressed by her use of colour and the bold statements made by her canvases. She had a strong following already and this, her second exhibition with Ellen, had cemented her success. Unusually, the man didn't stand in front of the painting for long. As he walked through to the front of the gallery, Ellen hoped she might at last have a sale on her hands.

'I love that painting, *Starship*,' he said. 'Every time I come in here, I'm drawn to it. I'd like to buy it but I don't have anywhere to hang it at the moment.'

'I could keep it here for you for a while, if you'd like.' She opened the drawer where she kept her red stickers and receipt pads.

'No. I don't think that would work. It might not suit whatever place I buy.'

'Are you moving to London?' Ellen's curiosity got the better of her.

That was how their conversation had begun. Within five minutes of him introducing himself, Ellen was offering him a coffee as he described where he'd been living in rural France. He'd run a small arts and crafts gallery there but felt after two years that it was time to come home, so had sold the business and was looking to start again in London. As they'd talked, they'd discovered that their shared interest in art and the business of running a gallery extended into the books they'd read, films they'd seen and even the stretch of Dorset coast she knew from her childhood holidays. As the time passed, Ellen had hardly noticed the bell signalling other customers, until one had interrupted to buy another of Caroline's pictures.

Oliver had waited, flicking through the prints folder, as she took the customer's details, then stuck a red spot on the label beside the picture. As she returned to her desk, he looked at his Rolex and asked if, at five to six, she was closing. Thrilled to have made the sale, she had had to phone Caroline first to tell her the good news, then happily agreed to go for a very quick drink before she had to rush home to cook the children's supper.

She smiled as she got on the bus, remembering those magical days of snatched encounters: coffee in the gallery, a walk round the local park, lunch, a drink in the pub. Oliver was funny, concerned and, most importantly, interested in her life. Despite her half-hearted attempts at resistance, she had felt like Alice tumbling down the rabbit hole into Wonderland, unable to stop herself, simultaneously curious and alarmed about what might happen next. At last, three weeks after they'd first met, the moment had come when she had turned to him as they stepped out of Bistro Pepe and he had taken both her hands and leaned towards her. She had pulled back, aware of and unable to believe what was coming, but he had pretended not to notice. It didn't matter to him that they were in a public place and that people might look askance at a younger man kissing a definitely middle-aged woman. As his lips touched hers, she felt as if she'd come home at last.

That night he'd accompanied her home and she'd invited him in for coffee. The day before, she had put the children on the train for Cornwall where, as always, they were spending the last five weeks of their long summer holiday with Simon's family just outside St Mawes. Without them, the emptiness of the house bore down on her.

One kiss had been all that was needed to puncture the ten years of overwhelming numbness she'd felt since Simon's death. Left on her own with two small children, then aged only five and three, she'd had no alternative but to batten down her emotions and concentrate on helping them cope with the lack of their father. What was important was that she kept Simon alive in their minds, making sure above all that they knew he'd loved them. To do that, she couldn't include another man in their lives, however frequently her friends and family said that was exactly what the children, and indeed she, needed. Until now. At first the sex was awkward, unfamiliar, embarrassing, but Oliver's confidence and consideration drew her out of herself until she relaxed and moved with him. Since that first night together, Oliver hadn't left except to go to pick up a few clothes and check out of wherever he'd been staying. And she had never wanted him to.

Ellen couldn't remember when she had felt so indifferent to what her neighbours thought of her. The net curtains of Oakham Road might be twitching as she and Oliver came and left together – let them! The only people, apart from her family, whose opinion she particularly cared about were Kate and Bea. She could imagine their faces when she told them about Oliver. After so many years of knowing her as a devoted widow and committed single mother, they would be completely taken by surprise. But keeping Oliver to herself made their relationship all the more precious, all the more intense. She didn't want that to end by going public, even though she knew that, once the kids came home, she would have to. If not sooner.

When she did, Kate would listen to her without interrupting but Bea would probe, making Ellen give away details before she was ready. Up until now, Ellen had treated Bea's own endeavours to hook a man with some scepticism, but suddenly she understood something of what her friend must be looking for. The discovery of Oliver had thrown a switch inside her that she had forgotten existed. That was all Bea wanted to experience. Ellen saw that now. With the menopause beckoning, they might have only a last few throws of the hormonal dice.

Musing on that unpleasant truth, she unlocked the door to the gallery, pushed up the security shutters and sorted her papers, ready for the usual steady flow of Saturday customers. She was in the back, looking at *Starship*, considering whether to buy the picture for Oliver as a memento of their meeting (so what if he didn't have anywhere to hang it?), when the bell rang. Perhaps it was too soon to make such a big gesture, but she had the rest of the morning to think about it. In the meantime she would put her back into some work and go through the programme for her next exhibition, making sure everything was on track.

She went through to see her first customer of the day, and was surprised to find Kate standing there, the only woman she knew who was over fifty and could get away with a skimpy pale pink T-shirt and white linen trousers. Suddenly she felt self-conscious about the old cotton dress she'd yanked off its hanger that morning. What they said about a moment on the lips was true. All those consolatory biscuits that she'd packed away over the years had made their home very comfortably on her hips.

'Kate! Good to see you. It's been ages.'

'That's why I thought I'd drop by. Where have you been hiding yourself?'

Ellen's mobile rescued her from having to answer. 'Just phoning to tell you I love you.' The sound of Oliver's voice transported Ellen into her garden where she imagined him sitting.

'Don't be silly. You've already said that once today.' Ellen laughed with pleasure.

'Three times if I remember right,' he corrected her.

'I'll see you later. Can't wait.' Ellen was anxious to cut the conversation short in front of Kate, who was staring at her open-mouthed. 'I've got a customer with me.'

''Bye, darling. See you soon.'

'Who on earth was that?' Kate was watching Ellen's face with amazement. 'You're absolutely glowing.'

Ellen couldn't stop a grin spreading across her face. 'I wanted to tell you,' she began, 'but I wasn't ready or it wasn't the right time. Look, sit down and I'll fill you in before the gallery gets busy.' An intense feeling of relief came with this unlooked-for opportunity to spill the beans as she launched into how she and Oliver had met.

When Kate heard that Oliver was only forty at most, she exploded: 'Does he know that you've got at least eight years on him?'

'Well, no. In fact, he hasn't mentioned age at all. I thought that was so tactful that I decided to go along with it.'

'But what will he think when he finds out?'

'He won't. Not yet anyway. He did ask me what my HRT pills were but I just told him they were contraceptives – if only – and I pretended the thread veins on my legs were scratches from the roses in the garden. And I told him I'd been grey since my early thirties! One of the drawbacks of having jet-black hair as a kid.'

'Ellen Neill! I didn't know you had it in you.'

'Neither did I. At least, I'd forgotten. But white lying's not the only thing I haven't forgotten how to do.'

'Not the only thing?' Kate was so absorbed in the story that the exhaustion Ellen had noticed disappeared as her face grew more animated. Suddenly she cottoned on to what Ellen meant. 'My God! How long have you known him? Four weeks? You don't hang around, do you?'

'I know. It does seem ridiculously quick but I haven't felt like this since . . . I can't remember when. Honestly, I feel like a teenager with a first crush. I think about him all the time, wondering what he's doing, if he'll phone. Do you remember that feeling? I'm as surprised as you are,' she said, watching Kate's expression. 'I never imagined anything like this would happen. I never wanted anyone coming between the kids and Simon but I don't think Oliver will. He's so kind and considerate. I'd forgotten how good it feels to be wanted by someone and to share all those endless day-to-day tasks that otherwise you deal with on your own. It's all happened so fast and – I know this sounds silly – I feel really happy for the first time since Simon died.'

'Do the children know?' As the most family-oriented member of the little group, Kate's first thought, after her friends' well-being, was always for their children, whom she loved almost as if they were her own.

'Not yet.' At the mention of them it suddenly occurred to Ellen that she'd been in massive denial. Of course she couldn't wrap this delicious secret about herself and pretend the outside world didn't exist for ever. What had she been thinking? Her children came first. 'But you're right. I must tell them. Now they're older, I hope they'll understand. Oliver loves kids and can't wait to meet them. In fact, I'm thinking of taking him when I go down to see them before the bank holiday.'

'Are you nuts? How do you think Simon's family will react, never mind the children? His parents will probably both have a coronary. I know Simon's mother's been encouraging you to find someone else for years but, all the same, you've got to take this slowly. The reality might be harder for his family to take than they imagine.'

Kate was always so sensible. Now the secret was out, it wasn't just about Ellen and Oliver any more. Ellen was going to have to confront and deal with the repercussions in the best way possible. If only she had kept her mouth shut, as she'd intended, and given herself a bit more thinking time – except she hadn't been thinking.

'You're probably right there too but I know it'll be OK.' A finger of doubt gave her a sly poke but she slapped it away. 'Oliver's not going to try to replace Simon. How could he? But I'm so sure he's going to get on with them.'

'I still think you should take it a step at a time.' Kate was obviously choosing her words, not wanting to prick the bubble. 'It's only been a month. You've got to be absolutely certain that you're not making a mistake.'

The bubble wobbled but remained intact.

'I've never been more sure of anything in my life.' As gentle a character as she was, a determined set came to Ellen's jaw when she fought for something she believed in. 'I've enjoyed keeping him secret so far, but now that's over, I want people to know I love him.'

'That's fine. But take it easy. The children will adapt but they'll find it difficult to start with. At least don't make them deal with this in front of their grandparents. They need to be in their own home, near their friends and everything that makes them feel comfortable.'

Ellen knew that, as usual, Kate was talking sense. The excitement of the affair had temporarily blinded her to the realities of the situation. Much as she was dying to embark on her new family life, taking Oliver to Cornwall would be a mistake. She saw that. She would go down on her own, as originally planned, come back for one last glorious week alone with Oliver before Em and Matt finally came home in time for the start of the new school term. Then she would break the news slowly and carefully.

5

In the car, on the way to her mother's, the voice of the Radio 4 presenter was overwhelmed by the noise of the motorway. Not that Bea noticed what she was missing. Her mind was on her son. These days, Ben was being less communicative than she could remember him in all their sixteen years together. He had barely mustered a grunt when she'd left, refusing to tear his attention from yet another old episode of *Skins*. Not even 'Have a good time' or 'Love to Gran'. She left him lying on the sofa, his glass on the floor under his discarded socks, a faint whiff of sweat and feet hanging in the air.

She visualised his worldly possessions scattered in his room upstairs where they'd last been used, then buried under the T-shirts, pants and socks dropped on top of them. His wardrobe door hung open, revealing a row of empty metal hangers and shelves with various knots of tangled clothing that had somehow spread their way across to his unmade bed. Whenever she nagged him to tidy his room, he put the whole lot in the laundry basket downstairs – much easier than hanging it up again. If the door was shut, she always knocked – she had done ever since he'd shouted at her to keep out of his business. She hadn't even commented on the last poster he'd Blu-tacked to the wall – two girls going topless, one touching the other's breast, both slightly smiling with their topaz eyes staring out from under their strawberry blonde fringes. Ben had bought it from a boy at school last year. When she'd seen it, she'd frowned but managed not to say a word.

This morning, despite all attempts to bite her tongue, she'd been less successful.

'I'm just off to Gran's,' she'd said, in her cheerful let's-not-get-off-on-the-wrong-foot-this-morning voice.

'Right.' Eyes fixed to the screen.

'Darling. You will tidy up, won't you?'

No reply.

'If you could just try to do something with your bedroom so we can at least see the floor . . .' The hope in her voice was met with silence. 'Well, I'll be back late tonight, then.'

'Yeah. Right.' He hadn't even glanced round.

Since Colin had left, Bea had watched Ben turn more and more in on himself. Apart from having to deal with the inevitable teenage hormonal soup, he'd had to watch the father he'd adored go off with his PA, a woman almost young enough to be Ben's older sister. Within a year, she had given birth to twins. Colin had never explained to Bea why he had fallen out of love with her. She sometimes wondered whether he had ever been in love with her at all. But, her own feelings aside, it had been hard to answer with any truth twelve-year-old Ben's endless questions about why Dad had gone. Apart from the obvious one, she didn't know the answers.

Together they watched as Colin morphed from a suit-and-tired executive into a complacent new husband and on into an even more self-satisfied but exhausted new father of two. Plumper than he had been, his skin shinier and more tanned, he oozed self-satisfaction. His hair, though greyer, was cut fashionably short; his clothes were no longer mail order (too busy to shop) but designer ('Carrie helps me choose'). The idea of the pair shopping together made Bea laugh. The Colin she knew would no more set foot in a clothes shop than he would in a supermarket. But she had to hand it to Carrie: that girl had got Colin wrapped round her little finger in a way that Bea never had.

As soon as he'd announced he was leaving her for Carrie, Bea had known it would be only a matter of time before they started a family. Carrie would want kids and the only way Colin would keep her was to give them to her. What she hadn't bargained for was the vigour with which he threw himself into second-time fatherhood. She hadn't bargained for how upset she'd feel either. Colin had discovered the joys of nappy-changing, of bottle-feeding, of getting up in the night. When he looked for sympathy, complaining of how tired he felt at having to do all this and go to work, the floodgates of Bea's fury opened.

'Tired? How many women do you think feel exactly the same and have been working and looking after children for centuries?'

'But, Bea,' he had protested, sheepish, 'that's not the same. They're used to it.'

'Bollocks they're used to it! What do you think I felt like

when I was still breast-feeding Ben and struggling to keep my job going?'

'But that was different,' he had protested.

'How? How was it different?'

'Well, you wanted to do it.'

'Wanted to? I only wanted to because I didn't want to lose my bloody job. I would have felt a whole lot better if I'd had someone else getting up in the middle of the night to help.'

'But they're so sweet in the night. Cora—'

'I know that, Colin. I was there with your firstborn. Remember? Shame you weren't there most of the time too.'

'Well, OK. I regret that now. I should have helped more. I wish I had. That's why I'm going to do it differently this time round. I'm going to be a good father.'

'Well, remember you're Ben's father too. That's all I can say.' Bea gave up. There was no puncturing his unbearable self-satisfaction. She refrained from pointing out the smear of baby sick that ran down from the shoulder of his expensively relaxed Etro shirt. Let him face the world with his badge of fatherhood. Carrie must be finding her two young daughters such hard work (Bea sincerely hoped so) that she hadn't noticed. This was not the man who had fathered Ben. She knew Ben recognised that too and was hurt by it. He didn't want to go round to Colin and Carrie's to have it rubbed in his face, but Colin didn't understand that. He thought that by including Ben every now and then he was completing his happy family. Happy families – huh!

Her attention was brought back to the road as she joined the exit to the motorway too fast and came screaming up beside a red Saab that had earlier overtaken her. The two young guys turned and the passenger screwed his finger to his head, mouthing something at her. For God's sake. She stuck her tongue out at them as they roared off. Not very grown-up, Bea, she admonished herself. All the same she felt much better.

Instead of returning to Ben, her mind flitted to Coldharbour. How safe was her job? She knew Adam Palmer's reputation as a ruthless, manipulative boss who would do anything to raise his staff's so-called performance levels. In his last incarnation, he'd turned round an ailing Pennant Publishing by wasting no time in getting rid of all the dead wood, building a small and fiercely loyal team who had successfully shaped and tightened the list. Would he be bringing any of them with him? If he did, how would that affect her?

As she approached the outskirts of Harmchester, she took a right into the narrow lane that led to her mother's house. She loved the drive down there, so familiar that memories of her childhood rushed into her mind as she turned into the open gate at the top of the drive, which led to the house that stood just as it had since she, Will and Jess had been brought up there.

She crunched over the gravel to the porch, a relatively recent addition to the faded but still elegant Georgian house. Gumboots crowded the small space below the ancient duffel coats and scarves that she, her brother and sister had forgotten when they'd finally left home. It was just as if they were about to return. Housekeeping had never been her mother's strongest point, she reflected, noticing the dried mud on the flagstones, and the cobwebs above her head. Even Miss Havisham might have set slightly higher standards. However, at least she and her siblings had been allowed to get on with their own lives, blessed with a mother who would take her independence to the grave with her, if she had any control over her future. And let's hope she does, Bea willed.

'Mum! Where are you?' she yelled, as she let herself into the dim panelled hallway. Bending to pick up a few scattered letters, mostly bills and mail-order catalogues from the floor, she balanced them in the minimal space available on the small gate-legged table that held the phone.

She called again, putting her head round the door into the sitting room. The knitting left mid-row on the comfy plum-coloured sofa and the voices from *Any Questions?* on the radio signalled that Adele couldn't be far away. The gilt mirror over the mantelpiece could have done with a good dusting and the hearth might have benefited from being cleaned out. The books were crammed higgledy-piggledy onto the shelves at either side of the chimney breast. Not for the first time, Bea thought her mother might benefit from moving to somewhere smaller. They had talked about the huge task it would involve, but Adele was waiting until the time was right. Whatever that meant.

'Mum!' She heard the familiar edge of impatience creep into her voice. Making a mental note to control it, she tried once more. 'Mum.' Better.

'Here, dear. I'm in the kitchen . . .' The crash that followed made Bea run down the flagged corridor past the stairs and through the door at the end of the passage. Her mother was on the floor, rubbing her leg, surrounded by saucepans and the rail that was supposed to suspend them within easy reach above the ancient Aga.

'What on earth are you doing? Are you all right?' Bea's relief at seeing her in one piece swiftly turned to exasperation. She righted a fallen chair to where it belonged under the table, trying not to let her irritation show.

'I'm absolutely fine. I was just trying to straighten the rail. I suppose I should have taken the pans off first. I just pulled a bit too hard and the whole thing collapsed.' Adele rubbed her elbow where she'd caught it on the Aga.

'But why didn't you wait for me to do it for you? We've talked about this thousands of times. You could have been hurt.' Bea couldn't stop the edge creeping back into her voice.

'Oh, rubbish, darling. I didn't want to bother you. Anyway, I wasn't expecting you,' she announced breezily.

As Adele got to her feet, brushing plaster dust off her cardigan, Bea registered that she was still wearing her pyjama bottoms and slippers. 'But, Mum, I've come to take you out to lunch. Don't you remember? We arranged it on Wednesday.'

Adele rolled her eyes to the Kitchen Maid adorned with damp tea towels and her underwear. 'Of course. How stupid of me. I'll just be a minute.'

'But you're not even dressed yet.'

'Nor I am.' Her mother dived into the laundry basket for some tights. 'It won't take me long, darling.' She disappeared along the corridor and up the stairs.

Bea stayed where she was, bending to pick up the pans.

Should she be more concerned about Adele? Her feelings of responsibility for her mother weighed heavy even though she knew they weren't wanted. If something happened to Adele, it would be her fault. After all, of the three children, she was the one who lived closest. Will had married his Australian girlfriend and won the bonus prize of a new life in Sydney while Jess was wrapped up in her perfect family of one long-suffering husband and two children (she'd have had the point-four if she could have arranged it) in spick-and-span heaven outside Edinburgh. Bea resolved to bring up the subject of moving house again, but not right now. She didn't want to spoil the afternoon ahead.

Tempted though she was to do the bit of washing-up piled by the sink, she ignored it, knowing that her mother would only take her help as a form of criticism. Instead she returned to the sitting room to put the fireguard in place before standing and staring out of the window at the long garden stretching towards the copse beyond. Just the sight of it brought back all those years of hide-and-seek, bonfires, camping. If only Ben could have enjoyed the place in the same way, but childhood was different these days. Nobody was thrown outside after lunch and told to 'go and play' for a couple of hours any more. She could imagine Ben's reaction if she'd ever dared to try.

'I'm ready.' Adele came into the room, having put on a taupe cotton skirt with a neat white blouse, car keys in hand.

'I'll drive, Ma.' Although Adele's doctor seemed to think she was still capable, the idea of her mother driving scared the hell out of Bea. She wasn't frightened for Adele but for everybody else on the road. 'You can navigate.'

'Where are we going again?'

'The Hare and Hounds in Ludborough. If we get there early enough we'll be able to sit outside.'

The lanes were almost empty as Bea drove, ignoring Adele's uncertain directions and relying on the satnav. They arrived without mishap and pulled into the already busy car park alongside the pub. Above the porch, darkened windows winked out from behind the profusion of vivid pink and red petunias, yellow golden eye and trailing blue lobelia crammed into the window boxes. Mother and daughter picked their way through the dim lounge bar, ordering their drinks en route, and out into the back garden, blinking at the sudden light.

It was the best kind of English summer's day – blue sky with puffs of cloud chased across it by a light wind. Sitting in the pub garden at a table in the shade of a whispering beech tree with a bowl of soup, a chunk of crusty bread and a glass of lager, the world seemed a better place. Inevitably, the conversation moved immediately to Bea's own life. As usual, her mother could be relied upon to put her mind to good use when listening to Bea, helping her to get matters into some sort of perspective.

Although she was of the generation of middle-class wives whose pregnancy had put an end to their ambition and who had stayed at home to bring up their children, Adele was an intelligent woman, whose husband had trusted her good sense when he had had to make his own business decisions. She had known exactly how his bank functioned, who worked there and what they did or didn't contribute and how he was able to manipulate them to his success.

As a result, she had developed a pragmatic stance from which to view life. So, as far as she could see, whatever happened at Coldharbour, there was nothing Bea could do to influence events. If she wanted to keep her job, or until she had decided whether or not she did, she should put her head down and work hard, adopting the stance that Adam Palmer expected: tough, go-getting. When she'd won his confidence, she'd be in a position to make a choice. As for Ben, had Bea ever seen a monosyllabic twenty-two-year-old who spent all day in front of the TV? Of course not. The boy would grow out of it, just like all the others. Bea had a nasty feeling that there were plenty of twenty-two-year-olds who never had.

Later, as Adele was laughing at the story of her daughter's latest dating fiasco, Bea's phone rang.

'Bea, it's Kate. You'll never guess.'

'Well, for God's sake tell me, then.'

'It's Ellen. She's got herself a man!'

For a moment Bea was thrown. 'Ellen? Hang on a minute.' She held up one finger and gestured to her mother that she wouldn't be long.

Adele nodded, quite content to watch what was going on at the tables around her while she waited for Bea to finish.

'Yes, Ellen. Your old university friend who's been single since her husband died. That Ellen.' Bea could hear Kate's excitement. 'I went to the gallery this morning and she told me. He's one of her customers!'

'You have got to be joking. After all this time? Who is he? When did she meet him?' Bea was ashamed to admit to herself that, instead of sharing Kate's evident pleasure, she was piqued by the idea that, after years of apparent indifference to the opposite sex, Ellen had beaten her to it. Somehow the natural order of things seemed to have been skewed.

'They just met and he's moved in with her already. Well, at least until the kids get back.'

'What?' For once Bea was speechless.

'It's true. He's not even forty. And she wants us to meet him. I said I'd tell you to expect a call from her.'

Moved in with her? That couldn't be right. Ellen would never do anything so hasty. Although she had made some canny snap decisions over the artists she took on at the gallery, outside her work life this was a woman for whom 'dithering' was a watchword. But what appeared to be indecision was really circumspection. And Kate didn't make mistakes. She listened, absorbed what she was told and considered her next course of action. She wouldn't have told Bea any of this unless she was absolutely sure it was true.

Bea ended the conversation more abruptly than she meant to. She couldn't share Kate's pleasure in the news, not just yet. She needed time to take it in, get over her own feelings of what felt horribly close to envy. She was ashamed of herself. What an unpleasant person she must be, if she couldn't share in a friend's happiness without thinking of herself first.

But why didn't Ellen tell me? Bea wondered. We've been friends for almost thirty years, seen each other through so much, and yet she told Kate. Kate, to whom Bea had only

introduced Ellen about ten years ago when Kate and Paul
had moved to London from Manchester. Bea disliked the
insidious needle of resentment that pricked her when she
was reminded of the strong relationship between her two
friends. But it was true that, having introduced them because
she thought they'd get on, there were times when she felt
the odd one out, such was the bond that had developed
between them.

'What is it, darling? I've lost you.' Adele's voice brought
her back to the present.

'That was Kate telling me that Ellen's got herself a man
at last.'

'But that's wonderful. She's been lonely for so long.'

'Lonely?' That wasn't the way Bea saw her friend at all.
'What makes you say that? She's had the kids, and Simon's
family have always supported her, as well as Kate and me.
She's always said she didn't want anyone else.'

'Bea, dear, try to be a little more understanding. Of course
lots of people have loved her and looked after her. But that's
not the same as being in love, is it? It's not the same as
having someone special to share things with, someone to
provide a buffer against the world outside, someone who
makes you feel safe and loved. Your father did all those
things for me – all those things that I know you're looking
for yourself, although you'd never put it that way.' Adele
reached across to grasp Bea's hand while Bea looked away,
suddenly self-conscious – her mother knew her far too well.

She wasn't in the mood to discuss the truth of her own
feelings so briskly changed the subject, making her mother
laugh as she regaled her with the story of the date who had

come to pick her up in his van. When she'd opened the door, the first thing she saw was a made-up double mattress in the back. All she'd let him see of her was her back as she beat a hasty retreat into her house.

By the time Bea and her mother left the pub, everything was back on an even keel and they headed into the nearby town to buy something for supper and to stock up Adele's fridge for another week.

6

When Bea had cut off their conversation so abruptly, Kate had understood exactly what was going on in her friend's mind. Bea's emotions were so transparent. But why couldn't she just accept that Kate and Ellen's friendship was inevitably different from the relationships Bea had with either one of them? And, more importantly, that it didn't matter. They were old, close friends who shouldn't be divided just because of Bea's irrational jealousy.

She picked up the newspaper that Paul had left spread across the kitchen table and took it outside to the patio. She sat down and began to leaf through the pages while working out which jobs to do the next day. She knew that if she didn't take the secateurs to the garden soon, the whole place would be a jungle. The white wisteria, while beautiful in flower, grew so vigorously that it was threatening to overwhelm the pergola and the apple tree beside it. The summer storms during the week meant that the weeds were pushing their way through her carefully planted borders and the shrubs seemed to have taken on a life of their own as they sprouted towards the sun, spreading sideways, fighting for space.

As she considered what to tackle first, she was interrupted by a sudden shout from inside where Paul, in khaki shorts, T-shirt and sandals – he'd got the message about not wearing socks with them at long last – was jumping up and down, sucking the index finger of his right hand.

'What's happened?' She got up. 'Are you OK?'

'I cut my finger on a bloody tin,' he muttered. 'Where are the plasters?'

As he moved across to the sink, Kate could see the large chrome Brabantia bin on its side, rubbish spilling across a sheet of newspaper on the floor with a green plastic bucket nearby. 'What on earth are you doing?' she asked, as she opened a cupboard to get out the first-aid box, then passed him a small box of plasters.

'I'm going through the rubbish – obviously.' Paul was running his finger under the tap, the water streaming scarlet. 'Perhaps you should have a look at this. Stitches or septicaemia – I don't know which would be worse.'

Years of experience of being married to one of the world's great hypochondriacs had taught Kate to ignore all remarks relating to his well-being. They were invariably exaggerated. It had always struck her as odd that a man with such an impressive City profile should be such a wuss behind his front door.

'Have you lost something?'

'No! Don't put that there.' Paul's attention turned from his injury as he grabbed the handful of orange peel she was about to return to the bin and tossed it into the bucket instead. 'The fruit and veg go in the bucket, the paper in the plastic box and everything that can't be recycled goes in the bin. How many times do I have to remind everyone?'

She stared, astonished, as he continued to rummage through the mess picking out potato peelings, teabags and leftovers from supper the night before.

'I'm the only one in this house who takes recycling seriously,' he added.

'I hope you're not saying I don't? Sometimes I forget, that's all. It's going to get mixed up once it's in the rubbish van anyway.'

'Kate, you haven't a clue what happens in the van – or at the recycling centre, come to that. I'm just trying to do my bit – well, our bit.' He separated out some pieces of egg shell.

'Isn't this a bit extreme? The odd bit of potato or orange peel in the wrong place isn't going to bring the world grinding to a halt.'

'If everybody talked like that . . .'

'Pinch me, please.'

'What?'

'Pinch me. I want to be absolutely certain that we're really having this conversation.'

She knelt down and began to help him sort out the rubbish, unable to stop a snort that turned into a stifled giggle. 'Look at us!' Within seconds, they were sitting side by side on the floor, laughing together like old times.

'Are you going into the surgery today?' Paul recovered himself enough to ask, satisfied that everything was in the right place.

'I haven't decided. It's such a lovely day but I suppose I ought to get on top of my referrals. Why?'

'In that case, I'll go down to the fishmonger's and get the stuff for that bouillabaisse I've wanted to try for ages. I've started making some panna cotta too.'

Kate smiled. 'Sounds good.' She considered her husband as he went over to pull out a recipe book. He was still so much the man she had fallen in love with so many years earlier. 'Will Jack be in?'

'God knows. You know what he's like. Saturday night? I doubt it.'

As if on cue, the sound of the bathroom door prefaced the sound of footsteps heading downstairs.

'Morning, Marge.' Jack hugged his mother. 'Anything for breakfast?'

Kate squeezed him back, feeling a great rush of affection towards the tousled twenty-two-year-old who towered above her. She leaned against his Chelsea strip, inhaling his sandalwood aftershave, yet again struck by the speed with which all her children had grown up and saddened by the thought that it wouldn't be long before they'd all gone. Jack was the last to fly the nest. 'Try the fridge. Are you going to be in tonight?'

'In? What, here? No way. I'm off to the Chelsea match and then I'm meeting some mates. There's a party in Chiswick somewhere.'

'So it's just us, then.' Paul pulled out a used envelope and began writing his shopping list.

'Again.'

'Don't say it like that. We haven't had a night in together for ages.'

'Yeah, Mum. Chill out. The old man'll cook something great and you can open one of those posh bottles of wine you insist on keeping under lock and key.'

'Only because I know they're not safe when you and your mates are around and we're not.'

'Just because we finished off that crate of Château-something-or-other when you were away. How was I meant to know it was so special?'

'My point exactly.' She put her arm around Paul's shoulders and kissed his cheek. 'It's a lovely idea. Let's do it.'

Fifteen minutes later, she was on her own with a valuable half-hour in which to do nothing. Paul had gone off armed with carrier-bags and Jack had left for Stamford Bridge, having rejected the contents of the fridge in favour of a sausage sarnie on the way. As she resettled herself on the garden bench with a coffee and the paper, her thoughts returned to Ellen. She had been glowing from the inside out this morning, giddy with happiness. Whoever this man was, he must be a good thing if he could bring about a change like that so suddenly. Kate could still remember what it felt like, the intensity of that first flush of love – the sense of there being no one but Paul in the world, that nothing else mattered – as if it was yesterday not thirty-odd years ago.

Paul had been such a maverick then, always the life and soul, unpredictable, fun. Their children would never believe how different he was from the man they knew today. She remembered the party where they'd met, the usual student thing: crowded, loud and with plenty of drink in the kitchen. She had been sitting in a corner where it was quieter, less smoky, huddled in conversation with a couple of other medics from St Mary's when Paul had come towards them. As soon as she saw him, her heart skipped a beat. Quite literally. She knew she wasn't alone in fancying him, but the difference had been that, incredibly, he felt the same about her. They went home together that night and that was that. For thirty-one years their rock-solid relationship had been the envy of their friends. But the sensations she knew Ellen must be experiencing had faded long ago.

Kate sighed and stretched out her legs on the bench, leaning back with her face angled to the sun and thinking about her marriage. If anything, it was like a favourite old coat: over the years, patches of fabric had grown thin, one or two rips had been stitched up so you almost couldn't see them – but you always knew they were there. Yet, despite its increasing shapelessness and the signs of general wear-and-tear, it still felt more comfortable than any new coat ever would. It was 'her'. She shut her eyes, pleased with the analogy, and felt the sun warm her cheeks. Perhaps she and Paul had come to take one another a bit too much for granted over the years but tonight would be a chance to patch one of those thinning areas. Seeing Ellen had made her realise she'd like to recapture a bit of that old pizzazz and she wanted to believe Paul would too.

*

'Darling, I can't find the corkscrew,' Kate yelled from the kitchen.

'It's up here. Come and sit down.'

She was surprised that Paul hadn't commented on her contribution to the evening, however minimal it had been. She was used to him being more appreciative. When she'd got in, relieved to be temporarily back on top of the endless practice admin that came with her job, the scent of the Mediterranean had stolen up the stairs to greet her. Paul was absorbed in his cooking and, to her relief, refused all offers of help. Instead she went into the dining room and laid the table with the Victorian lace cloth, got out the silver, replaced the candle stubs with new, then went into the garden to snip three Belle Isis roses, their pale flesh-pink petals in full bloom. Putting them in a vase, she inhaled their myrrh-like scent, then placed them in the centre of the table. She heard the bang of the oven door, then a muttered curse, and guessed she still had time to whizz upstairs and change into a simple dusky lilac linen dress, brush her hair and even dab on a lick of lipstick before adding a quick spritz of cologne.

Paul had docked his iPod to send a piano concerto she didn't recognise rippling round the dining room. She dimmed the lights and lit the candles, pleased with what she saw. The scene was set for seduction.

Paul came in carrying two plates. 'I've messed up the panna cotta. Not thinking.'

'That's not like you.' He normally got the results he wanted by adapting any recipe as he needed to. 'But this looks delicious.' The bouillabaisse, the garlicky croûtons and *rouille* breathed the South of France into the room. She watched him pull the cork on a chilled bottle of Montrachet and pour the pale, straw-coloured wine into their glasses. She lifted hers to clink with his. 'To us.'

As Paul smiled back, she noticed the slight bags under his eyes. He looked tired. Immediately she reproached herself once more for not paying him enough attention over the last months. With the children grown-up, it was too easy to give the time that she used to devote to them to her work. Apart from that, throwing herself into the practice and all it involved meant her mind was constantly occupied, giving her little time to dwell on how much she missed her two oldest. Now that she was a partner, and had upped her number of sessions a week, she didn't get home till nine most nights, too exhausted to do anything more than eat, doze in front of the news and go to bed. As she began to eat, she thought again about how little she knew of what really went on in Paul's world, any more than he really did of what went on at the surgery. They met at the beginning and the end of the day, caught up with all the jobs they didn't have time for at weekends, exchanging snippets of news as they passed each other – and so the months disappeared. An idea struck her.

'We should think about going to see Sam. We deserve a holiday.'

'Yes, we do. But Africa?'

'Well, it's going to be hard to see him anywhere else.'

'I can't possibly. Not now.' Panic crossed his face before he looked down at his bowl.

'No, of course not. But we can make plans.' If she pressed enough, she might be able to persuade him. Dreaming up and organising the trip of a lifetime might be just the thing to bring them together again. And combined with seeing their faraway son – what could be better?

'I'm sorry, but now isn't the moment.' He picked up his fork and took a last mouthful.

'Why not?' Why wouldn't he explain what was causing his withdrawal from her?

'It's been a heavy week.' Paul finished his meal and put his head into his hands. 'There's no escaping the fact that we're going to have to make more cuts.'

'But I thought you'd been through that.'

'We have. But our turnover's still down and we've got to cut our overheads even further if we want to stay in business.'

'But you'll be all right, won't you?' Perhaps that was what was worrying him.

'Oh, I'll be all right. But there are plenty of people who won't and it won't be easy for them to get another job in this climate. I had a young guy in the office this morning, crying, pleading with me to reassure him that he'll keep his job and I couldn't.' He sounded so despairing, but Kate knew she had nothing to say that would help him. The chasm that was opening between them was already too wide for her to reach across.

The mood of the evening had changed.

'I'm sorry, Katie. You're right, I'm still knackered. Another early night and I'll be fine. Coming?'

'Actually I think I'll stay down here and clear up. I've got a few things that I want to get done.' She began to gather up the plates and glasses.

'Well, OK. If you insist.' He leaned over and kissed her. 'Good night.'

Despite her earlier resolve, Kate recognised that tonight was not for romancing. The moment had gone. Pottering about in the kitchen, she relaxed in the heavy peace that descended on the house at this time of night, only ever interrupted by the odd passing car, distant police siren or the sharp, high-pitched bark of a fox. With everything put away, she made herself a cup of tea and switched on her laptop, clicking on her latest emails. At last there was one from Sam. She opened it with a happy sense of anticipation and relief.

Hey Mum
How are you guys? Can only get online when one of the boys takes me into town. That's why the long silence. Although I've only been in Ghana for a few weeks, I've been so busy I haven't had time to be properly homesick. Coming here has been one of the best things I have ever done. After a week of acclimatisation and getting to know one another and making sure we had all the supplies we'd need, the five of us were driven to this tiny village where we're now all living (photos to follow – have lost the lead!). I'm talking mud huts in a compound – the real deal. The villagers took to us straight away and have made us feel almost at home. I suppose they would, given we've come to help them build and run the school. Kev, our team leader, is dead keen that we should be helping the villagers help themselves. Enabling them by

teaching them the processes rather than doing all the work ourselves. I hadn't thought of that before but, of course, when we eventually leave, the whole point is that the project should be able to continue running without us. We haven't actually started building yet because we're waiting for more wood to be brought in, but in the meantime I spend hours playing football with the kids – not much of a strain! – and have even been taken hunting with the men of the village. When I'm not doing that we're trying to work out the beginnings of a sponsorship scheme so that kids from other villages will be able to come here too . . .

As she read on, Kate couldn't help feeling envious. What Sam was describing was as remote and intriguing to her as the photographs she saw in the pages of *National Geographic*, which they kept in the practice waiting room. She and Paul had always talked about how one day they would travel together but somehow they'd never got further than Europe. Early in their marriage, Kate had been happy at the centre of her new family, pitying her friends who were missing out on the joys of family life but were able to holiday where and when they wanted. But perhaps it was she who had missed out. In the end all her friends had caught her up: careers were chosen and babies were born but without the sacrifice of those early years of freedom.

She pulled down a favourite old photo from a shelf in

the corner. There were the three of them, Megan, Sam and Jack, sitting in a blue plastic paddling pool in the garden. How could she and Paul have produced three such contrasting children? Smiling out at her were nine-year-old Megan, fly-away brown curls, blue eyes under fine wide-apart brows, a tip-tilted nose and a gentle mouth; Sam, at seven, with blond curls, freckles, eyes already with that faraway look despite the broad smile at the photographer, which revealed a front tooth chipped when he had fallen out of a tree; and Jack, four years younger, with short darker hair, a determined chin and a slight frown. The photo gave away exactly the people they would become: Megan married to Ned and working in the drama department of the BBC in Bristol; Sam, out of easy contact, adventuring in Africa; Jack, confident, charismatic and too soon out of university to have found his way.

Suddenly there was an almighty crash from outside, followed by the sound of something being dragged along the street. She jumped to her feet and ran upstairs into the living room where she pulled aside the curtain. There, in the middle of the road, a mangy brown fox was tearing through the contents of their food recycling bin. So much for Paul's care in sorting out the rubbish. The animal had dragged the bin out of their front garden, forced it open, strewn everything across the road and was now sniffing round, scoffing the best bits. A sharp bark heralded the arrival of a second, which slunk between two cars further up the street, then loped towards its mate, eyes gleaming under the street light. Kate shuddered. Sitting on the back of the sofa, she knocked hard on the window to drive them away. For a moment they stopped, looked up. One stared straight at her, defiant, before going back to its feast.

The curtains drawn and lights switched off, she went upstairs to tell Paul but he was flat out, sound asleep, one arm flung across the bed, gently snoring. With a small sigh, she got herself ready for bed and slipped in beside him.

7

'I've got a surprise for you.' Oliver came through the kitchen door, looking relaxed in his blue cashmere sweater, his hands behind his back. 'Close your eyes.'

Oh, God. A present. Ellen knew she should have bought him the picture.

'Hold out your hands.'

Apprehensive, unused to being given anything unexpected, apart from the children's half-baked efforts from art classes, Ellen put out a hand. She felt something, a bag, being hung over her arm. Then two more. 'But I haven't got anything for you.' The part of her that had hesitated over buying the picture said that presents were reciprocal, to be given on special occasions; otherwise they were an unnecessary indulgence. Not even Simon had surprised her with something as spontaneous as this.

'Doesn't matter.' She felt his hand lightly on the small of her back, aware that if he moved it a centimetre lower, it would be lying right on the roll of fat pushed up by the too-tight waistband of her skirt. He didn't seem to notice or, if he did, to care. 'Right. Now you can open them.'

She moved away from his hand, opening her eyes to see three bags hanging off her arm, a small one from La Perla and two large ones boasting names she had never heard of. She became uncomfortably aware of her greying, almost elastic-free Marks & Spencer underwear that had absorbed the colours from everything else in the wash over the last couple of years, of her once comfortable skirt that had seen better days, and her loose disguise-it-all cotton shirt from the same period. Out of the tissue paper came a confection (there was no other word for it) of copper-coloured lace. At least he hadn't gone for a G-string, she saw with relief, as she separated a pair of flounced lace briefs in cotton tulle from a bra that frothed with more lace than she had ever seen on one garment. 'Oh, God! They're . . . well . . . beautiful.' (And totally unsuitable.) 'Thank you.' (Please don't make me try them on now.)

'There's more. Look again.' Oliver had sat down and was wearing a strange expression that Ellen didn't recognise. For a split second, it was as if the spontaneous, generous man she loved had disappeared, to be replaced by someone far more cool and calculating. Disconcerted, she looked away, reaching into the bag again, this time to find a white (more my colour) push-up (oh, no, I don't want to show off my wrinkled cleavage) bra with matching briefs.

'Now look in the other bags.' The Oliver she loved was back – caring and attentive. Uncertain what she should say, Ellen sat down without a word and continued to unpack. After five minutes, she was surrounded by his purchases – an elegant lime-green belted button-through linen dress, a floral silk skirt that hugged the hips, then flared in panels from just below to be paired with a simple grey T-shirt, and a second dress in lined smoky pink cotton lawn that was low cut and fitted at the top (too fitted), empire line (will at least hide my stomach) and sleeveless (has he not noticed my flabby upper arms?). Despite her reservations about their suitability, there was no denying that he had great taste.

'They're beautiful. I would never have bought them for myself.' Ellen was dreading the moment she was going to have to go upstairs and try them on, confident that she would look utterly ridiculous out of the comfort zone of her normal don't-notice-me-I'd-put-a-bag-over-my-head-if-I-could look. 'You've even got my size right.'

'I know you wouldn't. When did you last buy yourself something?' His question didn't need an answer. They both knew it must be months, if not as much as a year ago. 'But it's important that you look good at the gallery,' he went on. 'In charge.' What was he saying? That she normally didn't?

'What's wrong with the way I look now?' Ellen's voice sounded muffled as she began to fold the wrapping paper, returning it to the right bags ready for when she would secretly sneak the garments back to their shops. To her horror, she could feel her lower lip begin to quiver and her eyes sting.

'Nothing, darling, nothing at all. But just try them on to see. Please. For me.' She couldn't resist the appeal she saw in his eyes.

Oliver was pouring two glasses of chilled Sancerre when, half an hour later, she came back downstairs in the lime linen, having tried on the lot and been almost pleasantly surprised by what she saw. Having those moments alone had given her a chance to steady herself. Turning back and forth in front of the mirror, she could see that somehow he'd chosen lines that actually flattered her far from perfect body, taking attention away from the worst bits. Even her upper arms looked better than she remembered them. Was it a fluke that he'd done so well or did he have a good eye? And she had to admit that the touch of silk underwear gave her a frisson that didn't come with M&S cotton.

She'd picked up the photo of Simon she kept by her bed, wondering if he'd understand. He looked back at her: a confident man with a high forehead, thick dark eyebrows and a nose that had been knocked out of shape in a childhood bicycle accident. His eyes were kind, his chin strong and his mouth tilted up at the corners. He wasn't a man to turn heads but he had been a dependable, kind and loving one. He would never have thought to buy her clothes. That wasn't what their relationship was like. She had known that and hadn't wanted it any different. Her priorities had been him and their children, not the irrelevance of the way she, or indeed he, had looked. But things had changed. She wasn't the same woman she had been when he was alive. How could she be?

'You look gorgeous,' said Oliver, giving her a glass. 'Let me see. Mmm. I thought that green would suit your skin. I was right.' Despite her discomfort at being so closely scrutinised, Ellen was surprised to find herself simultaneously melting under his attention. Nobody had ever treated her like this. Even though she had only known Oliver for a short time, she realised he was already pushing her towards a reassessment of her relationship with Simon. She was beginning to see that there were perhaps sides to it that hadn't been quite as perfect as she had previously believed. Not that Simon hadn't adored her, but he was a man of few words and by nature not particularly demonstrative. A pat on the back or a slap on her bum was the most appreciative she remembered him being. And presents, other than on her birthday or at Christmas? Never.

'Now, tell me one thing.' Oliver took a couple of steps towards the french windows and looked out down the carefully planned and planted garden to the small greenhouse where Ellen had spent so many happy hours sowing her flower seeds, pricking out seedlings and potting them on. 'I am right in thinking that the gallery is closed on Monday, aren't I?'

'Yes. Why?' Just the two of them alone together. She'd like nothing more.

'I've booked you a hair appointment. No, wait . . . Let me finish. And they'll give you a facial and a manicure at the same time. I just thought you should have a day all to yourself, being pampered.'

'Oliver, stop. I can't possibly accept all this. It's too much.' She knew his generosity was well meant but, instead of adding to her confidence, paradoxically she felt the little she had gained over the past weeks with him ebbing away. 'Besides, I like my hair the way it is.'

'I know you do. But I want you to feel even better about yourself. I was just walking past that salon on the high street and I thought you'd like it. That's all.' The smile left his face and he began to snap his left thumbnail with the nail on his middle finger. 'I can easily cancel the whole thing, if that's what you want.'

Ellen had always thought of the beauty business as an excuse for absurd self-indulgence, something for women with more money than sense. Although Bea's and Kate's battle waged against the onslaught of time had always amused her, she had no wish to join them. Shouldn't women accept the inexorable march of time, and age the way nature intended? She was used to a quick trim with Angie at the small hairdresser's on the corner, with the result that style and chic had eluded her for years. But she was happy with that. Overcoming her discomfort and accepting Oliver's present gracefully would be hard, but she could see he was going to be so disappointed if she didn't. Weakened by his forlorn expression, she waved her hands. 'No, no. I'd love to go. It'll be a real treat. I haven't done anything like that for years. Thank you.'

'Right. Well, that's agreed, then. The other thing I wanted . . .'

Before he had finished his sentence, Ellen had picked up the empty bags and was halfway up the stairs with them, crying, 'Back in a minute. Let me show you the skirt . . .' She stuffed the bags into the bottom of the wardrobe, just in case she changed her mind and needed to return anything, and sat on the bed to take a few deep breaths. No more! This generosity was overwhelming. Since Simon's death she'd had to get used to being in control of her own life, but since Oliver had visited the gallery, her world was spinning off its axis and she couldn't right it. She had been swept into this unlooked-for relationship with a man she didn't know yet felt as if she'd known for ever. She was besieged by unfamiliar feelings that thrilled yet threw her off kilter.

Close by the photo of Simon, there was another of him with Emma and Matt on the last family holiday they'd had together in Cornwall. The four of them together on a family picnic at an isolated cove not far from Towan beach, a favourite spot that the summer tourists to the Cornish Roseland rarely discovered. The children were due to come home in just over a couple of weeks. What were they going to think of all this? She had wondered whether she should ask Oliver to move out until she'd told them, but she didn't want him to go. Their relationship had given her a new recklessness that had overthrown almost everything she'd held close. At the same time she was frightened by what was happening to her, not knowing how to pull things back under her control but at the same time not wanting to. She felt as if she had climbed aboard a giant switchback, increasingly petrified as it neared the top of each peak, her stomach rising into her mouth as it tipped over into the descent, screaming to get off yet wanting the excitement never to end.

She looked beside the radiator where she always left her shoes, never having got round to organising a shoe rack in the wardrobe. To her surprise, the jumble that she had left this morning had been transformed into a neat row of six matching pairs. She opened her underwear drawer in the hope of finding tights she could wear with the floral skirt. As she pulled out a pair, a cascade of red confetti flew up and fluttered to the floor. Startled, she bent down and scooped up the pieces only to see that each one was shaped like a heart.

Suddenly she felt an unfamiliar sense of relaxation. How wonderful that this adoring and adorable man had come into her life and wanted to look after her. However in control of things she had appeared, there had always been an ever-present underlying fear that everything was about to fly apart. If he would do something as special as buy her clothes, tidy her shoes without being asked, and add a sprinkle of romance to her drawers (she smiled at the pun), what else might he be capable of?

She slipped the skirt over her head, then the T-shirt, pulled on the tights and one of the four pairs of heels she owned and almost skipped back downstairs.

8

As her alarm cut through the clouds of sleep, Bea swam up towards consciousness and reached across the bed, congratulating herself on having remembered to change the sheets the previous morning. Not that she'd known what was going to happen then, of course. Anticipating the moment her hand would come into contact with a body of the male persuasion, she stretched out further, moving her arm up and down. Nobody. Suddenly awake, she opened her eyes. Definitely nobody. He must be in the shower. Or making them tea, perhaps. She curled round in the warmth of the duvet, luxuriating until he reappeared, piecing together for herself the previous day.

This time Let's Have Lunch had got it right. As soon as she had seen him walking towards her across the airy, minimalist Asian-fusion restaurant, she had known. A confident stride, a well-cut suit, brown eyes with a twinkle, a full head of hair, without a recessive gene in evidence, and, most important, an easy smile. If she half shut her eyes, there was definitely enough of a resemblance to Gabriel Byrne to make him extremely attractive. The second morning from hell since the arrival of Adam Palmer at Coldharbour Press had dimmed at the prospect of lunch in the company of Tony Castle.

She was not disappointed. There wasn't a moment of awkwardness as they introduced themselves, not a moment of hesitation as they weighed each other up. Lunch sped past in a haze of laughter and conversation with an undertow of sexual tension that had made itself felt almost immediately, only to intensify the longer they spent in each other's company. The dishes of sea bass with garlic, ginger and soy, oven-roasted lamb with fiery spices, flourless chocolate cake with raspberry sauce came and went, eaten almost unnoticed. Wine glasses were topped up with a never-ending stream of Sauvignon Blanc as they got to know each other. Lunch bled imperceptibly into the afternoon so that when Bea looked at her watch to see whether it was time to return to the office she was astonished to find it was already four thirty. It had hardly seemed worth going back for an hour, particularly when she briefly considered the glum faces that would surround her as they waited for Adam's axe to fall. Her decision was made in a nano-second. She was having a good time. Why stop? If questioned, she'd just say she'd been with an author.

The graphic-design company in which Tony was a partner seemed to have little need of him either so, instead, they agreed that nothing would be nicer than to cross the river to Tate Modern. They wandered between the rooms, both of them less than half intent on the pictures on the walls. In the darkened space of a video installation, she accidentally brushed her hand against his. Did he too feel the jolt of electricity that had travelled between them? They emerged into the glare of the gallery, Bea feeling as though something in the world had shifted.

Rather than seeing more, they decided to stroll along the South Bank, stopping to watch the river traffic, leaning over the stone wall by one of the Victorian wrought-iron street lights in the shade of the giant plane trees, dazzled by the sunlight on the water. It was unusual for Bea to feel so relaxed in a stranger's company but, she pinched herself, she really did. Tony must have kissed the Blarney Stone several times before he'd moved to London. His flow of conversation was effortless and amusing, his attention flattering, his company diverting. Everything she could have asked for in a date. As they took themselves into a small tapas bar, it dawned on Bea where all this was leading. And lead there it did.

The sex had been better than good, earth-moving, even. A half-smile slid across her face as she remembered how spontaneously and how well they'd connected. Her fear of embarrassment at getting her kit off in front of someone new had proved groundless. Tony hadn't recoiled in horror at the sight of her body, stranger to the gym as it was. In fact, she seemed to recall, as her smile broadened, quite the reverse. Nor was she the inhibited sex-starved singleton she'd worried she might have become during the drought since Colin's departure. To her surprise, she had found that her self-consciousness was disappearing with age.

What was keeping him for so long? Her thoughts were taking her in one direction and one direction only, and she was aware that there were a good forty-five minutes or so that could be put to good use before they both had to leave for work.

Not wanting to wake Ben by shouting, Bea edged herself out of bed, draping her faded but attractively Bohemian silk dressing-gown round her. Her attention was caught by the dust on the bedside table-top and the base of the light, all too visible in the sunshine leaking through the gap in the curtains. Not wanting Tony to realise her slummy side just yet, she grabbed the black cotton knickers she'd been only too pleased to abandon on the floor the night before and did a quick dust with them before hurling them into the laundry basket. Pleased with the result, she went to find him in the bathroom. To her surprise, the door was wide open. There was no sound of running water from inside, no steam misting the windows, as it did after the shower had been used. The blue and grey towels sat neatly folded, untouched. Turning to go downstairs, she noticed that Tony's shoes were no longer where she remembered him slipping them off by the radiator in the hall. She couldn't hear him opening cupboards, trying to find what he needed to make tea in a strange kitchen.

There was a good reason for that, as she discovered when she reached the ground floor and could see along the hallway to the long kitchen. Tony wasn't there. He had gone. Gone without waking her, without saying goodbye.

Mystified, not to say disappointed, Bea decided to make herself a cup of tea to have in the bath where she would ponder this turn in events. Why would he have gone off without saying anything the night before? It didn't make sense. Perhaps he had thought that mention of an early meeting the next day would interrupt the enjoyment of the moment. He had been right. She stood on her tiptoes and stretched, confident that he'd call her later in the day. Waiting for the kettle to boil, she began planning what they might do that evening. Or was that rushing things? But going that fast seemed to be working for Ellen, so why shouldn't it for her?

Except that, clearly, it hadn't. The rosy glow that had enveloped her on waking began to evaporate as realisation dawned. The bastard had legged it and, worse than that, he'd gone in the middle of the night with no explanation. She cast her mind back, trying to find one for him. Had he disguised his real reaction to her body? Had gravity, food, drink and childbirth taken the toll she feared? Should she have had the Brazilian she'd been meaning to endure and hadn't quite got round to? Perhaps she was even more out of practice than she'd thought and it had showed. What had been so good for her might not have been so good for him after all. But he had touched her, reassured her, even complimented her.

Puzzling over how someone could say the things he had without meaning them, her fury was compounded when she found the bathroom door locked. Could it be? Her hopes rose for a moment as she knocked – quite gently so as not to wake Ben. No reply. She tried again, louder this time.

'What d'you want?' Ben's voice boomed through the glass panel.

Disguising her disappointment, Bea yelled, 'For God's sake, hurry up. You know I've got to go to work.'

Work. The day ahead rushed towards her, tsunami-like. This morning she was having her first official meeting with Adam to discuss 'the future of the editorial department'. Being late was not an option. A headache that had until that moment been distant thunder on the horizon began to rumble unerringly in her direction.

'Ben!' she yelled again, rapping on the glass.

'OK, Mum. OK.' Ben unlocked the door and shambled out. 'Chillax.'

'If you say that to me once more, I'll . . .' For once words failed her as she pushed past him into the room that, minutes ago, had looked unused. Now it looked as if a whirlwind had blown through it. The pile of towels had been knocked to the floor beside an open magazine that lay half hidden by Ben's discarded T-shirt and pants. The basin was dotted with black stubble, the razor left lying by the toothpaste tube, which was leaking into the soap dish. Bea started the shower and, with a heavy sigh, pulled off a bit of loo paper to mop up the splashes on the floor round the toilet where Ben had missed – again. No amount of asking, telling, shouting or begging seemed to make any difference. Every day started in the same old way, except that this one was even worse than usual, thanks to Mr bloody Castle.

By the time she was strap-hanging on the tube, already wilting in the heat, Bea realised she had made a big mistake in the wardrobe department. The cotton shirt she remembered looking so great on her the previous summer and that had still looked great when she was standing quite still in front of the mirror this morning was now straining dangerously across her bust while her shoes, fashionably pointed, gripped the joints of both her big toes in separate agonising vices. However, her Nicole Farhi deep blue cotton jersey skirt was nothing short of perfect.

The insult (which was how she now saw it) dealt by Tony Castle had insinuated its way to the back of her mind where it lay temporarily dormant as she concentrated on the morning ahead, going over how she was to protect her staff's and her own jobs. Equally dormant were her concerns about how Ben might be spending his day and about her mother. She couldn't afford to let anything or anyone deflect her focus. As she saw it, everyone who worked with her did a valuable job and didn't deserve to lose it. They were relying on her to speak up for them and she would.

*

With the shirt problem righted with a large safety-pin (unpleasantly reminiscent of a nappy-pin) supplied by one of her younger colleagues, and unable to feel her feet, Bea knocked on Adam's door and went in to face the enemy as the ten o'clock reminder beeped on her phone.

He barely glanced up. 'Just one moment while I finish going through these figures.'

Rude, but at least it gave Bea time to sit down and assess her surroundings. In the couple of days he'd been there, Adam Palmer had made his mark, insisting that he take over Stephen's office from day one. Not a popular decision with the rest of the staff, who felt that after so long with the company Stephen hardly deserved to be so humiliated. He, however, had been unbothered by the move. 'What does it matter to me, Bea? It's just an office. I'll be out of here in a few weeks. I can see that he wants to make an impression and, let's face it, I did have the best office in the building.' Over the weekend, Stephen had moved into a smaller one on the other side of the open plan. Now that the axe had fallen, a change had come over him. Already, he looked like a man with a weight removed from his shoulders. He no longer wore a slightly anxious, distracted expression, as if something terrible was about to happen unless he did something to divert it. All those budgetary worries he had carried about with him for years had been parcelled up and passed on to Adam. He had been in the office as little as he could get away with as he silently prepared his exit. Bea was already missing his ready friendship.

She looked across the empty table to the bookshelves, where Stephen's accumulation of Coldharbour's titles had already been thinned so that the recent better-selling ones were standing face out to impress any visitor. Beside them were a select few that Adam had presumably been responsible for at Pennant, all having had an enviable stint on the bestseller list. Nothing like driving your success home where it's not wanted, thought Bea. On the walls he'd hung a couple of modern prints and on his desk stood a large, framed snapshot of an attractive woman, all blonde ponytail and cheekbones, and a freckle-faced curly-haired boy of six or seven.

So, like attracts like, thought Bea, as at last Adam looked up from his papers. She saw a lean aquiline face with steely grey eyes that appraised her for a moment before a slight smile was allowed to cross his lips. Beneath his casual but expensive striped open-necked shirt there was the suggestion of a well-worked-out body. A copper wristband sat just below the dark leather strap of his square-faced TAG Heuer watch. As he stood up to walk round the desk to join her at the table, she couldn't help noticing his jeans (with a crease), silk socks and soft tan leather loafers.

'So, you're Bea Wilde.' Far from unfriendly, his tone was more matter-of-fact.

Bea braced herself. 'Yes. I'm the publishing director, as I think you probably know.'

'I certainly do.' He leaned across the table towards her and got straight to the point. 'Would you say you've done a good job here?'

'Yes, I would.' Bea's hackles rose in preparation to defend herself.

'Let's see. What was the last book you were responsible for that made the bestseller list? Remind me.' He leaned forward. No smile now.

'Jan Flinder's *A Certain Heart.*'

'My point. That was spring last year. Why nothing since then?'

'You know as well as I do that that's an impossible question to answer. We've had a couple that made it close, others we had high hopes for. But everyone knows that publishing's not an exact science. If it was we'd all be rich.'

'Of course I know that. But, these days, one would hope for more success on a list than you've had here.' Adam smacked the palm of his hand on the table as he stood up to pace the room. For a few moments, he stared out of the wide plate-glass window across London. Then he turned to her. 'We've got to do some drastic housekeeping. I've been going through the figures and, of course, talking everything through with Piers. He agrees with me that we have to reduce our overheads if we're going forward. There's no alternative but to lose the slack from every department.'

Bea's stomach plummeted but she kept looking straight in his eye. This was what she'd been dreading. 'What are you suggesting?'

'Redundancies.'

'But we need everyone we've got in Editorial,' she protested. 'There are only six of us. There really isn't any slack. Everyone's working to their full capacity.'

'I know that. So I'm also proposing that we cut down the number of titles we publish per year. I want you to do fewer better. You won't need as many staff.' He tapped his chin with a manicured finger.

Already Bea was running through the people in the department. Stuart and Jade were indispensable. As for Alice, the managing editor who commissioned a few of her own non-fiction titles, and the two assistants, Becky and Warren, Bea couldn't reward their loyalty and enthusiasm by putting them out of work.

'I really don't think we can do without any of them. Stuart and Jade—'

She was about to start justifying everyone's employment when he cut her short. 'The decision's been taken, I'm afraid. I want you to lose two members of your department.'

'Two!' Bea's breath was taken away. 'I can't do that.'

'It's the only way I can make the numbers work. If you're

unable to help, then perhaps you should think about your own position. I'm only interested in keeping people who'll work with me, not against me. Think about it. We'll talk again in a couple of days or so.' He looked at his watch, then returned to his seat behind his desk and his papers, indicating that the meeting was over.

Bea was reeling from the brutal no-nonsense approach that she'd just encountered. Gone was Stephen's gentle old-fashioned all-around-the-houses method of broaching something unpleasant. He'd hated upsetting his staff – but (Bea failed to dismiss the disloyal thought) the company might not have been in such a mess if he'd adopted a more leader-like approach.

As soon as she was back in her office, Stuart and Jade made a beeline for her.

'What's he like? Is he as tough as they say?'

'Well, let's just say he apparently learned his management style at the knee of Genghis Khan.'

'What's he going to do to the editorial department? He's bound to want some changes, isn't he?' Jade's anxiety betrayed itself in her quieter-than-normal voice.

'Bea, you have to tell us what's going on.' Even Stuart, normally bothered by nothing, had dropped his customary laid-back manner.

'Nothing's going on.' Even to hint at what had been said at this stage wouldn't be in anyone's interests. 'All he wanted was a rundown on the staff and to go through the upcoming programme. That's it. As soon as there's something to tell, you two will be the first to know. Promise.' She was surprised to discover that she hadn't dropped the childhood habit of crossing her fingers to excuse herself when telling a lie. Just as long as they hadn't noticed.

The rest of the day disappeared as she caught up with correspondence, put together editorial notes on a manuscript whose author was coming in the following day, talked to the publicity and art departments about the approaches they were taking to a couple of her books, and dealt with all the day-to-day business of an editorial department. Whenever possible, she avoided speculative conversations with anyone about the future of the company.

Only when she had closed her front door, thrown off her shoes, poured herself a glass of red plonk and sunk into her deep red sofa, eyes shut, did she take time to concentrate on her first conversation with Adam. A tad disenchanted with her career she might be, but not enough to throw in the towel right now. And there was something about this ruthless management style that she found exciting. His macho approach was outrageous, but she was curious to see if he was all he was cracked up to be and whether he would be able to deliver. If he could, then perhaps she wanted to be a part of his new team. If he couldn't, it would be interesting, and maybe she would survive him. The challenge he presented was one she couldn't possibly duck. Adele was right. However, sacrificing two members of her staff, none of whom had shown anything other than enthusiasm for their jobs, was an almost impossible demand. She sat there wrestling with the problem, convinced that a bit of lateral thinking was all that was needed to solve it. Not so.

The front door slammed as Ben crashed in, hurling his

bag on the floor and himself towards the kitchen, yelling, 'What's for supper?'

Her 'Hi, Ben. Good day?' went unheard. Putting her work life to one side she concentrated on making a bowl of pasta and a green salad for them. Annoyed that she refused to let him eat his on his knees in front of the TV, Ben refused to answer her questions with anything other than grunts and monosyllables until he'd finished. Then he disappeared into the sitting room, dragging his bag behind him and muttering something about 'Bloody parents.' None the wiser about his life, Bea cleared up while returning to her previous musings, still getting nowhere.

Salvation came when the doorbell interrupted her ever more circular thoughts. Surely Tony Castle hadn't come back for more. She stood to give herself a quick once-over in the mirror on the kitchen wall. Mmm. Could be worse. She ran her fingers through her hair in an attempt at windswept-and-interesting, then turned the dimmer switch to a more flattering level without quite switching the light off. Taking a deep breath and pinning on her most winning smile, she walked down the hall and flung open the door.

9

'I'm sorry to arrive out of the blue, but I know you're cross with me.' Ellen stood on the doorstep, looking expectant, with a bottle of wine in one hand and a brown and white box that Bea instantly recognised with delight as being from Artisan du Chocolat.

'Of course I'm not.' Bea's disappointment at Tony's no-show wrestled with surprise, as she ushered Ellen into the kitchen. 'Let me find the corkscrew. You know where the glasses are.'

'I should have called you to tell you first but it's just that Kate came into the gallery, Oliver phoned and I couldn't stop myself. I wanted to tell you both days ago but I was so wrapped up in what was happening that I wasn't thinking straight. It's been crazy.'

'Slow down.' Bea was laughing as they settled themselves at the table. 'God, look at you. You're completely different.'

A blush began to colour Ellen's cheeks. 'I know. Oliver suggested I had my hair cut like this. Do you think it's OK?'

'OK? It's taken years off you. But what about the dress? I'm used to Ellen, the woman who single-handedly keeps

Levi's afloat. You look amazing.' She made Ellen turn around, taking in the lime dress, the slight heels, the dab of makeup, the urchin cut. Something had happened to her friend that had transformed her almost beyond recognition. 'I'm dying to know all about everything but tell me slowly. And in detail.'

Ellen understood how miffed Bea had been not to be told her news first. They had been friends since they'd met at university and were so familiar with the way each other's minds worked that they often didn't need to ask what the other was thinking. Ellen's coming round this evening was an olive branch. Bea took it readily.

Friends again, they raised their glasses in a toast, comfortable as ever at Bea's kitchen table. As they talked, the candles on the table flickered in the breeze that was also carrying in the sounds of the neighbourhood through the wide-open patio doors. Beyond them, the small back garden was lit with a few discreet outdoor lights – a mail-order bargain from an interiors magazine. The overhead dimmers were low, the under-unit lighting giving out just enough background illumination. Thanks to an uncharacteristic cleaning frenzy a couple of days earlier, the black granite worktops of Bea's kitchen were unusually tidy, apart from a disorganised stack of papers by the phone. The much-cherished double-door American fridge punctuated their conversation with the sound of ice cracking in the ice dispenser. Through the side window, they could see over the garden wall into the neighbouring kitchen where a woman stood with her back to them, round-shouldered with exhaustion, as she worked her lonely way through a vast, precarious pile of ironing. Down Bea's hallway, a strip of light escaped from under the door of the sitting room, with a not-so-muffled bass beat that indicated the defiant presence of Ben. It wasn't long before Bea had caught up on the unexpected developments in Ellen's life, the when, where and why answered.

Naturally sceptical about the concept of love at first sight, she nonetheless had to concede this seemed to have been what had happened to Ellen. Seeing her friend so happy was enough to dispel the negative thoughts that Bea had been trying to keep at bay. 'He sounds terrific – and just the man for you. What does he do?'

'Actually, nothing at the moment.' Ellen looked half apologetic in the face of Bea's badly hidden surprise. 'He hasn't been back in the country for long. But he's applying for curator and gallery jobs. There just aren't that many around, that's all. I'm sure he'll get something in the end.'

Bea decided to change tack to what mattered more. 'What about the kids? Do they know? When are they coming back?'

'That's just what Kate asked. I've thought so hard about them and, of course, I've talked to Oliver.' Her face brightened as she said his name. 'They've been having such a lovely time in Cornwall that I haven't dared hint at anything over the phone.'

'Well, you're going to have to tell them.'

'That's what she said too. But I don't know when.'

'Maybe you should take a few steps back. Get him to move out, then introduce him gradually into their lives.'

Ellen's face crumpled.

'It doesn't have to be for long, for heaven's sake. I may not be the best example of hands-on motherhood but I do know that if you're serious about him you have to do this properly.'

'You're right. You're a good friend not to let me make such a stupid mistake.' A note of resolve entered Ellen's voice. 'I'll have to get him to see that's the right thing to do.'

'Just as importantly, when do we get to meet him?'

'I'll think of something as soon as I get back from Cornwall. Promise. But I don't want to make him feel like something in the zoo with the two of you giving him the once-over.'

'Mmm. Sticking our fingers through the bars to give him a poke or a handful of nuts. We might be a bit much, I can see that.' Their laughter was that of old friends who completely understood one another.

'No. What I've got to do is sort this out. I think I'll go down alone to Cornwall for the second last week of the holiday as planned. I'll tell them I've met Oliver and they can meet him after they get back.' Her relief at having made a plan gave way to anxiety. 'Do you think they'll like him?'

'God knows. I hope so. But as I haven't met him how could I possibly know?' Bea was as relieved as Ellen that they'd reached a conclusion but was impatient to catch her friend up on her own news. As she was wondering, with an unusual degree of tact, how to change the subject, the sitting-room door opened, a shaft of light illuminating the hall, falling across the multi-coloured woollen rug Bea had lugged home from Marrakesh, regretting it every step of the way. Inveigled into a shop in the souk, she'd been unable to resist either the mint tea or the guile of the shopkeeper. The light hit the long mirror over the radiator, illuminating the reflection of the Bryan Pearce harbourscape hanging on the opposite wall, a reminder of family holidays in St Ives. Ben emerged from the sitting room to slouch into the kitchen, an empty glass in one hand and a plate in the other.

'Hi, Ben. How are you getting on? Must be nearly A-2s, isn't it?'

Bea envied Ellen's breezy chat-among-equals approach, not to mention her ability to ignore the expression of non-cooperation that was making itself plain on Ben's face.

'Yeah. All right,' he muttered, avoiding Ellen's eye by keeping his own fixed on the floor. He put the plate and cup on the side, before opening the fridge to take a beer.

'Darling! Not on a week night,' said Bea.

Ben returned the can with a grunt, exchanging it for a carton of milk and a yoghurt. He lifted the carton and tipped it towards his mouth.

'Ben! How many times have I—'

'Bea,' hissed Ellen.

'Sorry,' she muttered. 'But, honestly, I—'

Ellen silenced her with a glare. As Ben opened a cupboard and started piling biscuits on his plate, she tried again: 'Which subjects have you gone for?'

'Haven't decided yet.' Ben shook his fringe out of his eyes. 'Maybe English, history, media studies. Maybe I'll just leave school and get a job.'

Don't rise to it, Bea said to herself. Don't rise to it.

Simultaneously, she heard her own intake of breath and her sharp 'Ben! Don't be so bloody ridiculous.'

'Well, I might.'

'Perhaps now isn't quite the right moment to discuss it.' Ellen was the epitome of family conciliation as Ben disappeared, armed with his supplies, his thunderous mood adequately communicated by the hunch of his shoulders, the slam of the door and the increase in the music's volume. Bea took a swig of wine. 'Bloody child! Sometimes I think I can't get through to him any more.'

'He's only saying it because he knows exactly the reaction he'll get,' said Ellen. 'And you know nagging never works.'

'I can't help it. He drives me mad.'

'He's just at that age,' Ellen reassured her. 'You've got to ignore it. He's still a great kid underneath all that.'

'You think so?'

'I know so. Give him a couple of years and you'll see.' Ellen got up to put the kettle on. 'Now, where were we? I think it's your turn.'

'How long have you got?' So saying, Bea launched into her latest news from the work and dating front, giggling about Mark and bemoaning Tony Castle. For the next couple of hours, they would go back and forth over the same well-trodden ground, as they examined and re-examined their lives, loves (or lack of them) and children. They had spent countless similar evenings in each other's company, enjoying the friendship, discretion, support and advice. Even if Bea's feathers were ruffled from time to time, Ellen took that in her stride. That was what friendship was about, thought Bea.

Ultimately, nothing was strong enough to break the bond between them.

*

Before she went to bed, Bea made herself a cup of hot chocolate and took it to the sitting room, ignoring the debris that was evidence of Ben's earlier occupation. Mothers and children – who'd have 'em? She opened the box Ellen had brought and took out the distinctive brown tub of pink and black pepper caramels. As the fusion of sweet and savoury flavours melted in her mouth, she thought with affection of Adele and with some sadness of the last conversation they'd had together when she'd dropped her mother at home.

They had sorted out the shopping and sat down with a cup of tea before Bea had touched on the subject of Adele moving house. To her surprise, an uncertain look crossed Adele's face and she said what she must have been bursting to say all day.

'I've got something to tell you, Bea. I've been putting it off because I don't know how you'll react. Janey Blythe has asked me to move to Bournemouth with her. There.' She sat back, looking pleased but apprehensive, waiting to see the effect her announcement would have on her daughter. Janey Blythe was Adele's near neighbour, a sprightly, slightly younger woman who, like Adele, was widowed, with her children long established in their own lives. The two had grown particularly close after the deaths of their husbands and Bea knew they spent hours talking about their own and their children's lives. Janey was always keen to try new things. Her last idea had been to encourage Adele to go to the local pottery class with her. The three wonky vases on top of the old upright piano suggested lots of enthusiasm but little skill.

'Ye-es.' Bea was hesitant, worried she'd been wrong in her assessment of her mother's state of mind. She'd clearly completely lost her marbles. 'But where? And what about the house?'

'I'm going to sell it. I've been rattling around it for years. We've found two flats – actually, Janey has – in a new development principally for old crocks like us very close to the sea front.' Adele was beaming at the prospect of something so different.

'Mum! You can't do this without talking to us.'

'But that's what I'm doing – talking to you. I've always wanted to live by the sea . . .'

'Have you? You've never said anything.'

'Bea, I hardly see you. And when I do, we mostly talk about you or Ben.'

Bea was ashamed to admit that she was right. She'd imagined she knew all that there was to know about Adele's life. She had got into the habit of assuming that her mother's days and weeks followed the same inevitable pattern and that Adele was quite happy with that. Bea had never bothered trying to put herself into her mother's shoes to see how the world looked from her vantage-point. Of course, a woman of seventy-something (there – she didn't even know exactly how old Adele was) had the right to expect more out of life and still have ambitions, however modest. 'I'm sorry.'

'No, that's not what I meant. I love hearing all your news. But Janey and I have had more cups of coffee together than either of us can count, discussing what we might do with the rest of our lives. At the moment we're both relatively fit and healthy so it's not too late for us to start a new chapter.' Her eyes were bright with excitement.

'Why didn't you say something earlier?'

'Because I was enjoying hearing about you and Ellen. And I was nervous. I didn't want to spoil our outing, which I would have done if you don't like the plan.'

'But, Mum . . . the house.' Now that the idea of Adele's moving had suddenly become a reality, getting rid of the family home was unthinkable. Or was it? After all, she was the only one of Adele's children who visited with any regularity any more. Why should her mother have to live there alone, just so her children could revisit their memories every now and then?

'It's only a house, dear. It's given us plenty of good years but I like the idea of another family taking it over now. And I'd like a change while I can still enjoy it. If I move with Janey, we'll have each other for company as neighbours again. What could be better? And you won't need to worry about me.'

Selling the old place would be a huge wrench, not to say a logistical nightmare as they disposed of all those years' worth of accumulated belongings, but was that a reason to prevent Adele having one last shot at life? Bea looked around the room. She had grown up with everything in it: the faded furniture, the pictures on the walls, the green and white Penguin crime novels that Adele had collected so many years ago. Where would it all go? She turned to her mother, who was leaning forward in her chair, looking anxious for Bea's approval. In that moment, Bea grasped that whatever her feelings about her childhood home, she couldn't use it to deny her mother's right to her much-cherished independence. That Adele was embracing her future with another woman close to her age should be a relief, a way of taking some of the load off her shoulders. Adele was right. The house had done them well and at last the time had come to move on.

'You know what, Mum? I think it's a great idea. Go for it.'

The relief she saw in Adele's face told her all she needed to know. Adele's mind might have been made up but what she really wanted was her daughter's blessing. Though saddened by the nostalgia provoked at the idea of selling the old house, Bea was able to enthuse over the estate agent's details of the new flats. Soon she and her mother were making plans to travel down to inspect them as soon as they could.

By the time she left for home, she was almost as excited as Adele by the imminent change. She was confident Will wouldn't mind. He'd said goodbye to his childhood home long ago when he'd set off for Australia. As for Jess, she had no right to protest. She only ever visited when she felt she absolutely had to and spent much of her time eyeing up the furniture, as if mentally marking the pieces she liked with red stickers. No, this was a positive thing to do and Bea was going to support Adele all the way. Life would be easier for everyone.

Unable to resist another chocolate, she kicked off her

shoes and stretched out on the sofa as a feeling of relaxation stole over her. She wasn't sorry that Tony Castle hadn't turned up this evening. Having the opportunity to talk to Ellen was much more important to her. After so many years coming to terms with Simon's death, Ellen deserved her shot at happiness. Her obvious pleasure in her new man brought home to Bea how much she wanted the best for her friend. Besides, she admitted a small afterthought, if Ellen had found someone, then maybe there was still hope for her too.

10

'I'm not going. No way.'

They had reached stalemate already. The conversation that Ellen had rehearsed in her head a hundred times was proving far more difficult than she had envisaged. After she'd got back from Bea's the previous night, she'd lain awake going through exactly what she wanted to say to Oliver and the best way to put it. However much his temporary absence was going to hurt, she knew Bea's advice was right. He had to go, and for a short while they would have to pretend a different relationship in front of the children. Once Emma and Matt liked and accepted him, they could start their future together. All day at the gallery, she had been busy planning a new exhibition, speaking to two painters whose work she hoped to show and to customers, but her thoughts had kept running ahead to the conversation she must have. Dreading Oliver's reaction, she hadn't been able to broach the subject immediately. He'd welcomed her home as if he hadn't seen her for days, not hours, and she hadn't wanted to spoil the mood. His attention made her feel alive.

Eventually, as they sat down for supper, she'd told him that she was planning to go alone to Cornwall and began to spell out as gently and reasonably as she could what she felt was the best way of introducing him to the children. His response was as negative as she'd feared. As she talked, his expression had hardened. A barely perceptible steeliness slid into place behind his eyes. But she saw it. He pushed his chair away from the table and leaned back, folded his arms and waited, motionless until she'd finished. Then he spoke. Those five non-cooperative words.

For a second, Ellen's panic was eradicated by the fleeting thought of how sweet he looked, like a frustrated child about to stamp his foot. She swiftly brought herself back to the moment. 'Darling, at least try to understand.'

He reached for the bottle of Pinot Grigio and refilled his glass without offering any to her. 'I am trying. But what's so ridiculous is that I know deep down you don't want me to go either.' How true that was. 'Why do you think meeting me will be so difficult for them? I love you and I'll love them. It'll all work out.'

But will they love you? She pushed the thought away, annoyed that it had burrowed in through her defences. How lucky they were that she'd met a man so ready to take on her children as well as her. To find someone so big-hearted was a blessing. Of course they'd love him just as she did. She remembered the conversations she'd had with Bea over the years since Colin had left her. Bea had been convinced that any potential partner would run a mile once they'd got wind of Ben's existence. She could hear her now: 'Why would they take on a middle-aged woman at all, let alone

one with a child? Look at me. I'm like a leftover from a designer sale! Once a desirable bit of shmutter but still on the rail and no longer fashionable, desirable or even fitting.' Ellen was no different. But she mustn't waver.

Looking over Oliver's shoulder to the wall behind him, she could see one of the large picture frames that, over the years, she'd filled with collages of family photos and hung all over the house. A grinning Matt stared out at her, snapped just after he'd triumphed with a winning goal in a school football match. Higher in the frame was Emma, two years older with a pretty, elfin face, her grip tight round Bonkers, her silver-grey flop-eared rabbit. She seemed to be looking straight at Ellen as if she was trying to say something to her. Ellen strengthened her resolve. 'You don't know them.'

'I feel as if I do. You've told me so much about them. Everything you've said makes me sure we'll get on.' He clicked the middle and thumb nails on his right hand, again and again.

'But coming back to find your mother has moved a strange man into your home is a lot to take on board. They've been used to everything being the way it's been for so long that they're bound to resent you at first. Surely you see that.'

'Of course. But they'll get over it and be pleased to see you happy again. Think of that.'

'Not to mention the discovery that their mother's enjoying a sex life all of a sudden! I should think they'll be horrified, poor things.' Ellen laughed. 'But, most importantly, I don't want them to think they've lost me to someone else.

They've lost one parent – that's enough. If we're going to be together for ever, I want it all to be right from the start.'

But Oliver was not going to give in that easily. They carried on the discussion over the mushroom omelettes, the apple pie, the washing-up, the coffee. They took their mugs to the end of the garden where they sat in the near-dark on the bench, the summer smell of other people's barbecues drifting round them as they tried to reach a resolution that suited them both. Lights from neighbouring windows cast a glow over the gardens while the sound of voices travelled across fences with the last gasps of barbecue smoke. Over the previous years, Ellen had always drawn comfort from the proximity of her neighbours but now she wished they would hurry inside so she and Oliver could have the night to themselves.

They talked round and round in circles, until finally she invoked the one person she had hoped not to involve. 'I have to do this for Simon. I have to make sure that Em and Matt understand that I'm not writing him out of their lives or them out of mine. I know he'd want me to be happy but he'd want them to be happy too, so I've got to do this in the way I think will make that happen.'

They sat for a moment, neither speaking. Then Oliver took her hand and kissed it, pulling her towards him until she leaned against his chest, feeling the steady beat of his heart.

'I think you're the most wonderful selfless person I've ever met.' He bent to kiss the top of her head.

'I'm just their mother, that's all. I—'

'Sssh!' He stopped her saying any more. 'OK. I'll do whatever you want.' He ruffled her hair.

'You will?' His sudden agreement shocked her.

'Yes.' He took a deep breath. 'I don't want to, but I will.'

'Thank you so, so much.' She sat up to face him, taking both his hands in hers. 'Where will you go?' Now she was anxious at the idea of being separated from him again.

'I've no idea.'

'But you must have. What have you done with all the stuff you must have brought back from France?' She pulled her pashmina tighter round her shoulders, aware of a chill in the night breeze.

'I've stored it all at a friend's place near Cardiff. Yes, I could go there.'

'Near Cardiff! You never said.'

'You never asked and it didn't seem important.'

'But you must have friends in London?' This wasn't what Ellen had imagined at all. She had imagined him nearby, in easy reach, so that he could call in regularly and gradually become more of a fixture in their lives without the children really noticing.

'None. Not close enough to bum a bed from anyway – and I couldn't afford a hotel, not for that length of time. No. I'll have to see if Dan and Alice can have me for a few months. Do you think that'll be long enough to sort this out?'

Long enough? It sounded like a lifetime.

'But how will we see you, if you're living there? When will we see you?'

'It's only a couple of hours on the train. Ellen, this is what you wanted. Remember?'

'But I hadn't imagined you quite so far away. I'd thought

114

of you sneaking out in the early morning before the children were up. That kind of thing,' she said, her cheeks burning.

'I'd rent somewhere nearer, but my funds are limited and without a job . . .'

She thought of the clothes that he'd bought, guilty that he'd spent so much on her. 'Haven't you had any luck at all?' She knew how he spent his days while she was at the gallery, trawling through the jobs-vacant sites online and riffling through the papers, ringing the bigger galleries. He was doing his best.

'Nothing concrete. But I'm hoping it won't be long. I've got a couple of possibilities lined up. Once I've got an income again, things will be different, I promise.' He kissed her again, taking away her breath and her impulse to ask what the possibilities were.

'I can't bear to think of you so far away. There must be a better solution. Isn't there any way of borrowing some money till you set yourself up?'

'Who's going to lend money to someone with no obvious means of repaying it and no guarantees? Unless . . .'

She could barely see his face now the lights from the surrounding houses were going out one by one. She responded to the touch of his hand by moving closer to him. Sitting with his arm around her, their bodies tight against one another, Ellen felt she had never been more at one with another person. Even Simon. She shuddered.

'Unless what?'

'There's only one solution that I can think of.' She felt his body tense, his arm tighten round her. 'But I can hardly bring myself to ask.'

He didn't need to say more. A silence fell between them as the night grew darker.

*

'You'll never guess what she's done now!' Bea's shriek of indignation almost burst Kate's eardrum. She held the phone away from her ear.

'What?'

'She's only agreed to pay rent on a studio flat for Oliver until he gets a job. "It should only be for a month or two."' This last was said in a shrill imitation of Ellen's own justification to Bea only a couple of hours earlier. 'He hasn't got any money and otherwise he'd have to move out of London. Or so he says.'

On her screen, Kate saw there were no patients waiting. Her morning so far had been routine, filled with the usual minor ailments and one or two 'worried well'. She was glad of a break. Holding her phone between her shoulder and her ear, she began to straighten her room, hiding the carrier-bag of allotment vegetables given by a grateful patient, replacing the paper sheeting on the bed, pulling back the curtain surrounding it and putting away the toys that the last child had slung about in boredom while she was examining his mother. 'Where?' She held one of Sam's long-ago discarded plastic Ninja Turtles, turning it over in her hand and remembering those days when he was a small boy and would play with nothing else.

'I don't know where. Somewhere near Ellen, I suppose.

There wouldn't be much point otherwise. I just can't believe she'd be so rash.'

'Why are you so against the idea? Mightn't this be the best way to get what she wants?' She sat behind her desk, picking up her pale-blue cardigan, which she'd knocked off the chair-back, and glanced at the photograph of the view from the Tuscan villa she and Paul had rented two years earlier. Looking at the rolling vineyards, distant orchards, terracotta-roofed farmhouses and yew trees standing sentinel around a distant monastery gave her the sense of relaxation she remembered from that time spent together. On her desk calendar, a caravan of camels and white-clad nomads crossed the shadowy red dunes of the Sahara. Between them they did the trick of distancing her from her immediate surroundings, reminding her there was another very different world out there. Feeling better, she turned her full attention to the conversation.

'But she's only known him a few weeks. She knows nothing about him.' Bea sounded full of righteous anger.

'And neither do we.'

'You're always so damn reasonable.'

Kate could sense Bea's indignation waning. 'And you're always so quick to judge.'

'I know, I know. But, really . . . How do we know he'll pay her back?'

'You've read too many novels!' Kate had always thought that Bea's imagination was fuelled by what she did for a living. Her own attitude was much more practical. 'Of course we don't. But she's a grown-up and we have to trust

117

that she knows what she's doing. And we should give him the benefit of the doubt – at least until we've met him.'

'But all this is so out of character. I don't want her to get hurt.'

'Neither do I. But paying someone's rent for a few months isn't the worst thing that could happen.' Kate sat in her surgery day in day out, listening to people talk about their lives, about the sometimes bizarre and extreme things that some of them experienced. She had learned long ago never to be shocked by anything. Life had a way of throwing up the unexpected. That was what happened and you just had to get on with it. There was no point in overreacting.

'What's she paying with, though? The gallery can't be bringing in that much. And she needs what she's got for the kids.'

'No idea. I don't mind asking her when I next see her, though.' Kate straightened her papers and popped her pens into the holder at the back of the desk. 'I expect she's got a bit stashed away from Simon's life insurance or something. Rainy-day money. What better way to use it?'

'You sound as if you approve.' Bea seemed quite taken aback.

'I don't disapprove, I'll say that. Besides, it's all so romantic. Don't tell me you wouldn't give your eye-teeth to be in her shoes.'

Bea said nothing. Regretting her tactlessness, Kate attempted to smooth things over. 'Oh, Bea, I'm sorry – but you know what I mean. I'm as glad for her as I would be for you in the same situation.'

'You're right. If I'm honest, I suppose I am a bit jealous.

Why is it that I don't get lucky? It's not as if I wasn't making the effort.'

'Perhaps you're trying too hard. I don't know.' Kate's attention was taken by her screen alerting her to the fact that four patients were waiting. 'Bea, I'm sorry. I'm going to have to dash. Let's talk about this when we've got some time.'

'OK. Don't worry. I've got a meeting to go to in a minute anyway. I know you're right. I'll send the jury out again and won't decide on anything until there's more evidence. Fair?'

'Fair.'

As she put down the phone, Kate couldn't help think how lucky she was to have found two such good friends who understood each other so well. Despite the odd up and down in their history, there was always one of them who could see sense. Pleased by the turn in Ellen's fortunes at last, she didn't want anything to spoil it, least of all by Bea being over-protective or jealous. She would do what she could to stop that happening. If only Bea could meet someone for herself, perhaps she'd back off Ellen and leave her to make her own mistakes. Surely one of the agencies she'd applied to would throw up someone suitable soon.

11

Bea had been waiting for her appointment for just over half an hour. Her long-time principled allegiance to the NHS was being tested to its limits. Half a manuscript lay unread on her lap. She found it impossible to concentrate as women came and sat down or were called and disappeared down a narrow corridor where she could see a line of white doors, each with a red light that lit up when the room was occupied. She'd given up trying to puzzle out how the system worked. She had heard one of the nurses explain that, unusually, there was more than one clinic running today, which was why people who had come in after her had been seen ages ago while others who had been there when she arrived were still waiting.

She looked around her. The faded lino was the colour of dried blood. Below the thick green line painted all the way around the room at elbow height, the institutional cream walls were smeared black where chair backs had dragged along them. Above the line, one or two mass-produced exotic landscapes hung dusty and squint. In one corner, a TV was bracketed high on the wall, the sound not loud enough to hear but not quiet enough to ignore. Thin cotton curtains, too short for the grimy sash windows, blew in the breeze made by a fan putting up a futile struggle to circulate some air. The blue and red chair seats were worn and grubby. Everywhere, signs announced the department's imminent move to a spanking new building: presumably the reason why this waiting room had been allowed to languish, Bea thought crossly. Behind the large semi-circular desk by the door, one nurse sat almost hidden behind a tower of files that she was gradually dismantling, over-lapping them on the desktop, apparently to put them in some sort of order, with frequent tuts that could be heard across the room. A receptionist worked beside her, presum-ably unable to help thanks to her nails, which were long, lacquered works of art.

Bea got up yet again to go to the Ladies and sat there trying to breathe through the pain low in her stomach and the excruciating burning sensation that came as she tried to pee.

'Bastard!' she muttered, coming out of the cubicle and taking a plastic cup of water from the dispenser. Wash an infection through – isn't that what you were meant to do? Two days and God only knew how many gallons didn't seem to be doing the trick.

Back in the waiting room, she sat feeling angry with herself. A week after their encounter, having geared her mind up to forgetting Tony Castle, it looked as if that was not going to happen – or not yet, at least. Thank you, Tony! How could she have got herself into this situation? How many times had she embarked on the condom conversation with Ben, only to be told he knew it all? As did she. Unprotected sex leads to unwanted pregnancy or the GUM clinic – and to prove it here she was.

'Mrs Wilde.'

An unsmiling nurse stood, thin blue file clutched to her bosom, waiting. At last. Bea followed her along the corridor into a small room where an equally serious young woman sat bent over a desk. She looked up as Bea sat down. Kind, bespectacled eyes stared out of an exhausted face. She mustered a wan smile.

'I'm Dr McKay. What seems to be the problem?' She toyed with her red biro, seesawing it between the thumb and forefinger of her right hand.

As Bea explained her symptoms, the doctor's intent gaze didn't leave her face. Under such close scrutiny, she found herself stumbling over her explanation, embarrassed and furious with herself and with Tony. Dr McKay said nothing until she finished, then was sympathy itself.

'I'm sorry but I have to ask everyone these questions . . .' she began, before rifling through Bea's recent sex life – or lack thereof.

Bea was surprised to find that under these circumstances talking about what came naturally came quite unnaturally. Matters she would joke about with Kate or Ellen assumed a more sobering significance. She felt a sadder, more inadequate person than her usual robust self. No, she didn't have a regular partner; no, she hadn't had sex for some time (yes, some years) before this last episode; no, she couldn't exactly remember when; and no, she knew almost nothing about her most recent partner or, more worrying, about his own sexual history, recent or past.

'Hop onto the couch and I'll take some swabs.' Brisk and matter-of-fact, the doctor wasn't judging her for being so inept on the condom front. But lying there, eyes shut, legs apart, took Bea back to the last time she'd been in the same position. How very different she'd felt then. How short the journey from ecstasy to embarrassment.

'It's probably trichomoniasis.' That was reassuring. At least it was nothing worse. 'We should get the results within half an hour and I'll give you some antibiotics. There's no need to be embarrassed, Mrs Wilde. Relax.'

'I'm not embarrassed exactly. Just kicking myself for letting it happen.'

'You'd be surprised at the number of women over forty we get in here with similar problems. It's more and more common. They think they can't get pregnant but they forget about things like this.'

Knowing she was in good company didn't make Bea feel any better.

Three-quarters of an hour later, the result was confirmed, the antibiotics prescribed, advice on the use of condoms dished out and Bea was back on the street, breathing in the exhaust of real life. She remembered the doctor's advice: 'Even if the symptoms disappear quickly, you should still avoid having sex for a week.' That was a laugh. Avoid sex? She was *never* going to have it again. Not for a bit anyway. Well, not unless she got very lucky indeed. More worrying was the insistence that she should tell her 'partner' that he must be a carrier. She'd finessed the part where she should have admitted to knowing him for only half a day by adding a couple of extra dates. Dr McKay didn't need to know that even if Bea wanted to she had no idea how to get in touch with Tony Castle except through Let's Have Lunch.

She checked her mobile to confirm that she was running late. Stopping only to get her prescription en route, she rushed to the office where she had a twelve-thirty meeting with Adam. She arrived too hot and bothered to go straight in so decided to be five minutes late, having straightened herself out in the Ladies, then dipped into her office to get the papers she needed. When she knocked on his door, he opened it, obviously about to go out.

'I'm so sorry, Adam. I had a meeting outside the office and I've rushed back as fast as I could but the traffic . . .'

'Don't worry.' He straightened his pink and charcoal-grey striped tie before slipping on his tailored dove-grey suit jacket.

Don't worry and a smile. Had the man had a personality transplant? Bea stepped back to let him pass. 'Shall we rearrange for this afternoon?'

'I don't think we need to.'

'But I thought you said you wanted to go through the forward schedule?' And I've spent the last three days desperately trying to magic something together. If any of those authors don't deliver on time, I'm dead.

'I do. But I thought we'd do it outside the office. I asked Jade to check your diary and I think you're free over lunch.' Less of a question, more an instruction, Bea noted. 'Well, I was going to catch up with what I've missed this morning but, yes, that would be very nice. Thanks.'

'I noticed a new French bistro down the side-street by the tube. I thought we could talk there.'

Obviously not expecting disagreement, he strode out of the office, with Bea in his wake, clutching her future plan and praying it would look convincing under Adam's close scrutiny.

Sitting at a bare wooden table, tucked into a quiet corner of a small, almost empty room, decorated with posters for French cities, tourist sites and French advertisements, Adam suggested they took a moment to look at the menu before they got down to business. A tanned young maître d' came over and explained in a mouth-watering French accent the dishes of the day, all of which sounded to die for. Convincing herself that food was what she needed to support the antibiotics, distract her from her difficulties and give her strength for the meeting, Bea decided to go for the *galette de crabe* and then the *crevettes aux tomates*, leaving room for the cheese board on the other side of the room. Adam gave the menu a cursory glance, then unbuttoned his jacket.

'I'm glad to get out of the office. I thought we could do with a change of scene.'

'Good idea.' This relaxed version of the Adam Palmer she knew was rather unnerving.

'However, there's something I want to tell you before we start.' Not expecting to be taken into his confidence so early on, Bea nonetheless leaned forward to listen. He must have chosen this restaurant because he knew no one would be here to overhear whatever he was about to say.

'About a month ago I met a terrific-looking woman at a party. She was in really good shape.'

That was the last thing she would have expected him to

confide. Bea couldn't imagine where this might be leading. Not an idea for a book, surely?

'When I asked her how she kept herself looking so good, she told me that she ran twice a week and fasted for one whole day.'

'God. I could never do that.' Bea felt her waistband biting. Perhaps she should. But not today.

'That's what I thought too, but in fact it's quite easy. I've been doing it for three weeks now.'

As he opened up a little, letting something of the man behind the machine slip through, Bea suddenly saw that he might be quite attractive. Vain but attractive. To some. But back to the book in question.

'The only snag with our coming out at lunchtime,' he went on, 'is that today's my fasting day. You don't mind, do you? I just thought we could get more done here without interruption.'

'Of course not.' You bastard. 'I'm not very hungry anyway. I was only going to have the melon and the *salade maison*.' Whatever power game you're playing, I am not going to be fazed by it. She waved goodbye to the cheese.

Before the food arrived, she had refused the warm crusty French bread with peppery virgin olive oil and had, at his request, passed a copy of the publishing schedule for the next two years across the table. He spread it in front of him so there was little room for her place setting, making her feel crowded and greedy. No doubt another power ploy. As he quizzed her about the titles, she had to keep her wits about her, all too conscious that whenever she had to answer a question, her mouth was full.

'Obviously I looked at this before I took the job, but I wanted to see in more detail the books you expect to be delivered and those you plan to acquire. Some of this is speculative, has to be, of course, but it's more impressive than I was expecting.' He sipped his tap water.

'Thank you,' Bea muttered, through a mouthful of salad, acutely aware that a bit of olive (black, of course) had wedged itself between two of her front teeth. Why did this happen more and more often as she got older, and always at the most inconvenient moment?

'When you say "major autobiography" in October in both years, have you anything in mind or is that just wishful thinking?' Adam's grey eyes were on her face, as she tried to manoeuvre the piece of olive out of her teeth with her tongue without it being too obvious. 'Well?'

Success, just in time. Thank you, God. 'I don't have anything definite lined up but you know as well as I do that these things often come in very close to the wire. I'll brief Stuart and Jade and ask them to make a real onslaught on the agents, literary and showbiz. Of course I'll be doing the same so we'll divide the work between us. I'm confident that we'll find what we need. And that goes for the big fiction for spring in both years too.' In fact, she was far from confident, but he didn't need to know that. 'They'll be thrilled to have the extra responsibility and I'm sure they'll rise to it.' That was true. Under Stephen, they had been kept in the background, responding to the few manuscripts submitted to them or to those passed directly on to them by him or Bea. There was little room for initiative and their contacts were deliberately limited to the less important or fledgling agents not really dealt with by Bea or Stephen, who concentrated on the heavy hitters. 'And, of course, I know you've got your own contacts.'

'I'm glad you're responding so well to the challenge.'

Was that real warmth she saw in his smile? In his eyes as well? Surely not.

'When we last talked, I wasn't sure you would.'

'I don't give up that easily.' Power games might be his thing but Bea knew a few of her own. Following Adele's advice, she had decided to play the game his way until she knew what her position was. She was not going to relinquish control of her life to him. Perhaps reorganising the way they worked and putting new demands on herself and her senior staff would reignite her enjoyment of the job.

'Good. Now what about losing those two people from your department?'

'Becky, our most junior assistant, could go. I'd be reluctant to let her because she's bright and energetic. At the same time I know she'd find something else quite easily. But I simply can't see a way to losing another member of staff and getting the job you want done. You'll have to make the cut somewhere else.'

Adam shook his head. 'I can't.'

'Then you'll have to look at the budget again.' She didn't need Adele to tell her that the only way to fight a bully was to stand up to them. She knew that from school. When she was thirteen, Sally Armitage had orchestrated a campaign against her. The rest of the class were too wet to stand up on Bea's behalf so she'd worked out what to do for herself. One day, when Sally had pushed her off balance and snatched her KitKat to accompanying gales of giggles from her admirers, Bea had shoved her, hard, and grabbed back her biscuit. From then on, she had no more trouble, and within a year, she and Sally had become firm friends. Remembering that incident had often helped cushion her way through life. She went on, 'If we succeed in upping our turnover through the reduced but more profitable publishing programme that I'm proposing then we need the staff we have and, what's more, we can afford them.' Bea was not going to back down. She steeled herself for a fight.

'I'm sorry.' She caught a note of regret in his voice but it was tempered by certainty. 'I'd like to give you a chance but I can't.'

Bea's heart sank. 'Why not?'

'This is part of a larger corporate plan, and if I start making exceptions, it won't happen.'

'Being flexible isn't making exceptions.'

'I've made up my mind, I'm afraid. Things have got to change but I want you on side. I want your talent and your experience. You could make a fantastic contribution to the new Coldharbour, I'm sure of that.'

With flattery thrown her way, Bea had to think fast. Fortunately she'd already gone over and over the possible outcomes of their conversation. She had prepared herself for his insistence. If she continued to support her team, not only would some of them get fired regardless, she would be casting the remaining members adrift. If she didn't, she could look after those who were left as well as being part of what could be an exciting new start. She might have her reservations about Adam, but there was no doubt he'd done the business and saved Pennant. If he was going to do that again, she might enjoy being part of the effort. Her decision was made.

'All right.'

'You're sure? You don't want time to think about it?' He seemed surprised by the speed of her change of heart.

But what was there to think about?

'All I need is time to decide who to let go and the best way to tell them.' This was going to be hard although in her heart she knew who it should be. Stuart and Jade had different but complementary strengths; each of them was valuable in their own way. Stuart was less conventional but with extremely eclectic taste while Jade's taste was more middle-of-the-road and she did have some good contacts on the fringes of showbiz who might be useful.

'Done!' He stretched his hand across the table to shake hers. She couldn't help noticing the perfect squared-off nails, the neat half-moons, the dark hair at his wrist. Was it her imagination or did he hold her grasp for a fraction longer than necessary? Get a grip, woman, this isn't a Let's Have Lunch situation.

'And now,' he announced, 'there's one thing I'd really like.'

Thank God for that. He's human and we're going to celebrate. He's going to crack and have a brandy or at the very least a double espresso. Bea felt that their relationship was taking a stride forward and, despite the immediate hurdles she was dreading having to cross, she was even looking forward to getting back to work for the first time in ages.

Adam called the waiter over. 'Coffee for you, Bea?'

You bet. She nodded. Would asking for the cheese be going too far?

'As for me, what I'd love is a cup of boiling water with a twist of lemon.'

Well, perhaps they had a little way to go before they became soul-mates, but she liked the challenge he'd offered her. She felt excited but nervous about what the next few months would bring. The jury was out on how far she could trust him but she'd go along with him and see how things played out. By the time they reached the office, she knew what she had to do.

12

Knowing what has to be done is a lot easier than doing it, reflected Bea, as she strode into the office with renewed purpose. She noticed Stuart in Jade's office. He was stretched back in the one comfortable chair, arms behind his head and eyes half shut while Jade talked at him from the other side of her desk, wearing an unusually earnest expression. Those two spent far too much time closeted together analysing office politics. With one of them gone, the other might sharpen up their act. A reinvigorated twosome with a fixed goal in their sights might well be better than the three of them working together at half-cock. But was she right in her choice as to which one of them should go? Stuart or Jade? Who would make the better working partner? Jade was younger and probably more hungry, but her taste in books was very similar to Bea's. Stuart, on the other hand, although more world-weary, had a certain edge that might complement Bea better. She had to remember that her choice might make the difference between success and failure. Not just the company's but hers. And after that lunch, failure was something she didn't want to entertain.

Jade saw her coming and immediately leaped to her feet. Pencil thin, dressed in black as usual, she had a head of wild black curls that provided a perfect foil for the slash of bright red lipstick she always wore. She paused to listen to something Stuart was saying. Encouraging or discouraging? Bea couldn't tell. However, whatever it was didn't dissuade her from coming to her door.

'Bea! Could I have a word with you?'

'Not now. I'm sorry but there's something I've got to do. Later this afternoon any good? Or even Monday morning?'

'It can't wait, I'm afraid.' Jade could never be described as aggressive but she sure knew how to assert herself. That was one of the reasons Bea liked and rated her. She knew no one else who would contemplate doorstepping a celeb to persuade a book out of them. That wasn't what old-fashioned publishing had been about, but Jade was one of a new breed who thought out of the box.

'Well, I'm sorry, it's going to have to.' Bea had to get to her office to think. The last thing she wanted was a discussion with someone she might be about to make redundant.

'I just need ten minutes. Please. In about half an hour?'

'All right, if you really insist.' Bea conceded defeat in the knowledge that Jade would pester her until she gave in. Having such little time in hand would certainly help focus her mind.

Half an hour later, she was still undecided. Much as she would have liked to get the difficult conversation over with before the weekend – something that Adam, doubtless, would have done in her place – she needed more time to be absolutely sure she was doing the right thing. If only she could escape with her antibiotics, go home and start again on Monday. At least she'd be feeling better then. She shifted position to ease her discomfort, then sipped at yet another glass of water. A knock and then Jade put her head around the door. 'Now a good time?'

'Just give me another couple of minutes. I've got to make one call, then I'm yours.' Coward.

Bea stood up, straightened her skirt – rather a nice Marc Jacobs number that she'd spotted in the window of Flash for Cash and couldn't resist on the grounds that second-hand doesn't count – then picked up her phone and turned to face the window so no one could see she wasn't speaking.

When Jade came back, she was ready. She was going to pretend everything was normal, soothe any worries and take the next couple of days to be certain of her decision. Stuart and Jade might not be her best friends but they had been loyal colleagues and they at least deserved to be given serious thought and consideration. She owed them that. Even if they were going to think she was a two-faced cow on Monday when they knew the truth.

'Tea?' Jade had brought in two mugs with her.

'Thanks. Lovely.' Tea was not going to do Tony Castle's legacy much good, but in the interests of oiling the wheels, she took the proffered mug. 'Now, what's so urgent?'

Jade took a deep breath. 'I know you must be having a really difficult time at the moment.' Her customary confidence had deserted her. Keeping her eyes on her black-stockinged knees as she spoke, she kept turning a foolscap envelope that she held on her lap.

Bea couldn't avoid noticing the particularly brilliant

shade of Jade's newly applied red nail varnish – it still had the faint smell of pear-drop. 'Nothing I can't handle.' She was determined to remain cool and noncommittal.

'Everybody's saying there are going to be job cuts.'

Already the conversation had veered from any direction Bea had hoped it would take. 'Well, it does look as though things are going to be a bit unsettled for the next few weeks.'

'I saw you going out for lunch with Adam so – maybe I'm adding two and two together – but . . .'

'No decisions have been made, if that's what you're asking.'

'Not exactly.' Jade looked so uncomfortable that Bea almost felt sorry for her.

'Yes?' she said, in what she hoped was an encouraging way.

'I've been here for four years now and have loved working with you.'

Oh, no, she was going to plead for her job, citing out-of-work husband, young children, aged parents and, of course, an abiding love of the company. Bea braced herself. 'Honestly, Jade. Nothing's been decided.' Bring on the weekend.

'That's good. I thought perhaps I might be making things easier for you if I told you now that I've been offered a job at Harcourt House and I've decided to take it.' The last bit came out in a rush as she lifted her head and looked across the desk, straight at Bea, as if wanting her assurance that she had made the right decision.

Managing to refrain from leaping up and hugging her, Bea was nonetheless having difficulty in composing herself.

There is a God, after all. Thank you. 'That's wonderful news for you. Congratulations. What will you be doing?'

As Jade explained that the new women's fiction list was being reinvented and put in her charge now because the existing editorial director had moved to America, it became obvious that this was going to be an excellent career move.

'That all sounds fantastic. A great break for you. I'm not going to try to persuade you to stay because, the way things are, I think this will be a much, much better deal than anything I could offer.' That, at least, was true.

'I was hoping you'd say that. Thank you.' Jade was all smiles now the worst was over. 'Here's my resignation letter. I thought I'd better make it formal.' She passed Bea the envelope.

'Perhaps I should have a word with Stuart, just to put his mind at rest about what's happening here.' Bea couldn't quite believe how good fortune had played into her hands. 'Could you ask him to come in?'

Stuart entered her office at his most recalcitrant, his scar gleaming pearly white. He left on a high to go and celebrate with Jade. Bea had reassured him that his job was secure. Deciding to put all her cards on the table, she confided that Jade had in fact done him a favour. She hadn't wanted to lose either of them but she was delighted with the way the dice had fallen. He would have more responsibility and together they would make a strong team with a vital role in turning the company around. Fired with enthusiasm, they planned to meet the following week to discuss tactics.

After he'd gone, Bea spent a couple of hours catching up

with a backlog of work and tidied the office ready for a new start. For the first time in months, she went home fired up and looking forward to what was to come.

*

As she soaked in a hot bath, hoping that it would relieve the worst of her symptoms, she let her mind run to their source. Tony Castle. Why, when she had at last met a man, even if their brief acquaintance had been fuelled by alcohol, did he have to have been such a shit? Until that night, she'd almost forgotten how good sex could be. And now she wished she hadn't had the reminder. She slid down so the back of her head was submerged under the water. With the sounds of the radio dulled, a conversation she'd had with Kate over an Indian takeaway floated back into her mind.

'I don't know why you're so hell-bent on finding a man anyway,' Kate had said, as she piled up the foil trays. 'You've survived without one for long enough.'

'Sex. That's why. A bit of physical contact. Someone to talk to on a long dark winter's night. Someone to put out the bins. It's all right for you, cocooned in marital bliss with it all on tap.'

'Seems to me the only good thing about sex at our age is that once you've done it you know you don't have to do it again for at least another week, or even a fortnight if you're lucky.' Kate stabbed at the last bit of chicken korma with a fork, before taking the containers over to the retro flip-top pedal bin.

'Speak for your own libido. Mine feels as if it's been in

cold storage since Colin left. I've spent all my time throwing myself at my work unless I was trying to be a decent mum to Ben. Now I've decided to throw myself at a man instead. I've just got to find one.'

Why was it that married women really didn't get what it was like to be single at this age? Although they moaned about their partners and pretended to envy the single, even the celibate, state, she knew they, Kate included, would never embrace it any better than she did. Yes, she had the freedom to do exactly what she wanted when she wanted, but there were also times when the loneliness could be over-whelming. At home alone on a Friday night when smug couples were candle-lit dining with each other, when young singles were out pubbing, clubbing or smooching in the cinema, 'alone' was what she was. Ben had his own life now and was guaranteed to have skedaddled to a friend's house or a party as soon as humanly possible. She didn't dwell on the possibilities too hard. Scrambled eggs, a bottle of wine and a DVD were all well and good in their place, but on a regular basis, they lost something of their charm. And, however well she entertained herself, there was always an empty space beside her on the sofa. Most weekends she kept herself busy, even if only with the piles of reading she had from work, but some she spent huddled in a self-pitying heap beneath the duvet. What she'd said to Kate was right. This had to stop. She was only at the half-way point in her life: it was time to pick herself up and find the partner of choice. She hadn't yet lost all faith in Let's Have Lunch, so bring on the next four dates.

Dates? *Christ!* She had one with Mark this evening. 'Eight.

Don't be late,' he'd said. And that was exactly what she was going to be. Very.

Like a whale rising from the ocean, she surfaced with a huge splash, soaking the bathmat and dousing the three scented candles. How could she have forgotten? Cursing under her breath, she climbed out, wrapped a towel around her, mopped the floor with another and tore down the corridor to her bedroom. With the hair-dryer in one hand and her phone in the other, she did her hair and ordered a cab. She took a look in the mirror, then dashed back to the bathroom for some styling mousse and her hairbrush, which she found muddled up in Ben's things. Still, the fact that he brushed his hair at all was something to be thankful for, never mind what he did it with.

When she heard the hoot outside, she was almost ready, ramming her feet into the nearby fake leopardskin pumps, grabbing the thin cream jacket from the end of the bed and running downstairs as she transferred the contents of her office bag into her evening bag. Her only other bag, in fact. Her hair and lipstick could be remedied in the back of the cab.

Her heartbeat had slowed by the time they pulled up outside the bar, which was tucked away behind Regent Street. Outside, the pavement pulsed with people. Window ledges were littered with empty bottles and glasses, the street with cigarette butts. She pushed her way through the open doors into the dimly lit interior. Huge ceiling fans whirred lazily while the combination of voices and music provided a busy background hum. Edging her way past the mahogany bar, which was shoulder deep with braying cocktail drinkers, she eventually spotted Mark sitting in the quietest corner by the restaurant section, partially hidden behind a potted palm. Opposite him was an enormous wall clock, so he must be all too aware that she was nearly forty minutes late. On the table was an empty glass and a forlorn neon pink gerbera that was winning its right to droop, despite the supporting wire wound about its stem.

'I am *so* sorry.' Bea hurried up to him. 'I've had a helluva day and I had to rush home first to drop some things off, then I came straight here.' She hoped he wouldn't notice how newly bathed she was.

Mark looked at her, clearly relieved. 'I thought you weren't coming.'

'My God. I would never stand someone up. Never. Let me get you a drink.' She began to rummage in her bag for her purse. 'I'd have phoned you, but you didn't give me your card.' Despite being touched by his response to her arrival, she decided to pass the buck. It worked.

'I'm afraid I don't really have much time.' He sounded apologetic, as if it was his fault she was late. 'My ex has just phoned. She's had a major row with my youngest daughter and is insisting that I come and take her for the weekend.'

'Heavens. How old did you say she was?' Surely his children were old enough to look after themselves.

'Thirteen going on twenty-three.'

'Then you'll need a drink first. Hang on.' Bea negotiated the crush at the bar to return with two small glasses of Pinot Grigio and a bowl of nuts. 'What happened?' Any story of another mother's difficulties, however small, was usually music to her ears. Being part of the same sisterhood meant she relished any confirmation that her inadequacies on the parenting front were not unique.

'The usual. Alison, my wife – sorry, ex-wife – has a short fuse and Bella knows how to light it. She announced she was going to a party but when Alison called the parents of the party-giver to ask if Bel could stay the night – guess what?'

'No party!' Bea had been there.

'In one. So now they're never speaking to one another again. And I've got to tube out to Chiswick to persuade her to come back to my flat with me.' He sat back and sipped his drink, then let his shoulders fall and his eyes close as if wishing he could shrug off his warring women.

'Do you have to? Can't it wait till tomorrow?' Bea was not asking for herself. He looked tired. Even in the dim lighting, he gave off an aura of weariness and she could make out the shadows under his eyes.

'No. Really not.' He sighed. 'If I put it off, Alison won't speak to me either, which would make seeing the girls that much harder. I only see them at weekends and then only if Alison hasn't organised something else for them. Which she often does.' His wistful expression gave way to something more determined as he looked at Bea. 'But you don't want to hear all this.'

In a way he was right, she didn't. Yet at the same time she found she did. She had never given a serious thought to what it must be like to be at the losing end of the custody battle. Had Colin felt any of Mark's frustration those times she'd insisted on him seeing Ben when she was reaching the end of her tether? Not that she'd cared about that at the time. Dealing with teenagers alone was hard, especially if your ex was only an angry tube ride away. She used to imagine Colin out enjoying himself while she was imprisoned alone with Ben. But seeing Mark in this state made her think perhaps things weren't so black and white.

'No, I do,' she said, and meant it.

'I vowed I wouldn't bore any of my dates into the ground with my personal life. So that's enough.' His smile seemed more attractive than she remembered from their first meeting. His teeth weren't *that* uneven. 'You sound as if you understand, though.'

'Oh, I do. More than you know.'

'That makes me want to find out more but I really am going to have to go. I'm sorry.'

'No, no. I shouldn't have been so late. It's my fault. You go, and I'll finish my drink.'

'Are you sure?'

'Positive. I've always got a book with me.'

'Then could we try again next week?'

'Yes. I'd like that.' To her surprise, Bea realised she meant that too.

A book! As she watched him weave his way into the night, Bea dug into her bag for her regular Friday-night companion. She signalled the waiter to order a salad and another glass of wine. How stupid she felt, always moaning about the lack of a man in her life and then, when she'd had the chance to do something about it, she'd blown it by not turning up on time. But the opportunity hadn't been entirely wasted. He might not be the most attractive man she'd met so far but, on a second outing, he just might be one of the nicest. Something that her other recent date certainly was not. Perhaps she shouldn't underestimate that.

13

'What do you think? You can open your eyes . . . wait for it . . .' Ellen opened the front door and led Oliver through. 'Now!'

They were in a long, rectangular room, light spilling through a large window with wide french windows at the far end that opened onto a tiny terrace, just big enough for a metal table and chair and some bedraggled pot plants. To the right of the door a neat row of white and chrome kitchen units ran the length of the wall. Beyond the small glass-topped dining-table and two white leather and chrome chairs, a yellow two-seater sofa faced a small, wall-mounted flat-screen TV. The walls were freshly painted a uniform white, the perfect setting for the *pièce de résistance*: Caroline Fowler's *Starship*. The colours sang from the painting, taking attention from everything else in the room.

Oliver gasped. 'My God. It looks better than ever. You bought it?'

'For you.' Ellen enjoyed his obvious pleasure. 'It's a present.'

'I can't . . . you shouldn't have . . .' For the first time since she'd known him, Oliver couldn't find the words he wanted.

'I can. I have. Now, come through here.' She caught his hand and pulled him through a door on the left. Another light-infused room with pale Wedgwood blue walls and white woodwork, at the centre of which was a double bed made up with crisp white bed linen. There were blue and white checked blinds at the windows, a bedside table carrying a chrome Anglepoise reading lamp and a wide built-in wardrobe. 'And then, best of all . . .' Ellen almost skipped over to a final door, which she flung open to reveal a wet room, where the sun glanced off blue and white mosaic tiles, and a sheer glass panel divided the shower from the rest of the room. 'Well? Say something.'

Once they'd made the decision that Ellen was going to loan him up to three months' rent, and maybe more, if need be, she hadn't wasted time. While Oliver put his energy into finding the now more-necessary-than-ever job, she put hers into phoning the local lettings agents. One of her calls had been taken just minutes after this flat had been accepted on the agency's books. Because it was in a converted stocking factory within half a mile of her house, she had shut the gallery for a couple of hours over lunch and gone to inspect. The rent was a little higher than she'd budgeted for but she'd put down a deposit, frightened they would lose it otherwise. She had been so sure that it was perfect but, too late, the thought crossed her mind that perhaps she'd moved too fast and forced him into a commitment that he wasn't really ready for, despite what he'd said.

'It's nothing like I'd imagined.'

'It's not?' Her relief at his regaining the power of speech was tempered with anxiety that she'd made a terrible mistake.

'No. I thought I'd be living with cockroaches and damp. I never imagined anything like this. It's . . .' he paused '. . . absolutely breathtaking. I love it.' As he pulled her towards him, they fell back onto the bed, laughing. Then, as one thing led to another, Ellen stopped worrying that (a) he didn't like it, (b) she'd spent too much money, (c) she'd borrowed from the children's university account (but, of course, it would be paid back long before they'd be choosing where to go), and gave herself up to the moment.

Afterwards they lay in a tangle of duvet, the bed surrounded by the clothes they'd flung off in their hurry. Ellen's head rested in the dip below Oliver's shoulder as she half dozed in the afternoon light, marvelling on how blessed she felt to have discovered such a sense of harmony with someone else again. Oliver and she were a perfect fit. She couldn't imagine him ever not being in her life now.

'Funny to think that we're not going to see each other for a week.' She caught the woody citrus scent of his after-shave as he rolled to face her.

'Don't,' he said. 'I wish I could come with you.'

'I wish you could too.' She could picture them in Cornwall together, staying at a local B-and-B, introducing him to everyone, tramping the cliff path, pottering about in the family boat, eating crab sandwiches on the beach. He could even have come with her to visit the couple of artists she hoped to persuade to exhibit at the gallery. 'And next time you will. But I'll be back in a week and by then you'll be ensconced here and you might even have found some work.'

'Don't.' He groaned and rolled back again, his arms folded behind his head as he stared at the ceiling.

'Couldn't you widen the field a bit?' she asked tentatively.

'For God's sake, I'm doing the best I can. Just leave it to me.' He swung his legs over the edge of the bed and sat up, rubbing his head.

'Come back.' She ran her hand down his back, resting it on his waist. 'I was only making a suggestion.' But she couldn't stop herself thinking that the wider he cast his net, the sooner he would find something.

'I don't think so.'

Her heart sank. Why was it that, despite the intense closeness she felt they had, she sometimes had to tread on eggshells around him? It was as if there was still a part of him he kept hidden, despite the 'no secrets' pact they had made. She could put her hand on her heart and swear that he knew everything about her, her marriage and her family, her work, her hopes and fears. Would he be able to swear she knew everything about him? She thought not. Now was clearly not the moment to find out.

'I've got a better idea,' he said. 'Why don't we test-run the wet room together?' Smiling again, storm over, he took her hand and together they went next door, any tension between them evaporated.

*

As she replayed that afternoon in her head, she looked out of the train window, a slight smile on her lips. They were passing Dawlish, her favourite part of the journey south where the track hugged the coastline, waves slapping against the sea wall below them, the white and pastel houses of the town on the north side giving way to the rich red sandstone cliffs. She gazed south to the horizon where the sea and sky fused into one another, the vast expanse of inky blue water only interrupted by the flash of a white sail with seagulls wheeling above.

Her usual enjoyment of the journey had been hijacked by her memories of the last weeks, and by her projections of those to come. She felt as if her life had divided into two parts that she had to reconcile as soon as possible. Before and after Oliver. As the train rushed towards the before, she was beginning to acknowledge that the potential difficulties Bea and Kate had signalled were all too probable. As long as she was with Oliver, the realities of the situation were sufficiently misted to make it easy to ignore them.

As the train drew into Truro, she began to feel more and more nervous about how the children might react. What would she do if they didn't give Oliver the welcome she'd been so sure of till now? Then, there was no more time for thought. There they were, sun-kissed and smiling: Matt racing down the platform, flinging his arms around her; Emma holding back but looking pleased to see her. By the exit, Ellen caught sight of Mary, Simon's mother, a trim, diminutive woman in her late seventies who had refused to let age get the better of her. She was the picture of a proper countrywoman, with her unruly grey hair, ruddy cheeks, blue Barbour waistcoat and loose trousers.

'Mum, come on. If we're quick, we can get back in time

for you to go out in the new dinghy. The tide's just right.' Matt pulled at her arm.

'Hang on, hang on.' She laughed. 'Give me a chance to say hello to Em. How are you, darling?'

'She's got a boyfriend,' Matt mocked in a sing-song voice.

'Shut up, Matt. It's not true, Mum.' Emma hugged her tight.

'Yes, you have. You're always down at the beach with him.' He managed to dodge the slap aimed at him.

'Stop it, you two, I've only just got here.' Ellen walked between them to prevent any further disagreement. 'Hello, Mary.' She embraced her mother-in-law. 'Not too exhausted?'

'You know we always love having them. And you look as though you've benefited from the break.'

'Look at your hair, Mum. You look like M in the James Bond films.'

'Thanks so much, Matt. She's only about twenty years older than me. Don't you like it?'

'Very much indeed. Makes you look younger, whatever Matt says.' Mary led the way to her battered old Peugeot estate and they all piled in, shouting greetings to Tilly and Rex, the excited pair of springer spaniels bouncing around in the back. They drove down the familiar high-hedged narrow lanes, non-stop chatter from the rear seat, arriving at the Neill's family home, a large nineteenth-century stone farmhouse close to a small hamlet in the Percuil valley. During the school holidays, the house was Holiday Central, alive with cousins and their friends who dashed in and out, snatching up and dropping off riding kit, surfboards, wetsuits, swimsuits, towels, tennis rackets, car keys, bicycles, and distributing sand wherever they went. The two dogs followed the crowd, wagging and barking with excitement. Mary was immune to the hubbub, enjoying having the young life around her. Bob, Simon's father, hid himself in their private sitting room whenever it got too much. Simon's brother and sister, Pete and Julia, lounged around the garden with their partners, coming in to contribute to a meal, get a book or a drink, or give the youngest children a lift somewhere. The atmosphere was the same relaxed chaos that it had been every summer Ellen could remember being there.

By the evening, Ellen had been out in the dinghy without capsizing it, helped with supper and caught up with snippets of what Emma and Matt had been doing over the last weeks. She was helping with the washing-up when Mary said, 'Darling, you didn't eat much at supper. Are you all right?'

'Just because I normally eat like a horse, I know. No, I'm trying to lose a few pounds. Oliver's persuaded me it would be a good thing.' His name slipped out without her thinking and there it lay between them, large and glaringly obvious. Her prayers that Mary wouldn't notice went unanswered.

'Who? I don't remember hearing that name before, do I?' She put a plate back in the sink and stopped to scrutinise Ellen. 'I knew there was something different about you, apart from the new hair, of course.' Two and two made four with no effort at all.

'You're such a beady old thing,' Ellen protested. 'OK. Hands up. I was going to tell you but I was waiting for the right moment.'

'Seems like you've just found it.' Mary put a hand on

Ellen's arm. 'Don't worry. I've been expecting this for years. Can't think why it took so long. Anyway, I couldn't have wished for a lovelier daughter-in-law.'

As they washed and dried, Ellen poured out the whole story, grateful that they were having the conversation at a moment when they didn't need to look each other in the eye – exactly as she'd engineer an awkward conversation with Matt or Emma. She told Mary everything, feeling only a smidgeon of guilt when she omitted to include the minor detail of the rent payment. When she'd finished there was a short silence while Mary peeled off her rubber gloves.

'It all sounds a bit of a whirlwind.' She hesitated over her choice of words, obviously not wanting to give the impression that she disapproved. 'Are you sure you know him well enough to make such a commitment so soon?'

'I know more every day. And the more I know, the more I like.' Ellen brushed aside any potential objections, as she'd promised Oliver she would. If she let a chink of doubt appear in her armour, Mary would pounce, then worry away until it was much larger. 'I know you're concerned for Matt and Em, but so am I. I won't do anything to hurt them. Promise.'

'What are you promising?' Matt stuck his head round the door. 'Hurry up. I want to beat you at Scrabble.'

'Why? Has the TV broken?' Matt was usually impossible to prise away from the screen.

'Ha ha! No, but Em and Lucy are watching some stupid film. What *were* you promising?' Like his grandmother, Matt had a nose for what he wasn't meant to know. There was

151

no point in trying to fudge because he'd just go on until he'd succeeded in worming a satisfactory reply out of her.

'I was just promising that you'd like a new friend of mine.'

'Why? Who is she?'

'She's a he. And he supports Arsenal.' At least, she was sure he could be persuaded to, in the interest of good relations.

'A he!' Matt yelled, as if a male friend was the last thing he'd expect his mother to have.

'Yes. He liked the paintings in the gallery and we've made friends. You'll like him.'

'He's not a boyfriend, is he?' The disgusted emphasis put on the word 'boyfriend' was enough to warn Ellen not to say more. As was Mary's sharp elbow in the ribs.

'No, no. Don't be silly.' Time to change the subject. 'Come on, then. Scrabble it is. But you know I'm unbeatable.'

The challenge was enough to put everything else right out of Matt's head. 'No, you're not,' he objected. 'I won at least the last two times.'

That's boys for you, thought Ellen and she clenched her fist Andy Murray-style. 'OK, then. Bring it on.'

'You won't beat me, you know. Let battle commence.' With the gauntlet thrown, he dashed down the corridor to the living room, Ellen in hot pursuit.

*

By the end of the week, Ellen was exhausted and ready for home. She'd played all the games in the toy cupboard with varying degrees of success – Scattergories, Monopoly,

Articulate, The Nasty Horse Racing Game and Cribbage –
all old favourites that were brought out every year. She'd
walked the cliff path, straining up the steep bits, legs aching,
but relishing the open spaces, the wind in her face and the
time alone. She'd played tennis (badly), golf (even worse),
been out in the dinghy, and even been persuaded to catch
fresh mackerel for a barbecue supper. She'd visited her two
artists: one had already been snapped up by a gallery in
Bristol but the other was interested in her proposals. They'd
been through the work he had in his studio, selecting the
best of the figurative oils that had so readily captured her
imagination with their clever use of space and compos-
ition, and their suggestions of half-told stories. They agreed
he would paint another four over the following few months
so there would be enough for a coherent exhibition in the
back room of the gallery next spring.

Most importantly, she had had time to catch up with
her children and re-forge her relationships with them – if
not always in exactly the way she would have liked. Matt
was still the boy she had waved off on the train at the
beginning of the holiday. He remained a child of wild
enthusiasms, with the charm of his father and a love of
physical activity, cleaving to the band of male cousins and
their friends as if he'd never been away from them. Seeing
the gusto with which he joined in with everything they did,
however challenging for a boy of thirteen, always made her
smile. She knew his older cousins would watch out for him
whatever they got up to. However, there was something
about Emma that had changed during her three weeks away.
Watching her with the others, Ellen could see how she hung

on the words of Josh, a blond surfie who'd become a regular in the house. Whether or not he was the 'boyfriend' Matt had mentioned was unclear, but the lingering glances she had given him from under her eyelashes whenever he spoke, the alacrity with which she followed him about, made it obvious that she might not object if such a relationship were suggested.

Whenever Ellen tried to talk to her about Josh, Emma had avoided the conversation by either having something else to do or somewhere to rush off to. In fact, she spent as little time with her mother as she could, as if embarrassed by her presence. There was no doubt she was growing up fast, thought Ellen, wistfully. She wondered how Kate had coped with Megan at the same stage. Although Josh seemed nice enough, Ellen could see that his evident lack of reciprocal interest meant Emma might get hurt. All Ellen wanted to do was to help cushion the blow. This new lack of communication between them also meant that she didn't have a chance to talk to her daughter about Oliver either but, after a few days of being there, it hadn't seemed appropriate. Mary's measured reaction had confirmed the need to be more circumspect about him. As she relaxed into the holiday, enjoying not having to worry about her appearance and letting the diet slide for the week, she decided to wait until they returned to London. Better not to rock the boat just yet.

14

Ellen jumped off the Truro–London train, hefting her case down the steps to the platform. Joining the slew of people who were rushing towards the barrier, she craned her neck to see Oliver. The last time they'd talked, he'd said he couldn't bear to be apart from her any longer than he had to so he'd be waiting for her at the barrier.

She knew Oliver was hurt she hadn't spoken to the children about him. He interpreted her silence as a lack of commitment to him. However hard she tried, she couldn't get him to understand the situation from Emma and Matt's point of view, which to her was what mattered.

'If you loved me as much as I do you, you wouldn't be able to resist telling them about me,' he complained. Or 'If you were as proud of me as I am of you, you would be bursting to tell them.' And then, 'If you wanted to spend the rest of your life with me, you wouldn't hesitate.'

Hearing him say those things, she had wavered again. But she had found necessary strength in being with Simon's family. Despite her intentions, she'd been so busy that there was little time to dwell on Oliver. But once she was on the train home, she'd realised how much she was looking forward to seeing him again. They had spoken every day while she was away and every day she had struggled to explain how she was trying to sort out the confusion in her head, but he just didn't get it. He didn't understand why she had veered from their original plan. But being sucked into family life again, seeing fifteen-year-old Emma's new vulnerability, Ellen's priorities had shifted back to where they'd been for the last ten years. The familiar realities of Cornwall meant their seven-week affair had taken on the strange insubstantiality of a dream. If she didn't know better, she could almost believe she had imagined the whole thing. Every night, lying with her eyes shut, she had tried to conjure Oliver's face onto the back of her lids, but she could never hold it there. No sooner had she pieced his features together than they floated apart again. The intensity of their passion was just as elusive. She could remember what they had done together but it was more like an out-of-body experience, watching herself having the hottest sex of her life but without being able to call up the emotions that went with it. Without the reality of his presence, she had slipped back into her perennial role of daughter-in-law and mother, where she always came second.

Suddenly there he was. Ellen's heart did a somersault. He pushed his way through the crowd to her and almost swept her off her feet, so big was the bear hug, so intense the kiss. 'God! I've been longing to do that.' His smile was broad. 'I can't wait to get you home. The car's this way.' He took her case and led her out of the station. 'So, was it a success?' The words tumbled from his mouth with the excitement of seeing her again.

She tucked her arm into his, happy to be able to touch him again. 'Terrific. The kids are on great form, having the usual brilliant time with their cousins. They were glad to see the back of me for another week!'

'I'm sure they weren't.'

'Not really. But they were definitely pleased not to be coming back to London just yet. I wish you could have come with me.'

'But there was something I wanted to do here. I had the idea a few weeks ago and your being away gave me the perfect opportunity.'

'Why won't you tell me what it was?' He had been peculiarly mysterious about what he'd been doing in her absence. She hoped he was about to surprise her with news of a job.

'Wait and see.'

During the journey home, she regaled him with descriptions of the artists she had met, where they lived and the pieces she'd seen. Uncle Sidney had rarely expanded his existing stable of artists except by recommendation but she had soon developed a nose for the sort of pictures that the gallery could sell and believed that by widening their roster they would attract new customers. Oliver didn't offer much conversation in return but listened, occasionally asking the odd question, his hand on her knee whenever he could put it there safely.

Her stories were only interrupted by his swearing whenever a light changed against them or thudding his fist on the steering-wheel when another driver got in his way. Ellen pretended not to notice these squalls of unnecessary temper and just carried on talking.

When they arrived home, Oliver switched off the engine and turned to her, taking her face in both hands and kissing her deeply.

'Let's go in.' Ellen reached for the door handle.

'Hang on a minute! There's something I need to tell you.'

She stopped and looked at him. 'What?'

'It's your birthday next week, isn't it?'

'You know it is. We talked about going to the theatre. Why? Have you got tickets for something?'

'No.' He looked as if he was about to burst with excitement. 'But I have got you a surprise.'

'Don't say that. I'll be dying with curiosity for the next four days.'

'No, you won't. Let's go in. I just wanted to . . . well, warn you.'

'OK. Consider me warned.' Ellen got out of the car and ran up the steps. 'I love coming home. More than ever now that you're here. And we've got one whole week to ourselves.' She turned and put her key in the lock, immediately feeling guilty for taking pleasure in her children's absence.

'Hang on. Let me go first.' He edged past her. 'Let me take your bag upstairs. Then, while you freshen up, I'll go down and crack open the bottle of champagne.'

Having washed and changed from her jeans into her loose navy silk trousers and a beaded pink Indian kurtee that he had once said he liked, she came down the stairs into the kitchen. A slice of evening sunshine came through the side window, lighting the darkened room. Oliver gave her a chilled glass of champagne before leading her to the kitchen table.

'Mmm. What a welcome. Why don't we go out into the garden? It's a beautiful evening.' Ellen went over to the french windows. 'Why have you got the curtains drawn, anyway?' As she reached out to pull them back, Oliver grabbed her arm, making her spill some champagne. 'Ouch. Careful.'

'Wait a minute, darling.' He pulled her back to the chair, and pushed her down on it. 'Before we do, have a sip, then close your eyes.'

'What? You are funny but OK.' She did as she was told and heard the curtains being pulled back.

'Keep your eyes shut.' Oliver came to stand behind her with his hands resting on her shoulders. He took a breath. 'OK. You can open them now.'

As she looked out to the garden, her eyes widened and she gripped the sides of her chair.

'Well?' he said. 'What do you think?' She could hear the note of pride in his voice. 'Happy early birthday, darling.'

'Oh, my God, Oliver. What have you done?'

'Don't you like it?' Ellen could hear the click of his thumb-nail against another.

'I . . . well . . . I . . .' Words failed her.

'It's specially purpose-built so that you can use it as a studio. You said that you always wanted one of your own and now you've got one.'

'But the garden . . .'

'It's a bit of a mess, I know. They had to work so fast to get it finished on time. But there's nothing that can't be tidied up. We can do it together.'

'A mess . . . yes.' Ellen's voice faded.

Outside, her beloved garden that had seen her through her bereavement, providing so much pleasure and comfort over the following ten years, had been destroyed. The small lawn had been trampled over, and no heed given to her precious plants on which she had lavished so much time and attention. Two planks lay on the grass, their ends crushing the scented French lavender. The central bed and the two borders were devastated, the hellebores bent and crushed, her precious shrubs knocked about, her favourite lilac with a broken branch. And at the end, just hiding the greenhouse, stood an enormous new garden shed, painted a deep Scandinavian red. Facing the house were two glass doors through which she could see a skylight illuminating an easel inside.

'Don't you like it?' Oliver's voice came from somewhere miles away. 'The glass is special Pilkington double-glazed so you'll be warm in there, even in the dead of winter. Perhaps I should have asked you. But I was so sure you would.'

Ellen felt as if she had been plunged into a pool of water that was closing over her head. A rushing noise filled her ears as she struggled for breath. Her garden! How could he not have understood how important every plant out there was for her? He had watched her pottering about outside in the evening, dead-heading, straightening wayward stems, picking posies for the dining-table or the bedroom. He had sat beside her in bed while she planned the changes she would make for the new year, experimenting with new planting schemes, outlining a different shape for a flowerbed. He knew how long she spent poring over her plant books, her pencil poised over the graph paper on which she sketched her ideas. She remembered talking about the possibility of putting a tool shed on that bit of hard standing, but she had dismissed the idea in favour of a pergola. The space she had earmarked for it had disappeared under the footprint of his present.

'It's such a shock.' Ellen was desperately searching for something positive to say. After all, his motives had only been the very best. She had sometimes talked about having nowhere to paint but never would she have envisaged a studio at the expense of her garden. She stood up, walked over to the french windows and stared out.

Oliver put his arm round her waist. 'I know. The garden. I didn't imagine it would take such a battering or that the studio would look so big. I was stupid not to see that.'

She twisted to face him, wishing the extra four or five pounds that had effortlessly slid on while she was away would disappear instead of organising themselves exactly where his hand lay. 'But how could you afford it?' The words came out before she could stop them.

'I maxed out my last credit card and made up the difference by selling *Starship* the day you left for Cornwall. I looked through your customer index and phoned that collector, Dan Frost.' He smiled, pleased with his own ingenuity. 'He was thrilled to have the opportunity to buy another Caroline Fowler and gave me a very good price for it.'

'You sold *Starship*?' she repeated. How could he have sold the picture that had brought them together – and go through her confidential papers to do so? She backed away from him, her arms crossed over her chest as if she was protecting herself.

'But you don't mind, do you?' He seemed surprised by her reaction. 'Didn't you give it to me? And I made sure I found it a good home.'

'Well, yes, of course I did. But I thought it would mean more to you than that,' she mumbled, not caring how petty she sounded.

'Well, it did when you gave it to me, of course. But then I had the idea of doing this for you, and selling the painting was the only way I could afford to. It's just a picture, after all . . . Have I made a terrible mistake?'

The anxiety in his voice made it impossible for her to say yes. 'No, of course not.' She tried to sound happy and failed miserably. Her present, the painting that she'd believed he appreciated for its beauty as much as she did, had been 'just a picture' to him. In exchange for something that held so much significance for her, she had been given this shed. She swallowed. 'I just need a bit of time to . . . well, to get used to it.'

'You'll feel better once you've been inside.' His excitement had returned.

They picked their way across the garden to the door. He passed her a key on a loop of red ribbon. 'Happy birthday.'

'You open it, darling.' She didn't want him to see her hands shaking. As the door slid to one side, she saw how he had prepared for her. The sun lit up the pale cream walls and the scrubbed wooden floor, illuminating the few pieces of furniture that Oliver had provided.

'I picked up the plan chest on eBay. Look, it's perfect for

you.' He pulled open the top drawer. 'I've put all your paper-work from the gallery in here so you've got somewhere to keep it rather than spreading it all over the house.' But that was how she liked to work, she objected silently. 'There's watercolour paper in the drawer underneath and you can put all your sketches in the others. Come over here.' From one of the two shelves on the wall, he took a small card-board box containing tubes of watercolour paint. She took them from him so he could reach for the jam jar that he'd stuffed with various paintbrushes. 'I didn't really know what you'd want but they told me in the art shop that these should be enough to get you started. Well?' He was looking at her with such expectation, she couldn't possibly dis-appoint him. How much he must love her to do all this in secret. Just for her. 'I really am sorry about the garden.' He sounded so forlorn.

'We can fix that.' She found words at last. 'And, well, I have always wanted a studio of my own.'

She rifled through the paints, delighting in their colours. She twisted the top off the cadmium red and squeezed it until paint oozed from the end. That small action was enough to bring back hours spent in her studio space at art school. She began to feel more positive. Oliver was giving her the chance to reclaim a lost part of herself. And they really could fix the garden.

'Are you sure it's all right?' He still sounded doubtful.

'Of course.' And, at that moment, she almost was. 'The garden could do with a bit of a rethink and this gives me the opportunity to do it.' Standing there, surrounded by what he'd done for her, she felt an enormous rush of love for him. She wrapped her arms round his neck and they kissed, long and hard, until they pulled apart breathless, Ellen once again bowled over by the intensity of her feelings.

Oliver looked down at her. 'There is one more thing.'

'You've spoilt me enough.' She didn't think she could take any more.

'I thought we could put the sofa-bed from the playroom in here too so you've got somewhere to sit and think. Oh, and I forgot to show you these.' He bent down and, from behind the chest, he pulled a small electric travelling kettle, two Tate Gallery mugs and a small jar of Gold Blend. 'Coffee?'

'You know what, Oliver Shepherd?'

'What?'

'You've thought of everything. I do love you.'

'That's all I wanted to hear. Shall we go back inside? Or will you be resuming your artistic career straight away?'

'Mmm. Tempting. But I think I'll wait till tomorrow, if that's all right with you.'

'Perfectly. Since the kids are away, I've got other plans for us anyway.'

'I was hoping you might have something in mind.' She followed him back to the house, forcing herself to look away from the destruction around them.

*

Much later that night, woken by Oliver's rhythmic but insistent snoring, Ellen tiptoed downstairs and sat in the kitchen cradling a mug of hot milk. With the lights off, she could still see the huge hulk of the shed dominating the garden. She didn't need to remind herself of the damage its installation had caused. Her excitement at having a place to paint had waned, only for her first reaction to return: dismay. Her life was already so busy with the house, the business, the children and, now, Oliver that she couldn't imagine a time when she'd ever use the shed. If she had wanted to paint badly enough, wouldn't she have found somewhere to do it years earlier? What she wanted was actually to enjoy her garden again, to watch her plants grow. She wished the bloody shed was gone. But that would only cause more damage and, worse, it would be like a gigantic slap in Oliver's face. The last thing she wanted to do was hurt him.

But now, the more she thought about it, the angrier she became. How could he have sold the painting? she asked herself again, still not quite able to believe he had. How dare he ruin her garden? What had made him think he could do whatever he wanted to her home? Even though he would be living there one day, he wasn't sharing it yet. What was he thinking of, spending what little credit he had left on her while she was paying his rent? But, she had to remind herself, the point was that he had done it for her. It was an act of love – wasn't it? She heard the slap of his bare feet on the stairs.

'Ellen? Are you there?'

'In here.'

'What are you doing? Aren't you freezing?'

'Just thinking.' As he entered the room, he looked so tense, so vulnerable. All he had been trying to do was please her. Her anger disappeared. Him being there made all the difference. His presence gave her a feeling of security and a sense of being loved that obliterated everything else. This was what she'd been missing for years.

'Penny for them.'

'Nothing, really.' She drained her mug and stood up. 'Just being silly. You know what it's like in the middle of the night when everything seems worse than it is.'

'Look. You can talk to me, you know.' He took the mug and put it on the counter before pulling her into the warmth of his embrace. 'What's the matter?'

'Oh, I don't know . . . there are some things that aren't worth discussing. Let's go up.'

As they took the stairs together, she looked up at him, his face lit by the dim light from the casement window, his hair on end. What other surprises had he got up his sleeve, she wondered. This was the man she had believed to be her kindred spirit, but again, she realised she didn't know him well at all.

15

Caught by a gust of wind, the front door slammed behind Paul as Kate stared at the ingredients he'd prepared for her. Heaped on the work surface lay a pile of glistening grey tiger prawns, hand-peeled, de-headed and -tailed. Who else but Paul would have the patience? Next to them, he'd left plump white scallops that he'd halved, leaving their orange corals intact. He'd even cooked and skinned the halibut for her, cutting it into large meaty chunks. Next to them, his instructions were written in neat capital letters so she couldn't possibly make a mistake. He knew her well. Following them to the accompaniment of Mozart's string quartet in G, she combined the fish with the cold herby wine sauce that he'd laced with chopped cornichons, then spooned the mixture into his favourite red ceramic pie dish, which he'd bought when they'd spent that long weekend in Grasse. Finally she added some capers to the grated and buttered potatoes before forking them over the fish mixture, spreading them as evenly as possible. A quick scattering of grated cheese and the pie was ready for the oven.

She laid the downstairs table for three, placed the bowl of

green salad and the dressing Paul had mixed in its centre and sat down to wait for Bea and Ellen, flicking through a *National Geographic* she'd brought home from the surgery. She couldn't concentrate. Instead her thoughts drifted back to her relationship with Paul. How many other husbands would arrive home early with the shopping and organise a meal for his wife and her friends before going out to a business dinner? She should have been more grateful when he'd gone to so much trouble for her. True, he loved doing it, but as thanks he deserved more than a rant about the failings of the new district nurse as the reason for being too late to do it herself. Memo to self yet again: don't take him so much for granted.

The doorbell made her start. She found Bea and Ellen standing hunched together under an umbrella. Beyond them, the plants on either side of the path were glistening wet, bent over in the wind. She could see the rain driving into the road, spitting up from the tarmac.

'Come in, come in. Quick.' She took the umbrella and left it dripping in the downstairs shower while Ellen and Bea shrugged themselves out of their macs. Having hung them above the umbrella, they followed her down to the kitchen where Bea pressed a pale blue box decorated with a wild boar into her hand. 'Rococo ganaches – my new favourite of the moment.'

Kate took them with a smile and put them on the side for later.

'Something smells good.' Ellen walked over to the oven and peered through the glass.

'Let's hope. I just finished off what Paul started.' Kate opened the fridge door and pulled out a bottle.

'God, you're lucky. He's too good to you.' Ellen went to sit on one of the bar stools by the island.

'Don't – please! I know.' The weight of Kate's guilt increased. 'Anyway, *you* can talk, if things are as good as they were the last time we spoke. White OK?'

'Industrial alcohol would be OK after the day I've had.' Bea threw herself into the comfortable chair at the front of the room, letting her shoes drop to the floor so she could bend her legs underneath her. 'You'll never guess what that smooth bastard's done this time.'

'I thought you were on his side now.' Kate had heard the whole work saga when Bea had phoned during the week so knew exactly who she was talking about. She had agreed that Bea's chosen course of action was the best. For the time being, at least.

'I was. I still am – in a way. Except he called me in today to tell me he'd hired Amanda Winter, his editorial director at Pennant, as . . .' she made quote marks in the air '. . . "publisher". *Fait accompli.* Not even a word of consultation.' Her voice rose in indignation.

'But he can't do that. You're the publishing director. Isn't that constructive dismissal or something?' Kate found herself equally outraged on behalf of her friend.

'Nobody takes any notice of that any more. Once you get to a certain level you can hire and fire who the hell you want. Just wrap the new chief in another title and everyone turns a blind eye. Then get rid of another Indian to pay for it so you've got fewer people to do the essential jobs that keep the company going.'

'Where does that leave you, then?'

'Good question. On the bloody back foot. Again. Even though he protests he needs me and wants me to stay.'

'Perhaps he doth protest too much. Can't you do something?' She filled Bea's glass and moved the magazines on the coffee-table to make room for it.

'Like what? All I can do is sit tight, and make sure she doesn't take my job. That's what she'll have her eye on. But she's not going to get it. I'm going to be the one who decides when I throw in the towel. Not her.'

Kate watched as Bea arranged her jacket over the back of her chair, still fulminating against the shortcomings of senior management. Like so many of their friends, she had got blonder as the years passed, her hair artfully and regularly streaked for the cost of a small mortgage. Animated in conversation, her face was still striking, mostly thanks to her strong cheekbones and large, expressive mouth that still retained some of the fullness of her youth. She had forged her own style, throwing in the odd designer label with a bit of ethnic and using long tops, not too tight, and jackets to hide the worst bits: her midriff, thighs and a bum that she joked was sliding down towards the back of her knees. Now that she had finally shrugged off the hurt and humiliation of Colin's clichéd departure for a younger woman, Kate couldn't see why she was having such difficulty in meeting another man.

'I envy you, you know,' she blurted. The words were out before she had a chance to stop them.

Bea stopped her continuing rant mid-flow. 'I'm sorry?'

'I do. Things might be going wrong for you at the moment but you've still got that energy we all had when we started out.'

'What *are* you talking about?' Bea looked genuinely bewildered. 'What energy? I'm completely knackered.'

'You may be. But you still get excited about what you do.'

'So do you, you idiot. Saving lives is exciting, isn't it?'

'Saving lives is the least of it. I'm bogged down with admin, man-management, endless disputes and patients wanting me to sign sick notes when there's nothing wrong with them. None of the things I went into medicine for.' What did she sound like? She hated the self-righteousness that had crept into her voice, especially since what she had said wasn't really true. She did see plenty of patients during her sessions and house-calls. There was nothing like the feeling of having successfully diagnosed and treated a patient, not to mention being on the receiving end of their gratitude. Her job was constantly different and throwing up new challenges. The burden of admin must be skewing her sense of perspective.

'I thought working for myself was hard,' said Ellen. 'I'm always struggling to keep my head above water but you guys make it look positively pleasant.' She had opened a packet of peanuts and offered them round.

'Don't go all smug on us. I couldn't bear it.' Bea drained her glass and got up for a refill.

Kate had noticed Ellen's hurt expression. 'That's a bit harsh.' Sometimes Bea's humour could fall just on the wrong side of the line dividing funny and sharp.

'You know I didn't mean it, don't you?' Bea took a few nuts and smiled at Ellen who nodded, obviously not a hundred per cent convinced.

That was another of Bea's defence mechanisms – pretending

her tactlessness didn't terribly matter. But it did, especially when Kate knew Bea was as fond of Ellen as she was and would walk over hot coals for her if the situation demanded.

'New man, job you love. How lucky are you?' There had been an edge to Bea's voice that Kate didn't like. She must be minding about things more than she was letting on. 'Oh, sorry, El. I'm being foul. Too much on my plate and unlucky in love as well. Not much of a life-enhancer. Take no notice.'

'You should have called me,' Ellen offered. 'I'd have come round.'

'I did. I spoke to Oliver a couple of times, but he said you were busy and couldn't come to the phone.'

'Busy?' Ellen looked puzzled. 'When was that?'

'I can't remember. Monday, maybe. And then Tuesday. I did think it was a bit odd that you were too busy both times, but what do I know? Poor put-upon singleton that I am.'

'Oh, please.' Kate played air-violin. 'Stop now, before I burst into tears.'

Ellen laughed. 'I can't remember what I was doing unless it was when I was going through my wardrobe.'

'What? Your wardrobe's been set in aspic for years. You don't do "going through" your wardrobe.'

'She's right,' Kate agreed. 'I've never known you throw anything out.'

'Oliver went through my dresses and skirts when I was away and made some suggestions, then encouraged me to take a few things to the charity shop. Don't know why I've never done it before really . . . What?'

Kate and Bea were looking at her open-mouthed.

'He went through your wardrobe while you were away?' Bea said, incredulous. 'I'd kill anyone who went through mine.'

'Only because yours is such a shambles you don't know what they'd find.'

'It's not that bad. Just a tad disordered. But I wouldn't want anyone going through my things.'

'I didn't think of it like that.' Ellen looked perplexed. 'He was only trying to help.'

'I'm sure he was,' said Bea. 'But what was he doing there anyway? Hasn't he got the flat?'

'He has a key. Anyway, he was helping put up the studio-shed.'

'The what?' Bea got up to help herself to another drink.

'My new studio. It's a shed. Oliver thought he'd surprise me with somewhere I could paint. So he got the whole thing installed while I was in Cornwall.'

Both Bea and Kate stared at her as if they couldn't believe what they were hearing.

'He surprised you with a shed?' Bea spoke slowly as if she might have misunderstood. 'Completely out of the blue? He can't do that. He hardly knows you. What about your garden?'

'Put like that it does sound a bit unusual.'

'Unusual? I'll say.'

'But he's a man who acts on impulse. He wanted to give me something special for my birthday, and thought putting a studio into the garden was what I'd want.'

'Did you?'

'Of course.' She didn't sound entirely certain. 'And I'll enjoy planning and replanting parts of the garden.' As she went on to describe it, Kate could see that Bea's continuing interrogation was making Ellen uncomfortable. She obviously didn't like Bea's implication that Oliver had gone too far. Kate decided to change the subject. 'What about a job?' she asked. 'Has he had any luck yet?'

'Nothing.' Ellen looked relieved and grateful. 'But you know how difficult it is at the moment. There aren't that many jobs around and he isn't known on the circuit since he's been in France.'

'But he's not in a position to be fussy, is he? There must be something he could do.'

'I know.' Ellen sighed. 'I've said as much. But he bites my head off.' She seemed quite resigned to the way he was.

'Ah, so all is not one hundred per cent in the Garden of Eden, then?' Bea couldn't resist.

'Bea . . .' warned Kate. 'I'd better get the pie.' She was anxious to move the conversation on to a less controversial tack. After all these years, the last thing she wanted to do was throw cold water on Ellen's contentment. They still hadn't met Oliver, so were hardly in a position to judge him.

'Well, if Kate envies me, I envy you actually,' Bea volunteered suddenly, looking at Ellen, who had ignored her previous remark. 'Apart from the clothes thing, of course – that's a bit too controlling for me. But he's obviously mad about you.'

'You *will* find someone, Bea. Probably when you're least expecting it.'

'That should be about now, then!' She and Ellen went over to the table and sat down while Kate wrestled the pie out of the oven. 'Do you want a hand?'

'No. I'm fine. Ellen's right, you know.'

'Mmm. Maybe. But look at me! I'm beset by a hormonal teenager who, as far as I know, has as much chance of becoming a nuclear physicist as he does a mass murderer; an overbearing boss; a Mr Bean type in the City whom I've met for one drink; and some knob who left a calling card that took me to the clap clinic. And he left fake contact details with the agency so I can't even have the pleasure of passing on the good news. Bloody marvellous.'

Just then Kate reached the table. 'Put like that, I see what you mean. And who'd want to compete with them? Mind out! This is hot!' Her voice rose to a shriek as the tea-towel she was using as an oven glove slipped. The pie-dish pressed against the heel of her right hand. She tried to get it to the table in time. But, in agony, she let go a moment too soon, just before the dish was fully on the table. In horrified silence they watched as the pie arced over and down, the dish shattering into smithereens and the pie splattering across the pristine limestone-tiled floor.

The three women stared at it. Kate was the first to break the silence. 'Paul's favourite dish. He'll kill me!'

A clearing of Bea's throat was followed by a stifled cough from Ellen. Kate looked up to see that the two of them were trying to contain their laughter.

'God, look at us. It's not exactly *Sex and the City*, is it?'

As Bea choked the words out, she couldn't control herself any longer and, with an explosive snort, she cracked up completely. At that, Ellen followed suit, leaving Kate to join in as she held her hand under the cold tap. They laughed together till the tears rolled down their faces.

At last, when the only sounds to be heard were a few muffled whimpers from Bea, and Ellen was wiping her eyes with a bit of kitchen roll, Kate spoke: 'Fish and chips, anyone?'

*

A couple of hours later, Kate was alone again in the kitchen. The fish pie was in the bin, the fish-and-chips papers had been recycled and the plates and glasses were in the machine. Paul was still not back. Bea had left with Ellen half an hour earlier, prompted by a call from Oliver wondering where Ellen was. He couldn't be blamed, Kate supposed. He wasn't to know that the evenings they spent together always ran on into the night. There was always so much to catch up on, now more than ever, and none of them ever wanted their time together to be over. Oh, well. Possessiveness wasn't such a bad thing, she supposed. Better than not being wanted at all. Poor old Bea. If only she and Paul could magic up a single friend for her. She checked the clock. Half past midnight. It was unlike Paul to be as late as this.

She wasn't tired so made herself a cup of peppermint tea and took it up to the living room. She'd wait for Paul. She collapsed into the familiar comfort of their old sofa, currently reupholstered in an off-white calico (something she could never have chosen until Sam and Megan had left home) and scattered with the rose-print cushions she'd found at a *brocante* during the same holiday that Paul had bought the pie-dish. What a good weekend that had been. Was there this unfamiliar distance between them back then? She didn't think so. Something had definitely happened that had stopped them communicating in their old familiar way.

Or someone? Her sudden gasp caught her by surprise. The thought was as unwelcome as it was shocking. As she tried to shake it off, it only tightened its hold. Could history be repeating itself? Yet again she dismissed the idea. Now part of the warp and weft of their marriage, his affair was an incident they'd weathered and he'd promised there wouldn't be another. Surely this was one of the occasional downturns to be expected in a long-term partnership. But she didn't find the thought all that reassuring.

She put down her tea and stood up to look at herself in the large mirror over the fireplace. Stuck about with invitations and cards from the children, her reflection stared back, showing a thoughtful face only slightly lined and framed by fine dark hair. She could never be as open as Bea or Ellen in discussing her relationship with Paul: it wasn't something she wanted to air with them or with anybody, not in any detail at least. No, this was something she was going to have to work out alone.

She crossed to the assorted family photos ranged on the top of the console table and picked up their wedding picture, so old it was beginning to fade. There they stood, radiant and full of hope for the future. So much of that hope had been fulfilled, she thought. An abrupt miaow announced the arrival of Mouse, the grey stray that had adopted them about ten years earlier. Sam had found the bedraggled young cat in the bushes at the end of the garden. He had tempted him out with a saucer of milk and a bit of cold chicken, and ever since Mouse had been Sam's most devoted fan. He hopped up beside Kate now, rubbing against her hand and clawing at her trousers.

'Mouse! Stop it!' She lifted him up and laid him on her lap, stroking him until his rumbling purr filled the silence. 'There, you silly old thing. Where do you think Paul's got to?'

She picked up her book on Africa. Reading about someone else's experiences travelling through Ghana and other countries brought her a little closer to Sam and helped her understand something of the country where he was. She found her place, although she wasn't in the mood to read tonight. What would Paul say when she told him Ellen had invited them for lunch? Would he be as interested in meeting Oliver as she and Bea were? Probably. He liked Kate's friends and was pleased to see them when he did but wasn't as involved with their lives as Kate was. As far as he was concerned, they were a part of her life that was separate from him. However, even his interest had been piqued by the arrival of Oliver. Wait till he heard about the shed. He was cynical, like Bea, and curious about who Oliver was and where he had come from.

'I'm learning about him every day,' Ellen had protested, when cross-questioned earlier in the evening. 'He's lived in

France, somewhere in Centre, for the last two or three years and doesn't like talking about what went on there. He says it's still too painful. Something to do with the woman he lived with. But I'm happy with that. I'd rather not know. Anyway, he'll tell me when he's ready.'

'But, Ellen, you've got to ask him,' Bea insisted. 'God almighty, woman! You've got him practically living in your house, and your children will be home in a couple of days. Suppose he turns out to be – I don't know – a paedophile or something?'

'Don't be so ridiculous.' Ellen was outraged. 'If there was something like that, I'd know. Why can't you just take him as the loving, generous man I know he is? You're my closest friends, for God's sake. I just want you to be pleased for me. You'll see when you meet him.'

And then she had invited them to a family lunch. Bea had looked slightly ashamed of her suggestion, apologised and accepted. As had Kate.

Kate ran her fingers up and down Mouse's soft belly, making him stretch out his legs in pleasure. If Ellen was prepared to accept Oliver at face value, shouldn't they? As Ellen's friends, it was up to them to support her in whatever life choices she made. Who were they to question her judgement? Or should they, as her friends, be looking out for her when she was head over heels, possibly blind to anything that would spoil things? Kate knew Bea would take the latter view but for once she disagreed. She wanted Ellen to be happy. She wanted that for all of them. She sighed and began to read about the elephants of Knysna.

Outside, the gate banged, and Paul's key turned in the lock. She stood up to greet him, tipping an indignant Mouse onto the floor. At last. Late he might be but this was her chance to start making things better between them.

16

As they pulled up outside the house, Matt leaned forward, pulling against his seatbelt and blocking the window. 'Who's that?'

'Where?' Ellen didn't look up as she rummaged in her bag for her purse.

'There's a man standing on the doorstep, waving.'

Despite Oliver's attempts to persuade her, she had refused to let him come with her to Paddington to meet Emma and Matt and had asked for a couple of days alone in which the kids could settle back home. Reluctantly, he had agreed to be introduced into the household by degrees, without any fanfare. At the same time, Ellen enjoyed the thought of stealing out for secret rendezvous in the flat, keeping him a delicious secret for a little while longer, preserving the family's status quo. Deceit might be bad but it was surely better than telling the children too soon. She was at last confident in her control of the situation and relieved she had found the right way at last. That was what her friends and family would want.

But despite all they'd agreed, here he was.

'So, who is he, Mum?' Emma emerged from the gloom she'd been in ever since she'd set foot in the taxi. She had spent the entire journey home staring bleary-eyed out of the window. Ellen thought she'd caught her wiping away a tear but felt it better not to say anything. If Josh the surfie was the problem, nothing she could say would make a difference. The summer was over, they had to come home and Emma had to learn to live with disappointments thrown up by life, however painful. When they had time alone, she would try to console her.

'Have you been having something done to the house?' Emma looked anxious that her instructions to leave her garish Indian/hippie-themed bedroom might have been ignored and that she was going to find the tasteful lilac or gardenia walls that Ellen sometimes threatened.

'No. He's a friend, that's all. Come on, get out.'

'Not the one you told me about?'

Ellen cursed the sharpness of Matt's memory.

'Not the boyfriend?' He brought all the scorn of a thirteen-year-old to the last word.

'Boyfriend!' Emma was immediately all attention. 'You never said anything, Mum.'

'He's not a boyfriend. Oliver's just someone I met while you were away.' She struggled to pocket her change, before bending over to pick up the two cases, leaving the kids to their backpacks. 'You'll like him.'

Doubt was writ very large indeed on Emma's face. But she said nothing.

Torn between her fury at Oliver's turning up, her desire to tear down the path and fling her arms round him, and her anxiety as to the best way to introduce him, Ellen stood by the gate, a case in either hand. She breathed deeply, trying to control the sudden thumping of her heart. Instead, Oliver took the initiative and came towards them. He looked relaxed in his cream chinos and a dark blue open-necked shirt. She saw him as if for the first time, taking in his aquiline features, the startling blue eyes and dark flop of hair. His familiar slightly uneven smile gave a sharp nudge to all the emotions that she'd thought she had under control, sending them skittering through her. If she took a step towards him, she felt her legs would give way. As if he understood, he turned to the kids, giving her time to gather herself.

'Hello. You must be Matt and Em. Your mum's told me all about you. Good holiday?'

'Yes, thank you.' Emma's voice was tight with dislike.

'I thought you might all be starving after such a long journey, so I've brought some supper over.'

They looked at him in surprise, unsure what to say. Why on earth would a stranger bring them supper? Ellen could almost hear the cogs turning.

'How lovely. What a kind thought.' Under the close scrutiny of her children, she chose her words with care, not wanting to expose her cartwheeling heart. Matt could probably be deflected but Emma would pick up on the slightest clue. As they led the way to the front door, she lagged behind with Oliver. She fought back the urge to put her arms round him. 'What the hell are you doing?' she hissed instead.

'I couldn't wait for two days.' As he touched her hand, her stomach flipped. 'You don't mind, do you?'

'Yes, I do. And after everything I said.' A look of such abject disappointment crossed his face that she weakened. 'Well, no, not really. Oh, I don't know. You're impossible.' Whatever she said, it was too late. He was there and she was going to have to deal with it in the best way she could.

They'd reached the front door. Emma was already inside and had shot upstairs to check her room. Oliver leaned down to pick up his bag of shopping.

'What have you got there?' A sure way to Matt's heart was through his stomach.

'Only spaghetti carbonara.'

'Nice one! How did you know I liked it?'

'Your mum told me, of course. I've brought a salad as well.' He winked at Ellen. 'And I tell you what, Matt, England are playing tonight and my TV's broken. I wondered if I could watch with you. Only if you're watching, of course.'

'Oliver, I'm not sure this is such a good idea.' His brand new TV couldn't possibly be broken. How dare he try to win over her kids without consulting her on the method first? 'Shouldn't you get back home? We'll have to unpack and get ready for school.'

'Come on, Ellen.' His voice was like the smoothest honey, impossible to resist.

'Yes, come on, Mum. We don't need much at the start of term anyway.' Matt's eyes were shining with excitement at the idea of being able to watch the match. Normally Emma shouted him down if he dared even suggest such a thing.

Ellen was torn. She wanted Oliver to stay but she wanted him to go. At the same time she felt a guilty sense of relief steal over her. For ten years she'd been running this household, having responsibility for every decision, smoothing out every disagreement. Being able to share some of the daily grind suddenly seemed almost unbearably attractive. Despite all her anxieties, he had got Matt onside within minutes. Perhaps, with a little extra effort, he could work the same magic with the more resistant Emma. Why shouldn't she indulge him? What harm could it possibly do? She led the way downstairs to the kitchen. 'OK, I give in. Em and I can always do something else or watch TV in my bedroom, I suppose. Just this once,' she added, to stamp on any impression that this might be a precedent for things to come.

'Yes!' yelled Matt, his fist punching the air. 'I'll go and tell Em.' He shot upstairs before Ellen could stop him.

'Oh, God,' she groaned. 'Wait for the fireworks.'

Oliver slipped an arm around her waist.

'They'll be down in a moment,' she said. 'You really shouldn't have come, you know.'

'It's OK.' He looked at her, before just brushing her lips with his.

She was glad he realised how inappropriate it would be to do more.

'I'm going to make sure it all works out. Trust me. Let me get on with the cooking while you help them unpack.'

Lugging the cases up the stairs, she could hear raised voices from Emma's room. Unable to make out exactly what was being said, she decided to leave them to it, dumping the cases on the landing before she retreated to the safety of her own room. Sinking onto the bed, she fell backwards into its embrace. She automatically turned her head towards her bedside table. For the last ten years she had gone to sleep and woken up beside Simon. He had remained a constant in her life even though he hadn't been here to share things. Somehow she'd always drawn support from seeing him there, as if he was guiding her. Before she had a chance to think further, there was a shout, a slammed door and the sound of Matt laughing.

'Well, we are and you can't stop us,' he shouted, above the noise of his footsteps clumping down the stairs.

With a sigh, Ellen got to her feet. Peeling off her jeans, she once again cursed the weight she'd put on during her week away as she squeezed herself into a green stripy skirt that Oliver liked, leaving the top inch of her zip undone and crossing her fingers that it would stay put, then rummaged for her long cream top in the cupboard. Slipping her feet into her most comfortable flip-flops, running her fingers through her hair, she emerged for the fray. As she passed Emma's room, she noticed the door was ajar.

'Mum!'

Unable to gauge the tone, imperious or upset, she pushed the door open, careful not to bring down the red-and-yellow sari fabric threaded with gold that was draped over the entrance. Inside, Emma had thrown herself face down on the gaudy Indian bedspread embroidered with tiny mirrors that twinkled in the light. In her left hand lay Lolly, a once yellow now grubby and almost threadbare pig that had gone everywhere with her until about five years ago when he had been relegated to pride of place on the mantelpiece. Ellen watched her daughter's thumb working back and forth over the scrap of ribbon round Lolly's neck, just as she had when she was a toddler needing comfort. She tiptoed in, taking a detour round the colourful spiky star lampshade, which was at exactly the right height to poke her in the eye, and sat on the bed.

'Em. What's up?'

'What's he doing here?' Her daughter twisted round to face her, propping herself up on an elbow. She'd obviously been crying.

'Oliver?'

'Who else?'

Ellen was alarmed by how angry she looked. 'He's just a friend making us supper. That's all.'

'I don't want him here.'

'Why ever not? Nothing's changed, you know.'

'It has.' Emma threw herself on to her side and curled into a ball.

Ellen sighed and reached out to stroke her daughter's hair back from her face. Neither of them spoke. But deep down, Ellen knew that Emma was right. Something had changed in both of them this summer. They had taken an irreversible step in a new direction, she towards a new life with Oliver, and Emma towards adulthood.

'Listen, Em. Sit up and talk to me.' Ellen tried to engineer her into a position where she could at least see her face. But she wouldn't co-operate.

'I *am* talking to you.'

'I mean properly. I want to try to get you to understand.'

'I understand completely.' Emma turned herself over and pushed herself towards the bed head so that she could sit up against the pillows. 'The moment we go away you get some man who you think will take Dad's place before you're too old to find one.'

Wounded by the venom in her daughter's voice, but infuriated by what she had said, Ellen had to muster every ounce of self-control. 'Em, you know that's not true.' She edged herself up the bed until she was sitting beside her daughter. 'How could you say that? This wasn't something I meant to happen . . .'

'Then why did you let it?'

'I know it's hard for you to understand but as you and Matt grow up, get your own friends and start to go out more, I sometimes feel lonely.'

'What about Kate and Bea?'

'Of course they're my friends but they have their own lives too. Their friendship means everything to me but it isn't the same as this.'

'You mean sex.' Her tear-stained face twisted in disgust and she stiffened.

Ellen hadn't wanted to have this discussion, but having come this far, she had to show Emma respect by finishing it. 'Well, partly, yes. But it's also having someone I can trust, having a friend at home to share things with when you're out more and more.'

'Mum, you don't even know the man. You can't do.' Her voice sounded like a little girl's. Then she sniffed hard.

'Come here, Em.' As Ellen put her arm round her child, she felt her give a little. They sat together for a few minutes in silence again, leaning into one another just as they had always done. 'Why don't I go downstairs and make us some hot chocolate? Then I'll come back and we can talk about it together.'

'Well, OK.' Emma's tone was grudging but Ellen could tell she'd begun to soften. Not that that meant she would necessarily change her point of view.

Just at that moment she heard footsteps in the hall.

'Supper's ready,' Oliver shouted up the stairs.

'I don't want any,' Emma muttered, her thumb working away at Lolly's ribbon.

'Come on, Em. I know it's hard but do come down.' She sat there for a moment longer, then stood up. 'For me?'

Emma put Lolly on the pillow and looked up at her mother. Ellen couldn't read her expression, but decided to make one more appeal. 'Please.'

'OK, OK.' She stood up. 'If Freya did it for her mother, I'll have to try. But don't expect me to like him.'

Ellen remembered gloomily that Freya was one of Emma's schoolfriends whose mother had moved in a new lover before the ink was dry on the divorce papers. It had been the talk of the school for months. 'It's hardly the same thing. Freya's dad had only just moved out. And Oliver certainly isn't moving in.' She hoped she'd be forgiven for the lie.

'Isn't he? I'm not a fool, Mum. It looks pretty much like the same thing to me.'

They went downstairs together. Supper was not a happy affair. Oliver passed Ellen a noticeably smaller helping of pasta than anyone else and piled the rest of her plate high with leaves. She knew he was only doing it for her own good, having learned she had the will-power of a slug, but she wished he could have been a little less obvious about it. The conversation, such as it was, revolved around Matt and Oliver's assessment of various football players and teams, something in which she and Emma had absolutely no interest. Emma sat in silence, playing with her food, picking out the bits of ham and piling them on the side of her plate before announcing that she had become vegetarian. The minute they finished she said she was going round to see Freya. Ellen didn't stop her, hoping that Freya might make her see some sense.

When she finally found herself alone, a protesting Oliver having been chased out to his flat and Matt up to bed, she sat down to wait for her daughter with a cup of tea and a slice of cake that Oliver didn't know existed. This was going to be much harder than she had thought.

17

Standing on the balcony, a glass of champagne in her hand, Bea could see below her the race-goers milling like moths around the on-track bookies who were barking the odds, jabbering into mobile phones. She looked down on tweedy jackets, the odd designer outfit that had probably been pulled out of a perfect home-counties wardrobe or bought weeks ago for the occasion. Contrast Bea's – the result of a department-store dash two nights earlier. Just when she was being forced to give up, with the store closing, she had found a purple and blue swirled sleeveless silk dress, and a blue slightly fitted hip-length jacket. She just prayed she wouldn't get so hot that she'd have to take the jacket off and reveal what Ben insisted on calling her 'bingo wings'. Minutes later, on her way out of the store, by some miracle she had spotted a blue pillbox hat with a discreet pink trim. The whole outfit made her feel quite the thing, and a little bit Jackie O. Her new-found confidence was confirmed when she had met Mark at the station. From his expression she had seen that she'd made quite an impression.

They had arrived at Ascot early, at which point she could

see that his impression might have been that she was completely over-dressed. She'd imagined that the races would be full of women sporting the sort of outfits she'd seen photographed on Ladies' Day. But this wasn't Royal Ascot. The truth was a revelation. Brushing past more Barbours than she could count, corduroy trousers, brown trilbies and an overwhelming assortment of tartans and tweeds, she hoped the dress code would improve once they hit the Members' section. Her prayers were answered. As they made their way through the brand new grandstand, riding the escalator up through the airy state-of-the-art building to the corporate box hired by Mark's co-directors, she began to feel she wouldn't stick out like quite such a sore thumb after all.

In the dining room, a long table was laid with a smooth cream tablecloth, a vase of creamy roses in its centre. She counted twenty-four places laid with gleaming cutlery and sparkling wine glasses while in a corner a flat-screen TV was anticipating the start of the racing. 'I wasn't expecting it to be a sit-down do.' Bea was wishing she'd gone with her original impulse to refuse the invitation.

'Don't worry. I know you'll get on fine with them.' Mark's reassuring best was far from convincing. 'Although I don't really know their wives. Let's grab a glass of champagne and take a look at the course from the balcony.'

She followed him out, trying not to let her nerves make her drink too quickly. It was hard not to be impressed by the modern curved grandstand that looked over the course. Their box was positioned just before the winning post, giving them a clear view of the finish. They chatted easily together as gradually the other guests arrived and Bea was introduced one by one. As she relaxed, she began to think that perhaps the afternoon wouldn't be such an ordeal after all. Mark was turning out to be rather a considerate host who made sure she was never left standing alone but at the same time didn't stick to her side like glue. His frequent laugh as he chatted to colleagues told her that he was never very far away. She could turn to him if she needed to.

Just as they were gravitating towards the table for lunch, the last couple arrived. Bea saw the woman first. She was a head-turner: tall, gamine, with cheekbones to kill for, generous bee-stung lips, wide-set innocent eyes and brown hair pinned up with a yellow silk rose above her right ear. She was wearing a soft yellow figure-hugging dress that was slightly ruched below the narrow waist with a rounded neckline and no sleeves, showing off her perfectly toned, tanned arms and enviably firm cleavage enhanced by a tiny gold cross hanging from a fine gold chain. Standing slightly behind her, in the shadow of the doorway, his hand resting possessively in the centre of her back, was her partner. From a distance he looked slickly suited and as much of a crowd-pleaser as her. As they sashayed into the room together, smiling at the assembled group, Bea realised, to her horror, who he was.

Tony Castle.

She took a step back onto the balcony to compose herself. Thankfully she had seen him before he saw her, so she had the advantage. A deep breath or two later, she returned to the room and took her place beside Mark.

'Are you all right? You look a bit pale,' he said, solicitous as ever.

'Completely fine. I left my bag outside.'

Mark put his hand on the back of her arm. 'Good. Now, I want you to meet my new colleague, Tom Carter. He only joined the company a couple of weeks ago.' He steered her towards a place at the other side of the table where she could see that she'd be next to the man she knew as Tony Castle. What a crazy coincidence. Or was it some kind of bizarre joke Mark and Tony had dreamed up together? They must know that they both subscribed to Let's Have Lunch, surely. Tom Carter! He hadn't even used his own name. At that moment, to her huge relief, a portly older man insinuated himself into the chair, conveniently scuppering Mark's planned introduction, and tucked his napkin into his shirt collar.

'Damn. That's Brian Anderson, one of the chief execs. I can't ask him to move,' he whispered. 'Never mind. I'll introduce you to Tom later. There'll be plenty of time.'

'Mmm. Can't wait.' Her sarcasm floated over Mark's head as, instead, they found themselves places at the opposite end of the table.

As the starters were brought in, she caught Tom turning his head to look up the table. His expression when he saw her for the first time was a joy: shock and confusion jockeyed with fear, resulting in a dead heat. Bea was quite happy where she sat, opposite Mark and between a couple on his team who were bent on having a good day out. One of them was an old hand at the racing game and, with the benefit of his expertise, she was soon entering into the spirit of the day and marking up her race card. Occasionally, she'd look down the table at Tom, who had lost his initial swagger and seemed frequently preoccupied, toying with his food, paying scant attention to the people on either side of him and barely responding to the attentions of his female companion, whose laugh tinkled down the table as she extended an arm to persuade him to try a forkful of her meal. And at the end of that arm, Bea thought she saw the sparkle of a large ring. Well, she knew from experience how quick a worker 'Tony' could be.

Mark's laugh made her turn back in his direction. Since meeting him for their abortive drink, Bea had managed to arrive on time for their next drinks date and for the couple of dinner dates that followed, as well as speaking to him at length several times on the phone. He didn't send her lust-meter soaring but, each time, she had grown to like him a little more. He had never made a move that suggested he fancied her either, but there was no getting away from the fact that they got on well. Bea had talked to him about herself and her work, describing the strategies she was using to turn her list around, not to mention the attempts of Amanda Winter to get her feet under her desk – and lie down under Adam's, judging by the number of times she had shut herself into his office with him. Bea could see that Mark was impressed by her fortitude in the face of stress. God loves a trier and so, it appeared, did he. But, more than that, he was interested, asking questions and making sure he understood.

As the month had progressed, Bea had felt a new energy propelling her through her work. By the time she and Mark had last spoken, she was able to tell him that Stuart had stepped up to the plate and, between them, they had so far persuaded an already bestselling novelist that Coldharbour could publish him better. Bea herself was hot on the trail of one of the great theatrical dames and hoped to convince her that the time had come to write her autobiography. She knew the project had bestseller written all over it. More than that, she was reading a first novel from the States, *Bare Bones*, which reminded her of Donna Tartt's *The Secret History*. Everyone, including Adam, was going to read it over the next couple of days. With their support, she was confident they could make the book sell.

She took care not to completely monopolise their conversations and began to listen more carefully to what Mark had to say. She found it hard to follow the ins and outs of his career in a world so very different from her own but she stopped and asked him to explain when she got confused. The result was that she had become interested in the financial rigmarole of his working life. When she got him talking about his marriage and the children he only saw when it suited his ex, they had plenty to talk about. Eventually he had asked her to accompany him to his office jolly at the races. By the time the day dawned, she had surprised herself with the discovery that she was actually looking forward to seeing him.

'Bea!' Mark looked across the table at her. 'Tell me you're not putting your money on that nag, Heavenly Joker. Look at it on the screen. Fit for the knacker's yard, for God's sake.'

'Bollocks, Chapman,' Bea's neighbour and now racing adviser intervened. 'That is a horse in its prime. Take no notice, Bea. Your money's safe.'

Out of the corner of her eye, she noticed Tom getting up from his seat and turning their way. He'd obviously decided how he was going to deal with the situation.

'Well, I may put on a second bet just to cover myself,' she announced. 'Come on, Mark. Let's go down to the paddock and watch the race from the floor.'

'The floor? I thought you didn't know anything about racing.'

'I don't. I just overheard someone else saying it.' She grinned at him, all the time aware that Tom was threading his way towards them. The tinkling laugh sounded from somewhere behind him. Suddenly intrigued to find out what his game-plan could possibly be, she slowed down her rush to the exit.

'Hey, Mark. Good to see you.' Tom's overweening confidence had evidently returned, with a decision to brazen out a potentially awkward situation by establishing the upper hand.

'Tom. This is Bea, a friend.'

'How do you do?'

Bea took his proffered hand, giving it as strong a shake as she dared. She looked him in the eye, hoping to see him flinch. Nothing. Then came inspiration. 'How extraordinary,' she murmured. 'I could have sworn you were someone else.'

'Really?' He looked amused.

'Yes, you're a dead ringer for someone I once knew called Tony Castle. It's quite a relief that you're not, actually.' The combination of new-found confidence and champagne gave her a sudden feeling of recklessness. By his expression, she could see he was completely thrown by her line of attack.

Mark turned to her. 'Why?' he asked. He hadn't noticed that his colleague's smile had slipped a fraction. But Bea had. She had also seen Tom's eyes narrow as if he was working out what she might possibly say next. Suddenly he seemed less confident.

'If you'll excuse me, I must just get to the Tote before the next race.' Tom tried to slip by them but Bea stepped to the side to block his route. This was going better than she could have imagined. She put a hand on his arm to detain him as she leaned forward, taking them both into her confidence. 'You wouldn't believe it but this guy Tony was seeing a friend of mine. Then, one day, he stood her up. Wouldn't return her calls, nothing. Then she discovered that he'd only given her the . . .' She mouthed the word silently. 'Sorry, you don't want to know about that.' She looked at her audience. Mark seemed bemused that she was telling the story at all while Tom was staring at her as if he'd seen a ghost. That would teach him to leave fake contact details with the agency. He'd obviously understood exactly what she was saying. 'She never saw him again, so she had no way of telling him because he'd given her a wrong number. So it was good riddance, really, but bad luck for the next woman in his life.' The tinkling laughter rippled down the table again. 'What a bastard.' She squeezed his arm. Hard. 'Funny, Tom. You could almost be his twin.'

'That's bad.' Mark looked decidedly relieved that the story was over without any more intimate detail. Tom gave a weak shrug as he struggled to maintain his composure. He slipped a finger between his throat and the collar of his thinly pin-striped primrose yellow shirt, moving it back and forth as if giving himself more room to breathe.

'Isn't it? But it's true.' Bea smiled, triumphant. 'So you can see why I'm relieved Tom isn't him, after all. I wouldn't have been able to stop myself saying something to him and embarrassing everyone else. So, we must put our bets on the next race.' She dropped her arm from his and stood aside so he could get to the door. 'After you.'

They followed Tom out but turned the opposite way so they could take the stairs to the outside. Bea's heart was singing.

'What on earth was that about?' Mark asked.

'What?' All innocence. So what if Mark thought she'd behaved oddly? The important thing was that Tom had got the message. And she was sure he had.

'That story. Tom looked rather uncomfortable.'

'Did he? I'm sorry. It's just that the whole business with my friend makes me so cross, I didn't think. I hope I haven't embarrassed you.'

'Not at all.' He laughed. 'It would take more than that. Here, hold my hand so we don't get separated in the scrum.'

They stood at the paddock, watching the owners and trainers chatting by their horses, waiting for the jockeys to be legged up into their saddles. Led round by the stable-lads, the horses jinked as the wind caught them under their tails, ears flicking back and forth, heads tossing, nostrils flaring, sweat flecking their necks. A handsome chestnut that looked in peak condition, its conker-coloured coat shining, its stride full of purpose, immediately caught Bea's eye. She ran her eye down the race card. Blade Runner, trained by Ali Newsome with Jo Michaels up and sporting the owner's emerald and blue silks. 'That's the one for me. Number twelve.'

'Where? Bea, no. Look at the form. It hasn't completed two of its last races and it doesn't do well when the going's soft.'

'I don't care. I like the colours and its name and he looks cute. And it's been trained by a woman.'

'What sort of reasons are those?' he teased. 'Look at the odds.'

'Oh, come on, you do better, then. Make up your mind and let's get down to the winning post.'

By the time they eventually pushed their way through to the rail, Bea was regretting the rush of blood to the head that had made her put twenty pounds on the nose. She'd done it on a whim to show up the more cautious Mark but now she thought she might as well have taken the money to the Ladies and flushed it down the loo. He, on the other hand, had gone through the form, every runner's last three races, the weights carried, the distance run. If Bea didn't know better, she might have been convinced there was a science to it.

On the big screens, she could see the horses lining up on the far side of the course. The atmosphere tensed, heads turned in their direction, then they were off. The commentator's voice crackled indistinctly across the stands as Bea strained to catch the positions of her two runners. To begin with, Blade Runner was too near the back to get more than a mention while Heavenly Joker was up by the rails towards the front of the pack. After one circuit, they were racing down the back straight. At that point, Blade Runner picked up speed, edging his way towards the front, jockey bent forward, crop swishing. The crowd yelled encouragement, Bea loudest of all, as he moved smoothly forward until he was running neck and neck with Heavenly Joker with just one other horse ahead of them, in the way of victory. They came into the final turn, the ground vibrating with the thunder of approaching hoofs. Bea forgot about Mark, forgot about the people around her. Her fists clenched, she yelled, 'Come on, Blade Runner. You can do it. Come on!'

And suddenly it was over. The front runner had faded in the last few strides. Her horses had taken first and second place. 'Oh, my God. We won!' She flung her arms round Mark. As she turned her head to look back at the course, she realised too late that he was moving in to kiss her. His lips smacked awkwardly against her cheek. They backed away from each other, startled.

'I'm sorry.' Mark looked embarrassed.

'Don't be.' Bea wasn't going to let anything spoil her moment of victory. This was something they could discuss another time. 'Let's go and see how much I've won.'

Two hundred and five pounds later, they were back in the box, toasting her success as if nothing had happened between them. Tom and his friend were nowhere to be seen. Good riddance, thought Bea. The rest of the afternoon passed in a convivial blur of champagne for her, water for Mark, more socialising, a few bad bets, then a couple of wins for Mark and another place for Bea. Eventually they were being swept along in the wave of punters trudging towards the car park while helicopters thudded into the sky taking home the better-heeled members of the racing fraternity. From her bag, Bea caught the sound of her mobile. She fished it out and strained to hear her sister.

'Where have you been? I've been trying to get you all afternoon.' Jess never called unless there was an emergency or she wanted something. Bea waited.

'Mum's had an accident. She slipped on the path and was lying there for ages before Janey Blythe found her. They couldn't get hold of you so they called me. But there's no way I can get down there.'

'Where is she now?' This was the sort of news that Bea had been dreading for months.

'At the hospital. You can get there, can't you?'

'Of course.' Bea abandoned her plan of blowing her winnings on a slap-up dinner with Mark as a thank-you for the day. As Jess couldn't be there, she had to go. Her mother had no one else. 'I'll get there as soon as I can.'

As they reached the car, she hung up. Mark looked questioning.

'I was going to treat us to dinner but apparently my mother's had a fall so I'll have to go straight to hers when I get home.'

'Not a good idea. You've been drinking and I haven't. I'll drive you.'

'No, Mark. It's miles out of your way, and I'm sure you've got a million better things to do.'

'Actually, I haven't. Alison's taken the girls to her parents for the weekend. Didn't you say your mum lived in Kent somewhere? We can just go round the M25. Be stupid to go into town and out again.'

Bea hesitated, then said, 'That's incredibly generous of you. Incredibly.' Her urge towards independence was overwhelmed by gratitude and a sense of relief that matters were out of her hands. She let Mark take control while she had nothing to do but worry about what she would find when they got there and what on earth she should do to avoid it happening again.

18

By the time Mark finally pulled up at Bea's house it was well past midnight. To her horror, the lights were blazing from the front room and, even inside the car, the insistent throb of a bass beat could be heard coming from the house.

'Oh, Christ!' She flung open the car door and ran up the path, leaving Mark, who had apparently been about to say something of import, sitting slack-jawed behind the wheel. He climbed out and caught her up just as she retrieved the key from the depths of her bag, dropping her hat in the process.

'Bea, I was about to ask you—'

But she cut him off: 'Any other time I'd ask you in for a coffee but now is not the moment.' She jammed a key into the lock.

'Understood. Completely.' He stood there as if waiting for something.

'Well, goodbye, then, and thank you for everything. Oh, no!' she shouted in frustration – she'd got the wrong key.

'Here, let me.' He took the keys, slid the right one into the lock and opened the door. 'There.'

She ran towards the wall of sound. 'Thanks, again. Sorry. BEN! Turn that music down.' If Mark spoke again, she didn't hear him: she was too busy negotiating her way past two bicycles that were leaning against the wall, taking up most of the corridor, socks on the handlebars to stop them marking the paint. Thoughtful, but she'd have preferred them chained up outside.

At first glance, the sitting room was empty. The sofa had been pulled into the middle of the room, an island in a sea of empty pizza boxes, lager cans, a few crisps packets and much of their contents. Among them were stranded various large male trainers. In front of the sofa, the characters from an animated computer game scurried back and forth across the TV screen, awaiting their instructions from the gamepads that lay abandoned among the general detritus on the floor. At the back of the room, a boy she didn't know was lying asleep, his pillow a folded linen jacket of hers that she'd left hung over the back of a chair. Beside him Ben's iPod speakers were blasting out loud rock music she didn't recognise, the words indecipherable, the noise deafening.

The silence when she switched it off seemed almost as loud. She could imagine the neighbours' sighs of relief as clearly as the bunches of flowers that she would have to buy the next day to placate them. Neither side had teenage children yet, so they wouldn't understand at all. 'Just you wait,' snarled Bea, as she turned her attention to the youth coming to in the chair.

He ran his hand through the matted tangle that passed for his hair. 'Ben?' he muttered. As he unfolded himself, he proved taller than Bea but thin as a bean pole, his black jeans revealing the grubby elasticated waistband of his knock-off DKNY pants. His skimpy black T-shirt had a red scrawl across the front.

She kept very calm as his eyes gradually focused on her, alarm registering as he worked out who she must be. 'I don't know who you are,' she said quietly, snatching up her jacket and giving it a brisk shake, 'but I think it's time you went home. I'm afraid the party's over.'

'Yeah, right. Thanks.' He scuttled sideways out of the door, pulling on a tiny black leather bomber jacket as he went. Bea followed him into the hall, at the same time noticing that Mark had disappeared. For a moment, she felt a flash of regret that their evening had ended so abruptly but right now she had more important matters to attend to. The kitchen doors were open into the garden and through them wafted the sound of voices and the unmistakable sweet smell of cannabis. She stamped on the equally sweet sense of nostalgia that it provoked. The kitchen radio was on, pumping out more music but at an almost acceptable level. Instead of switching on the lights, she marched the length of the room in the near dark, reckoning that surprise was the best form of attack. So it proved. She neared the end to hear, 'Ben! It's your mum!' and a muttered 'Shit!' Before she'd got out of the door, she could see four silhouettes busily putting out a couple of spliffs and picking up lager cans.

'Ben, I'm back.' Pleasant but with a distinct warning note. Perfect.

'Some of the boys came over, Mum. But they're just going.' She recognised his if-I-behave-as-if-there's-nothing-wrong-she-might-not-notice voice. Too late, mate.

'Well, good night, then,' she said, firm but not unfriendly, eyeing up the two figures standing closest to Ben, about whom there was nothing visibly boyish at all.

The four figures materialised in the dim light of the kitchen, Ben and another boy, identikits of the one who had already left, and two girls who sported tiny vests and jeans. One had most of her hair in a scrappy ponytail. The other had a short spiky cut that revealed a dark pictorial tattoo of some kind running down the side of her neck. Without looking Bea in the eye, they mumbled, 'Thanks,' and scarpered with their bikes through the front door to join the first boy, who was waiting, still dazed, by the gate.

She could see from the set of Ben's shoulders, and his apparent preoccupation with something on his foot, that he was gearing up for a confrontation. But her day had been too long, too enjoyable, too disturbing to destroy it all with a row. She could only muster the energy for a weary 'Next time, do keep the music down.' As for the spliffs, she wasn't sure what to say. Rather than broach the subject now, when Ben was stoned, she decided on the spot to get Colin involved. His views on the matter were far more draconian than hers and, for once, he was likely to be more effective.

Surprised not to get an earful, Ben grunted something about tidying up. Bea pressed a black bin bag into his hand and decided to wait in the kitchen with a small whisky until he returned. Tidying up *his* tidying up could be done in the morning before she went to work. It was more important that he made the effort than she moaned about how inadequately it was done. Besides, she wanted a moment to straighten out her thoughts about her own evening.

The drive to her mother's local hospital had been straight-forward enough but by the time they got there Adele had long since been discharged into Janey's care. Bea discovered her tucked up in bed, shaken, with a bruised knee and hip, her arm in plaster. 'Darling, you shouldn't have come,' Adele had said, as soon as she saw Bea. 'It's only a broken wrist and Janey's looking after me so well. It's a bit painful but I'll be up and about again in a day or two.' Janey assured Bea that she could manage and was more than happy to – Bea was sure that Janey would be much more patient than she would ever be – then Bea kissed Adele, promising to come and see her as soon as she could.

All those hours in the car with Mark should have given the two of them plenty of time to talk, yet things hadn't quite worked out that way. She had known she wouldn't be able to get away with ignoring the kiss. And sure enough, as they left Harmchester, Mark broached the subject: 'What happened this afternoon after you won . . . well, I . . .'

'Yes?' Bea encouraged him, keen to get the conversation over with and move on to the next stage in the proceedings. Whatever that might be.

'Well, the truth is I – er, well, I do like you and . . . Oh, this is awful. I haven't done this for so long that I've forgotten how.' As Bea watched, a blotchy glow spread up his neck and into his cheeks. His knuckles were white on the wheel.

'While you're driving a car probably isn't the very best moment to try.' She felt genuine sympathy for him.

He stole a quick look at her and they laughed. 'No, I guess it's not. Shall I save it till we get back?'

'That's a very sensible idea and it'll give me time to think how I'm going to reply. Only joking,' she added, as alarm crossed his face. 'I like you too.' Had she really said that?

But did she like him enough? she wondered now, as she pottered about the kitchen straightening things up. The rest of the journey had been spent in a slightly awkward silence or in talking about whether Adele could or should cope on her own. She couldn't help but think how much simpler the proceedings had been with 'Tony Castle', despite the outcome. Not that she was in any hurry to repeat that experience. But what she had enjoyed about their meeting had been the lack of discussion, the way things had moved swiftly and seamlessly to the inevitable outcome. And the outcome had been good. Until he'd done his runner, leaving her self-confidence in tatters, confirming to her that whatever sex appeal she'd once had was in serious decline, and not, of course, forgetting that trip to the clinic.

She became aware that her mobile was ringing somewhere. She sprinted to retrieve it from her bag in the hall. Suppose Adele had suffered some kind of a relapse? She was relieved to hear Mark's voice.

'I just thought I'd check everything was all right.'

'Yes, it's fine. The pill-fuelled rave I'd imagined turned out to be rather tame and they were quite polite and took themselves off. Ben's even tidying up as we speak. A miracle in itself.'

'I'm glad. What I was going to say in the car . . .' She could tell he was nervous from the way his voice was picking up speed. 'I was going to ask you if you'd like to spend next weekend or the one after in Norfolk with me.'

'Oh!' From a foiled kiss to a dirty weekend in one bound.

Not what she had expected. On the other hand . . . The old worm of doubt wiggled its head as she thought of the wider implications. But why not? What was the point of Let's Have Lunch if she wasn't going to keep on trying? 'Well, yes. I would.'

'That's fantastic. My sister and I inherited a cottage on the north coast. It's nothing special but it's in a great spot near Holkham. I think you'll love it.'

'I'm sure I will.' She remembered the big skies, blowy walks and the broad sweep of Holkham beach from a visit some years earlier. 'But I can't do next weekend. I'm going to a friend's for a family lunch to meet her new man, and the one after we've got a work away-day on Friday, coming back on Saturday. It's the new regime – brain-storming, team-building, all that nonsense.' She felt quite lowered by the thought.

'Well, the one after that, then. But we mustn't leave it any later or the weather will be grim.'

As she hung up, she realised she was looking forward to spending a bit more time alone with him. Mark was no Tom Carter, but that might be a very good thing indeed.

The sound of the front door opening made her look up to see Ben taking the rubbish out to the bin. The sight of him trying to make good sent a wave of maternal warmth rolling through her. He was a good lad at heart. They just rubbed each other up the wrong way sometimes because there was no one else to defuse the tension between a hormonal teenager and his peri-menopausal mum who didn't want to be the grown-up all the time.

*

The next day she watched Amanda shut the door of Adam's office behind her once again. What could they be dreaming up, she wondered, irritated yet pleased she could rise (well, almost) above their petty power games. She was due to meet an author in an hour, which gave her just enough time to deal with her emails and work out exactly how to break the news that if he didn't deliver his long-overdue manuscript she'd have to cancel their contract and he'd have to repay the advance that he'd no doubt spent. She knew it wasn't going to be pleasant. As she sat down, her phone rang. 'Bea Wilde.'

'Tom Carter here.'

'Tom who?' She must have misheard.

'You know who.' She did. That deep Irish burr was all too familiar. She tried to ignore the butterflies trying to escape from her stomach.

'What do you want? I said all I had to say to you yesterday.'

'So it's true, then?'

So that was why he had phoned. To check his facts.

'Yes. And if you hadn't given the agency a fake name and contact details, I'd have told you sooner.'

'You're sure it's me?'

The cheek of the man. As if she'd been lucky enough to have a choice. But she wasn't going to admit to him her dearth of success in the Valentine's department. 'Don't insult me,' she said, with as much assertiveness as she could muster.

'I'd like to meet you again.'

A moment of silent incredulity, then, 'Are you joking?'

'I couldn't be more serious.'

'I don't think so. What about your fiancée?' This man

was unbelievable. He had the morals of a tom-cat (she liked the unintended pun).

'She won't know a thing. Nor will Mark. Just you and me. You know how good it was.'

'And I know that you left in the middle of the night.' He began to interrupt but she spoke over him. 'And you lied to me.'

She hung up, stunned by his sheer nerve.

At that moment Amanda slid into her room. She was petite, immaculate at every hour of the day (and even in the middle of the night, Bea imagined), with a kind of doll-like beauty that belied the steely determination that characterised her business dealings. Her short dark hair was cut with a long fringe that she swept across her left eye. 'Bea, Adam wants to see us both about the away-day.' She tapped her nails on the glass wall of Bea's office.

Bea followed her, part-mesmerised by the brilliant red pencil skirt, the chic black silk shirt and the vertiginous heels, and part-preoccupied by Tom's phone call. How had he got her number? The brief distance between her office and Adam's gave her long enough to register that she had to think more carefully about what she wanted from her lunch dates in future: hot, unreliable sex versus consideration and commitment. But why shouldn't she go for everything, preferably minus the unreliable? She hadn't yet reached an age at which she was prepared to exchange her sex-life for slippers. But then again, there was the weekend away with Mark to consider. It might be an eye-opener. With that thought, Tom was instantly consigned to the waste-bin of history.

'Bea, hi.' Adam gestured that they should both take chairs at the round table. She sat down, unnerved by the way they were both watching her. Adam took some papers from a file with a fluorescent label marked 'AWAY DAY' and thumbed through it till he found the one he wanted and put it on top. 'I want to talk about you and Amanda presenting the highlights of the spring list to the rest of the company.'

'And Stuart?' Immediately she was on the defensive.

'I think it should just be the two most senior members of the editorial team.'

'But Stuart's responsible for some of the best books and feels passionately about them. It's only fair that he presents them.' Out of the corner of her eye, she could see Amanda directing a pearly smile at Adam as if she was complicit in his suggestion.

'He can brief you both thoroughly. That should be enough.' Amanda nodded in support of this strategy.

But Bea was not going to let go of something she believed to be a matter of principle. 'That's not the point. If you want this to be a morale-boosting away-day for the troops then you need to let him take a role. Otherwise there'll be resentment, not to say a whiff of rebellion, in the ranks.'

He thought for a moment, steepling his hands in front of him and tapping his fingertips together. Then he stopped. 'She's right, Amanda. I do want everyone onside.'

So it had been her idea, as Bea had suspected. Of course, without Stuart's books, Amanda had nothing to present except the few Stephen had commissioned before he left. But how would Amanda be the star of the show with only a couple of worthy history books that would sell barely a copy and a self-help guide to positive thinking? Her opportunism reminded Bea of Tom Carter's. Anyone was expendable if they were in the way of what she wanted and, right now, Bea and Stuart stood shoulder to shoulder in the path to Amanda's goal. Bea watched her force a smile over her scowl as she obliged Adam with a gritted 'Of course.'

Fifteen love.

The rest of their discussion focused on the shape the day would take. Apart from the presentation of the new books, which was intended to excite the staff about the company's coming year, there were going to be talks by the different directors to show how they intended to revitalise their departments, and finally there would be a series of brainstorming sessions to give everyone a chance to contribute their ideas towards improving the status quo. As far as Bea was concerned, the last were probably going to be the most valuable and interesting parts of the day. The most enjoyable, however, would be dinner, along with the time at which she could tear herself away and go to bed. As she was contemplating that marvellous moment, she heard Adam say, 'Lastly, I think you can chair the editorial brainstorm together, pooling your different experiences.'

Before Bea had time to react, Amanda jumped in: 'I don't think that will work, do you? Each session needs one person to drive it or you run the risk of losing its focus. I think I should take the lead simply because I'm not associated with the old regime and can encourage more new thinking. No offence to you, Bea.' The slight smirk indicated there was plenty. 'But people might feel less able to be open with you because they know you too well and associate you with the past.'

Ace. Fifteen all.

'That's a very good point,' agreed Adam. 'Are you OK with that, Bea?'

She was aware that she'd used up all her ammunition too early in the discussion. After being so adamant over the presentations, she would appear uncooperative if she didn't agree to this. And she had to be careful not to be too aggressive or she would alienate Adam, which was not part of her game-plan. 'I don't honestly think that would happen, Amanda. After all, I've worked for a long time with most of the people who'll be there. So, on the contrary, I think they trust me and because of that would feel quite able to speak their minds.'

Adam pursed his lips. 'But Amanda needs to be given a role that shows where she stands in the company.'

Amanda nodded.

'I see that. But are you sure this is the best way?'

'It's that or being given more titles to present. I'm anxious the staff recognise that she's been given a position where she can breathe new life into the place. Because it's such early days for her in the company, I'm asking you to compromise.'

Bea turned over all the reasons why she shouldn't, unable to find one that she could voice without appearing petty and vindictive. Deciding the best course of action this time was to be conciliatory, she rolled over. 'Of course. But I'll be there to help if you need me.'

'Thank you,' purred Amanda. 'I won't let you down, Adam. And, of course, this time next year, things will be very different.'

Thirty fifteen.

You bet your life it will, thought Bea, as she excused herself. If I have anything to do with it. The game's not over yet.

19

Even from the outside, Ellen's house had undergone a transformation. Instead of sitting empty, the flower boxes on the ground and basement window ledges overflowed with deep red miniature cyclamen and trailing silvery green stars of ivy. The door-knocker and letter-box had been recently polished, the cream still smeared into the crevices of the deep blue beading. On the doorstep stood a single bay tree in a carved stone pot chained fast to the railings.

As Kate raised her hand to press the bell, the door swung inwards and Emma rushed past her, almost knocking her back down the steps into Paul. Ellen was hot on her heels.

'Em. Come back!' she yelled. 'You nearly sent Kate and Paul flying and Bea will be here soon. It's almost lunch time.'

Emma slammed the gate so hard that the railings shook. As she turned round to her mother, her small face was streaked with mascara, surrounded by a halo of messy reddish curls. 'I don't care. I hate you,' she spat. 'He's not my father and he can't talk to me like that. It's not his house.' She gripped the top of the gate.

'Em, he was only asking you to tidy up. I'd have done the same.'

'No, you wouldn't. Not like that.' Having exited without her shoes, she was uncertain where to run next.

'Em. We can't talk about this in the street so why don't you come back and at least have some lunch?'

'Do come back,' urged Kate. 'Paul and I haven't seen you for ages. I want to hear about Cornwall and I've brought you a belated birthday present.' Emma hesitated, clearly having second thoughts about running away. Not that Kate was entirely sure that the coral necklace she had wrapped up in her bag was going to be enough of an incentive to persuade her to stay for long.

Needing her shoes if she was to get much further, Emma unlatched the gate and slouched back up the steps, giving Kate a rather ungracious kiss on her way past. 'I'm glad you're here. Perhaps you can talk some sense into Mum.'

'Em!' Ellen's voice trembled with hurt.

'Well, it's true. This is our house as much as yours so I do have a say in what goes on here.' Emma stormed into the living room where a calm-looking Oliver and Matt were engrossed in a game of Risk. As she kicked on her shoes, Oliver looked up from her to Kate who was right behind her, and shrugged slightly, as if looking for support.

'Hey, Em. I'm sorry if it came out the wrong way. I was only asking you to help your mother.' He pursed his lips in apology.

'Yeah. Whatever.' She left the room and they heard her stamping upstairs. Oliver stood up and offered Kate his hand, welcoming her with a wide smile that he extended to Paul. 'I'm Oliver. I'm sorry about this. I seem to have blotted my copybook already.' Apparently realising that his little-boy-lost expression cut no ice, he offered them a drink, then disappeared downstairs to get a bottle of *cava* from the fridge.

Ellen collapsed into the comfortable red sofa and sat forward, elbows on her knees, hands over her face. Paul took one of the other chairs, looking mildly embarrassed at being part of someone else's domestic drama.

'I'm so sorry, Paul,' said Ellen. 'It's been a trying week but I had hoped you wouldn't have to see just how trying.'

'Never mind, Mum. I like him even if Em doesn't.' Matt stood beside her, twiddling a bit of her hair round his finger before he snuggled under her arm to give her a kiss. Satisfied that he'd done his bit, he extricated himself and went downstairs to help.

'And I'm sure we will too,' added Paul, earning Kate's undying gratitude for being so conciliatory despite his confessed wish to be at home, catching up with some urgent office work. He turned his attention to the three rows of art books in the alcove beside him. 'You've got quite a collection here.' He took out an old Tate catalogue of a Rothko exhibition. 'Never quite got him myself.'

As he leafed through the pages, clearly relieved at having something to do, Ellen turned to Kate. 'I'm afraid it's turned out just as I predicted in my worst moments. You can see for yourself. Matt's fine and Em's a nightmare. Oliver can't do anything right. She's being so selfish and unpleasant that I don't know what to do.'

'Well, when I've got a drink, I'll go up and see if I can

knock a bit of sense into her. Or do you think it would be better to wait for Bea?'

'Oh, Kate. Would you? She always listens to you.' Ellen's gratitude was touching.

'She does not! Whatever makes you think that? But I'll have a go.'

Oliver elbowed his way in sideways through the door, holding a wooden tray with five champagne glasses and a green bottle so cold that condensation ran down its side. He put it on the games box that doubled as a coffee-table, nudging the Risk board to one side, despite Matt's shout of dismay as some of the pieces fell to the floor.

'Matt! Pick them up, would you?' He corrected a sharpness in his tone. 'We can start again later.' He sat beside Ellen and put his arm round her. As she leaned into him, he pecked her cheek. 'I don't think we need wait for Bea, do you?' With the two women's agreement, he peeled off the foil, untwisted the wire and slowly loosened the cork, twisting the bottle away from it with his left hand. There was a muffled pop and he poured them each a glass. Kate took hers and raised it. 'Cheers. I'll just run upstairs and give Em her birthday present. She'll be wondering where it is. Back in a minute.'

Going upstairs, she could imagine exactly what Emma must be feeling. With a philandering father and a twice-married mother of her own, Kate's own family had been a disaster zone when it came to ideal parenting. She didn't need a counsellor to tell her that was probably one of the reasons she had worked so hard to keep her own marriage together. She still remembered the ghastly occasion when her father had introduced her sister, Beth, and herself to his first girlfriend, who had been noticeably much younger than their mother and the first in a series of increasingly youthful women. Beth and she had been thirteen and eleven when he had taken them out for supper, trying manfully to fill the embarrassed silences with questions about school, their friends, favourite pop groups and what they were doing at the weekend.

Meanwhile the three females had sat uncomfortably, playing with their food. Mandy, the girlfriend, had looked alternately bored and adoring, while Beth and Kate had absorbed her brassy blonde hair, tanned cleavage, her habit of laying her hand with its long ruby nails on their father's thigh whenever his attention wandered from her, the way her tongue darted from her lipsticked mouth after every forkful, checking for any stray bits of food. The sisters stored away every detail with which to regale their mother later, vowing they would never go out with him again. They hadn't anticipated their mother's tears and anger, which had sent them scurrying, alarmed, upstairs. Neither had they anticipated her bringing home her would-be second husband a mere six months later.

Just as she and Beth had been beginning to enjoy the all-female household and benefit from their mother having become such an easy touch when they wanted something, in strode Charles. Loud and brash, he was determined to lick the household into shape, just as he had his army command. Beth and Kate had felt lost, unwanted and no longer part of a family. Not until she was in her twenties, had Kate understood that her mother had fallen in love on the rebound, an error of judgement that she would regret for the rest of her married life, bullied and harried by Charles until his death.

Not that what Ellen had done was comparable, but Kate knew just how devastating it felt when a stranger stole your mother's attention and love, when permission was given to them to take control of the household. Now she understood that her mother's love for her and Beth had never faltered but had been temporarily outweighed by her desire to prove to her first husband that she was as attractive to other men as he was to other women; by her need to be loved for herself; and by her longing to share the responsibilities of the household with someone who would and could contribute towards the financial side of things. All of the emotional and practical considerations that Kate had seen operate in so many of her friends and patients had come into play. At the time, none of that had entered her young head. Back then, the world had only spun around her and Beth, and what they wanted for themselves.

The door to Emma's room was firmly shut. As Kate knocked, she could hear the music being turned down.

'What?'

Kate heard the misery in Emma's voice and longed to help. Perhaps she could use her own experience to help her see things differently. She would share with her what she had shared with very few in the hope that it might make her come round. 'It's me, Kate. Can I come in?' She pushed open the door.

*

Twenty minutes later they came downstairs together, Emma wearing the coral necklace. She immediately went over to Ellen and apologised, while Kate sat on the arm of Paul's chair, resting a hand on his shoulder. He looked up at her, questioning, but now was not the time to explain how, after exclaiming in delight over her present, Emma had been a captive audience for Kate's own story, briefly told. Emma was not a stupid child and when Kate tried to help her to see things from her mother's point of view, rather than her own, she had the grace to look shame-faced. Her agreement to join them for lunch was easily won. She didn't want to fall out with her mother or upset her, but was struggling to find a right way to communicate with her. The relief and pleasure on Ellen's face when her daughter hugged her was more than worth the effort. Kate prayed the truce would last into the after-noon.

Oliver refilled Kate's glass just as the doorbell rang. 'Matt, could you, please?' he asked.

Bea swept in wearing one of her more flamboyant outfits: narrow dark green trousers under a tunic that was a riot of multi-coloured swirls and curves, a necklace with gold beads almost the size of golf balls and matching gold pumps. The room stared in wonder.

'Don't say you don't like it.' Bea grimaced. 'I needed a shot of retail therapy and the girl in the shop convinced me to buy it. Of course it cost the earth. I wasn't so sure by the time I got it home. Too much, do you think?'

'It's extremely flattering,' came a voice. 'I'm Oliver, by the way.'

'Of course you are.' She shook his hand. 'How rude of me. Hi, Paul. Em, good to see you. How was Cornwall?'

'Wicked. I learned to surf.'

'So did I,' chimed in Matt, anxious not to be outdone. 'Standing too.'

'That's brilliant. Did you find the perfect wave?' Without waiting for him to reply, she gave Emma a small box wrapped in silver paper tied with shiny red ribbons. 'I've brought you something for your birthday. It's only little.'

All eyes were on Emma as she tore open the package and gave a small gasp of delight when she saw the collection of different lip-glosses and nail varnishes. All eyes except Kate's – she had turned at the sound of what she saw was Oliver clicking the nails of his middle finger and thumb. Aware of her attention, he stopped and smiled. 'I should go downstairs and get lunch on the table.' While the rest of them were encouraging Emma to try out the glosses, he slipped out of the room almost unnoticed.

With all the fickleness of youth, Emma's mood had done a complete about-turn and, with it, so had Ellen's. 'I love that plummy one. Can I try it?'

'Mu-um! You're worse than having a sister! But OK, here you are.' She took out a couple and passed Ellen the deeper-coloured one. 'Anybody else?'

'Well, if you're offering . . .' said Paul.

'For you? No way. Bea? Kate?'

'No, no.' Kate was laughing. 'They're for you. Come on, let's see.'

'You're not going to make me feel guilty!' Ellen crossed

to the fireplace and, using the mirror above it, painted her lips a rich, glossy purple.

'That's so cool. Let me.' Emma followed suit with a subtle baby pink that was much admired.

'Lunch is ready!' Oliver shouted up the stairs. As if in response, Ellen swiftly wiped her lips with a forefinger and thumb, smearing off the gloss. Only Kate noticed, but said nothing.

Downstairs, an individual pear and Roquefort salad was laid at each place. Oliver was standing beside the table, the smell of roast lamb drifting from the other end of the room. 'Now, where would you all like to sit?'

'Well, I want to sit beside you,' Bea said immediately. 'Kate, why don't you sit on his other side?'

Taken aback at the speed with which his role as host had been taken over, Oliver pushed his hair out of his eyes, adjusted the oven gloves draped over his shoulder, smiled and pulled out their chairs. 'My pleasure.'

'Go easy with him,' Ellen whispered to Bea.

'You can rely on me.' Bea sat down.

'That's just what I'm worried about,' muttered Ellen, just loud enough for Kate to hear. 'Paul, Em! Come and sit by me.'

'This looks delicious.' Bea changed the subject. 'Did you make it?'

'I did, but it was very easy,' admitted Oliver. 'What about you? Are you much of a cook?'

'Me? I'm utterly useless. I've even been known to burn frozen peas. The one you should talk to is Paul. He's a genius in the kitchen,' Bea enthused.

'I wouldn't say that exactly,' Paul said.

'Don't be so modest. You're brilliant. Isn't he, Kate?'

Kate nodded, before turning back to Oliver. 'Enjoying food is half the battle, though, isn't it? You must have loved being in France – the food's so delicious there.'

'Certainly did. Do you know France at all?'

Responding to his cue, Kate and Bea sprang into reminiscences about their various trips to France. The conversation ebbed and flowed around them, with Matt volunteering his disgust at the idea of frog's legs and snails and Paul chipping in to describe a favourite meal he remembered once having in Paris.

While Oliver made gravy, Ellen brought the lamb pricked with garlic and rosemary to the table. Matt and Emma distributed steaming bowls of button onions and peas, glazed carrots and crispy roast potatoes round the table. The earlier disruption appeared to have been forgotten. Bea sat between Emma and Oliver, managing to turn her attention either to one or the other without drawing them into the same conversation. Then the general talk turned to the well-being of her mother and the consequences of her fall until, tired of the subject or at least by her inability to resolve it, Bea turned to Oliver. 'Have you got any ageing parents?'

'No. They're dead now.'

'I'm sorry. Where did they live?'

'My father worked for BP so we lived all over the world when I was a child. Hong Kong, Africa, the Middle East. By the time I left home, they had settled in the north of Scotland. So home for me is wherever I hang my hat.'

'But you're staying in London?' Kate glanced down the table at Ellen. She was eyeing them anxiously as they quizzed him.

'Of course. I couldn't leave now I've met Ellen.'

Emma chose that moment to leave the room to make a phone call, slamming the door behind her.

Oliver looked up the table at Ellen, who gazed back. 'I can't believe my luck.' He got up to stand behind her, his hands on her shoulders. 'Shall we bring on the pudding?'

'Of course,' she replied, squeezing his hand. 'Pear *tarte Tatin* and almond ice cream – or should we have cheese first?'

'Oh, cheese, definitely. I'll get it, though. You sit where you are.' He collected the plates and returned to the table with a plate of water biscuits and the cheese board. Emma followed him in.

'Yuk.' Matt turned in his seat. 'What's that? It looks totally rank.'

'That, you little savage, is Époisses. The finest cheese known to man. Delicious. Try it. Go on.' He bent over Matt, offering him a spoon to break through the reddish-orange rind.

'No way.' Matt wrinkled his nose. 'But I'll try a bit of that one.'

'Comté. Good choice. We'll make an expert of you yet. But visitors first. Kate?'

As the cheese did the rounds, only Emma and Ellen passed. No one commented but Kate was certain that Bea must have registered this uncharacteristic self-denial. Then, when it was time for the melt-in-the mouth *tarte Tatin*,

Ellen gave herself the smallest sliver by far. Kate noticed her looking across to Oliver. She was talking to Paul but always kept an eye on what her lover was doing. If the conversation opened out to include the whole table, she would look to him for approval after voicing an opinion. And he always gave it, with a wink, a smile, a nod. Each time, she seemed reassured, strengthened. As the meal moved into coffee, Emma excused herself again, this time to go and visit a friend. Bea seemed to take this as her cue to begin a new round of her cross-questioning.

'How's the job-hunting going, Oliver? I guess it's tough times at the moment.'

Ellen looked alarmed by the turn of the conversation, but he seemed quite unperturbed. 'No, no. I've got a few irons in the fire. I'm sure something will work out. It can't be easy in your business at the moment either, is it?'

'It's not. But you really don't want to get me going on that.'

'Yes, don't,' confirmed Kate. 'Once she starts on how things have changed since the good old days, she's impossible to stop.'

Bea gasped as if mortally insulted. 'Well, it's true,' she protested. 'But I take the point. Anyway, I'm dying to know about your gallery in France. Tell us more.'

'There's really nothing to tell. I wanted to move away from England. The gallery kept my head above water but I sold it once I understood that selling pottery was not what I was good at.'

Bea leaped rather too obviously at the opportunity to draw him out a bit more. 'What are you good at, then?'

'Bea!' Ellen sounded shocked.

'No, no. I asked for that,' said Oliver, pouring a little milk into his coffee. 'The truth is, I don't really know the answer. I think I could be very good as some sort of curator or doing gallery work that involves paintings or sculpture but I need the chance to try. What about you?' He turned to Kate. 'What would you do if you had to start all over again?'

'I wouldn't want to change from being a doctor,' she said firmly. 'Ellen?'

'I'd like to be a painter if I could ever find the time but I'd still want to run the gallery. Paul?'

'Anything that doesn't involve having to work at weekends. Like my dear wife's, my time-management is rubbish.' Paul put his napkin on the table. 'And on that note, I really think we should go. Can we offer you a lift, Bea?'

'That would be great. I've got a pile of submissions that's threatening to take over my bedroom. I've got to make inroads tonight.'

They offered their thanks and goodbyes before trooping upstairs and out into the street to where Paul had parked the car.

20

Bea could barely contain herself as she climbed into the Peugeot and slammed the door. 'Well, what did you make of him?'

'He's hot,' said Kate, incurring a mild tut of disapproval from Paul as he flicked the key in the ignition. 'And Ellen obviously adores him, but he's got his work cut out with Em.'

'Not my type. Too flash for me. But that's not what I meant. Did you find out anything about him?' Bea leaned forward as far as she could without the seatbelt throttling her, keen for a decent post-mortem on the lunch.

Kate imagined she could feel Bea's breath on her neck but she kept looking straight ahead. Her brow furrowed. 'Like what?'

Now that she'd met them together, she felt it would be disloyal to tear into Oliver behind Ellen's back. If Ellen wanted to throw in her lot with him and he made her happy, that was good enough for Kate. Outside the car, the streets were slick with rain. A bunch of teenagers yelled and shoved each other at the gateway of a park; pedestrians trudged home, heads down against the rain; a stray dog ran in front of them, dodging between the parked cars at the side of the road.

'Well, like anything,' Bea insisted, thrown backwards as they rode a speed bump. 'He was so cagey. Every time I asked him about where he lived in France, what he was doing about looking for a job, what he was interested in – all those things – he virtually stone-walled me, then headed the conversation off in another direction.'

'He wasn't very keen to talk about himself. I agree.' Paul was thoughtful as he waited to turn across the road that ran up to Alexandra Palace. 'Maybe . . .' he paused for effect '. . . he's got something to hide.' He turned quickly to give Bea a conspiratorial smile.

'Don't be silly. You heard what we talked about,' said Kate, on the defensive. Suddenly she didn't want to tell Bea about seeing Ellen wiping off the lip-gloss or taking smaller than usual helpings. She was sure to attach more significance to them than they probably deserved.

'No, I didn't. When I was talking to Em, I was very careful to block him out and concentrate on her. I got a feeling things weren't good between them.'

'You should have been there when we arrived,' said Paul.

Kate poked him in the thigh. 'I thought you didn't want to be involved!'

Ignoring her, Paul related what had happened when they'd arrived at the house and Kate's subsequent rescue mission.

'There you are. See?' said Bea, almost gleefully.

'No, I don't see,' Kate said. 'I thought he was lovely and

I'm really pleased to see Ellen so happy.' She turned round in the hope that Bea would understand that, as far as she was concerned, this was the end of the matter.

But Bea completely ignored the look, if she noticed it at all. 'There's something odd about him that I can't put my finger on. Something's not quite right. I hate the idea that she's supporting him. And apart from that, since when did Ellen ever think of dieting? She's always been completely against anything like that in case she put ideas into Em's head. But now she's practically starving herself.'

'Don't exaggerate. You're scaremongering. She didn't eat much pudding. What's the big deal?'

'But you noticed too, right?'

'You're making way too much of it. So she wants to look nice for him. What's wrong with that?'

'Nothing. But it's so out of character. Put that with the new hair, the new clothes and him not letting me speak to her those couple of times I called her in the evening. Bit Stepford wife-ish, isn't it? And what about the shed? Didn't look as if she'd used it.'

'I think it's great. Good for her. Much better to make the effort than not. It's just that you've forgotten what that first flush is like, that's all.' Kate regretted her last words as soon as she'd said them, but Bea laughed.

'Thanks so much for reminding me! Again. OK. I'm the tiniest bit jealous. I admit it. Better?'

'I still think you're being too hard on them. None of us is perfect after all, less so now than ever.' She talked over Bea's groan. 'So it's all about compromise. Of course we want the best for her, but perhaps Oliver *is* the best.'

'Kate's probably right,' added Paul, the diplomat once more. 'She usually is.'

'Maybe,' said Bea. 'But we have to watch out for each other and that's all I'm doing. And all that lovey-dovey, touch-me-touch-me stuff. Get a room, for God's sake. Spare us.'

'Leave it,' Kate insisted. 'You're reading too much into things. Give the guy a chance.'

'OK. But the jury's still out. That's all I'm saying.'

*

'Your friends are a pretty formidable pair,' commented Oliver, as he finished loading the dishwasher. 'Not what I was expecting.'

'Oh? What *did* you expect?' When Ellen had shut the front door behind them, she had been relieved that everything had gone so well. Her friends had seemed to like Oliver, and whatever Kate had said to Emma had had the desired effect.

'Well, they're so different from you. Here, you wash the glasses, I'll dry.' He took the tea-towel and waited.

'What do you mean?' She struggled into the yellow Marigolds that he'd bought her, then dipped the first glass into the foamy water.

'Well, take Kate. She's like a bird, isn't she? So tiny and fine-boned. I thought she was lovely, very calm and considerate, but I bet there's a steel fist in that velvet glove. Am I right?'

'Mmm.' Ellen had never thought of Kate in quite that

way. 'She's managed to keep so many balls in the air for years, so I guess she must have something like that. Though, funnily enough, she seems a bit lost now the kids have all but left home. Jack's still there, of course, and at least Megan's only in Bristol, but I know she desperately misses Sam. She'd love them to go out there and see what he's up to, but Paul's too busy. Not that she's ever said that in so many words. She always holds back when it comes to talking about herself. Unlike Bea.'

'But you said she's lost. Why lost? Isn't when your children leave home the moment you get your life back?' He seemed surprised at the idea of anything different.

'No! I can't imagine my life without Matt and Em being here. What would I do?' The thought of that inevitability both appalled and scared her.

'You'd be a lot less fraught, that's for sure,' he said, as he turned to put the last glass into the cupboard. 'You'd have more time for the gallery and your painting.' He ignored her sceptical laugh. 'And, besides, you've got me now, haven't you?'

'Yes, of course. And you do mean everything to me but the children—'

'They mean more.' As he finished her sentence, he slammed the cupboard door.

Ellen flinched at his flash of jealousy. 'That's not what I was about to say. You know you mean everything to me. But they're a part of me that I'll find hard to let go. Without Simon, we've been so, so close. If you had children of your own, you'd understand.'

He crossed the room to her side and she took his hand.

He pulled it away so he could hug her to him. 'I know. But selfishly I can't wait to have you all to myself.'

Staring over his shoulder, out of the window, she could just see their faint joint reflection. In that imperfect mirror, her finer wrinkles were blurred out of existence and a younger, slimmer version of herself gazed back. Was this the person he saw? she wondered. Or was it the more raddled one she gazed at in the bathroom mirror? His left hand reached out to pull down the blind and the reflection disappeared. Peculiarly, the mood of the moment disappeared with it.

Oliver moved away and started wrapping the cheese, ready for the fridge. Watching his long fingers – musician's fingers, she sometimes thought – moving with precision so that each piece looked almost shop ready, she brought the subject back to her friends. 'What about Bea, then? Did I give you a better description of her?'

'She's a great woman, a real larger-than-life character, isn't she? Says what she thinks and probably does what she wants too. Bloody terrifying.'

'She's not that bad,' Ellen protested. 'Maybe she's become a bit more full-on since Colin left her but that's her way of looking after herself.' Yes, that's exactly what it was, she thought. Over the last few years, Bea had constructed a second, more extravagant, personality for herself: when life got too tough, she showed the world another side of her character altogether. Only Kate and Ellen knew about her insecurities and occasional fears of growing old alone.

'Sitting next to her was like being interrogated. No

wonder she hasn't got a man. She had "needy" and "high maintenance" lit up in neon across her forehead.'

Ellen laughed and, standing behind him, put her arms round his waist. 'Now you're being unfair. And rude. She's my oldest friend.'

'I'm joking. All I'm saying is, I'm glad you're not like that.' He turned around to face her and she found her indignation melting away as he concentrated his attention on her. 'I'm glad you're you and that I found you.'

'Has anyone ever told you that you've got the most perfect bedroom eyes?' She touched his cheek, running her finger along the deep laugh line.

'All the time.' He leaned towards her, batting his eyelashes.

'Oh, you!' She pulled away, dragging him towards the stairs.

'Hang on. We haven't finished down here yet.' He flicked the tea-towel at her backside.

'I'll do it later.'

'What about Matt?'

She had made him agree that there'd be no bedroom activity whatsoever unless the children were sound asleep or away. His flat was the place for impromptu assignations until their relationship had been accepted by one and all.

She hesitated and in that moment the phone rang.

'Leave it,' he begged.

But Ellen had already picked up the receiver. It was Emma. She dropped Oliver's hand and pulled out one of the chairs to sit down. 'Em. What's wrong? Slow down, darling. I can't hear what you're saying.' Listening, she turned away from him, elbows on the table, cradling the phone by her ear, occasionally making noises of encouragement. 'Of course I'll come and get you.' She heard Oliver sigh. 'No, I don't mind. No, he doesn't either. Give me fifteen or twenty minutes.'

She put the phone down and turned to Oliver, who was staring at her with an expression she couldn't decipher, his lips pressed together, the corners turned down. 'I suppose that last idea's off, then?' He started picking up the coffee cups and folding the mats.

'Don't be like that, darling. She's had a furious row with Freya, her so-called best friend, and she's stranded at the Angel. The tube's not running. I'll have to fetch her.'

'For God's sake, she's fifteen. Can't she make her own way around London?'

'She may be fifteen but she's my daughter. She's upset and she's asked me for help. Of course I'm going to fetch her.'

'Of course you are. Sorry.' He gave her the funny crooked smile that made her knees weak every time. 'Another time.'

'I'm sorry too. I don't want us to fight over the children. I'll be back soon. Or,' she looked at him, 'perhaps you could come too.'

'Not a good idea. No, I'll stay here and finish tidying up. I'll scoot off before you get back. I think it might be better to make myself scarce.'

She adored him for how considerate he could be. Then a long, tantalising kiss lifted her onto cloud nine and, for a moment, she forgot her obligation to her daughter. She had begun to abandon herself to it when he pulled away. 'Off you go, then.' He smiled that smile again but made no move to release her.

She groaned. 'Why did she have to phone?'

'You could have said no, but you didn't. Go on, get outta here.' He let her go and the magic was broken.

*

Later that night, lying on her back alone in the dark, eyes turned to the ceiling where a feeble sliver of light cut across from the gap at the top of the curtains, Ellen let her thoughts circle at random. How many nights had she lain like this since Simon's death, concerned that she wasn't being a good enough parent, worrying about Matt and Emma's schoolwork, their friendships, their fallings out and, more than anything, the lack of a father in their lives? But now she'd introduced the possibility of one, things were worse rather than better. Perhaps she'd left it too late.

Having photos of Simon by her bed had always helped calm her when she couldn't see a way out of even the simplest problem. Sometimes, in the small hours, she had found that talking aloud to him had a therapeutic effect and helped her work out her worries. Despite Oliver's presence in her life, she couldn't give up on her original soul-mate, not just like that. Not after so many years. She could just make out the shape of the frame nearest her, but the photo inside was imprinted on her memory: Towan beach where a proud Matt knelt with Ellen beside the fortress they'd made in the sand while Emma tried to wrestle her sunhat from Simon's head.

Emma had been such an open, cheerful child until Simon's death. Matt had been too young but Emma quickly understood that her father was never coming back. She had sobbed herself to sleep in Ellen's bed night after night. Then, as she got used to his absence, she began to hold a part of herself in reserve as if afraid to trust anyone completely. If her father could let her down by disappearing without warning, then anyone could. Was that what was eating away at her now? Even all these years later, was fear of losing her mother fuelling her resentment of Oliver? If only Ellen could think of a way to reassure her, to show her that wasn't going to happen. But on the journey home tonight, when she'd tried her damnedest to get her back onside, Emma had clammed up. No doubt she was preoccupied by the argument she'd had with Freya – but was that the real reason? And why the hell was she fighting with Freya anyway? They were inseparable and never rowed.

The thoughts buzzed and swarmed in her head. Oliver had proved himself so good with Matt, why hadn't his charm worked with Emma? Ellen blamed herself for not being able to find some common ground where they could meet and get on. The antagonism that existed between them had to be her responsibility so she had to resolve it. Perhaps if she had handled everything differently from the beginning they wouldn't be in this mess. The blame lay with her for falling in love, the one thing she'd sworn she'd never do.

But was she really in love? What did that mean? Any neat answer eluded her. She had loved Simon, she was sure. Yet the feelings she remembered having for him were quite different from those Oliver aroused. What she felt now was an intense sharpening of her senses when they were close, a sense of incompleteness and a constant deep-seated longing that made it difficult to concentrate when they were apart. But she missed the total trust she had shared with Simon and their acceptance of one another for the people they were. He had loved her despite, or perhaps because of, her failings, just as she had him. He wasn't interested in what she looked like or what she wore. He had never judged her appearance. He hadn't minded when she'd put on weight after the babies. 'More of you to get hold of,' he'd joked. If she'd had a second piece of cake, he'd have one too without comment. He certainly wasn't worried if the house wasn't quite as tidy as it might be. He had never suggested she should try to change herself to please him.

All he had wanted was a life companion who would share the ups, and to whom he could turn during the downs. What pleased her was what pleased him. The fireworks in the bedroom may not have been the full-on pyrotechnics Oliver provided but neither had they been a total failure. What she remembered more than anything was the way they talked and laughed, always happy in each other's company. But then he had been diagnosed with advanced-stage pancreatic cancer. He had died within three short months of being told, three months that were overtaken by his treatment, then his swift but brave decline. No time to do any of the things they'd planned to do together, not enough to say all the things that were left to be said. Perhaps if he'd lived, things between them would have changed, but that was something she'd never know.

A taxi chugged to a halt outside and she heard the door slam, the voices and laughter of the young married couple across the road, the click of their gate and their front door jamming before it shut with a bang.

What was confusing her was the difference she found in her relationship with Oliver. There was so much about him that she adored – his eyes, his laugh, his consideration and love for her, his willingness to take her children under his wing. She was drawn by his impulsiveness, his desire to please and surprise her in so many different ways. When she thought about the way he'd sold *Starship* to raise the money for her studio, she smiled. Her initial reactions of dismay and anger had vanished as she accepted his gesture for what it was: a spur-of-the-moment loving act. She didn't doubt that he loved her and already understood some of her own self-doubt. He was trying to help her become more confident, but by encouraging her to make the most of herself, he sometimes succeeded only in making her feel she wasn't quite good enough. She wasn't sure he'd understand, even if she could begin to explain.

She loved the way he tried to introduce some order into her life but sometimes she worried he seemed not to know when to stop. When she'd searched for the company accounts, she'd been unable to find them. She remembered moving them from her home office, a.k.a. the dining-table, to make space for lunch but they had vanished from the end of the worktop where she could have sworn she'd left them. After a half-hour search she found them on the bookshelf, neatly squared off between a couple of cookery books. Perhaps not the most meticulous of housekeepers and certainly the most disorganised of accountants, she nonetheless employed some method in her arrangement of her papers, a method based on the fact that she could always remember – well, almost always – in which random pile of loose papers she'd left any particular item, based on its position relative to the other piles. He had completely messed that up by clearing them away. Before she could do any work at all, she would have to reorder the whole lot.

Alone in the dark, her thoughts kept spinning round her head. Had she made a mistake in introducing Oliver to the children too soon? She turned on her side, staring towards her photo of Simon. But not even he could help her now. She resolved to quell any doubt and make things work out. She longed to talk all this over with Bea or Kate but that would be the wrong thing to do. She didn't want them to think she had even one second thought. Friendship was a funny old thing. None of them was always quite as open and honest with the others as they professed to be. They'd never lie but they were occasionally guilty of sins of omission, like the times when she hadn't confessed Oliver had bought her the underwear or that he'd sold the picture to raise enough to buy the studio. She was sure the others did the same. She worried what they might think – she shouldn't but she did. And Bea could be so quick to criticise. No. Voicing her fears would make them assume an importance they didn't really have. She had to keep shtum. She had to sort out her jumbled thoughts and work out a strategy that would include Emma and make her see what a good and kind man Oliver really was.

Overhead the thrum of a police helicopter grew louder as it circled over the area. A siren wailed in the distance. She shut her eyes, turned on her side and drew up her knees.

One of her last waking thoughts was that love had to be about give and take. Working towards accepting the aspects of Oliver's personality that occasionally niggled would be the battle half won. All she was experiencing were teething troubles that would disappear as they grew to know each other better. This was to be expected after such a speedy romance. She had found a man who loved her. She had come too far down the line to think about going back now.

21

By summer, the two-storey seventeenth-century farmhouse would be hidden under Virginia creeper. Now the honeyed Cotswold stone could be seen through the leafless vines that reached up the façade and over the slate roof to the big chimneys at either end. Smoke drifted into the featureless grey autumn sky. Lights glowed in welcome from the two large bay windows on either side of the stepped porch to the front door. Bea carried her overnight bag into the reception area, looking into the beamed hotel bar on the right in the hope she might see a colleague. No one she recognised sat in the chairs arranged round low wood tables, so she turned to the desk in the oak-panelled lobby and checked in, then followed instructions to the second floor where she would find her bedroom.

Everything was tastefully neutral: pale cream walls and ivory bedspread, beige upholstery on the small sofa at the foot of the cream-fringed four-poster. The only splash of colour came from the patterned rug and the delicate sprigs of flowers on the cream swags of curtain. Outside she could see the conference centre and spa, attached to the main building by a covered walkway through the garden. Could Coldharbour afford this? Not your problem, enjoy it, came the swift reply.

She made herself a cup of tea and unpacked, putting away her things in the Georgian mahogany chest of drawers and a wardrobe so discreet she almost missed it. She had spent what felt like hours packing and repacking as she had debated which clothes to bring. She knew Amanda would be looking her sharpest, so the big question was, should she attempt to compete? Not, when it came to it, that she had much of a choice. When she delved into her wardrobe, attempting to flush out the ideal outfit that would make her feel her best and Amanda feel her worst, there was nothing. Not that her wardrobe was bare – very far from it – but none of the snappier outfits that might have had the desired effect fitted quite as they once had. She couldn't bring herself to throw them out so they hung there, waiting for the day when she'd be able to wear them again: a triumph of optimism over experience. In the end she had decided to go for simple but elegant, with a bit of layering in the hope that she could outwit any incipient hot flush by taking something off. In other words, she would look herself and to hell with Amanda.

Bea's professional life had improved immeasurably over the last couple of weeks. She was feeling particularly bullish after winning her colleagues around to supporting her acquisition of *Bare Bones*, her American novel. They had all admired the quality of the writing and also, like her, saw its commercial potential. The auction had dragged on over two weeks as the agent went backwards and forwards among the competing publishers, driving the price up. As it rose, Bea had begun to wobble, knowing that at fifty, sixty, seventy thousand pounds, it was no longer the sure-fire boost to the budget she had intended. But Adam had held his nerve. 'Let's try to close the others out by making one *last* bid that'll frighten them off.'

When Bea had still hesitated, he had been firm. 'If you're making a mistake, it's not the ten thousand you're adding to our bid now, it's the seventy-five thousand you've already got on the table.'

She wasn't altogether sure whether that made her feel better or worse. 'I'm not making a mistake.'

'Then raise the stakes!'

So that was what she had done and the strategy had worked. Their competitors had folded, and yesterday the deal had closed at eighty-five thousand: Coldharbour would be the British publisher. There hadn't been such an excited buzz in the company for months. No one had expressed a moment's doubt, apart from Bea, and, if she was honest, her anxiety was only about whether the book would justify the money she paid for it, not about its quality. She thought she had seen Amanda purse her lips at the level of the advance but she said nothing. That alone was enough to strengthen Bea's resolve. She would have to make it work.

Adam had invited the directors to stay two nights at the hotel so that they could bond over dinner on the first night and present a united front when the troops arrived next morning. Preparing herself for the evening, Bea decided on a long bath, using all the Molton Brown freebies lined up in the bathroom. Afterwards she relaxed on her bed in the hotel's soft white towelling robe and slippers, TV on, tea and a half-eaten piece of shortbread that she'd failed to resist at her side. She was woken by the shrill sound of the phone.

'Bea? Adam here. You OK to meet in the bar in about twenty minutes?'

'Of course. I was just reading. I'll be right down.'

She looked at the bedside clock. Shit! She must have dozed off. She leaped off the bed and pulled from the wardrobe a pair of Caroline Charles black crêpe satin trousers (expensive but worth every single penny) and a deep purple silk blouse (inexpensive but looked good) with a smoky green pashmina. Standing in front of the mirror, she pulled in her stomach but draped the pashmina to hide it anyway, just in case. Mmm, passable. In the bathroom, she laid out her tools for the usual repair job. First she leaned in and, with the slightest pressure of her hands, pushed her jawline up and back towards her ears. That small movement took about ten years off her. She sighed. But face-lifts were expensive and even the so-called non-invasive treatments weren't always the answer. She pictured the flat, frozen forehead of her crime author Beth Raymond, and the repetitive tic at the corner of her otherwise motion-less top lip – as if her face was rebelling against the grip of the Botox. No. Every wrinkle tells a story; they just need careful managing. Especially the ones emerging around the corners of her mouth. Dabbing Touche Éclat under her eyes, she watched the blue shadows recede. A lashing of Mac concealer put into check the tiny patches of hyper-pigmentation (yes, she knew it was sun damage by any other name but that one made it sound as if she were less responsible) and the most delicate wrinkles so that all she needed was a dab of colour on her cheeks to emphasise her cheekbones and a slash of lipstick. As she applied the first coat of mascara, the phone rang again breaking into her concentration so she smudged black on her eyelid.

'Bea, it's Kate. Something weird's happened.'

'Are you all right?'

'Yes, fine. Listen, can we meet over the weekend?'

'Of course. Sunday? But why?'

'I'll just be a minute . . . Sorry, Bea. I'm still at the surgery and Pete wants to talk to me. Come to ours at about three, OK? I'll tell you then.' And she was gone.

Preoccupied with removing the mascara, Bea wondered what on earth Kate could have been talking about. She began to speculate what might have happened to one of the children or at Kate's work, but had to push her thoughts aside. The evening beckoned. She looked at the finished result, with and without her specs. Better without (a plus for the short-sightedness that came with age) but not bad with, and five minutes to spare. She made her way downstairs to the bar, choosing the staircase over the lift. As she rounded the turn above the ground floor she caught sight of Amanda heading into the bar ahead of her. Predictably she was looking trim and glamorous in a little black dress, red shoes with those fuck-me heels again and a tightly fitting red jacket. Bea gathered the pashmina round her. Why was it that she couldn't 'eat sensibly' for longer than three or four days without succumbing to temptation just as the slimmer her was emerging? On the other hand, she reasoned, as she crossed the foyer to the bar, where she saw inviting little bowls of peanuts and olives on every table, life was too damn short. Adam was ordering drinks for everyone as they came in. Despite the glares from other guests, Amanda had commandeered a couple of tables surrounded by enough comfy chairs to seat them. One by one they settled themselves and the evening began.

*

The following morning Bea woke early, regretting the delicious syllabub dessert and the cheese that she could still feel sitting in her stomach along with the brandy that Adam had insisted she had as a nightcap. Right, she said to herself, for the umpteenth time in her life. Today was the day she would start a sensible regime – with exercise. Eat less, exercise more. Simple as that. And this time for good, she promised herself. The first thing she would do in the spirit of endeavour was visit the spa for a swim. She hadn't known what made her put her swimsuit into her case, but now she was glad she had. Most important was to get down there before any of the rest of the team did. Much as she liked most of her colleagues, she didn't particularly want to get sporty with them. She donned her cozzy, and a twirl in front of the mirror was enough to convince her that she wasn't too much of an embarrassment, despite gravity's attempts to discredit her. Wrapped in her robe, she headed downstairs, full of resolve.

The spa was in a converted stone barn with a high vaulted wooden ceiling. By the entrance, a small gym boasted an exercise bike, a couple of cross-trainers, a multi-gym, a stacked set of weights and a couple of pearlised exercise balls. Bea turned her back on them to see what the treatment room had to offer despite the large 'CLOSED' notice on the door. In the short pool an elderly woman was breast-stroking up and down, up and down, her head held regally above the water level, little wisps of grey hair emerging from her pink rubber cap. Beside her a young man was slowly but more professionally doing the crawl, water streaming from his mouth each time he raised his goggled face. On the wall, above one end of the pool, a large clock ticked away the minutes. Bea took a cushioned wicker recliner and watched them for a moment. Now she was here the whole exercise idea had lost most of its appeal. She was sure she could smell the fresh croissants and coffee for breakfast in the other building. As the young man drew near, she could make out several distinct spots on his back, even from where she sat. This was crazy. She wouldn't want to share her bathwater with these people. Why was she even thinking about joining them?

As she debated the alternative merits of a warm bath, the door from the changing area swung open and in walked Adam in a pair of checked swimming shorts. He dived straight in without apparently noticing her and swam swiftly to overtake the swimmers at the opposite end of the pool. She had noticed him, however, unable to avoid taking in his slim hips (nice arse), broad shoulders (but not too broad), lean tanned torso (well-defined pecs and more than a mere suspicion of a washboard) with its sprinkling of dark hair and his long muscled legs. Her original idea of huffing and puffing her way through the water now seemed quite out of the question. She reasoned that it wouldn't make that much difference to her body anyway, although entering the pool might make a difference to her relationship with her boss, and not necessarily in a good way. No, she would beat a hasty exit while the going was good.

As he touched her end of the pool, he spotted her. 'Bea! Are you coming in?'

Too late.

'Er, no. I've just finished.' Would he notice her hair wasn't wet? She roughed a hand through it as if drying it. 'I'd better go up so I'm ready for when the others arrive.' She stood up, bent over to pick up her towel and trod on the end of the belt to her robe. As she stood up, her robe fell open to reveal just how completely dry and untoned she was. Damn! 'Must fly.'

She thought she could see mockery in his amused stare and, even more humiliating, quite possibly something that might be revulsion.

'See you later, then.'

'Yes. See you.' He had known she was lying. He had seen her near naked. And, worse, he had probably guessed she'd decided not to take the plunge because he had got there first. She wouldn't have wanted anyone to know she was governed by such self-consciousness, least of all him, or to give him any ammunition that he might later use against her. So she pulled her robe together and retreated, mortified, to ready herself for the day ahead.

Upstairs, she went to extra trouble to make herself presentable, until she was happy with a chocolate brown suit and dusty pink V-neck – effortlessly stylish was the look she was going for in the hope she could obliterate Adam's memories of her as nature intended.

*

The company arrived at nine in time for tea or coffee. At nine thirty exactly they assembled in one of the general conference rooms to hear Adam welcome them, give a short, upbeat talk and explain the order of the day. All the directors sat ranked beside him, with Amanda on his right looking cool in straight black jeans and a green shirt. While Adam talked, Bea scanned the faces in front of them until she found Stuart and sent him a supportive glance. Before the presentation of the list, he came up and joined her.

'How was dinner last night?'

'Very good food, friendly talk, but no gossip. It was all very civil – even Amanda.'

They settled themselves side by side in readiness for their presentation. Before they kicked off, Adam introduced the directors (pointlessly, since most of them had worked with the company for years) before giving the big welcome to Amanda. To Bea's surprise, Amanda got to her feet to give an unscripted thanks. She went on: 'I know this has been a difficult time for many of you but I want to assure you that I have every intention of working with Adam, and Bea, of course, to restore the Coldharbour list to where it belongs. Back in the top ten. To do this we're going to have to make some exciting, well-judged acquisitions and I'm delighted to be able to tell you that the first of those is *Bare Bones*, honestly one of the best novels I have ever read. I was completely spell-bound after the first page . . .'

As she briefly précised the plot, Bea stopped listening. She was concentrating on being furious. Without actually taking the credit for buying the book herself, Amanda was making it look as if she was directly responsible for the acquisition. Just as infuriating, she had stolen the opening to Bea's presentation when she had been going to announce the book to her colleagues herself. Bea took a couple of deep breaths and looked down the row of directors. Everyone was watching Amanda come to the end of her show of one-upmanship, their faces unreadable. As she sat down looking pleased with herself, Adam raised his hand.

'I want to add one thing to what Amanda's just said. We should also congratulate Bea for the way she's got us all behind *Bare Bones*. She recognised the novel's quality in the first place and insisted we read it so we all shared her enthusiasm – as you've just heard. It's a great acquisition of hers that I'm sure will mark a turning point for us.' He turned towards her and smiled while the audience joined him in applause. Amanda turned her head, tight-lipped, but clapping along with the rest.

Bea couldn't believe what she'd heard. She could feel herself blushing, surprised but delighted by Adam's public vote of confidence. That could only be good news for the book too. Perhaps he wasn't always the bad guy after all. And, more importantly, perhaps she'd got the battle lines wrong. Perhaps they weren't drawn up so she was against him and Amanda. Perhaps he stood squarely between the two of them. Suddenly the day looked a lot better.

The presentation of future highlights went smoothly, as

did her overview of how they planned to develop the list. She didn't want Amanda to have a chance of hijacking that as well. Stuart was an edgy and entertaining speaker. How he made people – even her – laugh during a pitch for a football book was beyond Bea, but he did, as well as bringing out the best in his more off-the-wall non-fiction titles. Afterwards they both found themselves surrounded by an enthusiastic group of colleagues, wanting to congratulate them or know more. The fact that they had generated so much support made her feel good. As did the small surge of satisfaction she felt when she saw Amanda alone and cornered by the financial director – a man who could bore for England. Amanda must realise how badly she had misjudged her opening remarks. She had underestimated the staff of Coldharbour, most of whom had worked with Bea for so long and who, thanks to Adam's pointed intervention, could see through her. She was going to have to work hard in the afternoon brainstorming session to win them over.

And work hard she did. Bea had to hand it to her. Amanda did not give up easily. She appeared after lunch with the bounce back in her step. By the end of the afternoon, she had succeeded in regaining the confidence, albeit wary, of her new colleagues. She listened to what they had to say, threw open their ideas for discussion, drew Bea in when necessary, noted down the consensus of opinion and promised to act on it. She was respectful, funny and modest. It looked like a bravura performance, unless Bea had overestimated her. But she knew she hadn't.

*

'So, how do you think it went?' Adam leaned back, clasping his hands behind his head.

Bea was watching the orange sparks being sucked up the back of the chimney from the blazing log fire. 'Soldiers going into war' was what Adele called them, as they glowed brightly before being extinguished in the darkness. 'Good, I think,' she replied. 'Everyone seemed glad to be made to feel part of something again.'

Most of the staff had returned home while some of the directors and senior management had stayed over to continue the discussions that had arisen from the brainstorming sessions. Now dinner was over, a couple had drifted to their rooms while others were down in the snooker room. Bea, Amanda and Adam had ended up in the bar. Bea was still too wound up to be ready for bed, and snooker offered no temptation whatsoever. Adele's late-night addiction to BBC's *Pot Black* had never rubbed off on her daughter. The promise of a nightcap by the fire was too good to refuse.

'I agree,' said Amanda, sipping her tonic water. She sat opposite Bea, in an identical leather armchair that threatened to swallow her tiny frame. If only it would, mused Bea.

'Anything we should have done differently?'

'I don't think so — although I should have let Bea announce *Bare Bones*. I wasn't thinking.'

'Not like you.' Adam narrowed his eyes and turned his head towards her.

'I know. But I hope I've made up for that over the rest of the day.'

Was that an apology? Looking across at Amanda, who had changed into a short woollen dress that clung in all the right places, Bea realised from her body language that the answer was a definite no. She had turned towards Adam, her left arm across her body, her left leg crossed over the right, effectively blocking Bea from the conversation. Her attention was directed solely at their boss and Bea saw how, for that moment, he was mesmerised. Amanda was admitting to him that she knew she'd messed up and that it wouldn't happen again. It had nothing to do with Bea. The collegial role she'd played all afternoon had been a necessary strategy to take her to the front of the race.

'The session I sat in on seemed to go well.' Adam tore himself away from her gaze. 'Didn't you think, Bea?'

'Mmm, yes,' she murmured. What gorgeous brown eyes you've got.

'Can I get you another?'

Her glass of brandy was already combining with the dim lighting and the warmth of the fire to make her drowsy. But not too drowsy to realise that staying down here any longer would be a mistake, if not potential career suicide. She was aware that she had drunk enough at dinner to loosen her tongue, unlikely to be a good idea in this company. Tempting as it was to stay, she was still coherent enough to know that she was reaching a point at which she might say something she'd regret. Her differences with Amanda should be dealt with in the most discreet way possible, while flirting with Adam (yes, she was drunk enough to admit to herself she wanted to) would be a huge mistake. Mixing business with pleasure nearly always got messy and there was always a 'morning after'. Best leave all that to Amanda.

She shifted to the edge of her chair. 'Actually, I think I'm going up. Thanks, though. I'll leave you to it.'

The relief on Amanda's face was all too evident.

Once standing, the lure of Bea's pristine bedroom became irresistible. Congratulating herself on doing the sensible thing, she wished them good night, and headed towards the lift. There was no doubt in her mind that the day had worked in her favour. When she reached her room, she took her mobile from where she'd left it charging. A missed call from Kate reminded her of their earlier conversation. It was too late to call her back now but surely nothing could be so important that it wouldn't wait until they met tomorrow.

22

'Are you absolutely sure it was Oliver?'

'I'm one hundred and ten per cent certain. They came out of that restaurant on the corner of Clerkenwell Green. He had his arm round her, then he kissed her and he pushed his hair off his face in that way he does, and they headed off together towards Farringdon Road.' Kate was impatient at having to repeat what she'd seen.

The two women sat on her sitting-room sofa, mugs of coffee ignored on the table in front of them. The curtains were already drawn against the fading light, the fire was lit and the room snug. Paul was out. Mouse was curled between them, eyes half shut and one white-socked paw stretched towards Kate's leg.

'I'm sure there must be a perfectly innocent explanation,' she added, wondering if she had been right to call Bea, who was bound to blow the whole thing out of proportion.

'Did he see you?'

'God, no.' Kate sounded appalled. 'I stopped just long enough to be sure it was him, then carried on. I wish now that I'd gone over. Then he'd have had to introduce me.'

That was exactly what she should have done, of course. If she had, they wouldn't be sitting here now. Or if they were, at least they'd be talking about something else.

'You should have followed them.'

'Don't be ridiculous,' Kate exploded. 'We weren't in an episode of *Taggart* or something.'

'All right. Calm down. Tell me what she looked like.'

'Young. Dark hair tied back. Smartish in one of those black sheepskin coats with a shaggy collar. Boots, black with a heel. Definitely attractive from a distance. Maybe I've jumped to the wrong conclusion but they looked so, I don't know . . . comfortable together.' Or had they? Perhaps she was imagining this intimacy. Having supported Oliver in the face of Bea's scepticism, she almost didn't want to doubt him now.

That particular Friday morning had been difficult with a patient who had nothing more than a sore throat kicking up a fuss about the wait time. He had insisted on jumping the queue in front of other more obviously needy patients, who accepted that Kate was running late. His uncalled-for aggression, which had ended in him throwing a chair across the waiting room, had upset the reception staff and meant that Kate was still fuming when she saw the patients who had followed him. Her mood had hardly improved by the time the session had overrun by three-quarters of an hour, and she was left with a mound of paperwork to finish and the blood reports to check before dashing off to Bart's. She'd promised Mrs Fairweather a visit and couldn't break her word.

The old lady had been such a good neighbour for years,

keeping an eye on their house and feeding the ever expanding and shrinking menagerie of pets whenever they went away, as well as remembering the kids with a fiver at Christmas and Easter. Now she'd been admitted to Bart's in the last stages of metastatic breast cancer and she had no one left to visit her. Kate had decided that she could catch up on her missed work by staying late after the evening surgery and finishing off on Saturday morning. Again.

Now she wondered whether being so stretched might have made her read a meaning that wasn't there into an entirely innocent meeting. At the time, she had been thinking about Paul, wondering what he was up to. His behaviour of the last weeks had continued to disturb her and, despite her attempts to bridge the distance between them, they seemed as far apart as ever. Recently, he'd been paying more attention to his appearance than she remembered him doing before. When he wasn't in the office, he spent so much time at the gym he was in danger of developing a six-pack; he'd returned from the hairdresser with a new buzz cut, plus some fancy aromatic aftershave, but when she'd asked if anything was bothering him he'd accused her of being so stressed she was imagining things. She believed him when he said he was going through a tough time at work but, nonetheless, a little voice still nagged away at her, suggesting there was something more going on than that. Weren't these all the tell-tale signs of a man having an affair? She had risen above the temptation to look through his pockets or check his mobile for messages. Instead she had decided she would find a moment to confront him directly. After all these years of marriage, the least he owed her was respect. But back to Oliver. Perhaps her own anxiety about Paul had led her to misinterpret what she thought she had seen him doing.

'I remembered that Ellen said he didn't have friends or family in London, but perhaps it was someone visiting. I shouldn't have called you.' She got up to poke the fire, collapsing the embers to make space for a couple of logs she took from the large wicker basket.

'Of course you should. You always want to see the best in people, even when it's not there.'

'It's not that. I just don't want to spoil things for Ellen.'

'Better they're spoiled now than later when she's in even deeper.' Decisiveness was what Kate had always considered one of Bea's strengths. She was never afraid to go straight to the heart of the matter, then act immediately. 'I think we should tell her.'

'Bea, we can't. If he's really having an affair, it would kill her.' Exactly as it will me, if I find out that's what Paul's doing, she thought.

'(a) It won't. Not really. But (b), just in case, we'd better find out for sure before we talk to her. There are too many things that don't quite stack up. I'm not going to stand by and watch her get her heart broken. I still can't believe that shed. What was he thinking? Ellen said he didn't have any money and that's why she's stumping up for his rent. God knows how she's doing that. And look what he did to her precious garden!'

'When I last spoke to her, she was still torn between being thrilled that anyone would do something like that for her and sad about the garden. She didn't talk about the money.

I didn't know what to say.' Used to listening to so many people in so many different forms of distress at the surgery, Kate normally prided herself on having an answer to suit every situation. Years of general practice had taught her that there was little variation in the range of human experience. The differences came from the way people reacted to the circumstances in which they found themselves. She wanted to support Ellen – but how? Oliver's motives in erecting the shed were either presumptuous and overbearing or generous and loving. Bea thought the former, Ellen seemed to think the latter, while Kate was caught somewhere in between.

'I can't understand how she can let a man take over her life so completely and so quickly. It doesn't make sense to me.' Bea had always been so much clearer than her two friends about who was in charge of her life. She had never really let go of the reins for anyone and that was probably what had done for her relationship with Colin, thought Kate.

'Of course it doesn't. But see it from her point of view. The sex is probably great, he makes her feel good about herself and she can't say, "Stop," over the small things because she's scared it'll put him off.'

'Which means he can take advantage of her,' Bea concluded decisively.

'She doesn't see it like that.'

'OK, you're right. But I can't let it lie. She may be happy to know nothing about who he really is but I'm not.'

'What are you going to do?'

'Not sure yet. A bit of digging.'

'I wish you wouldn't.'

'Then why did you call me? But don't worry, I'll be *so* discreet.' Bea laughed as she reached for her coffee but Kate could see that she was quite serious. When she was in that mood, there was no point in trying to dissuade her.

'Right. Not another word about him,' Bea said firmly. 'I'm dying to tell you about Mark, the away-day, *and* I want to know what's going on at the coal-face of medical practice. You first.'

As Kate launched into what had been happening at the surgery, she relaxed. She would let Bea do as she chose. She couldn't stop her even if she wanted to and if she didn't turn anything up immediately, which she probably wouldn't, then she'd soon lose interest and that would be that. Within minutes, Bea was exclaiming at the incompetence of the practice nurses who, despite their training, had apparently failed to learn how to read the thermometer on the Labcold fridge and had cost the practice their entire supply of vaccines. Then Kate had embarked on the story of the sad end of one of her patients. A woman had phoned the police because of the swarms of bluebottles clustering on the inside of a neighbour's window. No, she hadn't seen him for a few weeks, now she thought about it. Turned out that the poor old sod had been lying there dead for at least a fortnight.

*

Kate was still laughing to herself about Bea's story of her aborted swim and wondering how long Mark would stay in the picture, when she heard the front door slam. Bea had left half an hour earlier, muttering about the number of scripts she had to read and having no time to take Adele and Janey to look at their new flats. That half-hour had given Kate enough time to think about what she wanted to say to Paul. The advice she always dished out to her patients with marital problems was to talk to each other. But that was so much easier said than done. There were always plenty of reasons to put off an awkward conversation, given all the demands life made on her and Paul and, of course, she wasn't altogether sure she wanted to hear what Paul had to say. But talking about Oliver and Ellen had driven home her need to get things into the open. Once she knew her situation for sure, she could work out the best way to face it.

She turned as Paul came into the kitchen, slim in his black tracksuit and trainers. 'Are you all right? You look exhausted?' Too much shagging and not enough sleep, no doubt – forget the sympathy.

'Thanks. You really know how to make a chap feel good about himself.'

'I'm sorry. Come and sit down.' She patted the seat beside her. 'I want to talk to you about something.'

He went over to the fridge and poured himself a large glass of cranberry juice, then turned towards her. She was shocked by how serious he looked.

'And there's something I must tell you.'

Her stomach lurched. So this was how it happened. This was how twenty-nine years of marriage came to an end. No fanfare, no bells or bunting – just a quiet announcement that would irrevocably change the course of their lives. Not only their lives, but their children's too. While her world stood still, the world outside kept turning. As if to underline the point, a burst of laughter came from people passing the house and a car horn sounded.

'Jack in?' He walked towards her, looking as if every step cost him an effort, then sat on the other leg of the L-shaped sofa and lay back against the cushions with his eyes shut.

'No. I don't think so.' Her voice emerged as more of a whisper than she'd intended.

'Good.'

Kate said nothing. She wasn't going to make it easy for him.

'I had no idea this was going to happen.' He sounded tired and beaten.

'I can imagine.' She could hear the bitterness and anger in her own voice.

He opened his eyes, surprised. 'You know? How?'

'I'm not an idiot, Paul. All the signs were there.'

'But I didn't see them, so how on earth could you?'

'What do you mean you didn't see them? We've become so distant over the last weeks. No . . .' She raised a hand to stop him interrupting. 'Let me finish.'

He subsided against the cushions again, all the fight gone out of him.

'There are all the little things like the hair, the aftershave, how particular you've got about the ties you wear, the gym, the number of times you've stayed late at the office. Shall I go on?' She let her anger take over as she realised the injustice of what was happening to her. 'Have you considered the children? What will they think?' She stood quickly and, in the ensuing silence, walked swiftly to the sink where she ran herself a glass of cold water. 'Paul, how could you?' As she turned back to confront him, his groan became a sigh.

'My God. You think I've been having an affair.' He sat up on the edge of the sofa, elbows on his knees, head in his hands. 'If it weren't so far off beam, it would be funny.'

She stood in the kitchen, staring at him, relief flooding through her. But if he wasn't having an affair, what could possibly be the matter? She realised then that it wasn't so much that he looked exhausted but that he looked old. Fear took the place of relief. She crossed the room and sat beside him, taking one of his hands. He didn't resist. 'Whatever's happened?'

Paul looked up at her, his eyes empty. 'I've been fired.'

Kate gasped. 'What? I don't understand. When did this happen? Why didn't you tell me what was going on?'

Paul drained his glass and made to stand up. 'I think we need something stronger, don't you?'

'Let me.' Kate went over to the drinks cupboard and emptied the remains of a bottle of whisky into two glasses. He took his and gulped it down. 'Go easy,' she said. 'Tell me what's happened. The last I heard, you were the one doing the firing.'

'Oh, I was.' He gave a hollow laugh. 'That bastard Tom Jenkins, jumped-up little prick, got me to do his dirty work for him. He got me to negotiate the redundancies of fifteen people. Then he fired me.'

'When did this happen?'

'Late yesterday afternoon. He called me in, thanked me

for my efforts, then told me they had no further use for me, that my job was now redundant. I tried to call you but you were tied up.'

'But not all night,' she protested.

'I know, but then I went for a drink with Chris Phillips and when he went home . . . well, I suppose I wanted some time to absorb it on my own. When I got back, you were asleep and when I woke up, you'd gone to work.'

She remembered how the bedroom had smelt like a bar when she'd got up, as if alcohol was seeping from every pore of his body. Angry, she had decided to leave him to it, hoping he'd have a hangover from hell. 'I still don't understand why you didn't call me on my mobile.'

'I wanted to tell you face to face.'

'I'd have come home.'

'Would you? You thought I was having an affair, remember?' He smiled. 'Never, Kate. Never. We've been through that and we'll never go through it again. I meant the promise I made you then.'

'But what about the hair, the gym . . . ?' The penny dropped. These hadn't been tactics employed to impress a new woman. They were to impress his colleagues, the young bloods now running the show who judged a man finished if he'd seen the wrong side of forty, let alone fifty. Paul had clung on for as long as he could but now he was facing the fact that, whatever he did, he wasn't one of them any more, and never would be again. Her heart went out to him. She knew how much it mattered.

'I know it's a bad time, but there must be other jobs.'

He shook his head. 'Come on. It's over. They salve their

consciences with a big pay-off and I walk into the sunset. I've got to face it. I'm fifty-seven and too old to start again. It's consultancy work and non-executive directorships from now on. Want another?'

She shook her head. While he went off to find another bottle, she remembered Bea talking about her need to control the timing of when and how she left Coldharbour, if it ever turned out that she had to. Paul must have felt the same way. For the last weeks he had sensed the control slipping from his hands without consciously realising it. The shock and humiliation must have been terrible. She could imagine how low he must feel right now. At least money wasn't the issue, thank God. And at least she could help, now that she knew what was going on. How selfish she'd been.

When he came back, she got up and hugged him tight.

'Whoa, hang on. I'm going to drop the bottle,' he gasped, extricating himself to put it down, then returning to her arms. 'What's all this about?'

'I am so, so sorry,' she said, leaning her head into the hollow beneath his collarbone. 'I'm such an idiot to have doubted you.'

'I don't blame you. I should have talked to you but then I would have had to admit to myself that something was wrong. And we've both been so busy.'

'I know. I thought when the children left home life would be easier but that's not how it's turned out. I suppose I've thrown myself into work so I don't have to think about them living their own lives – Sam thousands of miles away. Emails are great but they're not the same. I was so pleased when Pete and the others asked me to be a partner in the practice that I didn't think of the effect the extra workload might have on us. And I can't backtrack now.'

'I wouldn't want you to. This isn't your fault. I've seen plenty of men my age go the same way, some of them even sooner. Deep down, I've known that I couldn't last for ever, but I didn't want to acknowledge it. I should have prepared myself better.'

They sat down and talked, leaning against one another on the sofa. Kate knew it would take time to repair the damage to Paul's self-esteem, and for him to decide where he wanted to go next in life. But the best thing to come out of this evening was that there was nothing fundamentally wrong with their relationship, nothing that a little time and attention couldn't put right.

23

Despite having her left wrist in plaster, Adele had managed to make her trademark minestrone, learned during her and Bob's lifelong love affair with Italy, and eaten by the family for Sunday supper ever since. Sitting with her at the scrubbed pine table in front of the Aga, grating Parmesan, Bea was, as always, transported back to her childhood. The blue and white patterned plates had never changed, replacements easily picked up at car-boot sales or in the covered market, the Duralex tumblers likewise. There was the familiar semi-circular burn on the table from a casserole that should have been put on a mat, the W scored by Will's compasses when he was bored doing his maths homework, its patina darkened with age. She remembered the whack he'd got when their parents had finally noticed it. The large dresser was littered with correspondence, notices of what was going on locally, snapshots of the grandchildren, unopened mail-order catalogues, anything that hadn't been found a home when the table was cleared for a meal. Above her head, a fraction nearer the Aga, the Kitchen Maid was hung with Adele's tights, a bunch of dried lavender and a couple of tea-towels. The smell of newly baked bread drifted round them. She closed her eyes to the thin layer of dust that coated the less used surfaces. Whenever she came here, she was at home.

Bea had noticed with some sadness that, now Adele had accepted an offer on the house, she had made a start on sorting things out. The cupboards upstairs were virtually empty apart from Adele's own wardrobe, and the furniture she was expecting the local auction house to shift was marked with large red stickers. Books had disappeared from the shelves, pictures from the walls and in every room boxes waited to be packed, marked 'junk' and 'to go'. Bea felt so proud of her mother. She admired her determination to get what she wanted from life, even at her age. Just shows, she thought, it's never too late. At the same time, she couldn't help that feeling of nostalgia. Adele's move would mark the final death knell to her childhood.

'Well?' asked Adele, who was looking particularly spry today.

'Well what? You're the one who said she had something to tell me.' Adele had asked her over for an early supper because she had something she wanted to say. With Ben at football until nine that evening, Bea had agreed, but not without pressing her mother to tell her what was so special.

'No. I need to think about it a little more. All things come to she who waits.' With that Delphic remark she hung up.

That was so Adele. If Bea had heard her say that once, she'd heard it a thousand times. She sometimes felt as if she'd been kept waiting all her childhood: for sweets (two a week), for surprises (birthdays and Christmas), for pets (a cat, two dogs and a small assortment of rodents scattered over eighteen years), for decisions (after the subject had been thrashed to death with the rest of the family), for information (after begging to be told). Had she enjoyed any of them more for the delay? She thought not. Adele had been a mother bringing up her family not long after the war when things had been scarce and, as she never failed to remind them, treats were all the more special precisely because they were few and far between. She was determined not to spoil her children and had succeeded. It didn't take a genius to work out how differently each of the three had reacted to their upbringing. Will had escaped to Oz; Jess was leading a life in which every whim could be satisfied immediately; and while Bea would in some ways have liked that, she affected to despise her sister's lifestyle and tried to accept delayed gratification as part of her own. Or so she believed.

'Come on. Spit it out,' Bea encouraged her mother.

'That can wait for a moment. How's it going with Mark?'

'Far too soon to say.' Bea felt like screaming with frustration but knew better and decided to play along.

'I thought he was a good man when you both came down. You could do worse, Bea.' Adele's eyes crinkled at the corners with a hopeful smile. As she pushed her hair back from her face, Bea could see the attractive younger woman she must have been.

'It's early days but he seems to understand me better than Colin ever did.' Bea laughed.

'You thought he understood at the beginning.'

'Oh, yes. What was to understand? A woman with a

wickedly sweet tooth whose biological clock was ticking and who liked a good book. Do you know, we stayed together for almost fifteen years? That's nearly as long as a minimum life sentence for murder. And I can tell you that sometimes it felt as if it might become one.'

They laughed, and Bea cut a couple of slices of the still warm loaf, spreading hers with butter that melted immediately.

'But you like him? Mark, I mean.' There she went again. A little nudge that would become more insistent until the whole lot came spilling out. Bea looked across the table at her mother, diminutive and kindly in her neat duck-egg blue twinset and stripy red and white apron. She'd never lost interest in what went on in her daughter's life.

'Why are you suddenly so keen to partner me off with him?' For a reason she couldn't quite put her finger on, she was irritated by her mother's insistence.

'I thought that was what you were looking for. Otherwise, why all that dating malarkey?'

She had a point. After all, Bea had often travelled down to bore her for hours with her deliberations over the different men she'd met and their total unsuitability to become anyone's life-partner, let alone hers.

'I know, I know. That was why I started doing it, but the more I think about it, the more I realise I don't want someone cluttering up my house again with their razors and shoes and opinions. I like having my wardrobe to myself and, to be honest, my bed too. Don't get me wrong, Mum.' Adele was looking a tad dubious. 'I love the sex and all that but it's the extras that come with it. Who wants the snoring and duvet-snatching every night of their life? Meeting all those guys, some more desirable than others admittedly, and seeing Ellen and Oliver together has taught me something: lover, yes; live-in lover, no.'

Adele began to laugh again. 'You're a dear girl after my own heart.' She gathered up their plates and, having stacked them in the old sink, foraged in the freezer for her homemade elderflower ice-cream, one of Bea's childhood favourites.

'Mum!'

'Not the sex bit. Not any more anyway, more's the pity.' She ignored Bea's look. 'It's the independence thing. When your father was alive, I never thought of myself as anything other than his wife, but after he died I realised I had a choice. I could either do nothing and moulder away or I could decide what I wanted from the rest of my life and grasp what it offered before it was too late. You're the same. If staying apart's the kind of relationship that's going to work for you and Mark, then I'm not going to argue. You'll do what you want to do anyway. You always have.'

'Not strictly true. Anyway Mark and I aren't even close to living together. We haven't even slept together. We're going to Norfolk next weekend and we'll see what happens. Early days. Besides, I've got far too much on my plate at work to think about that at the moment.'

'I thought things were better on that front.' Adele pulled open the table drawer for the teaspoons before reaching down the blue bowls from the top shelf of the dresser.

'So did I. But I was wrong. The ghastly Amanda is getting her talons into Adam and her knives out for me. I don't think I've got a chance. The all-too-brief honeymoon's over.'

'Then why don't you think about leaving?'

'Leave?' What a question. 'I couldn't possibly. What about Stuart and my authors?'

'If Stuart's as good as you say he is, he'll be fine. And the authors will find their own way, you know.'

'No. It's not an option at the moment.' Yet oddly, as she spoke, she was aware that a little seed had taken root in her mind. 'Besides, I couldn't afford it.'

Adele scooped out a couple of good-sized dollops of ice-cream. Bang went those resolutions again. 'Thanks to Colin, you haven't got a mortgage.'

'Thanks to that divine barrister who did the divorce settlement, you mean. I wouldn't have minded getting to know him a little better.' He had been like a character from Central Casting, she recalled with a flutter. A young Gregory Peck without the American accent.

'Honestly, Bea! Have you no shame? Apart from the roof over your head, you've got enough clothes to last you a lifetime and alimony to help you with Ben. So you don't need all that much. But that does bring me to why I asked you down tonight.'

At last.

'I've decided to share some of the profit I'm making on the house with you, Will and Jess. Don't worry,' she stopped Bea's protest, "I'm keeping most of it to cover the worst eventualities that might happen when I finally reach life's departure lounge. Though I hope I get struck down long before that. But if the time comes when I can't look after myself there'll be enough to cover some sort of care home, God help me. The only catch is that I must keep going for another seven years, so there won't be any tax to pay on whatever I give you. Bloody government.'

'Mum, I don't want it anyway. It's yours.'

'That's not how I see it. This house was all of ours. So all of us deserve something from its sale. And perhaps this might buy you a bit of time to think about doing something different with your life. Anyway, it would give me enormous pleasure to see what you do with it. Better than waiting till I'm dead and gone. There's no more to be said.'

'Something different?' It was an absurd suggestion. She wasn't trained for anything else and had no idea what she could possibly do outside the world of books.

'Why not? I am, so why can't you? Think about it, Bea. That's all I'm suggesting. If you decide you don't need the money, you can always save it for Ben.'

Bea looked across the table at her mother, returning her sharp gaze. Her iron-grey hair framed a determined expression. Bea had learned long ago there was no point in arguing with Adele when she had made up her mind. The only thing to do was to make up her own, and in that split second, she did so. Pushing back her chair, she stood up and walked around the table to give Adele a big hug.

'Thank you. It's going to be really helpful when, and if, I make a change.'

'That's just what I hoped you'd say. Now, what else have you got to tell me?'

'I want to talk to you about Ellen.'

*

Looking back over the day, Ellen could see that storm clouds had been gathering all afternoon. Oliver had arrived just as she was putting together a scratch sandwich lunch. Matt was in a state of high excitement at the prospect of a friend's football party and sleep-over – on a Sunday! Emma had patched up her differences with Freya and they were now inseparable again. If they weren't together, Emma spent hours closeted in her bedroom, giggling with Freya on the phone. Now she announced she would be staying overnight at Freya's.

Normally Ellen drew the line at the children being away on the night before a school day but she had managed to convince herself to bend the rules. Their absence meant that she could have Oliver to herself. For once, they didn't need to snatch a hurried hour or two at the flat but had the whole evening together.

That afternoon, though, the children were being particularly trying, so she made allowances for his tetchiness with them. Why should he be consistently pleasant when his attempts to forge any kind of relationship with Emma were met by a brick wall? She was either dismissive or plain rude. Ellen felt like shaking her, embarrassed that her daughter could be so ill-mannered, but at the same time she didn't want to cause a scene by saying anything. Meanwhile Matt wouldn't keep still or quiet. He dashed around the house, noisy and insistent. Aware of Oliver's worsening mood, Ellen had taken her son to one side and asked him to calm down – with no effect whatsoever.

By the time they had left, she felt completely ragged, exhausted by the efforts she'd made to keep the peace.

She'd been careful to make Oliver's ham sandwich with just the amount of mustard that she knew he liked. She'd uncorked a bottle of his favourite Sauvignon. She insisted he didn't help but sat him in a quietish corner with the *Observer* and a drink. She suggested Emma and Matt went upstairs to pack their stuff. But she couldn't stop the frenzy of family life intruding and Oliver plainly wasn't in the mood to tolerate it. He fortified himself with a couple of glasses of wine but, judging from his thunderous expression, they didn't improve matters.

At last the children left and a blessed silence descended on the house. However, Ellen's hopes that the atmosphere would change with their absence had been misplaced. The children might not be there, but they had clearly irritated Oliver beyond the point of no return. He remained monosyllabic, clearly not in the mood for conversation. They ate supper on their knees in silence, watching a dullish episode of *Midsomer Murders*.

On the way to bed, their exchanges had been kept to a minimum. But what did she expect, she asked herself, as she brushed her teeth. He didn't have family of his own and wasn't used to the pandemonium, the constant demands and changes of mood. It was unreasonable to imagine he would adapt immediately, especially when Emma was making things so difficult. She would be patient and do whatever it took to smooth over this difficult period of transition. Everyone was allowed an off-day or two, including Oliver.

When she returned to the bedroom she found him standing by her side of the bed in his boxers, her photograph of Simon in his hand. A slight frown creased his forehead and a pale blue vein she'd never noticed before had appeared at the left side of his temple. She imagined the blood pumping through it.

'What's the matter?' She crossed the room to stand beside him, touching his arm.

He flinched, then moved away from her, almost bumping into the chair where she'd left her clothes.

'What's wrong?' she persisted. 'I know the kids have been a pain today but that's what they're like. They'll come round in the end.' But how many times am I going to have to reassure him before they do?

'It isn't the children.' He sounded terse, angry.

She sat on the edge of the bed, mystified. 'Well, what, then? The job-hunting?'

'I wish you wouldn't go on and on about that. I've told you I'm doing my best.' As he turned to face her, he was flushed with anger. 'I don't know what else you want me to do.'

'Don't be like this. Please,' she appealed, patting the duvet beside her. 'Sit down with me. Let's talk about it. I know things have been more difficult than we'd envisaged since Em and Matt came back but I'm trying my best to make everything work. That's what I want more than anything.'

'Do you?' She was shocked by the force of his question. 'Do you, really?' Instead of sitting by her, he began to pace the room.

'Of course. You know I do.' How could he believe anything else after all they'd said to each other? 'What's happened to you? I really don't understand.'

He ignored her last question, stopping to stare at the photo in his hand. 'Why do you insist on sleeping with this by your bed?' His voice was low, unloving suddenly.

'My picture of Simon? He's always been there. You know that.' A cold arrow of anxiety found its way to her heart.

'Have you ever thought about how I feel, with him watching us all the time?'

She couldn't read his expression – or perhaps she didn't want to try. 'You've never said anything before.' She cursed herself for not having moved the photo weeks ago, but whenever she'd thought about it, something had always stopped her.

'I'm saying it now.' His mouth twisted as he thrust the frame towards her so she was looking straight at Simon. 'How can you expect me to make love to you with your husband looking on?'

'I honestly never thought . . . but it's only a photo. I can easily move him.' Ellen didn't understand how or why things had deteriorated so badly between them. She wanted to defuse the situation, but Oliver's temper had made him unreachable all day. Now more than ever. She reached for the picture but he raised it above his head, out of her reach.

Then he threw it across the room with as much force as he could muster. Seconds seemed like minutes as she watched the frame spin through the air and smash against the wardrobe. The noise reverberated around the room as the glass shattered, flying from the frame, leaving Simon looking up through the few remaining splinters. For a second, both Ellen and Oliver stood staring at each other, stunned by what had just happened. The noise seemed to have shocked Oliver out of his rage: a hand covered his mouth and his eyes were wide and unreadable. Ellen was the first to move.

'Have you completely lost your mind? There was absolutely no need for that.' She snatched up the picture and ran from the room.

'Ellen! Wait.'

But she had no intention of waiting. Nothing that had happened during the afternoon had justified this. Her only thought was to get as far away from Oliver as possible. She ran downstairs and into the kitchen. She wanted to be alone, to think, but there was nowhere she could escape him. She could hear him moving about upstairs. Then she saw the key to the shed gleaming on the hook by the french windows. Within moments she was padding barefoot across the damp grass and unlocking her studio. She sank onto the sofa bed, her head spinning.

She had no idea how much time passed before she began to notice how cold she was. The house was in darkness. The half-moon was hazy behind cloud. Oliver hadn't even tried to follow her outside. She replayed that afternoon and evening again. Everything had obviously got on top of him so she should try to understand that. But to break something he knew was so very precious to her? That she couldn't understand. However, she didn't want to stay in the shed all night so she steeled herself to return to the house and a confrontation. He couldn't be allowed to get away with that.

Turning the handle of the kitchen door, she thought she caught a glimpse of movement on the stairs. Then it was gone. She turned the handle again. She was as sure as she could be that she had left the lock unsnibbed. Not now. She shook the door. There was no question: it was locked.

'Oliver!' she whispered, as loudly as she dared, not wanting to wake the neighbours. 'Oliver!'

No answer.

Had he followed her down, watched her let herself into the shed and then shut her out? Surely not. He had snapped out of his temper when the glass smashed. She had seen for herself how shocked he had been by his own action. But how else could the door have locked? Could she have been mistaken about the snib? Perhaps in her haste, she hadn't secured it properly. She didn't want to admit to herself what she knew to be the truth.

A light drizzle had set in. Wrapping her arms round herself in a useless attempt to keep warm and thanking God she'd had the presence of mind to grab an old cardigan from the back of a kitchen chair, she retreated to the shed to consider her options. The bedroom was at the front of the house so he wouldn't hear a stone against the back windows. The safety glass she'd installed to protect the children meant she couldn't break in. The overgrown trellis around the garden wall prevented her climbing over. In any case, there was only a faint landing light glowing from one of the neighbours' houses. They had obviously all gone to bed. She would have to spend the night wrapped up in the two blankets she remembered were trussed in the base of the sofa-bed and hope she didn't freeze to death. Furious, she put Simon's photo on the table where she could see it and began to organise herself.

*

Ellen woke, rigid with cold, as dawn cast a flat grey light through the shed windows. For a second she didn't remember where she was but then, as the events of the previous night came back to her, she sat up, confused. What had happened had taken on the insubstantiality of the dreams that had possessed her during her few hours of sleep. Something had made Oliver snap. How responsible was she for that? She couldn't help him with a job but she should have been able to deal better with Emma than she had. Perhaps then this might have been avoided. She found it almost impossible to credit what had happened but the broken photo frame was proof. She got up and started moving about in an effort to reboot her circulation.

She made herself a cup of coffee and decided that as soon as she was safely indoors she would have it out with him. However badly the children provoked him, his behaviour was totally unacceptable. It was then that she noticed the blood that had flowed onto her nightdress from a cut on her finger.

Eventually she saw the light go on in the kitchen. Moments afterwards Oliver was running across the grass to the shed. He flung open the door. 'Ellen! My love! What happened?'

'You locked me out. Why?' She was determined not to give an inch.

'But I thought you'd gone into Em's room to get away from me. I didn't blame you after what I'd done. I had no idea you were out here.'

She was almost convinced but couldn't stop herself stiffening as he put his arms round her. If he noticed, he ignored it.

'You must have been freezing. I'm so, so sorry. I can't apologise enough. I don't know what came over me.' He stroked the hair from her forehead as if she was a child. 'Everything got on top of me. I know that's not an excuse but I promise, absolutely promise, nothing like that will ever happen again.'

Her resolve to maintain her distance dissolved as she felt the warmth of his body, his touch. She let him lead her back to the house where he ran her a bath, fetched a clean towel and then her clothes. Nothing was too much trouble. At last, won over by his repeated apologies for his unwarranted display of temper, his assurances that there would be no repeat performance, his explanation of his frustration with the children, which he had tried to control, and his anxiety about finding a job, she forgave him.

She wanted their relationship to work. She wanted a stepfather for Emma and Matt, however reluctant they were to have one. After so long, she wanted someone to look after her as well. She didn't want to entertain any doubts that would spoil what they had. Her certainty that he was the man for her would surely pull them through. This episode had been a hiccup that in time they would forget.

24

Between the thin cotton curtains, Bea could just make out the skeletal outlines of trees through a blurring of mist. Drops of condensation trailed down the panes of glass, pooling on the window ledge above the woefully ineffective night storage heater. The throbbing above her right eye intensified as she tried to roll back up the slope of the mattress away from Mark, gathering the blankets round her as she did so. How she longed for the easy warmth of her multi-togged duvet and her pocket-sprung mattress at home. She tried to ease the grip on her memory of last night's events but they refused to let go.

Ben had gone to spend the weekend with his father amid many complaints. She had managed to guilt-trip him into agreeing to go by pointing out how long it had been since he'd seen his half-sisters, how much his father missed him, then slipped in the added temptation of Carrie's excellent (damn her) cooking. After he'd left, she dipped into an unpromising manuscript until Mark had eventually picked her up to drive to Norfolk. He was running too late for them to find somewhere open for supper on the way.

Instead, having failed to spot even a chippie, they'd stopped at a Spar garage on the A11 to stock up with a few emergency rations before finally arriving at the cottage close to midnight. Nervous of what the rest of the night had in store, they both rushed to open the first of the two Cabernet Sauvignon wine-boxes. Even the almost teetotal Mark glugged back the large glass he poured himself with obvious relief.

Then he had given Bea the two-minute tour, drawing the curtains and turning up the storage heaters as they went. The front door opened straight into the dining room where three chairs circled a round table with a dusty dried-flower arrangement. To the right, a tiny whitewashed kitchen held an old-style gas cooker with eye-level gas grill, a butler's sink with wooden draining board, a fifties yellow metal cabinet and a large chopping-board sitting on an ancient fridge. So, cooking would be basic to non-existent, she registered with some relief. At least he wouldn't be expecting her to knock up a three-course gourmet meal. Back through the dining room to the sitting room, where some tired armchairs and a sofa focused on a gaping inglenook fireplace with an aged TV to one side. At the far end there was a door to the garden with a nine-mile-an-hour draught racing in over the tiled floor, until Bea replaced the jolly snake draught excluder that had been kicked to one side. On the right was the bathroom with a single-bar electric fire that Mark switched on with a pull of its cord. O Health and Safety, where art thou? Bea cast her eyes heavenwards and saw dark patches of damp bubbling the plaster on the pale blue walls.

Upstairs in the eaves there were three bedrooms, one leading through to the next. All Bea noticed was the sub-zero temperature, the dead flies on the windowsills and the extremely uncomfortable-looking double brass bedstead (the only one) that they'd presumably be sharing later. Cue another drink. Swiftly followed by another when she spotted mouse droppings back in the kitchen.

As he showed her around, Mark continually apologised for the lack of a decent heating system, the mice ('Sweet little field mice – you'll see'), the long drive, the lack of shops. Bea countered with repeated reassurances that every-thing was just as she'd imagined. However, not for a moment had she imagined that when he'd said 'basic' he'd meant it. She hadn't realised how basic things could get in the wilds of Norfolk. As he set about lighting a fire, Bea busied herself making cheese on toast with the plastic Cheddar and cotton-wool bread they'd picked up on the way, and took it through.

The strains of James Taylor came from the record player at the back of the room. Bea could see several LPs that she recognised at a glance, strewn on the rag rug beneath the listing standard lamp: Dory Previn, Fleetwood Mac, Nick Drake, Leonard Cohen, the Lovin' Spoonful, Country Joe, the Byrds and, of course, the daddy of them all, Dylan. A record collection speaks volumes about a man, she thought.

Fortified by yet another glass of wine, they sat huddled together on the sagging sofa in front of the fire, plates on their knees. The flames roared up the chimney, taking most of the heat with them. Bea and Mark kicked off their shoes and stretched their feet into the fireplace as near as they dared.

'It's always like this to start with at this time of year. I should have warned you,' said Mark. 'By tomorrow it should feel much warmer, now I've turned the heating up. Here, have my sister's gloves.'

Bea could feel that he was beginning to relax a little now, just as her initial misgivings were surrendering to the influence of the wine. As she slipped on the knitted fingerless gloves, she realised her feet were suddenly burning hot and pulled them back with a yelp, almost knocking her plate to the floor. Within seconds, they were freezing again and she gingerly moved them nearer to the fire. He laughed and took her hand. 'What would you like to do tomorrow?'

They were on safe territory here. 'Whatever you recommend.' She extricated her hand so that she could pick up her last bit of toast.

'Perhaps we should wait and see what the weather's like. The forecast isn't great but we should be able to get out for a bit.' He put his plate on the floor, then straightened up and made a sudden lunge for her. She swiftly swallowed her toast, then gave herself up to him, wanting to enjoy whatever he had to offer. This was, after all, one of the reasons they had come. His tentative kisses grew more insistent as she lay back, trying to ignore the spring that threatened to work its way through to her spine. He smelt of lemons and cedar and his skin was soft against hers. She felt his tongue against her lips, promising and not too pushy, but when she opened her mouth in response she was appalled to find herself locked into the fast cycle of a washing-machine, his tongue everywhere, their teeth clashing. She pulled back for a moment, wiped her mouth as subtly as she could and took a sip of her wine. 'Let's take it slowly.'

'Is something wrong?' He looked so anxious that her heart went out to him.

'Of course not. I'm just a bit rusty, that's all. Just need a bit of Dutch courage.' She leaned forward and decided to take back the initiative with one or two gentle hints as to what might float her boat.

Next morning, the veil that Bea would have preferred to draw over the rest of the evening kept snagging on incidents that refused to be forgotten. For a start, just as things were hotting up, techniques improving with use, they'd had to call a halt because Mark remembered he'd forgotten to make the bed. He sprinted down the path to the car where the laundered sheets were chilling on the back seat. By the time they'd turned the corners and replaced the blankets in the glacial atmosphere of the bedroom, all desire had frozen. Undressing each other would take too long so they hurled their clothes onto the floor and leaped between the icy sheets, grabbing each other for warmth. Minutes later, Bea was out of bed searching in her bag for socks before her feet got frostbite. Later again, Mark remembered he'd forgotten to put up the fireguard and was worried they'd burn the place down. Then he couldn't find the condoms in his wallet and, with a flailing arm, Bea knocked her glass of wine over the bedside table. Eventually came the crowning memory of her consoling him when he had, as he put it, 'severe hydraulic failure'.

'Plenty of men can't get it up the first time,' she soothed, uncertain that there was even a grain of truth in what she'd said.

'Are you sure?'

'Absolutely. I've known several.'

'Really?'

Even in the dim glow of the bedside light, she could see he was somewhat taken aback.

'Well, not *all* of them with me, of course. I just read it somewhere.' She didn't want him to think he'd ended up, after all, with a complete ball-breaker. She was only making it up to reassure him. 'I'm happy just lying here with you. Honestly.'

So that was what they'd done, talking and sipping wine until they could talk and sip no more. And now she was paying the price.

After such an inauspicious start, her heart sank at the thought of the weekend ahead. The weather was clearly going to be grim and they would be imprisoned in this basic cottage, trying to have sex or not trying at all. Oh, God. She groaned.

'What is it?' As he turned towards her, drowsy, shifting the balance of the mattress, she slid back down into the middle of the bed and his arms. She felt too fragile to resist, despite her desire to avoid a repeat performance. Sleepily, slowly, they embraced as she came to realise that the malfunction of the previous night had quite definitely been rectified. Relaxed by sleep, the cautious fumblings she'd rather not remember had been transformed into something approaching a technique. Despite her nagging headache, she let herself go with the flow only to be pleasantly surprised. Quick maybe, but spontaneous, sexy and definitely with the promise of greater things to come. As the weekend took a turn for the better, the veil that she'd been trying to draw over the last evening slipped into place.

He ran her a bath and, while she tried to find the courage to abandon the warmth of the water, he knocked up breakfast: bacon and eggs, toast and cafetière coffee. Dressed in leggings, trousers, thermal vest, a T-shirt, two jumpers and the fingerless gloves, Bea began to feel she was getting to grips with this living-in-the-country lark. 'It's not the weather that's the problem, it's the clothes you wear': that was what Adele used to say in the days before they'd got central heating.

With the curtains open, she could see that they had arrived at a pretty brick-and-flint cottage surrounded by a rudimentary garden with a couple of flowerbeds on either side of the path between the front door and the gate. Beyond the garden there were fields to right and left with not another house in sight.

'By this evening, the old place should be quite snug,' Mark said, a trifle on the optimistic side, Bea felt. 'Why don't we go for a walk, find a pub for lunch and then see where we go from there? The mist'll probably lift by lunchtime.'

Parking in Queen Anne's Drive by Holkham Hall, they passed several optimistic birders armed with high-powered binoculars. Mark pointed out to her some black-headed gulls, Brent geese and a sparrow hawk but nothing more exotic. They took the sandy path at Holkham Bay through the silent pinewoods, eerie in the mist, emerging onto the dunes towards Burnham Overy Staithe. Clambering through the marram grass down to the beach, they walked along the wet sand, kicking at stones and knots of seaweed, picking up pieces of sculpted driftwood, puzzling over the mysterious presence of a large red fire extinguisher, talking all the while. When Mark took her hand, Bea didn't object. From Gun Hill, they crossed back over the dunes and turned down beside the creek, taking the raised path across the wide expanse of marsh. As Mark had predicted, the mist had begun to lift so they could just make out the windmill, its black body capped white, its sails still, beyond the neat brick and clapboard buildings of the village. As they approached, the faint jingling of halyards carried across the mud flats towards them. A short walk took them to the coast road and the Hero, a gastropub where they ate a good lunch, Bea surprised by how comfortable she felt.

Afterwards they set off again, walking quickly, aware that they hadn't long before dark. Their path took them inland towards Holkham Hall, through its landscaped estate, past the lake and the Hall itself, then following the drive through a herd of deer back to where they'd parked.

'God, I'm exhausted.' Bea collapsed into the car, feeling as if her legs and back were fused in a long line of pain.

'Was that too far for you?' Mark looked concerned. 'I'm sorry. I love that walk because it packs in so much that's great about this part of Norfolk – beach, woods, marshes, countryside and the formal grounds of the Hall. I wanted you to see it all.'

'It was just a tiny bit longer than I'm used to, that's all.' Only about five miles longer, she thought, as she unlaced her shoes, rejoicing in the overwhelming feeling of release that spread through her feet and up her legs. She might never be able to move again.

'Come here.' Sitting in the encroaching darkness, Mark pulled her towards him.

Then again, perhaps she would.

*

Back at the cottage, now warmed through as he'd promised, Bea realised how much she wanted the weekend to go on. The promise of dinner in Wells, a bed stuffed with hot-water bottles and a jigsaw if the weather didn't improve the next day was all she needed. Stuck in the middle of nowhere with a man she was beginning to like rather more than she'd expected, she felt that London was part of some other life. When Mark went out to get more logs, she settled herself by the fire only to discover that she couldn't concentrate on the proof of an over-hyped American novel she hadn't been able to stop herself packing just in case she had a free moment.

The previous week at Coldharbour had whizzed by. Not for months, even years, could she remember feeling so positive about her work. She'd rediscovered some of the enthusiasm she'd thought she'd lost for ever. Adam's way of working was a refreshing change from the way things had been run in the past. He had brought a new energy into the office, not that she trusted him. Once the initial shake-up was over, he'd gone out of his way to encourage and refocus everyone who'd stayed. Not a man who managed from behind a closed door, he spent a good amount of time walking around, getting to know everyone and talking to them about what they were doing.

After an initial flurry of resentment at what was seen as distrust of their working methods and concern that he was just looking for a way to get rid of them, most people had settled down to appreciate his direct involvement and the trouble he was taking. Despite his alarming reputation, he was a dynamic leader who, for all the market problems, still believed in editorial integrity and leadership. He liked people who played their hunches and gave them the scope they needed. He wanted the back-up of sales projections but would support his staff when he saw belief and commitment, just as he had when Bea had bought *Bare Bones*. By the same token, she didn't doubt for a moment that he'd show no mercy at the first slip-up.

The fly in the ointment was Amanda. She'd shown her colours at the away-day so Bea knew exactly what she was up against. Already she'd heard from a number of agents that Amanda was presenting herself as senior to Bea, as well as implying that any decisions about the publishing programme had to be sanctioned by her. In other words, they would be best advised to submit material and any concerns straight to Amanda, cutting out Bea altogether. But two could play at that game. Without making a fuss, Bea had assured the same people that nothing had changed. She was sure they would remain loyal to her.

The latch on the front door rattled and she heard Mark's shout. Reluctant to leave the fireside, she tore herself away to find him on the front step laden with a boxful of logs.

'Should have done this much earlier. I could hardly see

what I was doing. Still I was right, wasn't I? The second night's always much warmer than the first.'

'In more ways than one, I hope,' replied Bea, as suggestively as she dared.

'I'm sure we can make it as warm as we want.' He grinned as he lugged the box through to the inglenook.

And, indeed, by the time they left at Sunday lunchtime, Bea had no complaints. The weather had closed in, with a gale that howled in from the coast, so after Mark had gone out for the Sunday papers, they settled themselves round the fire with Radio 4 in the background and relaxed. She had even come round to the concept of 'basic' and, before they left, had promised that she would visit again. In the spring, perhaps.

*

By the time she got home, the prodigal son had returned from Colin's so Bea set about killing the fatted calf (rather, roast chicken and potatoes – his favourite) for his supper. As she pottered in the kitchen, she thought about Mark and how well they had got on. Once they'd relaxed with each other, the inauspicious start had given way to something much more satisfactory that demanded further practice, she decided. Perhaps Let's Have Lunch had something of an instinct for these things after all.

As she served up, Ben sloped in, like something out of an ad for heroin chic. Thinner than ever, shoulders hunched and hair all over the place, he took a seat at the table, crossing his legs. Bea decided against mentioning the risk his jeans must be posing to his circulation or asking if he was aware of the two cigarette burns in his T-shirt.

'How was your weekend?' she asked, as she bent to take the chicken from the oven. Long experience had taught her that conversations without eye-contact were the ones that went most smoothly.

'OK. Pity Dad's such a jerk.'

'Why?' She ought to discourage him from being derogatory about his father, but she couldn't resist the snippets that he brought her about her ex-husband's new life. The frisson of *Schadenfreude* was too delicious to ignore.

'He's decided he wants me to call him "Colin" instead of "Dad". "You're not a child any more." He had Colin's voice to a T. '"I think of us more as equals." What makes him think I want to be the equal of someone who made such a tit of himself leaving us for someone half his age? Everyone at school was pissing themselves about it. And I don't want to be *her* friend either. He keeps telling me we have so much in common, but we haven't.' His left foot swung back and forth, kicking the table leg. 'Anyway, the girls call him "Dad" and he is my dad too.'

'If you don't want to call him "Colin", then tell him so.' Bea was often irritated by Colin's inability to understand that, despite appearances, Ben was still a child in so many ways. Couldn't he see how difficult his son found adjusting to the idea that his father had another family? Obviously not. He would never try to get Ben in a heart-to-heart. They were alike in that way. Better to brush anything emotional under the carpet and carry on without making things worse or more uncomfortable by talking about them. However hard Colin worked to keep his relationship with Ben smooth, his underlying fear of being rejected for what he'd done was quite obvious to Bea – and maybe to Ben too.

'I did.' Another kick to the table leg. 'You know, I don't remember him ever taking me to the park. Did he?'

'I'm sure he did. Yes, of course.' In fact, she was far from sure. Colin's attitude to parenting back then had been of the hands-off variety.

'Don't bullshit me. I know he didn't.' Ben's face lit up as he smiled at her. Her heart melted. 'I don't mind that, but I don't understand what makes him think I'd want to go to the park for an hour to stand with him watching Coral and Maudie.'

'Perhaps he thinks it gives you a chance to talk to each other.'

'Mum, listen. I got an hour's lecture about why not to touch drugs. Way I see it, either I'm an adult or I'm not. He can't have it both ways.'

Bea felt a sliver of guilt as she remembered that she had asked Colin to address the drugs question. But she had assumed he would use a modicum of sense and timing. What a plonker. Whatever he'd said had obviously been dismissed, thanks to the way he'd handled things. 'He has a point about drugs,' she murmured.

'I might have known you'd side with him. Don't try and guilt me too. It won't work.'

'I'm not. Really, I'm not.'

'Where have you been anyway?' (Change the subject.)

'I went to Norfolk with Mark.' (Keep it casual.)

'That the guy you met through the dating agency?' (I'm not that interested.)

'Mmm. That enough chicken for you?' (Want to know more?)

'Good time?' (Not really.)

'Do you know? It was. We didn't do anything much but I really did enjoy his company.' She could tell that she had already lost Ben's interest. Whom she went out with didn't bother him, or affect his life, as long as she maintained a full fridge and biscuit tin, provided a laundry service, occasional company, and kept out of his affairs unless he asked for advice. But telling him about it was a way of going back over the time she and Mark had spent together. The man might not be the most obvious match she'd met, but she wouldn't put the brakes on just yet.

25

Standing at the top of the step-ladder, Ellen screwed a new halogen bulb into one of the two lines of track lighting that illuminated the gallery. She remembered Uncle Sidney's alarm when she'd told him how much her latest idea would cost and the disruption it would cause while the old wall lights were removed and the 'new-fangled' ones installed. Then, when he had seen how well they allowed the subtleties of colour in the paintings to combine, he had come round to her way of thinking.

The ring of the opening door made her turn a little too quickly so she put out a hand to steady herself before taking a step down to greet Oliver. Her heart leaped as he crossed the threshold and looked up at her.

'What on earth are you doing?' He sounded put out. Where was the 'Hello', the 'How's it going?'

She took a deep breath. Aware that her stress over the imminent exhibition was making her unnecessarily quick to criticise, she didn't want to feel irritated with anyone, least of all him. 'I'm just changing a bulb. They usually last for months but for some reason that one keeps cutting out.

I'm going to have to call the electrician.' She came down to greet him properly.

'I could see that. But what were you doing up a ladder dressed like that?'

She looked down at the full black skirt with the pale embroidery motif that they had chosen together. 'Don't worry, I'm not going to fall off. It's not like one of those pencil skirts that hobble you at the knees.'

'I'm not talking about falling off, I'm talking about customers. Wouldn't trousers be more suitable?'

'Yes, but I'm not wearing any and the job needed to be done.' She decided not to remark on such an absurdly old-fashioned view. After all, he was only thinking of her and the impression she might make.

'One bulb could wait, couldn't it?' The two slight creases between his eyebrows deepened with his frown.

'No, I don't think so. I've got Jed Sawyer coming in later to take a look at everything so I want it to be perfect for him.'

'I could have done it for you.' He snapped the step-ladder together and leaned it against the newly painted white wall. She hoped it wouldn't mark but said nothing.

'Yes, but I didn't know you were coming in. Why have you anyway?'

'I was on my way to the Portrait Gallery and I wanted to see you. But you're obviously busy.'

Why did he sound so huffy?

'Don't be like that. You know I love you dropping by.' She planted a kiss on his nose. 'Will I see you later?'

'Depends what time you're planning on being back.'

300

That same tone. She hated it when he went into victim mode, as if the world was against him and now even she was failing to offer the love and support that he felt was his due. He'd used it a couple of times recently, once because she'd supported Emma against him when he'd asked her to wash up and she'd had homework that had to be done and again when she'd wanted to meet up with Bea and Kate without him. The initial shine was definitely beginning to rub off their relationship. But that was life, she guessed. He knew what her business meant to her and how important it was to her financially. Every exhibition was at least as important as the last and had to be got absolutely right. 'I can't be too late because of the kids but I've no idea how fussy Jed will be. Some artists take ages until they're happy with how their pictures are hung. I can see why.' She paused. 'You could say there's a lot hanging on it.'

Although Oliver groaned at the pun, she was relieved to see him smile.

'Which reminds me, I must check when the drink's being delivered for the opening.'

'Why don't you let me do that? I could be useful around here.' He went over and sat behind her desk, flicking through her papers.

'I know you could but I prefer to do all these things myself. It's not that I don't trust you . . .' She stopped. Oliver looked so dejected that she almost changed her mind. 'Really.'

'I know.' He got up and started looking through the framed pictures that leaned against the wall. 'You've built the business up and you can't let it go. I'd be the same.'

301

She bit back her warning to be careful. If any of the glass broke now . . . 'You would?'

'Of course. You carry on and give me a call when you're through. Maybe I'll come round or, even better, you could escape to the flat.'

'I'll try but no promises.'

As he shut the door, he turned and blew her a kiss, then disappeared down the street. Ellen put the steps away and switched on the lights, ready to start hanging the pictures where she and Jed had planned the day before. She locked the door and put up the 'CLOSED' sign so she wouldn't be disturbed. Looking at the paintings, Ellen thought how much she loved these 'abstract landscapes', as he called them. Strong and atmospheric, the broad textural strokes and powerful use of colour conveyed the light and power that Jed saw in the land patterns and skies of the Lake District.

While waiting for him to arrive, she put the hard work off for another few minutes by sitting down with her checklist to make sure that everything would run smoothly the following evening. She ran through the invitation list to the private view, firing off reminder emails to anyone who hadn't replied. She called Emily Kirkbride, whose exhibition she had just taken down, to make sure she was expecting back the pictures that hadn't sold. Ellen was keeping three for stock and would take more once those went. She confirmed with *Time Out* that their reviewer would turn up and rang her friend Cressida at *Art Finder* magazine to check she was coming too. Majestic confirmed they would deliver the wine, ice and glasses the following afternoon.

With nothing left to do, she began to distribute the pictures around the gallery, leaning them against the walls where they'd look best. The largest went on the wall dividing the back and front room to draw visitors into the heart of the gallery. Then she shared out the rest between the two rooms, making sure the strongest works would be in key positions so the punters would keep moving around. She made a start on the hanging, stepping back every so often to make sure that each picture had enough space to speak for itself without having so much that it destroyed the effect of the whole. There was no doubt in her mind about Jed's talent. Apart from the abstracts that they were keeping towards the front of the gallery, he had recently started painting still-lifes in oils, choosing the simplest subjects – a sweet, a cherry, a small bowl of eggs or a plate of apples – most often painting them larger than life size, always concentrating on texture, light and shade. She grouped twenty together to hang on the short right-hand wall of the back room deliberately to surprise the punters with their impact. These were the ones that would sell first, she was sure.

As she worked, her mind went back to Oliver. He had gone to so much trouble all week to make up for that terrible night, constantly reassuring her that nothing like that would happen again. Although she could hardly forget the episode, she had made every effort to put it behind her. At the same time she had vowed that if he ever so much as threatened a repeat performance, he would not find her so forgiving. Constant re-evaluation was what every new relationship must involve, she reminded herself. Everyone packed the odd surprise into their emotional artillery and Oliver was no exception. She should try to be more generous.

However confident she felt, one nagging doubt still surfaced when the two of them were apart and she had time to look at their relationship objectively. Had she been too hasty in committing herself to him? Should she have waited until she knew him better? Everything had seemed so right to begin with but she had to acknowledge that their relationship had changed from how it had been during those first blissful weeks. But there were so many pressures on them now: children, rent, job. She wanted things to be as they had been but she couldn't ignore the demands of everyday life for ever.

If only he hadn't wasted all that money on that crazy romantic gesture of the shed. Despite all intentions, it stood unused (apart from the freezing night she had spent in it), a constant reminder of what she wasn't achieving and of the fact that he had paid for it while she was paying his rent. She hadn't expected their arrangement to continue beyond two or three months and her funds were already running low. One solution would be for him to move into the house, but much as she might welcome the idea, Emma was far from ready for that to happen. She knew other women in her position wouldn't let that stop them, but she wasn't one of them. Her children came first.

The previous week, two jobs that Oliver had been so certain were in the bag had come to nothing, one at the Dulwich Art Festival and the other at Marshalsea Arts, a small private gallery known to her only by name. Despite his obvious disappointment, she was pleased that he remained positive about finding something else. Having an uncertain future was difficult, but at least they knew they would be together. She smiled at the thought. Of course that was what she wanted.

There was a knock at the door. A tall, burly man in his fifties, with a head of cropped grey hair, a weather-beaten face and a short grizzled beard, stood outside. His dark-green corduroy trousers were topped by a heavy-knit brown jumper over an open-necked shirt, and he wore scuffed brown loafers on his feet.

'Jed, hi.' She shook his hand. 'I've made a start, but you may want to change things again once you see how they look.'

He came inside and stood still, taking in the room. Then his face lit up with a wide smile. 'This is fantastic.'

'Come through to the back.' Ellen led the way.

Again he took a moment to study what she had done. 'Yes, I still like your idea of putting these together and this wall's ideal.'

For the next hour or so they worked together. Jed had a clear idea of how his paintings should hang to be seen at their best but he listened to Ellen's reasons for placing the key works in certain spots. Between them they agreed exactly where everything should go and spent the rest of the day hanging them in place. Eventually Ellen left him to take a final look at both rooms. She went back to her desk and waited. She was aware of him stopping in front of each picture as if greeting an old friend. After a few minutes, she forgot about him as she concentrated on her paper-work, lost in the effort of double-checking her accounts for the show she'd just taken down.

'I was wondering whether to swap those two round.' Jed

broke her concentration and she looked up to see him pointing to two of the larger abstracts, one in autumnal, the other in winter tones. 'But now I look again, I can see that they resonate better the way they are. It works. I'm happy.'

'Are you sure?' Ellen wanted reassurance. 'We've got time to change them over.'

'I don't need to. Can I buy you a quick drink as a thank-you?'

'Let me buy you one,' she said, easy now she knew she had a good hour in hand and time to answer any of his questions about the next day. 'I should make a couple of calls first.' He nodded and went into the back to give her privacy. She dialled Oliver but was sent straight to voicemail where she left a message. Then she called home, promising Emma and Matt to be home by seven thirty.

The pub was busy but they found a seat in the back room. She pushed through to the bar to get Jed's pint and her glass of wine, then returned to join him. He sat with his back against the oak bench while she perched on a small round stool across a table that was marked with rings and covered with beer mats. She wanted to talk him through the private view, making sure that he was happy with every aspect. When she'd finished, there was a short silence.

'You've thought of everything. I don't know what to say.'

'Don't say anything until we've sold a picture or two. Then we'll know it's worked.'

'Just seeing my work displayed like that is almost enough. Honestly. If you hadn't come to Kendal last year and found me, this would never have happened.'

'If I hadn't found you, someone else would have. Jeannie was busting to tell someone about you.' Ellen remembered the woman who owned the B-and-B where she'd stayed. Small, round and aproned, she was a fount of knowledge as to what was going on in the area. Ellen had gone up there to see an artist whose work had been featured in a magazine but Jeannie had insisted she visit the painter who had rented 'the artist's place' just outside town.

She had followed directions to a small stone cottage where, alerted to her arrival, Jed had welcomed her inside. The place was furnished minimally but comfortably, giving the impression that he wasn't particularly interested in material things. At the back of the house was the studio, a large room with a north-facing window that looked across uninterrupted countryside scattered with sheep. She was immediately bowled over by his work as was he about her proposal to show it in London. Since then, they'd corresponded and spoken on the phone, making sure there was enough work to show, Jed photographing each new picture so she could see what to expect. She hadn't been disappointed.

Jed was endearingly straightforward and Ellen liked that. When he talked about the recent death of his wife, Anne, she had empathised. As the years had passed, she'd found she wanted to talk more about the devastation she'd felt when Simon died and her long journey back from there, but as time had gone on, fewer and fewer people wanted to listen. After a while, you were expected to be adjusting, not needing to grieve openly any more. Finding someone who understood that loss and could talk about it was an unexpected gift. Unlike Simon, Anne had taken her time to die. Her protracted death from cancer had been difficult for Jed, who had had to watch her ebbing away over years as her suffering increased. At least Simon had been spared that slow decline.

'That was why we ended up in Kendal,' Jed explained. 'She grew up there and we had family holidays there and she wanted to spend the last few years of her life there. When we thought she'd recovered after the first bout of cancer, we decided to move, you see. We didn't believe it would come back. You don't. Or we didn't want to. When it did, my painting became a way of coping. Anne said she liked to think of me out in the fells when I wasn't with her, recording them so she could see them too. Then, when she needed me in the house, I painted the objects around us. It turned into a kind of game as she tried to find more and more difficult challenges for me. I hadn't shown anyone else what I'd been doing till Jeannie sent you along.'

'Thank God she did. I know the show's going to be a huge success.'

'I hope you're right. Thanks to you, I'm beginning to feel as if I might have some sort of a future without Anne now.'

'I know that feeling. I was the same when Uncle Sidney asked me to work with him at the gallery. I was lost after Simon's death but working here gave me a new direction and made me feel as if I could somehow cope. And I have.'

'Let's drink to that.' He raised his glass.

'What do you think you'll do next?'

'I may look for somewhere to live in London.'

'Really?' Having seen the landscape he woke up to every day for herself, Ellen couldn't believe her ears. 'Why? How could you give up the fells?'

'Everything up there reminds me too much of Anne's death. If I'm going to start again, I've got to move away. We started out together in London, so I still have friends here. Life's about taking chances and this is one of them.'

'But will you be able to find the same inspiration down here? I'm sorry. That's naïve of me. But the landscape up there's so magnificent and so different.'

He laughed. 'You'll be surprised. This is where I began, after all. I was forced into teaching history once we'd had our boys so I never painted as much as I would have liked to back then. This will give me a chance to catch up on missed opportunities that I haven't forgotten. It'll be an interesting challenge.' He smiled at her as he drained his glass. 'You'll see.'

'I hope so.' She looked at her watch. 'The time! I must go, I'm afraid. My kids will be wondering where I am.'

'Of course.' Jed stood up to shake her hand. 'And I must find somewhere to eat.'

'Where are you staying?' She felt bad that she hadn't asked before. Perhaps she should have recommended something nearby.

He looked embarrassed. 'Er . . . right round the corner.'

'From here? Where?' There weren't any hotels as far as she knew, apart from the one that was heavily over-subscribed by Social Services to give people a roof while they waited for council housing.

'I'll show you. Come with me.' She let him take her arm and guide her to Conway Street.

'But there isn't a hotel anywhere near here,' she said, puzzled.

'Did I say anything about a hotel?' Jed laughed, a deep infectious rumble, and pointed to a maroon VW campervan. 'It's got everything I need: a bed downstairs and a pull-out two-berth shelf in the roof, a kitchen, wardrobe and bags of storage space.'

'But it must be freezing at night.' Ellen couldn't imagine anything worse than not being able to sleep in a comfortable warm bed.

'A little on the cold side, maybe, but nothing a good sleeping bag can't solve.' He opened the door to show her the tidy, snug interior.

'But you can't stay here.' Ellen couldn't bring herself to ask what he did about his washing arrangements. She could see that parking the van where you could pee in a field was one thing, but in a London street?

'It's not ideal, true. But I promised my son Ian that I'd bring it down for him. He's flying in from Germany to come to my show and then he's taking it through Eurotunnel. He'll drive it to Hamburg where he's living. Seemed a waste of money to book into a hotel. To be honest, I didn't really think it through.' He laughed again.

'Well, you must come home with me. I insist. At least I've got a shower and running water. I'll give you a key, introduce you to the children and you can come and go as you please.' Although she hadn't known him for long, she felt that she could trust him completely.

Jed raised a bushy eyebrow. 'Really?'

'Why not? It's the very least I can do.'

His face creased into a smile. 'Then leap aboard and I'll drive you there, my saviour.'

*

'You've let some artist you hardly know have free run of your house? I don't believe it.'

'I know, I know.' Ellen took Oliver's hand and stroked the side of his face. 'But the artists I look after are almost like my family. I had to help him and it won't be for long.'

'Family!' He snorted. 'I get thrown out and a near stranger gets to move in. How does that work exactly? Do explain to me.' He threw back the duvet and got out of bed.

'Come back. You know that's not what it's about.' He was not going to make her lose her temper. 'Come on.' She watched him turn, his body taut and strong. She could see his expression soften as he looked at her. His displeasure vanished as quickly as it had come.

He climbed in again then rolled over onto his stomach. He kissed her collarbone, suddenly penitent. 'I'm sorry. Of course I know all that. I'm jealous of him, that's all. I want to be living there with you.'

'I know. And you will. Just a few more months. That's what we agreed.' A few more months that she could barely afford unless Oliver started contributing. Perhaps if she worked harder on Emma they could bring the date forward.

She felt his hand move under the duvet until it was resting on her stomach. She rolled over to meet him and, as they touched, all thoughts of a practical nature left her head. She hadn't been too hasty. This was what life was for.

26

After the divorce, Bea had earmarked Colin's study in the loft extension for herself. As soon as he had moved out, the decorators had removed any trace of his occupancy. The striped wallpaper was stripped and the walls painted a soft off-white. His second-hand bookcases went to the tip and in their place four long thick shelves were fixed to the wall, manuscripts on the lowest and books above. Having finally persuaded him to take away his antique pine partner's desk, Bea chose oak trestles with a glass top instead. On it, in stark contrast to her office desk, sat her laptop, a phone and a Bestlite desk lamp, nothing more.

She'd put in recessed ceiling lights on dimmer switches that she rarely used, and four discreet Artemide wall lights that washed the walls with a soft glow. The manky blue carpet had given way to seagrass with a couple of strategically placed deep red wool rugs. The only other notable piece of furniture, apart from her office chair, was a chrome and black Corbusier chaise longue. How arty she felt when reclining to read, a standard Anglepoise behind her, the read pages of a manuscript turned onto the coffee-table at her side, a chocolate or two within easy reach. On the walls were three large prints that she'd bought from one of Ellen's artists: richly coloured and carefully patterned domestic still-lifes that reminded her of the work of Mary Fedden but without the price tag.

No one came here. Just Bea. Sometimes, when she felt the need for human contact, she took her work downstairs but most often she was happy to hide away up here where the atmosphere was reliably untroubled. Tonight, she had brought up her mug of coffee and settled herself at the desk. The blind on the window to her right was up so she could see across gardens and rooftops, the orange glow of the street lights blurring into a starless night sky. On the other side of the room, she'd pulled the finely striped cream blind so no one from across the street could see in. She'd lit her favourite scented candle, the Diptyque Figuier that Ben insisted smelt like cat's piss – but up here he didn't have to smell it. From the two tiny black speakers floated the soothing sounds of Dire Straits.

She switched on her laptop and quickly Googled 'Oliver Shepherd'. Might as well start with the obvious. She gazed awestruck at the possibility of nine million entries. How could there be so many Oliver Shepherds in the world, even allowing for a few repeats? She clicked on a few of the sites, finding nothing remotely relevant so quickly gave up. She'd have to narrow the search. He'd said he'd lived in France but where exactly? She picked up the phone.

Kate answered immediately. As she explained, Bea could sense Kate's disapproval.

'Did he mention the name of a town or anything? I can't

remember a thing, as usual.' Bea's anxiety about her senile moments had become a joke among them.

'Ah, the joys of alcohol-induced amnesia. You'll be able to ask him again and be just as interested in the answer as you were the first time then.'

'You must be able to remember. Your brain functions much better than mine.'

'Didn't Ellen once say something about Centre? I think it's a region around the Loire valley somewhere. Does that help?'

'Well, at least it gives me somewhere to start.'

'Go carefully, won't you?'

'Kate, stop it. This is for Ellen. I'll call you later or tomorrow if I find anything. And I probably won't.' She put the phone down and carried on Googling. After an hour, she was still not much further forward. All she had was a list of the four major towns in the area, the names of a few galleries, a couple of British-sounding artists who lived there, and no idea where to go next. As she debated how to narrow the search again, she was interrupted by the phone. It was Mark.

Within minutes, she had told him what she was up to and how she'd reached an impasse. Mark had heard enough about Oliver to be intrigued by his reticence about his past and backed her decision to do a judicious bit of digging into his non-background.

'Why don't you call a gallery or two in the major towns and just ask them if they know of an Oliver Shepherd or of an English gallery in the area?' he suggested.

'That's a bit of a long shot, isn't it? The area's huge. Anyway, my French is so rusty it's corroded.'

'But mine isn't. Maybe I could do it for you.'

'Would you? Really?'

'You've told me so much about this guy that I'm as curious as you are now. Of course I will.'

They agreed that during his lunch hour the next day he would try three or four galleries that they chose at random and then report back. Shutting down her laptop, Bea concentrated her attention on him and what he had to say, and for the next half-hour they chatted about their week so far and planned to see a film the following week, both admitting how much they were looking forward to seeing each other again. By the time she went to bed, Bea felt she was definitely on the way to putting her own small world to rights.

*

By lunchtime the next day, she felt quite different. A major disagreement had blown up with Amanda over a book jacket. Where Bea was anxious to send the illustration back to the illustrator, asking him to play up the humorous side of the novel, Amanda wanted to use what he'd already done so they could meet their production schedule. In the end Bea had stepped down, uncharacteristically brow-beaten into defeat, then spent the rest of the morning fuming, furious with herself for letting Amanda get her own way. She knew it was more important that the jacket was right than that they met the bloody schedule. When Mark called, she was debating whether or not to involve Adam. If she did, she might be shifting her rocky relationship with

Amanda into another gear. How much did that matter to her?

For a moment, she forgot her problems as she listened to what Mark had to say.

'I drew a complete blank with the first two in Châteauroux and Moulins. They sounded rather suspicious of me and couldn't understand why I wanted to find a gallery when I didn't know where it was or what it specialised in.'

Bea held her breath. She had a feeling something was coming.

'Then I called Jean-Claude Épicier, *une galerie d'art*—'

'OK, you're not speaking to them now! Stick to English with me,' Bea interrupted, rather more rudely than she'd intended but she was impatient to hear the rest of the story.

'Sorry. The chap who answered the phone said he didn't know any Oliver Shepherd but . . .' He paused for effect. Bea had to stop herself shouting at him to hurry up. '. . . there was an art gallery run by an Englishwoman close to where his father lived in the old town of Bourges. He couldn't remember its name but said he'd call his dad and get the number for me. Ex-pats in the same business are bound to know each other, aren't they? I'm calling him back in an hour.'

'Well done, Holmes. That's brilliant. Let me know as soon as you get it and I'll call her this afternoon.' Bea enjoyed the excitement of any chase, however fruitless it might turn out to be.

She spent the next two hours in suspense, unable to concentrate on anything, having to apologise to Stuart three times for making him repeat himself while pitching to her a book about Hitler's regiment in the First World War. Otherwise she fiddled about, answering emails and composing one to Adam about the controversial book jacket. She'd decided it was important to fight her corner, not for herself but for the welfare of the book. Her relationship with Amanda would have to weather the disagreement. Every time the phone rang, she grabbed it in a fever of anticipation only to be disappointed. At last, at twenty-five to five, Mark rang.

'It's called Art Space and is definitely run by an Englishwoman. Apparently it's been there for about five years.'

'Do you really think I should phone her?'

'Don't get cold feet now. Not after all I've done! If this comes to nothing you can think again. But what harm can possibly come from one call?'

He was right. She'd probably get nowhere but at least she'd have tried. Promising to call him when she'd spoken to them, she put the phone down, then hesitated. What gave her the right to interfere in her friend's life like this? Perhaps Kate was right and she should accept Oliver and his relationship with Ellen at face value. Then she thought of Ellen, the terrible bewildering period after Simon's death and how she had picked herself up and slowly built a new life for herself and her children. Kate and Bea had been so proud of her. Back then, Ellen had relied on them for support when she needed it. Bea was not going to let her down now, whatever Kate said. She had to find out if Oliver was who he said he was, for Ellen's sake. Although what she would do if he wasn't, she didn't dare think. Besides, it was only one little phone call. Mark was right. What harm could it possibly do?

Putting off the moment, she Googled 'Art Space Bourges'. All that appeared was the name, address and phone number of the gallery and a map showing the street it was on. At the same time, an email from Adam pinged into her inbox, asking her to come to his office at a quarter past five. She had twenty minutes. Galvanised into action, she dialled the number. Listening to the long beeps, she quickly considered what she was going to say. A click.

'*Allô, oui*?' A woman's voice.

'Do you speak English?' Bea decided not to embarrass herself by even attempting anything in French.

'Yes, I do. I am English. Mary Keeting speaking. How can I help you?' She sounded pleasant, friendly, of a certain age and with a slight northern accent that Bea hadn't expected.

'I'm looking for someone. I know he owns an art gallery somewhere near Bourges and I'm phoning various galleries and artists in the hope that someone will know him.' How feeble did that sound?

'If I can help I will. What's his name?'

'Oliver Shepherd.'

Bea heard an intake of breath. 'Who is this?'

'I'm Bea Wilde. I'm from London. Do you know him?' Her grip tightened on the phone.

'I do know *an* Oliver Shepherd, yes.'

'Well, the one I'm talking about is around about thirty-eight, handsome, tall, dark-haired . . .' Bea racked her brain to think of one distinguishing characteristic. 'And he owns an arts and crafts gallery somewhere in the Centre region.'

She winced at her own accent. 'I know this is like looking for a needle in a haystack but I must try.'

'Owns?'

Bea thought she detected a sense of outrage in Mary's question. 'Yes. That's what he said.'

'The Oliver Shepherd I know worked with a friend of mine until recently.' She emphasised the 'with'. 'He owns nothing.'

Bea could feel her heart pounding. 'But he said . . .'

'I'm sure whatever he said was extremely plausible. If he's the same person, it would be. He lived with Suzanne Berthaud, a friend of mine, who has a small but very successful arts and crafts gallery outside Bourges.' Mary stopped as if she was about to say more than she wanted.

Bea heard the ring of a bell in the background, something said.

'I'm sorry, it's a customer. *Bonjour, Madame. Un moment* . . . I'll have to go. Let me give you Suzanne's number. I'll tell her to expect a call from you this evening.'

Bea put down the phone as a hot flush overtook her. She flapped the neck of her blouse and removed her jacket, frustrated, excited and puzzled. With her elbows on her desk, she rested her head in her hands to think for a moment. Perhaps she should leave matters there. He'd said he'd owned a gallery and she'd found it. Perhaps he hadn't owned the place, but he'd told some version of the truth. But as she went over the conversation, she realised there had been something in Mary's voice that pricked her curiosity. She picked up the scrap of paper on which she'd written the number she'd been given and put it into her purse.

Stuart stuck his head round the door. 'Anything wrong?'

'Nothing.' Bea looked up, annoyed by the interruption. 'No. Just something I wasn't expecting.' Suddenly cold, she put her jacket back on.

Stuart understood that she wasn't going to say more and withdrew. She watched as he returned to his office and bent over whatever he was reading. She wanted to talk to someone but she hadn't time to call Mark or Kate. Besides, Mark was bound to be in some high-level meeting, and she'd never get past that dragon on Kate's practice reception. She decided to call Mark after she'd spoken to Suzanne and texted Kate to ask her round after supper. But, first, she'd have to wait and kill time doing battle with Amanda. She stood up to go to Adam's office, having just noticed Amanda tottering towards it.

*

By the time she and Ben had finished their fish pie that evening, she had calmed down from the confrontation. Adam's support for her over the jacket had provoked a stinging attack from Amanda in which she had accused Bea of costing the company an untold fortune, thanks to her frequent failure to meet the publishing schedules. Which was totally unfair. Well, almost. Bea had hit back, defending herself by pointing out that her prime concern lay with the books and their successful publication, not with being a schedule-slave. 'That's how I see my job,' she concluded. 'Like it or not.' She remained as calm and aloof as she knew how.

Adam had waded in to keep the peace, pointing out the right on each side and asking them to try harder to accommodate one another. However, he added, in this instance the schedule would have to be adapted to allow for getting the right illustration. Both women had stalked out without speaking and returned to their offices. Bea had heard Amanda's door slam.

'Sounds like a bloody kindergarten, if you ask me,' was Ben's verdict when she told him what had happened.

She laughed. He was absolutely right. Yet despite recognising their playground behaviour, she knew she wasn't going to be able to back down now. Amanda and she had crossed swords too many times for that. At least Adam appeared to have no favourites and supported whoever he thought was right, which must be particularly galling for Amanda, if office gossip about their increasingly 'close' relationship was true.

Once everything was put away, she left Ben in front of the TV while she went upstairs to phone France.

Suzanne picked up immediately. She listened without interrupting as Bea told her the story she'd thought up earlier, having decided not to tell the whole truth until she'd heard what the other woman had to say. If she turned out still to be a friend of Oliver's, despite Mary's apparent antagonism, Bea didn't want him or Ellen to find out what she'd been doing behind their backs. Not yet, at least. Instead she explained how she'd met Oliver through a friend some months ago when she was in France. He'd talked about his gallery and offered to look at Bea's pottery (as if – but the idea amused her), advise her and perhaps help to sell some pieces for her. When she finished there was a silence. She lay back on the chaise longue (however elegant it looked, she never failed to be surprised by how uncomfortable it actually was), hoping that Suzanne wouldn't see through her story, and waited for her to speak.

She began slowly although her English was fluent. 'I'm sorry to let you down but, if he is the Oliver I know and it sounds as if he well may be, then he had no right to raise your hopes. Mary and I talked about this and we agreed that I should tell you the truth of what happened.'

Bea could hardly breathe, not knowing what to expect next.

'I met my Oliver Shepherd when I was visiting England about two and half years ago. I bumped into him at the Serpentine Gallery, we got talking about the paintings and he asked me for a coffee. That was it. Within weeks of my coming home, he visited for a few days but then never left. He moved in with me and Isabelle, my daughter. My friends warned me to take things slowly, but it was impossible. We were in love. Or so I thought.'

Bea lay still, unable to believe the similarity with Ellen's story. But could she really have tracked him down this easily? Not possible, surely.

'I'm sorry, you don't need to know all this.' The momentary bitterness in Suzanne's voice had gone.

'But I'm really intrigued,' Bea reassured her. 'He seemed so genuine.'

'That's his great gift. I trusted him completely and he almost destroyed my business. Now I realise that he was a – how you say? – a conman who got what he wanted, then disappeared.'

'But Oliver said he owned a gallery. He can't be the same person.' By now, Bea wanted more than anything for him not to be.

'The Oliver Shepherd I knew said a lot of things. He worked in the gallery with me for maybe two years. I was pleased to help him earn some money. After the first year, he persuaded me into signing over half the business to him. Mary and her husband tried to stop me but I wouldn't listen. I wanted to prove to him how much I loved him. He often made me feel as if he doubted the strength of my feelings. This was a way of showing him. How stupid I was!'

She paused but Bea said nothing, astonished by how open Suzanne was being.

'I gradually cut myself off from most of my friends and let him take over my life, but I liked doing whatever pleased him. I really thought we would be together for ever and this gift was a sign of my commitment to him. But I've told you far too much. This isn't why you phoned. I'm sorry.'

'In a way it is, though. I think I'd better explain.' Apart from the similarities in the two stories, there was something in Suzanne's voice that made Bea trust her. Relying on her instinct, she made the snap decision to tell her everything. When she finished, there was a long pause. Then Suzanne said what they were both thinking. 'He must be the same man. He's doing the same thing all over again. You have to tell her.'

'I can't.' Bea was wishing more than anything that she hadn't made the phone call. Perhaps knowledge wasn't always such a good thing.

'You must. Let me finish the story and you'll see. Because,

having given him forty-nine per cent of the business, the only way I was able to get it back was to buy it. He made me pay for what I gave him. He may have been relying on me not being able to raise the money. If I hadn't he could have bought my share, then sold the place and walked away with the profit. Selling to him would be the only way I could sever ties with him. But he hadn't thought of my brother, who rescued me, thank God. By that time, I had no idea where Oliver had gone. Everything was being handled by an Edinburgh lawyer on his behalf.'

'Edinburgh? Are you sure?'

'Yes. I've still got the correspondence. So, you see, *if* he's the same man, you must say something.'

Bea needed time to think. Why did Suzanne make it sound so urgent? She had the oddest feeling that something had been left unsaid but she didn't feel comfortable in prompting her to say any more. She'd said so much. Before she had time to say anything, Suzanne caught her breath. 'Of course. I'm going to be in London in three weeks' time. We could meet then and I'll give you photos and anything else I can find to help.'

Three weeks seemed a long way off but Bea had to be content with that. She was curious to meet Suzanne in person and welcomed the opportunity to gauge her reliability for herself before she tried to convince Ellen. The two women said their goodbyes with a promise from Suzanne to be in touch nearer the time.

A huge weight seemed to be crushing Bea's chest. She sat upright and took several deep breaths as she absorbed everything she had just heard. Although she had been suspicious of Oliver, she had never imagined his background would contain anything like this. The one thing of which she was certain was that she must not go rushing to Ellen on the basis of this conversation alone. She remembered what Suzanne had said: '*If* he's the same person . . .' There was still a chance that he might not be. She had to talk to someone. She picked up her mobile. Ten o'clock.

Kate had texted back earlier to say she would be too exhausted after a day on call to come over but Bea could ring her any time before ten. So, too late. In any case, she wasn't sure she really wanted to share this with Kate just yet. She had a feeling that Kate would blame her for nosing around where she shouldn't. Without this conversation, they could all have carried on as before. There was no chance of that happening now. But she had to talk to someone she could trust and rely on for sound objective advice.

She flicked open her phone, found Mark's number and dialled.

27

Despite the cold, five or six people holding glasses of wine stood on the pavement outside the gallery. Wrapped in overcoats and scarves, they were wreathed by a pall of cigarette smoke. Inside, there was still a throng. Standing on the other side of the street, Kate was relieved to see things were still going strong, even though it was past eight o'clock. She had meant to get there much earlier but just as she was about to leave work she'd been called out on a home visit.

Only thirty minutes earlier, she had been a fifteen-minute drive away in a large, run-down estate, standing in a small bedroom: no paintings, no books, one wardrobe with a lock on the door, a few knick-knacks, clothes draped everywhere and a mirror on top of a chest of drawers that was missing several handles. A faint smell of urine hung in the air, almost masked by the distinctive, unmistakable smell of death. In the centre of the room was an old double bed in which Mrs Thomson lay, quite obviously dead. At its foot, her two middle-aged daughters were weeping. Kate had offered them awkward condolences. It was hard to know what to say in the circumstances. Her job was to give the body a full external examination but, with the audience, it seemed hideously inappropriate. She decided to get by with the bare minimum. She got out the stethoscope and torch from her bag, aware that to reach the body, she was going to have to crawl over the bed.

Now, across the road from the gallery, watching the party, she could still feel the twang of the springs as she had knelt on the mattress, aware of its sag taking her towards the middle. She had shone the torch into Mrs Thomson's sightless grey eyes and checked for a heartbeat. Nothing. Just the sound of her daughters' sobbing as they watched her poke and prod their dead mother. At the age of ninety-five, the old woman had simply faded away. Nothing untoward had happened. Kate hurried to do her bit so that the body could be removed, then left the flat with relief and the dull sadness that she always felt after the death of any patient. She would have preferred to go straight home to take stock alone, but she knew how much it meant to Ellen when they all showed up at her private views. She thought she saw Paul through the window, beside Ellen's desk, so, bracing herself, she crossed the road.

Inside the gallery it was hot and noisy. She crossed towards her husband just as he began to make his way into the back room, not having noticed her arrival. She followed him, glancing at the paintings she passed. At every private view she was impressed by Ellen's ability to find such varied but talented artists. She seemed to have a real eye for what people wanted. Kate stopped short by a wall of vibrant still-lifes, their labels already peppered with red dots. She was pleased for Ellen, knowing how personally she took the success of her exhibitions. She felt a tap on her shoulder. Bea was standing right behind her, suited and booted from the office, bold electric blue swing jacket over a calf-length black skirt and boots.

'I've been trying to get hold of you.' She was obviously bursting with whatever it was she had to say.

Kate's heart sank. If only she hadn't called Bea after she'd seen Oliver with that woman. Bea was like a terrier when she got wind of something and wouldn't let this go until she'd shaken the life out of it. Just like the time when she'd suspected Colin of having an affair. Kate still remembered her own shock at Bea's tales of checking Colin's mobile and emails, then going through his pockets and briefcase until she eventually found the clichéd tell-tale evidence: the Bath hotel receipt. It was almost as if Colin had wanted her to find it and take on the responsibility of unravelling their marriage for him. He must have known that once Bea suspected something she wouldn't let it rest until she'd got a result. But to Kate that kind of detective work was an invasion of privacy. It was wrong. If Bea had been burrowing into Oliver's affairs in the same sort of way, she didn't want to know. She made a snap decision.

'Not now, Bea. I've had a long day and I'm bushed. Let me get a drink first and look at the paintings. Please.'

'But we must talk about Oliver. So if not now, when?'

'Why don't you just let it rest?'

Bea stared at her, obviously taken aback by her un-expected vehemence. 'But I thought . . .'

'Whatever you thought, you thought wrong. I really don't want to be part of it. I've got enough on my plate right now.'

The hurt she saw in Bea's face made her instantly regret her rebuff. But too late. She'd said what she felt and couldn't take it back. 'Bea, I'm sorry . . .'

'Well, I'm sorry too. I thought we both had Ellen's interests at heart. I was obviously wrong.' Bea turned and headed to the drinks table where she refilled her glass before heading to the front of the gallery.

An almost unbearable weariness settled over Kate. After a day of patients and colleagues all wanting a little piece of her, she simply didn't have enough left for Bea. She poured herself some tonic water and scouted the room for Paul, finding him in a corner studying one of the abstracts. That new haircut had taken years off him, as had losing his job. Seeing him so relaxed made her realise how stressed he must have been in the last months. Habit and the everyday demands of life made it easy to miss such changes. She went up behind him and slipped her free arm around his waist.

'Darling! You *are* here. I was beginning to think you weren't coming.' He pecked her cheek. 'Aren't those still-lifes something? Though I'm not so sure about this. What the hell's it meant to be?'

She smiled. His predictability was endearing. He only ever appreciated the figurative artists Ellen found.

'Doesn't the title help?'

'*Landscape number three*? Nope. Looks like random brushstrokes to me.'

'I don't think it matters if you don't know exactly what it is. It's your response that counts.'

'What – total bewilderment? That can't be right.'

'In that case, if you've had enough, I'm ready to go home.'

'But you've only just got here.'

'I know, but I'm dead on my feet. We can say goodbye to Ellen on the way out. She won't have noticed I've only been here a few minutes.'

As they moved together towards the front of the gallery, they heard Ellen's raised voice. 'How dare you?' Then a hissed 'I think you should go. Now.' They found Oliver, Ellen and Bea standing together in the short passage between rooms. Ellen was obviously battling to control herself, not wanting to make a scene in front of her customers; Oliver stood expressionless, silent; Bea's face was flushed as if she was angry and upset. One or two heads had turned to see what was going on. The situation clearly needed to be defused before the evening was spoiled.

Taking matters into her own hands, Kate slipped her arm through Bea's, ignoring her attempt to shake it off. 'Time to go, Bea. You can sort out whatever this is another time.'

'Bea's said what she has to say. There won't be another time,' said Ellen, slipping her arm through Oliver's.

'You can't mean that,' said Bea, disbelieving.

'I do. Just go. Please.'

Oliver nodded in Ellen's support.

'Fine. I can manage on my own, thanks.' Bea shook off Kate's grip and left the gallery.

'What on earth's happened?'

Ellen was close to tears and Oliver still looked rattled, but Kate's question seemed to focus him. 'Nothing. Bea's had one drink too many, that's all.'

'How dare she?' Ellen said under her breath. 'My oldest friend.'

'It doesn't matter. There's nothing I wouldn't have told you if you'd asked. You know that.' Oliver's self-assurance was back. 'Forget it. She'll see sense in the morning. Let's enjoy the rest of the party.'

'Oh, my God! Jed! Yes, we must.' The mention of Jed's name seemed to jog Ellen back to the present. Apparently shrugging off whatever had been said and forcing a smile, she was the owner of the gallery once more.

Paul said their goodbyes but Kate hung back as he left. She couldn't leave Ellen without a word. 'Will you be OK?'

'Don't worry, I'll be fine. I thought Bea was above something like this.'

'But what's she done? Tell me quickly.'

'In her wisdom, she's decided to poke about in Oliver's past. I don't know what she thinks she's found out and I don't want to know. Just the fact that she would do such a thing behind my back is enough.'

'I'm sure she did it for you.'

'Did you know about this?' Ellen scrutinised Kate, making her feel awkward. 'Actually, you know what? Don't bother answering. I can see that you did.'

'She did say she was going to do something but I didn't think—'

'To stop her? I suppose that would have been too much to ask. Call yourselves friends? Oh, forget it.' She cut across Kate's stammered attempt to explain. 'I'm going back.' She merged into the party again where Kate saw her approach a grey-bearded man to introduce him to a couple of besuited clients who appeared to be discussing one of the larger abstracts. If it weren't for the heightened colour in

Ellen's cheeks, no one would have guessed that anything was wrong.

Somehow Bea had managed to lob a bomb at their friendship, and simultaneously cemented further the relationship between Ellen and Oliver. Long experience told Kate that there was no point in trying to piece things back together while Ellen was in this mood. Things would no doubt look very different to all of them in the morning. As she reached the door, she turned and caught sight of Oliver. He was standing alone by the big abstract behind Ellen's desk, watching her. As he caught Kate's eye, he inclined his head, his mouth in a taut half-smile. But his gaze was icy.

*

The cold night air hit Bea like a smack in the face. She strode down the street, barely aware of where she was heading until she stopped to take her bearings. At once, she was aware of the adrenalin rushing through her body. Her legs felt shaky and her heart was still pounding as the red fog of rage began to lift. Ellen's expression when she realised what Bea had been doing behind her back was imprinted on her memory. She had only seen her look like that once before, when a school friend's mother had accused Emma of lying. Ellen protected those closest to her with a formidable ferocity. Once crossed, she didn't forget or forgive.

Ellen's belief that Bea had betrayed their friendship had brought the shutters crashing down between them. She didn't understand that Bea had been acting out of concern for her, and now it would be twice as hard to persuade her. Bea cursed her big mouth. Adele had always warned her to think before she spoke: sage advice that she'd failed to follow yet again. As she began to walk, more slowly now, she rewound the evening and began to play it back to herself. How pleased she had been to see Kate. Through the day, she had texted, emailed and left a message on her voice-mail, but typically Kate had been too busy to reply. Not that she wouldn't have wanted to but Bea knew those sessions on call could be interminable. Mark's advice had been to talk everything through with Kate. He was as shocked as Bea had been by what she had unearthed but agreed that now she had the knowledge she couldn't bury it – for Ellen's sake – but he had also suggested she take things slowly. She had to be absolutely certain that the facts were incontrovertible. And, she cursed herself again, that was exactly what she had failed to do.

Trying to tell Kate what she knew at the end of a working day and at the private view had been unbelievably stupid. Nonetheless her friend's unexpected rebuff had hurt badly. That and two glasses of wine on an empty stomach had been enough to tip Bea into that dangerous zone between sobriety and recklessness. So when Oliver had approached her, in dark jeans and pink cashmere sweater, a smug glow emanating from him, her hackles had instantly risen.

'Enjoying yourself?' His opening remark had been innocuous enough.

'Mmm. Thanks.'

'Ellen's got a wonderful eye, hasn't she? I'm so proud of her. She's worked so hard on this.'

'As hard as Suzanne used to, I expect.' Why had she said that?

Standing in the street now, she could see that her response had popped out for all the wrong reasons. His patronising attitude towards Ellen had irritated her beyond belief. She didn't need him to point out aspects of her friend she had known for years as if he was the first to spot them. Was that because she was as jealous as the others joked she was? At last the answer was clear to her. Actually, no. As she'd explained to Adele, she wanted a man, yes, but she didn't want one who would take over her life. The first months after Colin's departure had been hard, but now she was used to having control of the TV remote, of having the food she wanted in the kitchen, of not having to eat at night if she didn't want to or of just having a couple of well-chosen chocolates and a glass of wine or two, of making her own decisions. Having a man in her life was great but only as long as she could keep a bolt-hole for herself.

She had intended to do as Mark advised and say nothing to anyone until she had cast-iron evidence but she hadn't been able to hold back, and now she knew the two Oliver Shepherds were one and the same person. During the brief second in which Oliver's mask slipped, she had seen all she needed to see.

'Suzanne?' He cleared his throat. 'I'm sorry, you've lost me.'

'You know exactly who I'm talking about,' Bea said, louder than she meant to. 'I could see it in your face.'

'I don't know who you've been talking to but I advise you to stay well out of my affairs.'

She saw him click one nail against another. 'We're not

going to talk about this now, but be very clear, I'm not going to let you hurt Ellen.'

'I don't know what you think you've found out but I've got absolutely nothing to hide.'

'You can bluff as much as you like but I know about the gallery in France and I will tell her.'

He was about to say something, his eyes narrowed with dislike, when Ellen materialised at his elbow. 'Is everything all right?' She had only to take one look at both of them to know that it was anything but. 'What's going on?'

'Nothing to worry about, darling.' Oliver slipped a proprietorial arm around her and kissed her forehead. 'Bea seems to have been digging about in my past on your behalf.'

'You've been doing what?' Ellen turned to Bea, all warmth gone from her expression.

'I made a couple of phone calls,' Bea had blurted out. 'I found out one or two things about Oliver that I think you should know.'

'How dare you?' Ellen's voice had trembled and even though she was making a huge effort to control herself, her anger was obvious. She had taken Oliver's hand and looked up at him, then at Bea. At that moment, Bea had known she had lost her. 'I think you'd better go. Now.'

Then, to make things worse (if that were possible), Kate and Paul had chosen to appear. With neither friend on her side, her only course of action had been to beat a retreat. But what was she to do now?

She started walking slowly towards home, letting the cold night air clear her head, thankful she'd chosen her flat boots that morning. She berated herself for knocking back that second glass of wine. Without it, she'd probably have kept her mouth shut. But there was no point in dwelling on what might have been. Despite being wounded by Ellen and Kate's rejection, she would find a way to put things right. Her long-time friendship with Ellen and what she knew about Oliver meant that she couldn't possibly walk away.

She passed a parade of shops where a small branch of the Co-op was still open. Having picked up half a dozen eggs, some mushrooms and new potatoes for Ben's and her supper, plus milk for the morning, she skirted a group of hoodies lurking near the entrance with their beer cans and fags. Turning right, she passed a new police sign asking for witnesses to a fatal incident that had occurred three nights earlier. She quickened her step, tightening her grip on her bag, aware that the short cut she was taking through the estate was not entirely well advised. The sounds of reggae and rock floated from a couple of dimly lit windows. Knots of disaffected youth hung about on corners, shouting and smoking, but to her relief, none of them appeared to notice her. For once, she thanked the Lord for the anonymity bestowed by middle age.

She emerged onto the main road feeling calmer. She took her mobile out of her pocket to call Mark. To her annoyance, she saw that the battery was almost dead. As she walked on, she thought about how considerate and sensible he'd been when she'd regaled him with Suzanne's story. What would he say to her now? He'd lean back in his chair, rub his right cheekbone with his fingertips as he thought, close his eyes and exhale loudly. Then he'd talk slowly as if weighing every word. His advice would surely be what it had been all along: she must obtain her evidence and she must talk to Kate. Of course.

Hastening down her street, she was relieved to see the light in their hallway, like a beacon welcoming her home. Ben was back from football practice. She made omelettes and chatted, catching up with as much of his day as he'd allow. Then she excused herself to go upstairs where she could talk to Kate uninterrupted.

As she took to the chaise longue, she remembered the last phone conversation she'd had from there. She put her cup of coffee on the side table. If Kate would only listen to her, she would surely understand.

The phone was picked up after a couple of rings. She explained to a rather hesitant Paul that she had to speak to Kate. 'I know she's knackered but this is really urgent, Paul. Please put her on.'

'She's gone to bed, Bea. I don't think I can . . .'

He was a hopeless liar.

'Please, Paul.' She hated begging but there was little else she could do.

There was a short silence in which she guessed they were mouthing a conversation between each other. Then, 'I'm sorry but she doesn't want to talk to you at the moment. It's too late.'

'I see.'

'Why don't you both sleep on it? Things will look different in the morning.'

Bea hung up. She thought about calling Mark. But falling out with both of her friends wasn't something she wanted to discuss with him. Besides, she was ashamed at not having stuck to the plan he'd suggested. This was something the three of them would have to sort out themselves. The last thing she wanted was to lose their friendship. Ellen had every reason to be angry with her. Bea would probably feel as incensed herself if she thought someone, particularly a close friend, had been poking around in her, or even Mark's, private life. But Kate was another matter. She had chosen to side with Ellen without bothering to hear what Bea had to say. The injustice of this fuelled Bea's determination not to let the matter rest. Normally, if any of them fell out over anything, they would be on the phone to each other the next day to sort matters out. This time, it felt different. If Kate and Ellen were going to stonewall her, then she would leave them to stew for a few days and get on with things her own way.

She went downstairs to get *The Times Atlas of the World*, a present to Ben from a well-intentioned god-parent, but only Bea ever used it. She opened it at the map of France, then switched on her laptop and started Googling. When she found the site she wanted, she picked up her phone and dialled Suzanne. Half an hour later, with a return airline ticket booked for the next day, she stood up feeling happier, switched off the lights and went downstairs to watch TV with Ben.

28

'What the hell am I going to do?' Kate flopped, despairing, on to the living-room sofa and hugged a rose-print cushion to her stomach. 'Bea thinks I'm siding with Ellen against her, and Ellen thinks I've ganged up with Bea. How ridiculous is that? But if only I'd stopped Bea trying to dig about in Oliver's past, this wouldn't have happened.'

'I should think stopping Bea when her mind's made up would be like trying to stop an express train. You couldn't have done anything even if you'd wanted to.' Paul pulled the small table that bore a vase of lilies back from the window and drew the curtains behind it, then walked to the fireplace and stood looking at her, warming the back of his legs.

'I guess you're right.' She groaned, bending double over her knees. 'But I feel so responsible.'

'Don't. I've already told you.' He came over to sit beside her, careful not to disturb Mouse, who was showing his pleasure at being back on his favourite cushion with a full-throttled purr, twisting his body so his stomach was on offer to anyone who'd rub it. Paul placed his hand on the small of Kate's back and began to stroke it as she relaxed into his touch. 'You've got enough on your plate with the practice.'

'But they've been such good friends and they matter to me. They really do.' She was astonished to realise there was a tear on her cheek. She wiped it away and sniffed.

Paul put a hand over hers. 'You're exhausted. You're working too hard, you know. Couldn't you cut down on your sessions?' Before he'd lost his job, he'd suggested this occasionally but now he was home alone he'd mentioned it several times.

'You know I can't. It'd look as if I didn't care any more. Just because you've taken to the life of Reilly!' She picked up one of the magazines neatly stacked on the coffee-table, flicked a few pages then put it down, regretting her outburst. 'Anyway, my work isn't the point here. My friends are. I've got to sort this mess out somehow. If I don't, no one will. I know them.'

The phone rang. Paul got there first. 'Bea! Hi.'

Kate reached out to take the phone from him. But he stood listening then said, 'She's gone to bed, Bea. I don't think I can . . .'

He put a finger to his lips, then walked to the back of the room, saying nothing as he looked out over the garden. He listened to what Bea had to say, his back to Kate so he couldn't see her mouthing at him to give her the phone. When she got up and tried to grab it, he held it above his head so she couldn't reach, whispering, 'Trust me.'

She collapsed back into the sofa and waited the conversation out, then let rip. 'What the fuck do you think you're doing? You can be such an annoying man sometimes. That was for me. Now give me the phone and let me call her back.'

'No.' Paul was adamant. 'Listen to me. I did that for your own good. It *is* too late to begin to sort this out now. Like it or not, you're tired, tempers are frayed, Bea's had one drink too many and you don't want to make things worse. If you leave it until everyone's calmed down, you'll sort this out much faster.'

Kate gave a deep sigh, putting her head into her hands. 'You're probably right, dammit. But I won't be able to call either of them tomorrow because I'm tied up all day and then we've got a partners' meeting in the evening and you know how they go on and on.' She thought for a second. 'I think I'd feel better if I spoke to her now.'

'Leave it, please. For once, I'm right.' He put the phone on the mantelpiece among the clutter that had accumulated there over the years.

She suddenly hadn't the energy to stand up and get it for herself. What was it about his brand of male certainty that made her wilt into submission? Every working day was chock full of action to be taken, decisions that had to be made – from diagnosis to treatment, from referrals to sick notes, from what to put on in the morning to which sandwich to have for lunch. Normally she would stand up to anyone in the interests of whatever she thought was right, or wanted to do, but this evening a part of her welcomed the decision being taken out of her hands. The weariness that she'd felt earlier on in the gallery was enveloping her again and she felt utterly drained. Yes, she knew Paul was right. She was putting too much physical and emotional energy into the practice but what alternative did she have? Her commitment had always been to medicine, even when she was working part-time as a salaried GP bringing up their young family. She leaned back and closed her eyes. 'OK, I give in.'

'Good. In that case, if you've got a jot of energy left, let's talk about Africa. I've been trying to pin you down for days.'

Her eyes snapped open. 'Africa? Are you serious?'

'Yes.' He walked over to the mahogany roll-top desk that they'd inherited from Paul's grandfather, the laptop on its surface at odds with the Victorian design. He pulled some papers from one of the drawers. 'Have a look at these. I've been looking at flights to Accra and seeing if we could combine seeing Sam with a bit of an adventure of our own. I think I may have to put us in the hands of a travel agent in the end, but at least I've made a start.'

She stared at him, disbelieving. Was this the man who had been turning into a middle-aged conservative eco-warrior, to whom the word 'holiday', let alone 'air-miles', had become anathema? 'What's brought this on? I thought you didn't want to go there.'

'That was when all that trouble was going on at work and I couldn't think further than the next meeting. Now I'm at home, with nothing imminent work-wise, I thought I might as well investigate. I know how much you want to go. And what's the point in having a socking great pay-off if we can't enjoy some of it?'

'What about your carbon footprint?' she teased.

'Sod it.' He grinned. 'This is in the name of Sam and in the name of us. What do you think?'

'I can't think of anything I'd like more.' The idea of seeing Sam again, finding out how he was living, seeing the work he was doing and meeting his friends thrilled her beyond measure.

'In that case, have a look at these flights and stuff and tell me what you think. February sound good to you? It'll be baking, but we'll miss the rainy season.'

'Sounds amazing. You have done your homework.' She took the printouts from him and began to look at the flight prices and thumbnail summaries of what Ghana had to offer. She was amused to see he'd ringed the eco-tourism section of one of the Ghana tourism sites. To be expected! But as she was bombarded by images of exotic wildlife, colourful native costumes, long, secluded beaches and more natural and cultural highlights than she had imagined existing there, she caught her breath with excitement.

'Have you told Sam? What about Jack?'

'I thought I'd leave Sam to you but I have spoken to Jack. I thought he might want to come but, believe it or not, he wants to make his own trip to visit his brother, without us. He's getting a job to earn the money!'

'He wants to work? Pinch me – am I dreaming?'

'That's what he says, so I think we should leave him to it. My only hope for him was that a life of lotus-eating in London would pale as his money ran out. And that's what seems to be happening.'

'What's he going to do?' She couldn't believe that her youngest was finally entering the adult world. The thought of her children so grown-up made her feel ancient. But it also confirmed that the time had finally come for her and Paul to start thinking about the next stage of their life together.

'Lord alone knows. I'm leaving that to him. He's got to find his own way.'

'So, just us?' She looked down at the picture on her knee of the hippos in the Wechiau Sanctuary. They were really going to see them and so much else together, at last.

'Yes, just us. Shall I find out more?'

The sheer pleasure she saw on his face made her leap to her feet and hug him, her exhaustion almost forgotten. 'Absolutely.'

'And now can we forget about your two friends for this evening and go to bed?'

*

With only a few stragglers remaining, Jed suggested that he take Ellen and Oliver to supper at the small Turkish restaurant round the corner. Ellen couldn't refuse, despite Oliver's badly disguised reluctance. Not that she had any appetite for food after what had happened, but overall the private view had been such a roaring success that she knew they should celebrate. The interest in Jed's paintings had been phenomenal, better than any other view she remembered putting on.

'I think I'll go home. Got a splitting headache,' muttered Oliver.

'Home?' Ellen couldn't believe he'd duck out of coming with her.

'To the flat.'

'Oh, do come with us,' she pleaded, when they found themselves in a quietish corner. 'I'd like you be there.'

'I know you would. And I'd like to be there too. But the best way to deal with these migraines is to lie down until they've gone. If I go now, I'll catch it before it sets in. We'll talk tomorrow, I promise.'

She couldn't remember him ever having mentioned that he was susceptible to migraines and wondered briefly whether it was a diplomatic illness. But he must know how much she'd appreciate him being with her. 'I'm so, so sorry about Bea,' she apologised. 'I don't know what she thought she was doing.'

'Let's not talk about it now. I don't want your evening to be any more spoiled than it has been. I'll tell you about it another time – the little there is to tell.'

'You don't have to.'

'I know. But I want to.'

They said their good nights, Ellen wishing he would stay and come back to the house with her. She clung to him, hoping he'd change his mind, but he pulled away and left her in the emptying gallery. Suddenly she felt very alone.

She and Jed didn't take long over their meal. He saw that something was preoccupying her, and when she declined to explain exactly what it was, he had insisted on treating them to a taxi home. He had refused the offer of a nightcap, seeming to understand that she needed to be alone, and, having used the bathroom, took himself off with a final 'thank you' to the campervan. Ellen saw him down the path as the implications of Bea's interference began to gallop through her mind.

Looking down the hall as the front door shut behind her, she saw the house as Oliver must see it. However hard she tried to look after the place, she couldn't hide the evidence of children that she knew he found so frustrating. Despite her repeated reminders about not touching the walls, a faint line of fingerprints ran at hip height along the hallway and up the stairs. Shoes were kicked higgledy-piggledy down the hall to where the end of the banisters was hung about with school bags and coats. Would he ever adjust to their chaos or would he be tidying up after them and tutting about it for ever? Like Sisyphus doomed to roll his boulder up that hill through eternity. The thought amused her. She tiptoed upstairs and looked in on Emma first, neatly curled with her back to the wall, then Matt, who lay sprawled across the top of his duvet as if he'd been dropped there from a great height. She gently eased it from under him and covered him up. She kissed them both. This was the one time when she could do that with a cast-iron guarantee that neither would object.

Her mind still racing, she decided to have that nightcap on her own. In the kitchen, she was greeted by a mess of pans that had been used for chicken Kievs, mashed potato and beans. At least one of the plates had been put into the dishwasher but the rest were scattered with the half-emptied lunch-boxes around the worktop. When she'd finally got the place back to looking as if a hand-grenade had exploded, rather than a nuclear bomb, she made herself a cup of best builder's tea and sat at the table to take stock. She attempted half-heartedly to bring some order to the opened bills in that morning's mail but she had too much on her mind to concentrate.

How grateful she was to Jed for taking her out and giving her time to unwind. His insistence had meant that in fact she'd avoided a potentially difficult evening with Oliver, and Bea and Kate had been relinquished to the back of her mind, which, right now, was where she wanted to keep them. But they were refusing to stay put. For years they had looked after her when she needed them and she loved them for that. But this time they had overstepped the mark. Whatever their motives, she realised she didn't want them to treat her as if she was some sort of victim any more, unable to look after herself or make her own decisions. They had fallen into the habit of casting her in that role but the time had come for her to take responsibility for her own life. If she made a wrong choice, then she would have to deal with it herself. She'd chosen Oliver and, whatever Bea had to say about him, she was going to stick with that choice. If being with him meant losing Bea and Kate's friendship, so be it. Big decision, but that was how strongly she felt.

As she sipped her tea, having allowed herself two sugars to celebrate the success of the evening – and because Oliver wasn't there to see – things gradually became clearer. She was sure there was nothing that couldn't be explained and that he'd do that in his own good time. She was happy to wait and certainly didn't need Kate or Bea's interference. Jed was right. Life was about taking chances, or what was the point of it? To show Oliver that whatever her friends said made no difference to her, she reached another a decision. Instead of wasting any more time, she would ask him to move in with them now. Emma would have to grow up and accept that her mother deserved a life of her own. A little tough love wouldn't do her any harm. Matt would be thrilled with the addition of a fellow sports and games fanatic to the family. She hugged herself with delight, thinking of how pleased Oliver would be. This, after all, was what he wanted too.

Staring out at the dark shadow of the shed, another plan began to crystallise. As she had yet to find the time to use it, why not let someone else? As long as Oliver remained unemployed, he couldn't contribute financially but, if she let the studio space to another artist and sublet the flat until the lease was up, it wouldn't matter. The sound of the campervan door slamming outside the front of the house prompted a memory of the plans Jed was beginning to make for his future. She smiled to herself. At last everything was falling neatly into place.

29

As the plane flew through turbulence, Bea clutched the arms of her seat. The seatbelt signs were on and the crew had abandoned their trolley duties to strap themselves into their seats at the front and rear of the cabin. A baby, two rows ahead of her, was yelling its head off. She shut her eyes, trying to pretend that she was in a rocking chair, a very unsteady one. Nothing to worry about, she kept repeating to herself. Planes survive much worse than this. It was a blessed relief to land in France twenty minutes later.

Contrary to Paul's prediction, sleeping on matters hadn't made them better. If anything, in the sober light of day, they looked worse. Even if flying to France on a whim meant she acquired some tangible proof of Oliver's identity, there was no guarantee she'd persuade either Ellen or Kate to listen to her. Ellen had made her feelings crystal clear and Kate could be as stubborn as a mule. She'd shown that last night.

Apart from that, Bea hadn't been able to let the office know she wasn't going to be in today. She was meant to be presenting *Bare Bones* to the booksellers: a crucial moment for the success (or not) of any book. But the impulse to save her friendship (and possibly her friend) had taken priority over everything else. She had justified her decision to take the day off in the knowledge that Stuart would make a brilliant stand-in. However, the fact she hadn't been able to get through to him yet to warn him was making her anxious. She would try again as soon as she got out of the airport.

The unfamiliar early start had left Bea feeling like something from the night of the living dead. By the time she caught sight of her reflection in the unforgiving glare of the lights in the Ladies at Tours airport, her hair had taken on an uncontrolled life of its own and, without makeup, her face was ashen, with purplish shadows under her eyes. What she looked like was neither here nor there. Last night's events had galvanised her. The look she had seen on Oliver's face had made her realise how much she distrusted him. Thanks to her inability to keep quiet, she had forced matters to a head too soon. So be it. She couldn't wait for Suzanne to come to London in three weeks' time: she needed whatever information there was right now. The previous evening, when Suzanne had heard what had happened, she had immediately agreed to drive from Bourges to meet Bea in a pâtisserie in the centre of Tours, just as soon as Bea could get there.

As Bea stood shivering outside the low white terminal building, queuing with the other passengers at the taxi rank, only twelve hours after they'd spoken, she switched on her mobile to call Stuart. One missed call from Kate. It could wait. Before she had a chance to dial, the phone rang.

'Bea?'

'Yes.' Adam! The one person she didn't want to speak to right now.

'Where the hell are you? The key buyers are due in twenty minutes. I thought we were going to run through the presentation.'

Shit! In the heat of the moment, she'd completely forgotten the run-through. But there was nothing she could do about it now.

'I'm in, er . . .' How could she break it gently?

'Where? Where are you? When are you going to get here?' His rage communicated itself only too effectively over the airwaves. There was no way she was going to be able to wriggle out of this one with the old fail-safe of gastroenteritis. He would have recognised the continental ring tone.

'In France.' She held her breath and waited.

'In France?' he repeated. 'What the fuck are you doing there?'

'I'm sorry, but I had to come here at very short notice. It's something of an emergency.'

'I'm not interested, Bea.' There was no mistaking the chill in his voice. 'The presentation has been in the diary for weeks, as you well know. As far as I'm concerned, it should have taken precedence over everything else. The fact that you couldn't even be bothered to let any of us know that you were taking off signals to me that something very serious is missing in your attitude towards this company.'

'Adam, I'm sorry. I tried to get hold of Stuart. He'll do a great job in my—'

'There's nothing more to be said right now. Amanda will step in for you.'

I bet she will, sighed Bea.

'We'll talk whenever you deign to come back.' Without waiting for her to say anything, he hung up.

Bea was cursing under her breath throughout the fifteen-minute taxi-ride into the centre of Tours. As far as her career was concerned, she had messed up big-time. The honeymoon was well and truly over and the divorce court beckoned. Adam's reputation travelled ahead of him. Fall foul of him and there was no way back. What made it worse was that she could imagine the alacrity with which Amanda would step into her shoes and the presence of mind with which she would fulfil the role so unexpectedly thrust on her. Bea might as well have put herself in front of a firing squad and given the order to shoot.

The sky was heavy with unfallen snow. The temperature was freezing and the good citizens of Tours were well wrapped up to protect themselves against it. The window of the Pâtisserie de Paris was stocked with fat, curled crois-sants, gâteaux and tarts of every size and description. As she nudged her way through the door, Bea was hit by the rich smell of coffee, the steamy hiss of the espresso machine drowning the voices of the customers who packed the small café. A waitress dodged among the tables, carrying orders, cups and plates to the high glass counter that displayed various tiny biscuits and an array of chocolates, behind which two other girls dashed back and forth, narrowly avoiding one another, shouting requests. Heavy overcoats and macs hung crowded on the wooden coat-stands. Round the dark, panelled walls hung familiar photos of Notre

Dame, the Sacré Coeur, Versailles, the Arc de Triomphe and other Parisian landmarks.

Bea checked out each table until she lighted on one tucked into a dark corner at the back. Sitting in a low leather chair was a slim woman in her forties, not wealthy-looking but elegant in a simple air-force blue fitted coat, a patterned scarf at her throat. A boyish haircut and a fine-boned face, with large, dark, hooded eyes and a long straight nose, made her stand out from the crowd. She saw Bea and smiled. As she negotiated her way through the tables, Bea felt a growing sense of anticipation, her anxiety about Adam temporarily forgotten. She noticed that beside the woman's coffee cup was a thick manila envelope.

'Suzanne?'

The woman nodded, shy, and waited as Bea shook off her coat and ordered a *café crème* from the waitress who'd followed her. As she sat down, Suzanne pushed the envelope towards her. 'I've brought photos so you can be sure we are talking about the same person. I've also brought the letters from the solicitor so you'll know I'm telling the truth.'

Bea pulled out the contents of the envelope. Oliver was standing in the main street of a small French town in front of the large window of an art gallery, his arm around Suzanne, smiling at the camera. 'It's him,' she murmured. 'I was so hoping it wouldn't be.'

There he was again, lounging on a cushioned bench in a sunny garden. And with a young child, whom she took to be Suzanne's daughter. And standing by a table, leaning on it, looking at a piece of brightly glazed pottery. Bea stared at them, torn between relief at not having wasted

354

her journey and dismay at what to do next. Suzanne said nothing, letting Bea take in the contents of the envelope in her own time. Then she inched one of the papers towards her. The embossed letter heading belonged to a firm of Edinburgh lawyers, McKitterick, Drummond & McKay. Below was a contract of sale drawn up between Oliver Shepherd and Suzanne Berthaud, dated almost a year earlier. But what particularly puzzled Bea was the address given for Oliver.

'But this says he lives in Edinburgh. I don't understand.'

'That's where he comes from and where his wife lives.' Suzanne must have anticipated Bea's reaction.

'His *wife*?' She was leaning back in the chair and gripping the table with both hands as if it was anchoring her to the floor. Winded, she swallowed. 'You've got to be joking!'

'No.'

'But I thought he didn't have any family.'

Suzanne straightened the photos into a pile. 'When he was packing to leave, I found a letter half written to her. That was when he told me the truth for the first time. There was no longer any reason for him not to. He admitted that he had been charged with assaulting her but although a court order, I think you call it, prevented him going near her, he had been writing because he wanted to see his daughter.'

'Assault!' This was moving too fast for Bea. When she'd set out to dig a little dirt on Oliver, she hadn't dreamed she would discover something so worrying.

'Yes. Of course, when he moved in with me, I had no idea. I told you, I was really in love but things turned very bad.'

'But he didn't hit you . . . did he?' Bea looked towards the street, not wanting to hear but knowing what the answer was going to be.

'This is the one thing I haven't told you.' Suzanne leaned forward, both elbows on the table, as she lowered her voice so their neighbours couldn't hear. 'It's something I never wanted to talk about again, ever. To anyone. But I've been thinking since we spoke and I must, for your friend's sake.' She sipped her coffee as if gathering strength from it. She kept her eyes fixed on the photos, perhaps remembering happier times.

'What do you mean?' Bea felt a knot of anxiety assemble itself in the pit of her stomach.

'He didn't hit me often and never very badly and he was always so, so sorry that afterwards I forgave him every time. There were just a few slaps at first. Once he slammed a door on my hand, and another time he threw a plate at me.' She hesitated and took a sip of her coffee. 'I'm sorry. It's painful to talk about. As time went on, he became more short-tempered but he was so kind to me in so many other ways. I felt his life had not turned out quite as he wanted and I was sorry for that. Then one day he hit me in front of my daughter, Nadine. Just once. But that was enough.' Bea pulled out the photo of the young girl with Oliver. Suzanne nodded, then started making patterns with the sugar in the bowl, her mind somewhere far away. 'That was when I knew it was over. I couldn't forgive him that. I asked him to go. He agreed . . .' She paused, lost in whatever memories she was not sharing. 'I'm not proud of what I put up with. All you need to know is here.' She pointed at the documents that lay on the table under the photos. 'When he eventually left, he went back to Edinburgh.'

'I can't take all this in. What you told me before was bad enough, but now . . . You don't think Ellen's in danger, do you? I'd never forgive myself if something happened.'

'How would I know?' She shrugged her shoulders.

Bea looked at her. How could she be sure she could trust everything this complete stranger told her? Suppose this woman had some agenda of her own that made her want to blacken Oliver's name.

Suzanne started talking again, nervously tapping the table with a finger. 'I've told you because I think she should be warned. I put up with it to begin with because I loved him. He could be so loving, so generous, that I thought I was the one at fault and that perhaps I deserved his anger. But no. I know that now.' She still couldn't bring herself to look at Bea. 'I'm so ashamed of myself and for my daughter.'

'Don't be. You've made up a hundred times by being generous enough to tell me.'

'What will you do?' Suzanne began to pull on a pair of deep blue leather gloves.

'I'm not sure. I need to think. Can't I get you another coffee?'

'No, thank you. I must get back to see someone in Bourges this afternoon. But you may keep these, if they're helpful.' She indicated the envelope and then she was on her feet, pulling a blue beret over her hair, picking up her bag. She gave an embarrassed smile. 'I hope I've helped.' Bea's heart went out to her – she looked suddenly so vulnerable and unsure of herself. Was Oliver responsible for her being like this? If there had been more room between the tables, Bea would have hugged her. As it was, she had to make do with standing as straight as the chair pressed into the back of her legs would allow and offering her hand. However, Suzanne leaned forward so they could exchange awkward kisses.

Bea watched the slight figure making its way out into the cold before ordering another coffee and, as an afterthought, a slice of chocolate ganache. She ought to phone the office, but that could wait. She needed to make a plan.

*

Ben had sloped off to watch a DVD at a mate's house so when Bea got home the rest of the evening stretched ahead of her. She'd had a shower, washing away the worst of her day and borrowing Ben's razor to shave her legs and underarms. He'd be disgusted, but he wouldn't notice. If he did, she'd buy him another. Besides, the older she got, the less hair she seemed to have to shave (except for the random dark ones on her chin that were appearing with alarming regularity and needed more serious treatment), so she wouldn't be borrowing the damn thing for much longer. Afterwards she hung up her clothes (must lead by example or there was no hope) and donned her embarrassingly old-fashioned pink floral winceyette pyjamas. Combined with the stripy cashmere bedsocks that Kate had given her the previous Christmas and her White Company towelling robe they made the most comfortable get-up she'd ever owned. Yes, she looked as if she had wandered in from a hotel bedroom somewhere but she didn't care. Who was there to see?

Downstairs she knocked up her favourite supper of scrambled eggs and anchovies – a combination she couldn't remember discovering, she'd loved it for so long. Many friends had remarked on it and not always favourably. She put the pan in the sink, vowing to wash it up before Ben came home but, because it always took so long, not just yet. She carried the plate through to the living room where she put it on the coffee-table while she slipped a DVD into the player. Then she sat with her legs stretched out on the sofa, arranged the cushions behind her, picked up her supper, resting it on a copy of *Hello!* (secret vice number one) and waited for the opening credits of episode 109 of *The West Wing* (secret vice number two). A whole forty-five more to go, she reminded herself, with a small frisson of pleasure.

At her feet lay a manuscript demanding a response to its agent. It wouldn't be read tonight, but having it there made her feel as if she might make a start. She thanked God she'd seen sense and finally taken notice of Ben's insistence that their lives weren't worth living without a flat-screen LCD TV. At last she'd put out the monolithic old set and replaced it with this streamlined dark-surround job that fitted neatly into the alcove by the chimney-breast. If there was anything guaranteed to clear her mind of the fact that she'd fallen out with the three women – if she included Amanda – who were closest to her, this was it. She leaned back and had her first mouthful as the strings took her soaring over to the White House and all that was good and bad about America.

But tonight the fate of a fact-finding congressional delegation to the Gaza Strip failed to grip her interest. Her mind kept wandering off to Suzanne, Mark, and what she had decided do next. As she was contemplating the alternative joys of episode 110 or the manuscript – no contest, really, but she felt better if she went through the motions – she was saved by the phone.

Mark had finished work late and was anxious to find out what had happened in France. After listening, he agreed that there was only one course of action open to her. Before she returned Kate's calls or even attempted to speak to Ellen, Edinburgh beckoned. Mark offered to book himself a ticket so he could come with her.

'But you don't need to,' she protested.

'I want to. Moral support. I'll book us into a swish hotel and take Friday off. How does that sound?'

'Well, brilliant, actually. I'd really appreciate it if you were there.'

'Then that's where I'll be. Leave it to me.'

Bea hung up and pressed the play button for episode 110. Mark was really quite intuitive. His company on the trip to Edinburgh was exactly what she wanted. As the strings swelled once again, she swiftly put the manuscript by the door ready for its journey upstairs – a sleeping partner who wouldn't snore or take most of the bedclothes yet might entertain her – and settled back on the sofa. But not before she'd grabbed her bag and unearthed her pudding, a box of four Paul A. Young hand-made chocolates (not-so-secret vice number three).

In *The West Wing*, events were spiralling out of control

in Gaza when Bea heard the front door slam and familiar footsteps dragging down the hall. She pressed the pause button as the door opened.

'Hey, Mum. What's up?' Ben dropped his bag in the middle of the room and plonked himself down beside her. She just bent her knees in time. 'Not *West Wing* again?'

'You know you love it, really. You just need to keep up.'

'If I did that, I'd be some saddo who stayed in with his mother most nights. Just because you've got a box-set habit doesn't mean I have to have one too.'

'True enough.' She ruffled his hair. 'Have you eaten? Hey!' She slapped at his hand, which was inching towards the remaining chilli truffle and raspberry ganache. 'Mine! Well, OK. You can have one of them, provided it's the raspberry.'

He puffed out his cheeks at her. ''S all right, but I might see if there's something in the fridge.'

He joined her for the remainder of the episode with a yoghurt and two cold sausages. They sat together, Bea catching him up with the plot as they went along. The smell of tobacco on his breath and smoke on his clothes reminded her of the failure of Colin's man-to-man chat. But Bea didn't mind. Just sitting with her boy, she felt contentment sweep over her. He wouldn't be there for ever, she knew that, but when he was and they were getting on, there was nothing to beat that feeling, as strong now as it had been when he was born. At last, for the first time that day, her mind stopped whirring and she allowed herself to relax.

30

The night after the private view Oliver came round for what was a slightly awkward supper with a monosyllabic Emma and a garrulous Matt. He waited until the children had disappeared upstairs before suggesting they took their coffee to the sitting room where they could talk. To Ellen's relief, the place was reasonably tidy. She put the tray on the blanket box she used as a coffee-table, then sat down beside him. Aware he was nervous about whatever he was going to say, she kept silent, waiting for him. After a few moments, he took a deep breath and began.

'I didn't feel ready to talk to anyone about this before but Bea's interfering made me realise I've got to be completely honest with you. I'm worried there may be misunder-standings if I'm not.' She felt him press a little harder on her arm while he paused, as if struggling to find the right words.

'Honest, yes,' she agreed. 'But you don't have to tell me anything you don't want to just because of what she's done.'

'I don't know who she's been talking to but I can only think she's found out about what happened in France.'

He shifted position so she had to readjust her own. 'You know that I lived with a woman there – Suzanne.'

Ellen concentrated as he began to detail the complexities of their relationship. However, she was soon lost among the intricacies and influences of Suzanne's numerous interfering relations and friends. She caught up again when he was talking about how they had grown apart. He'd lowered his voice so she could only just hear him. 'The first time she hit me with her mobile, I didn't think it meant anything.'

Ellen was listening in astonishment. He must have heard the catch in her breath.

'I know how stupid that must sound. But then she attacked me again. And again. Every time she apologised, crying and promising she'd never do it again. She didn't know what had come over her. But she got worse. Once she even burned my arm with the iron. I tried so hard not to provoke her but I never knew what it was that I did to trigger her off. She couldn't seem to help herself. I can't tell you how ashamed and useless I felt, yet I tried so hard. What sort of man am I to prompt that sort of behaviour, then sit back and take it?' His voice broke.

Ellen sat completely still. He hadn't looked at her once while he spoke as if he couldn't bear to see her inevitable disappointment in him. She reached across to hold his hand as he continued.

'She had only just opened the gallery when we met but I worked hard for her, helping her build it up. In return, after a year, she gave me a half-share in it to show her gratitude. She really believed we were in it for the long haul.

For a while we were a golden couple but nobody knew what was happening between us behind closed doors. I promised not to tell anyone, not even her family, and I kept my word. But the pressure built between us until we had a terrible fight, and in her rage, she said some appalling things to me. That was what gave me the courage to leave her there and then. I realised that if I didn't she was going to destroy me. She was devastated, begging me to stay. I needed every ounce of my willpower not to. You've got to believe me.'

'Of course I do.' Having heard him out, Ellen could barely speak, but she wanted to reassure him of her support.

'So I left. The only thing we had to sort out was the property because of course half the gallery was in my name. She insisted on buying it back. I would have given it to her gladly but I think she felt guilty about her behaviour and somehow this was a way of buying my silence. More than that, I think she was genuinely grateful for all I'd done to build the business. And I'd done a lot. So I agreed to accept well below the market value. That's the money I've been existing on and it's pretty much come to an end now. Thank God, you helped me by paying the rent.' At last he looked at her directly. 'There. Now you know the whole sorry tale. I didn't want to tell you because I was frightened you'd think . . . well, that I was some kind of wimp, or something. And perhaps now you do.'

'Of course I don't.' This was so far from what she might have expected, she wasn't immediately sure what more to say. Instead, she just squeezed his hand. What courage it must have taken to tell her. Instead of diminishing himself in her eyes he'd erased any doubt in her mind about their relationship. He wasn't less of a man for having endured what he had. If anything, she admired him more for his stoicism and the patience he'd shown towards Suzanne.

'No wonder you didn't want to talk about her,' she said, understanding. 'But you know what? I love you even more for telling me. We shouldn't have secrets from one another if we're going to live together.' He started to say something but she carried on, encouraged by his obvious relief. 'I've decided, if you still feel the same, that's what I'd like. Why don't you move in with us? Any time you want.'

He clearly hadn't expected this. 'Is this what you really want?'

When she nodded, he pulled her towards him. 'Despite everything I've told you?'

'It really is. What you've told me happened between you and Suzanne. I'm not her. I don't see why it should make any difference to us.' Resting her head on his chest, Ellen could feel the beating of his heart through his jumper.

'And the children?'

'The children will be fine. At least, Matt will be. We both know Em's going to be harder to pull round.' She heard herself echoing what she'd said weeks ago, knowing there was no reliable evidence that she was right. 'But we'll work on her together and, in the end, she'll have to accept it.' She wasn't entirely convinced things would pan out that easily but she wanted to believe they would. And if she believed it, perhaps that was what would happen. As far as she was concerned, Oliver had vindicated himself. Bea's accusations, whatever they were, were unfounded.

'Well, I don't want you to do anything that doesn't feel completely right,' he said.

She felt his hand on her head, tracing her hairline, down the side of her face to the back of her neck.

'This feels completely right. Everything fell into place after I'd had supper with Jed and he told me he was looking for a place down here. I was thinking about everything and realised we could sublet the flat to him. I know strictly speaking it's breaking the terms of the lease but who's going to know? I'm pretty sure he'll jump at it.'

'Can he afford it?'

'Of course he can. The paintings he's sold already will cover six months' rent and we've still got plenty of interest in the rest. I'm dying to see what he'll do once he starts working down here.'

'But the flat's tiny. How's he going to manage?'

'Well, yes. There's one more thing I haven't told you.' This was the bit that Ellen had been putting off mentioning. She looked up at him.

'What?' His hand was still on her head.

She waited for a second, then admitted, 'I'm going to tell him he can use the studio.'

His face darkened. 'But I got that for you.'

She felt his grip tighten on her hair till it hurt. She reached up to make him let go. Then, sitting up, she twisted round to face him. The blue vein had appeared in his temple again. She reached out to reassure him, but he inched away, his right fist repeatedly clenching and unclenching. 'I know you did, and I will use it one day. But I'm so busy with the gallery and the kids that I just don't have the time right now. This way Jed will be able to produce more paintings that we can sell at the gallery. And he's going to pay rent.'

'We?'

'What?' She watched his fist relax.

'You said, "*We* can sell at the gallery."'

'Did I? I meant "I".'

'But that's a brilliant idea. Why not "we"? I could come in with you. We'd be a great team. You've got the eye. I've got the organisational skills.' His expression had been transformed with excitement and enthusiasm. He grasped her hand as if willing her to agree.

But she didn't want to share the gallery with anyone, not even Oliver, with whom she was about to share her life. Perhaps she was being unfair, especially when he was having such difficulty on the work front, but she had made the gallery what it was and she didn't want to compromise. He might not think she could run a business efficiently, she thought, slightly annoyed by his implication, but she had done well enough until now. 'Steady on. You're crushing me.' She removed her hand from his grip and massaged her knuckles. Reluctant to break the change in mood, she hesitated before replying, wondering how to let him down gently. Living with him was one thing. Sharing her business was another.

'Come on, Ellen,' he broke in. 'I could learn so much from you. Perhaps we could even extend to renting the floor above.'

He knew just which of her buttons to press. Taking the floor above the gallery had long been a dream of hers. For years, the same landlord had used the two small rooms for storage, accessing them through the back of the building.

And for years, Ellen had imagined being able to open the front staircase and use the rooms herself, perhaps widening her stock to include some of the pottery and jewellery she'd seen on her travels. She steadied herself. 'That's a fantastic idea and perhaps, one day, we could. But not yet.'

His face fell.

'Let's take one step at a time. I'm not saying no,' she added hurriedly. 'Just not yet.'

'But you do think it's an idea?'

She couldn't refuse the hope in his voice. 'Of course I do. Let's get you in here and the children sorted. Then, if you still haven't found the right job, we'll think again.'

'I've got another idea.'

'What?'

'What if I were to help just on Saturdays? You've always said that's the busiest day. And that way at least we could spend the whole weekend together. Or, when you decide that you trust me, you could spend more time with the kids while I cover for you.'

'It's not about trusting.' But now he'd pressed another button. The guilt she had felt at not being around on Saturdays since Uncle Sidney's death had weighed on her for a long time now. She had managed, thanks to her neighbours, to Bea or Kate, and to occasionally shutting when absolutely necessary or during the quiet winter periods, but it had never been ideal. If she agreed, she would be able to go to Matt's football matches, spend more time with Emma and perhaps even ease her daughter into seeing that gaining Oliver was not the same as losing her mother. That final consideration decided her.

'All right, we'll give it a—' She hadn't finished the sentence when the breath was all but squeezed out of her by his hug.

'You won't regret it, I promise.' His smile was wider than she'd ever seen it, his eyes brighter. 'And then, if you think I'm any use . . .'

'No promises.' No thin end of the wedge. There would only ever be one person in control of her gallery and that was her. Not even Oliver would change that. She had always said she would never take on anyone in any capacity on any kind of a regular basis. But his delight made her feel as if she'd just given him the best present in the world, not to mention a sign of her commitment to him.

'OK. I get it. But this calls for a celebration.' He hugged her again, this time more gently, and then they kissed.

31

Things had hardly gone as Bea had planned. In an attempt to make up for her dash to France she had got into work early on Thursday morning. Yelling, 'Good morning,' in the direction of the post-room, she had crossed to the door of her office. She was surprised to see the vertical blinds drawn down. She rarely closed them, believing it was more egalitarian, given she had one of the few enclosed offices, to let everyone in the open-plan area see what she was doing. Reading and typing; typing and reading; and talking. The cleaners must have been being unusually thorough. As she leaned on the handle, she thought she heard a noise inside. Puzzled, she let the door swing open. Amanda was stepping out from behind her desk, a file in her hand. Looking her usual chic, unruffled self in a neat aubergine suit and lime green boat-necked top, she smiled as if it was the most natural thing in the world to be found there. 'Morning!' she chirped, nonchalance personified.

'What the hell are you doing?'

'I was just looking for the original Archer contract.'

'Couldn't you have waited for me to come in and then asked?'

'I could. But we didn't know whether you'd be in today or not.' A smile played at the corners of her mouth. Amanda was clearly revelling in her rival's sudden fall from grace. But Bea had expected no less.

However, Amanda having the brass neck to snoop round her office exceeded her expectations. 'What made you think you'd find it behind my desk?'

'I thought you might keep author files in the drawers.'

'Amanda, that's the lamest excuse I've heard for years. Surely you can do better than that.'

'It's the truth,' she protested, as cool as ever. 'And now you're here, perhaps you could give it to me yourself.'

'The contracts are all filed in the rights department, as you well know. I suggest you look there.'

Bea crossed the room so she could check her computer screen. It was blank, thank God. She had remembered to log off before she left on Tuesday to go to the private view. What a long time ago that seemed.

Amanda was edging her way out of the room. As she reached the door, she turned, her composure fully recovered. 'Oh, by the way, Bea, the presentation went well. Thanks for asking.'

Before Bea had time to react, Amanda had gone, gliding apparently without a care across the open-plan area to her own office. 'Cat' and 'cream' were the two words that sprang to Bea's irate mind. Having safely locked her bag into her drawer, she glanced over her desk to see what might have interested Amanda. Most of her correspondence with agents about possible or upcoming projects was on email so she couldn't have taken advantage of anything there. In fact, apart from the submissions, which were all logged in for anyone to see, she didn't think there was anything that particularly mattered. Relieved, but still furious at the intrusion, she hung up her coat and strode over to Adam's office to protest and apologise – if he would let her.

'Adam, can I have a word?'

When he nodded her in, she stood in front of his desk, knowing she'd be well advised not to let her anger show. She waited to be asked to sit down but the invitation was not forthcoming. A bad sign.

'So, you've decided to come back.' He continued to study the sales screen on his computer, without even a glance in her direction.

'Look, I'm really sorry but there was something I simply had to do.'

Behind him, she could see the London skyline sharp against the clouds. A small aircraft circled like a gnat somewhere towards the river. She became aware of the steady tick of a new clock that he'd had installed beside the door behind her.

'But you can't tell me what it was?'

'I'm afraid not.' For once in her life, Bea was at a loss as to how to handle a situation. She obviously hadn't just blotted her copybook with Adam. She'd torn it up and thrown it away. He wouldn't understand if she explained what she'd been up to and he certainly wouldn't consider it justification for missing such an important meeting. Meanwhile Amanda was hovering, waiting for any opportunity to better her rival, and Bea was making it easy for her.

'Bea, I've been talking to Amanda who incidentally did us all proud yesterday.' He tore his eyes from the screen and directed his attention fully on her. 'She's come up with some good ideas about how the editorial department could work more effectively. Talking to her persuaded me she's right. Particularly after you pulled that stunt yesterday. That, of course, was one of several things that came up in our discussion.'

I bet it was, she thought. His Beach-Barbie wife and son stared out at them both from the photo. Was there more credibility in the office gossip than Bea had thought? Had Amanda succeeded in flexing the boundary between her professional and personal relationship with Adam? If so, she might be getting a lot more of her own way in the future, which in turn would mean that Bea was going to find it almost impossible to scramble back into Adam's good books.

His face was unreadable. 'Not coming in yesterday and not warning anyone of your absence suggests to me that I can't rely on you in the way I'd hoped.'

'That's ridiculous, Adam. It was just one day. You know full well that I do a good job.'

Adam continued as if she hadn't spoken. 'You have to accept that Amanda is part of this company now.' He sounded as if he was talking to an educationally challenged five-year-old. 'She has a job to do here just as you have. She's told me how hard she's found it to work with you. You need to be more collaborative.'

'Even if I find her snooping about my office?'

'That's not Amanda's style.'

'Then how come I've just found her in my office, behind my desk, with the blinds closed?'

'I'm sure there was a good reason. Ask her.'

'I have.'

But Adam had already turned his attention back to his screen. His hands moved quickly over the keyboard. The discussion was closed. Bea gave an exasperated sigh and left him. She stormed over to the coffee machine for a polystyrene cup of the black sludge that passed as espresso. She took a double shot, marched back to her office and shut the door. She grimaced at the first taste. Heart-starter or heart-stopper? she wondered, and pushed the cup out of reach.

As she thought about what had just happened, she realised that her working life was about to become more difficult than ever. Finding her way back into Adam's favour was going to be difficult, perhaps impossible. Besides, did she really want to put herself through the humiliating procedure of trying? Her working life had taken a serious nose-dive from which it would be hard to recover. The seed that had been sown during her talk with Adele began to germinate. Perhaps she had reached a point at which she had to take control of her working life instead of going where it took her. Perhaps she would be able to survive outside the confines of Coldharbour, after all.

Adam was out of the office for the rest of the day. That meant she had the whole weekend to plan what she would say to him on Monday. She had no qualms about telling Amanda she had to go to Edinburgh to visit Audrey Balfour, a needy but much-needed bestselling author, who had asked her to travel up to discuss her next historical novel. Amanda had rolled her eyes at what she obviously felt was a further dereliction of duty, but Bea ignored her. Neither did she explain that her real reason for going was to find someone called Marion Drummond.

*

Bea sipped half-heartedly at her warm champagne. She turned to her left where Mark was hidden behind his copy of the *Financial Times*, a cup of coffee to hand. She thanked God the Edinburgh-bound budget airline had curtailed the jingle that had repeated itself *ad nauseam* before take-off until she thought she might scream or tear the plane apart with her bare hands until she found the off switch. But at least this time, on her third flight in two days, they hadn't hit any turbulence. On Thursday night she and Mark had rushed to meet each other at Liverpool Street after work, each clutching an overnight bag, and boarded the train. As they sped to Stansted, she told him at length about her day and the life-changing decision she had made. Judging by his reactions, Bea guessed that while he envied her impulsiveness, it made him a little nervous too. But there was nothing she could do to change her nature. Besides, her sense of anticipation about what lay ahead was clearly infectious.

Apart from that, the thought of a hotel room with crisp white sheets, a super-king-sized bed and a like-minded companion beckoned – what more could a girl want? What this one wanted was confirmation. And she was determined to get it. In her bag, stuffed into the phone pocket so it wouldn't disappear into the depths, was the address and phone number of Marion Drummond, otherwise known as Mrs Oliver Shepherd.

The flight was crowded and already delayed by three-quarters of an hour. By the time they finally disembarked into the icy sleet at Edinburgh, there was little traffic on the roads so their taxi found its way to the boutique Bruntsfield hotel in about twenty minutes, arriving just before they stopped serving dinner. It was the first opportunity for a week or so that she and Mark had had to sit down together. The dining room was discreet, dimly lit and came highly recommended by a colleague of his.

Within minutes of sitting at the table, Bea felt as relaxed as she ever had in the company of a lover. More so, perhaps. The diminutive starters were not much bigger than the *amuse-bouches* that had preceded them. Their palates were cleansed by a searingly acidic mixed citron sorbet before the minuscule main courses of monkfish steaks (for her) and rack of lamb (for him). Dithering over the wine, they decided to compromise and order by the glass so they could both enjoy the colour they preferred. Their conversation ranged over the children (gratifyingly and unusually well behaved at the moment), his wife (currently monstrously ill behaved with her demands rocketing now she knew he was seeing someone else), their work (anxious times given the current climate for him; her future hanging in the balance) and, of course, what lay in store for the following day.

'I still think you should have phoned her before we flew

up. Suppose she's not there?' As ever, Mark was the calm voice of reason.

But Bea was not. 'No. I've got to meet her in person and I want the element of surprise on my side. I didn't want to risk her refusing to see me or leaving town once she knew I was on my way.'

'And if she's not there?'

'I'll talk to her neighbours. I'll stay another night and wait for her. I don't know! I haven't thought it through but I must know exactly what I'm talking about when I manage to see Kate. I want her to grasp how thorough I've been. I'm not making the same mistake I made on Tuesday night.'

'I'm glad you've learned your lesson.'

'OK, Mr Smart Arse. That sounded just the teeniest bit smug.'

'You know I didn't mean it. So, how do I fit in?' His absolute willingness to help her was like having her favourite hot-water bottle in bed – reassuring and comforting.

'I thought we could find the house together early tomorrow morning. It's somewhere in Morningside, so she can't exactly be short of a bob or two. Then I'll go and talk to her on my own. I won't be long. After that we could go to the new wing of the National Gallery and have a sandwich there. Then I'll meet the tiresome Audrey Balfour for a couple of hours' worth of tea and ear-bashing and then we'll waste time together until we get the plane back. How does that sound?'

'Militaristic.'

She laughed.

'I'm exhausted just by the sound of it.' He pulled a face. 'Shall we head upstairs to get some rest ahead of time?'

'Thought you'd never ask.'

'Coffee or dessert?'

'No coffee. And I've got a small box of Godiva chocs that you're going to love. I thought we could just accompany them with a little something from the mini-bar.'

'Sounds perfect. Lead on, Macduff.'

*

The night fulfilled every one of Bea's hopes and expectations. It was extraordinary how much things could improve with practice, she mused, as they went downstairs for breakfast. Since their first awkward night together in Norfolk, Mark's confidence as a lover had grown so there were certainly no complaints on that score.

Mark had got a city map from the reception desk and over the full Scottish they hunted together for Cluny Drive. 'Got it!' Bea exclaimed, pointing with her knife and spreading egg yolk over the spot.

'It's a bit of a hike from here, but there must be a bus.' Mark borrowed her reading specs and squinted at the tiny numbers marked on the different roads.

In the end they took a taxi, Bea arguing that time was hardly on their side. She ignored Mark's suggestion that Marion might have left for work by the time they got there. The Edinburgh streets were bleak. Bad weather had rolled in from the north-east. Pillows of grey cloud swelled above the terraces, dark with rain. Car headlights beamed through the gloom. At least Bea and Mark had come prepared, Bea with her three-quarter-length loose black coat with a fur trim that, while not the most flattering, was a sure-fire barrier against the most Arctic of winds. On her head she had a fake (of course) silver fox Dr Zhivago hat. Mark was similarly well wrapped up in a heavy navy coat, bright orange scarf, gloves and a wide-brimmed waterproof hat that gave him a rather dashing outdoorsy look.

Turning off busy Comiston Road, the taxi entered a leafy residential area, pulling up outside a substantial semi-detached Victorian villa with a light shining from the ground-floor bay window. Mark took both of Bea's gloved hands and squeezed them. 'Good luck,' he said. 'I'll wait in the cab to see whether someone's there. If you go in, I'll find a coffee on the main road. If not, we'll be waiting round that corner. If you need me for any reason, call me and I'll be there.'

Giving him a peck on the cheek and an apprehensive grimace, Bea climbed out. Bracing herself against the wind, she waved, then turned under a small rustic arch and up a long, straight path that divided a scrappy front lawn down the middle. At its end was a white front door, surrounded by the naked stems of climbing roses. To the left of the door was a large bay window, curtains half closed, but she could hear music playing within. She could just make out a mirror above the fireplace and the reflection of a modern chandelier. To the right, four rectangular windows, two above two, stared out into the morning, blinds raised, lights off.

Bea reached out to the bell beside the door. It wasn't too

late to turn back. Instead she could spend the morning with Mark and give up this potentially pointless enterprise. But a voice inside her head said, *No. Finish what you've started. Wouldn't you want a friend to go to such lengths if they were worried about you?* Her resolve shored up, she pressed the lower bell marked 'Drummond' and heard five dissonant notes ring out inside the house. After a few seconds, she heard a shout, 'Hang on. Just coming.' A chain was unhooked, a mortice unlocked and the handle turned.

Bea stared at the woman in front of her – not the beaten-down victim she was expecting at all. In her forties, she had a round face cushioned by a double chin, deep-set blue eyes under eyebrows that had never glimpsed tweezers, and a pair of ruddy round cheeks. She was holding a towel to her pepper-and-salt hair. A certain stoutness was half hidden under a plaid dressing-gown. As she waited for Bea to speak, her initial smile began to fade.

'Yes?'

Bea pulled herself together. 'I'm so sorry. Are you Marion Drummond?'

'Yes, I am. And you are?'

'My name's Bea Wilde. I've come about Oliver Shepherd. I just want to ask you a few questions.'

Marion's face changed. Bea wasn't sure whether she was frightened or furious. 'Are you the police? Has he done something?'

'God, no. Do I look like a policewoman? I need to find out about him so that I can help a friend. Please let me explain.'

'You'd better come in before we freeze to death.' Marion

pulled the door open and welcomed Bea into a large hall. 'Now, how can I help you? It'll have to be quick or I'll be late for work.' She tossed the towel onto a chair before leading her through to a room at the back of the hall where the emphasis was on comfort rather than style. At one end, a sofa draped with a bright paisley throw was angled in front of a TV. A pile of magazines littered the floor between them. At the other, an oval table was covered with a patterned oilcloth. A dark-haired girl was sitting at it, eating breakfast. 'This is Natalie, my daughter.'

Bea nodded a greeting, remembering Kate's description of the young woman she had seen with Oliver. She told herself not to jump to any conclusions but to wait until she knew more.

They sat down together, and while Bea removed her hat and coat, Marion poured them all a cup of strong coffee from the cafetière, then offered round a bottle of milk. With the two women watching her, Bea embarked on her story once again, making sure she kept everything in the right order and didn't leave anything out. Marion listened carefully, giving the impression she'd heard it all before. Natalie looked upset but resigned, and continued eating her toast. When Bea produced the photos she had of Oliver, they both gave the briefest of nods and returned them without saying more.

When she'd finished, Marion asked Natalie to make some more coffee and to phone each of their employers to tell them they would be a little late. 'Only a little, mind,' she added, to emphasise the point. 'She's a PA at the Royal Bank of Scotland on Princes Street, God help us,' she explained, with a chuckle. 'And I've got to get down to a primary school in Merchiston but they'll manage fine without me for half an hour.'

While Natalie was out of the room, she spoke quickly and quietly to Bea. 'Oliver's Natalie's father so I won't say too much. Of course she knows he was violent and she was there one awful night when he was in his cups, grabbed me by the hair and smashed my head against the door, yelling and shouting. In fact, she was the one who called the police, but . . . years have passed and, after all, he is her dad.'

'What happened? Do you mind me asking?'

'Not at all. It was all over the local press so it's no secret.' She looked weary at the memory. 'Oliver was a possessive man, who had to know exactly where I'd been and who with. He'd give me the odd tap if he didn't like what I'd done but nothing too bad. I got clever at spotting the signs and keeping out of his way. But that particular night he came home from the pub, fixated with the idea that I'd been seeing someone behind his back. Somebody had said something that he'd twisted around in his head. Nothing I said would convince him otherwise. He started tearing the place apart, looking for a note – anything – to prove I was lying. I'd never seen him so out of control. I don't remember exactly what happened, but one minute I was yelling at him to stop and the next he had me on the floor with his hands around my neck. The noise woke Natalie up and she called the police. That was it. He gave himself up to them without a fuss. They took him away and he never set foot in here again. When he'd sobered up, he was terrified by what he'd done and so sorry, but I wouldn't have him back after that. I had a child to protect. While he was on bail, he wasn't allowed anywhere near us. He got three months suspended, then disappeared down south.'

Natalie returned with the coffee and Marion paused while her daughter refilled their cups.

Bea was trying to take the story in, appalled by its implications. 'Have you heard from him since?'

Marion glanced at Natalie.

'Not until about a year ago. He didn't come here but he rang asking if he could use this address for a legal matter. I agreed he could. Silly, really, but I suppose I felt sorry for him. After all this time he's still apologising.'

'He's stopped drinking now, though.' Natalie spoke for the first time, with a softer Scottish burr than Marion's. 'He told me that.'

'Yes. Natalie's seen him. You visited him when you were in London, didn't you?'

The girl nodded. And Bea refrained from mentioning the wine she'd seen Oliver enjoy. No point in puncturing his daughter's beliefs. This was not about her.

'But you're divorced?' Bea couldn't help asking.

'Lord, no.' Marion threw back her head and roared with laughter. 'I'm afraid not. We should be but that seemed the least of our worries. To be honest, I was so relieved he was away at last and I didn't want to do anything to rile him. I don't want him back here threatening me or causing trouble again. And he's never asked for a divorce.'

By the time Bea left, her head was spinning. She had come to Edinburgh to be certain that there was no mistaking who Oliver was. What she'd come away with was the awful certainty that her closest friend was involved with an abusive conman who had a wife and a daughter he'd never mentioned. She had photos to prove he was the same person, and legal documentation about the sale of Suzanne's gallery. Now she had to find a way to make Kate listen to her and together they would decide how to break the news to Ellen. If Ellen decided to do nothing with the information, that was her business.

The rest of the day sped by. Wandering round the National Gallery, she hardly noticed the pictures they were looking at. Over lunch, she toyed with her soup while telling Mark everything.

'I'm glad I was with you in case something happened,' he said. 'And after last night I reckon we make quite a good team, you and me.'

'You know what? I'm beginning to think we do too.'

They kissed across the table, ignoring the snorts of derision from the schoolchildren at the couple of tables nearest to them. Walking briskly along Princes Street, leaning into the biting wind, Bea stopped thinking about Ellen for a minute or two as she remembered Mark's words. He might not be the most prepossessing of men at first glance but, like it or not, she had meant what she said. They did work well together, in more ways than one.

As she approached the Balmoral Hotel, she changed her focus to Audrey and how she would counter the woman's objections to the way her last book had been published. She walked past the kilted footman through the revolving door into the grand lobby and a different world. She turned towards the sound of a harp drifting in from the Bollinger Bar. Audrey had installed herself at a banquette facing the bar and was already halfway through a glass of champagne. She was a particular type of Edinburgh lady, tall, thin and refined, not a hair of her waved bob out of place, the colours of her tweed skirt toning exactly with her cashmere twinset. She beckoned Bea over with an imperious wave and the briefest of smiles. The small-talk was exactly that, as Bea ordered the Balmoral tea for two, then listened to what Audrey had to say, making the right noises and defending the publishing strategy when called on to do so. She was virtually working on autopilot until she was pulled up short.

'Amanda Winter tells me you'll be rejacketing my backlist.'

'I'm sorry. Who said that?' Bea thought she must have misheard. Suddenly Audrey had her full attention.

'Amanda Winter. A darling girl who phoned me yesterday to introduce herself. I understand she's in charge of the publishing now, although I know you'll still be my editor. Will you be all right, after all this time?'

'I'll be absolutely fine, thank you, Audrey. Just fine.' So the scheming witch was already cosying up to Bea's authors behind her back and demoting her in the process. Amanda must have known that Audrey would repeat the message. As far as Bea was aware, there had been no planned rejacketing programme, although she agreed it was long overdue. In fact, she'd been fighting that corner on Audrey's behalf for months. The forces at Coldharbour were already moving against her, but they would be too late. It seemed that

Audrey, unwittingly, had put the final seal on Bea's own plans.

Eventually Bea made her escape, agreeing to keep in contact over the new treatments they might use and giving repeated assurances that she would put Audrey's new novel about Anne of Denmark to the top of her pile when it came in. And, yes (through gritted teeth), of course she would share it with Amanda. Never has an escape felt more divinely pleasant, she thought, as she made her way back through the sleet to Mark and the long journey home.

That night, while Mark cleared up supper she went upstairs, relieved that Ben had been so polite when they'd got back. Perhaps he welcomed the idea of another person in their lives who might take the heat off him from time to time. She had left them to it so that she could call Kate, as she and Mark had agreed she should. All the way home, she had gone over with him what she might say, how she would manoeuvre her way past Paul, if necessary. She had no idea what sort of reception to expect. She lined up two Rococo chocolates on the small table beside her, a lavender and a rose cream, then dialled.

Within moments Kate picked up.

'It's Bea. Don't hang up, please.' She hadn't meant to sound quite so desperate.

'Of course I won't, you idiot. I'm so glad you've phoned. Where have you been? I've tried calling you but you never picked up.'

'I've been dying to talk to you,' confessed Bea, intensely relieved that Kate wasn't going to cold-shoulder her. 'I behaved so badly on the night of the private view and I'm sorry I got caught between the two of you. I would have called back but I wanted to get my facts straight so I had to go to France and Edinburgh, believe it or not. But now I've really got something that we must talk about.'

'God, Bea. You know I'm not happy about this. It's why we all fell out, for goodness' sake.'

'I wouldn't ask if I didn't believe it was important. Please.' If Kate didn't listen to her, she would never convince Ellen. She waited as her friend deliberated.

'OK. OK. I give in.' Kate thought for a moment. 'Let's meet for lunch in Carluccio's tomorrow. You can tell me then. I've got a few things of my own to tell you, too.'

Bea picked up the lavender cream as she hung up. She had a feeling that everything between them was going to be all right. Now there was one more thing she wanted to do before she went back downstairs. She popped the lavender cream into her mouth and turned on her laptop to draft her letter of resignation.

32

That Friday night, Oliver and Ellen sat down to supper with Matt and Emma once more. Nothing was much different from the last time, except that Ellen's stomach felt as if butterflies were clog-dancing through it. Oliver irritated her by advising her to relax. How could she? They had talked to Jed, who had jumped at the idea of moving into the flat. His son had delayed his arrival until the weekend and was picking up the VW on Sunday, by which time Oliver would have moved out. Perhaps Jed was right, Ellen thought. Perhaps Fate was offering a guiding hand. In which case, the time had come to tell the children about all this.

Emma had come in late from school and had gone straight to her room to change. The laptop under her arm suggested she wouldn't be seen until supper, Facebook being so much more alluring than any conversation with her mother and Oliver. Matt had followed her in, bouncing a football down the hall. Ellen had felt Oliver wince as it rolled down the stairs to the basement. He picked it up and shoved it into a cupboard. She smiled to herself, knowing his sharp 'tut' came as he struggled with the door as the cupboard's contents fought to get out.

Matt was oblivious to the fate of his ball as he jumped down the stairs two at a time, his school bag bumping against the banisters. He submitted to Ellen's hug before untangling himself to head straight for the fridge. His over-long trousers wrinkled over his scuffed lace-ups, his shirt was untucked from his waistband and his tie hung from a trouser pocket.

'Matt, we're about to have supper . . .'

'Why so early? I want to see that *Top Gear* we recorded last night. Anyway, I'm starving.' He poured himself a glass of milk and took a Twix from the biscuit tin.

'Em's going out, that's why. Matt! Must you put your feet on the seat? Someone's going to sit there.'

'But they're not now, though, are they?' He moved them as Ellen advanced with a floor cloth in her hand. 'Anyway, guess what? I've been picked for the first team tomorrow. Billy's been dropped and I'm in.' He high-fived her.

'I thought you were looking pleased.' The years had taught her exactly how much being selected meant to Matt. 'That's fantastic.'

'So will you come and watch the match?' The eagerness in his face willing her to say 'yes' almost broke her heart.

'You know I want to more than anything, but I can't.' She went to pull the lasagne out of the oven.

'You never do.' He jumped off the chair and headed for the stairs.

'That's not fair. I would if I could.'

'I know – it's the bloody gallery's fault. Again.'

'Matt!'

Then Oliver intervened: 'I'd like to come. Would you accept me as a substitute?'

He had slipped in his request before Ellen could reprimand Matt for his language. She saw the pleasure in Matt's eyes at the idea of having someone to cheer him on, although he was grudging in his acceptance nonetheless.

'Yeah. OK. As long as you cheer for the right team.'

'What do you take me for? A complete numbskull? Of course I will. That's settled, then. And perhaps your mum could go next time. What do you think?'

'She won't. She never does.'

'Well, maybe we've got some news for you that you'll like.' Oliver smiled at him. 'No, I won't tell you. Not yet. And I've got tickets for the Arsenal match next week.'

'Wicked!' Matt's face lit up.

'Your name's on one of them if you lay the table.' He held out the knives and forks, which were ripped from his hand.

Five minutes later, the four of them were sitting down together. Emma was silent, eating rapidly, the quicker to get out of the house. Ellen had refrained from commenting on the skimpiness of her skirt, which barely covered her bum, or on her almost sheer glittery top. Didn't she feel the cold? Matt and Oliver were discussing the finer points of Fabregas's game. Ellen was finding it impossible to do anything other than play with the food on her plate, knowing that what she was about to say to them would mean things could never be the same again. But, she told herself for the umpteenth time, this was what she wanted to do. As they came to the end of the course, she cleared her throat and decided to plunge in before Emma disappeared through the front door.

'Listen, kids.' She tried to control the forced jollity she could hear in her voice. 'There's something that Oliver and I want to tell you.'

'What? Don't tell me. Oliver's moving in.' Emma didn't even look up but Ellen didn't need to see her face to register her disdain.

'Well, yes. But there's more to it than that.' Ellen had been preparing what she was going to say for the last forty-eight hours and, with one swipe, Emma had just taken her legs away.

'How can there be? It's been obvious that's what you've been waiting for so you might as well get on with it.' She still didn't lift her head, her fingers moving below the table.

'Would you mind not texting when I'm trying to talk to you?' The hope and optimism that she had nervously brought to the table were leaving Ellen and into their place rushed anger. 'I want to explain to you both how I hope things might work out.'

'Whatever.' Emma's chair shrieked against the tiles as she stood up, taking her denim jacket from its back.

'What are you doing?'

'Going out. I told you ages ago that I'm going to meet Freya.'

'SIT DOWN!' All three faces turned to Ellen in surprise. Even she couldn't remember when she had last raised her voice to them. 'NOW!' Just in case there was any doubt about what she meant.

Shocked into submission, Emma returned to her seat, slipping her mobile into the pocket of her jacket and fingering her bead-drop earrings.

'I know you don't want to hear this, but I want you to listen all the same.' Watching her daughter's pinched, resentful face, Ellen regretted shouting. Their living arrangements were making her experience emotions that she was still too young to understand, so Ellen had at least to try to explain. She had never shied away from telling her children what she thought were the essential truths of life and this was every bit as important. This was the moment she had chosen to tell them, and she was going to do it – calmly.

'I want you to understand how much Oliver means to me.' She ignored the muttered 'per-lease' from her right. 'But I also want you to know that him being here makes no difference to how much I love you both. I know Daddy would agree that if I'm happy you'll be happier too. And Oliver being here does make me happy. Yes, Em. He does. That's why he's going to live here with us.' She ignored her daughter's furious look. 'And he'll make you happy too, if you give him a chance.'

'I don't think so.' Emma stood up again. 'You can do what you want, Mum, but that doesn't mean I have to accept it.'

'I'm sure we'll get used to one another,' Oliver chipped in. 'Look, I'm not going to take your mother away from you. In fact, we've decided that I'll help her in the gallery on Saturdays so she can spend more time with you at the weekend.'

Ellen rather wished he'd left it to her to tell the children this. Too late.

'The gallery!' Emma's face was suddenly suffused with colour. 'So you're not just content with the house and Mum, you're getting in there too. That's her special place.' She dashed away a tear that ran down her cheek.

'Em!' Although shocked by the strength of Emma's feelings, Ellen was also dismayed to realise how much her daughter must be hurting. She had never heard her speak to anyone like that. She went to embrace her but Emma twisted away, raising her left shoulder against her to shut her out.

'Don't touch me. I'm going out. I'll stay at Freya's tonight.'

'When will you be back?' Ellen asked hopelessly. 'I'd thought we might all go to that new cartoon at the Vue tomorrow night.'

'For God's sake, Mum!' Emma's scorn was painful to hear. 'I'm not ten any more. Take Matt. He'll love it.' And she was gone, so quickly that Ellen had no time even to ask her to change her skirt.

'Well, that went well,' offered Oliver. 'What about you, Matt? Think it's a good idea?'

'It's OK,' Matt muttered, although he looked shaken by the fall-out between his mother and sister. Ellen was aware of him watching her, his face screwed up into a frown. 'Do you think Em'll come back?'

'Of course she will, darling. She's just got to get used to the idea.' Yes, given time, Emma would find other things to obsess her; what was happening at home would eventually take second, third or fourth place.

'Oliver? Will you be getting a season ticket for Arsenal if you're going to be living here?'

They laughed.

'Maybe, just maybe, I will. You never know.' To Ellen's ear, Oliver didn't sound terribly convincing but Matt didn't notice.

'Wicked! Can I watch that *Top Gear* now?'

Ellen gave in. 'Go on, then.'

As they watched him take the stairs two at a time, the only one of them still smiling was Oliver.

33

As Ellen let herself in through the front door on Wednesday evening, she was thinking about the success of Jed's show when she noticed that all the paintings in the hallway had been moved around. She looked up the stairs to see that the familiar pictures that belonged there had been changed too. Oliver must have rehung her entire collection. She sat at the foot of the stairs, giving herself a moment in which to ready herself for the evening ahead. However well meant, his inability to leave her house alone was getting too much. She usually looked forward to coming home but she knew the atmosphere downstairs between him and Emma would be tense, Matt would be unhappy, and she would have to referee as well as being grateful for Oliver's latest efforts.

In the few days since he'd moved in, he had already reordered the kitchen drawers ('so much easier to find everything'), moved her books around ('alphabetical means you can find them'), tidied away things she wanted to places where they couldn't be found ('a tidy house is a tidy mind'). Without intending to, he was turning the place into something that no longer felt like her home. Why didn't she say anything? She'd asked herself that question over and over again. The answer boiled down to her fear of any conversation that would confirm her deep-rooted suspicion that, by overreacting to Bea's interfering, she had made a snap decision that was too difficult to unpick without causing more damage. Loss of face with her ex-friends was one thing, but to go back on everything she'd said to the kids, the promise of a happy future together that she'd held out to them . . . that didn't bear thinking about.

Any laughter and shared family pleasures seemed further away than ever. And, if she had to acknowledge the truth, the problem didn't lie with her or the children but with Oliver. She had imagined that he would approach them and the whole house with the sensitivity and charm that had attracted her to him in the first place. How wrong she'd been. Ever since he had arrived with his suitcase and taken his things to her room, she had felt uneasy. Fortunately, his judicious editing of her wardrobe meant that there was now plenty of room for his clothes. As she watched him hang his suits, jackets and trousers in Simon's side of the cupboard, she felt a renewed familiar ache at the loss of her husband. Would it never go away? Somehow Oliver's physical presence in the space that had only ever been occupied by Simon made his absence more final. Oliver in her bed was one thing. His using Simon's cupboards and drawers, putting his toothbrush into the slot that had always held Simon's suddenly seemed something else altogether. She told herself not to be so stupid.

The only thing that hadn't changed was the sex. Behind the bedroom door, Oliver was as attentive and loving as ever. When she was alone with him, although she rarely was now there was no flat to run to, Ellen still knew exactly why she wanted to spend her life with him. But outside the bedroom, he was a different man. The dual nature of his personality completely baffled her. If she tried to approach him about it, he changed the subject, persuading her that they had done the right thing, but he was tense about his lack of a job, his relationship with the children. Yet, despite all his earlier promises, he appeared to do nothing about rectifying either. Not wanting to accept that things might have gone wrong so fast, she was nonetheless beginning to wonder who the stranger she had let into her home really was.

She roused herself, knowing she couldn't sit on the stairs all evening. After all, she was the one who kept the show on the road. Without her to keep the wheels of the family oiled, everything would grind to a halt or, at the rate they were going, crash. She always consoled herself with the thought that perhaps the next evening would be different. Eventually something would have to snap into place to make things work. As she approached the top of the basement stairs, stopping to look at the pictures Oliver had chosen to hang there, she realised he had done her a favour. Seeing the paintings and prints in their new positions made her look at them in a new light. She paused in front of the Caroline Fowler print she'd bought for herself as a reminder of her meeting Oliver.

Absorbed in Fowler's trademark vibrant colours, she was brought back to earth by Oliver and Emma shouting at each other. She couldn't make out what was being said, but as she raced to the stairs, she heard the unmistakable and shocking sound of a slap, followed by a silence, then Emma yelling, 'If you ever touch me again, I'll kill you.'

Ellen dropped her bag and ran down the stairs to be confronted by her daughter, a hand pressed to her right cheek, her eyes welling with angry tears. 'Mum!'

'Whatever's going on?'

Oliver was standing by the french windows, his face flushed, his body rigid. He was rubbing his right hand against his thigh and in the left he held a tiny orange jumper. Startled by Ellen's appearance, his expression changed. The anger that she had read in his narrowed eyes and clenched jaw immediately mutated into something approaching shame and embarrassment. If anything, he reminded her of a dog which knew it had been caught doing something wrong. Then, just as quickly, his self-confidence began to reassert itself.

'I'm so sorry. I snapped. I should never have done that. I'm sorry, Em. I really am. But it is my favourite jumper.'

Ellen remembered the gorgeous burnt-orange sweater that he had worn when they had eaten out a couple of nights earlier. A tiny bit of her wanted to laugh at its demise but the situation demanded a different response.

'I was only trying to help.' Emma choked out the words between sobs. 'I didn't know it was in the basket.'

Ellen instinctively went straight to her, putting a protective arm around her shoulders, giving her a kiss on the cheek. She could feel the tension in her daughter's body yield a little. Matt sidled over to stand beside them, the three of them together.

'You hit Em because your precious jumper's been shrunk?' She spoke slowly, weighing every word, disbelieving and outraged. 'Is that what this is about?'

'It was a mistake.'

'Damn right it was a mistake. Are you OK, Em?' She got a nod and a sniff for a reply. 'Good. Then why don't you guys go upstairs and watch a bit of telly? I think Oliver and I have some things we need to say to each other.'

As the children trooped upstairs, Ellen could hear the clicking of Oliver's nails, one against another. Her own hands were shaking, her fury making her feel sick. She sat at the table, shocked to the core that she could have misread Oliver's character so completely. She contained herself until she thought Matt and Emma were out of earshot, then spoke, her voice soft but icy clear. 'How dare you lay a finger on either of them? I know she can be difficult but nothing gives you the right to punish them like that. Nothing.'

'Ellen. Calm down. It's not as bad as it looks. It was just a tap and she's overreacting.' A hint of a smile hovered on his lips, then disappeared as he realised she was not going to be so easily reconciled.

'A tap! Since when did you start "tapping" my children?' She felt as if she might explode with anger.

'Look, I've said I'm sorry and I am. I truly am. It won't happen again. I'd spent the last half-hour trying to talk to her and she snubbed every attempt. She was sullen and rude. When I saw what she'd done to my jumper, it was the last straw.'

'But this is a difficult time for her. You're an adult, for

God's sake, and you should be able to understand. As for your jumper, she didn't do it on purpose.'

'Are you sure?' He pulled out a chair and sat opposite her, his expression designed to appeal to her sense of fair play. He laid the jumper between them.

'You're suggesting that she deliberately ruined it?' She spoke with disbelief. It certainly wasn't beyond Emma to have put the jumper in the wash on purpose, but even so, Oliver was way out of order.

'Nothing would surprise me. She hates me.'

'You're a grown man, not a two-year-old,' she spat. At that moment she knew for certain that bringing Oliver into their lives had been a terrible mistake. And the sooner she undid the arrangement, the better for all of them. It was as if a light had been switched on and she could see the way forward at last. With the realisation came a new strength of purpose. Everything had changed between them in the last fifteen minutes. Never mind what had happened over the last few months, his unforgivable lack of control had brought things to a head. Without thinking, Oliver had given her the opportunity to put things right. She closed her eyes and took a deep breath, trying to keep herself steady.

'I think we need to talk. Don't say anything.' She stood up and walked over to the sink where she leaned with her back against the worktop. 'I've been thinking a lot over the last few days—'

'I know I haven't been myself,' he interrupted, apologetic, pushing his chair back.

Ellen raised both her hands, palms towards him,

signalling that she didn't want him near her. 'Just listen to what I've got to say.' She spoke slowly, with purpose. 'Your moving in here isn't making any of us happy. The children are miserable and the atmosphere's unbearable. I've tried so hard and really hoped things would change and we could make it work, but now this. I'm sorry, but I think it's better to end things now, before they get any worse.' There. She'd said it.

'You don't mean that.' His shock was evident as he slumped back in his chair. Yet within seconds he had begun to recover himself, sitting up and gazing at her in that compelling way he had.

'I do. I really do.' To her frustration, she began to cry.

'Ellen, Ellen. Think about what you're saying.' His voice was soothing, seductive. 'We've just got off to a bad start, that's all. I know I'm to blame for being such a moody sod, but I've had a lot on my mind. Give me another chance and I'll show you how good it can be.'

'I can't.' She wiped the tears from her cheeks with the back of her hand. 'Don't you see how much there is at stake here for me? You've hit one of my children.'

'But I'll make it up to her. I can do that.' He was calm, reassuring, persuasive.

'I doubt it. I know her. It's almost as if you've gone out of your way to alienate her and now it's too late. Can't you see that?' She sniffed and reached for a bit of kitchen roll. 'You've got to move out before things get worse.'

'Where to?' His face was hidden, bent over the table, but his voice was a whisper.

'I don't know. Go to your friends in Cardiff or wherever they are!'

'Cardiff? There aren't any friends in Cardiff. There's no one.' He looked up at her at last, his voice steady, his eyes glittering. 'I understand that you're shocked and angry but you can't throw away everything we have. I won't let you. Look at me,' he pleaded. 'Look. This won't happen again. You have my word.'

She shook her head, muttering, 'No, don't,' as he stood up. But he ignored her and crossed the room to stand facing her. He held both her arms, trapping her.

For a moment his touch cancelled out everything, then the image of Emma's tear-streaked face with one cheek splotched red came back to her. She couldn't possibly love a man who lashed out at her children. It changed everything. She could forgive a lot but not this.

'You've got a week to find somewhere. And don't you dare lay a finger on Em again. However bolshy she may be.' She tried to move out of his grasp.

'I knew you'd understand. I'll prove to you that I can make it work. Nothing like this will ever happen again, I promise.' He tightened his grip on her right arm while he stroked her hair off her forehead with his other hand.

At that moment she realised this wouldn't be easy. He was going to try to win her over, just as he had before. He hadn't listened properly to a word she'd said. Why not? Because he didn't understand the gravity of his offence, or because he didn't want to? Torn by her own feelings, which still split her so neatly down the middle, Ellen didn't know how to respond. He had crossed a boundary and would have to leave.

She would insist when the week was up. But a tiny shaming bit of her was glad that she would still have him for a little bit longer. That it wasn't quite over yet.

*

That night after Oliver had gone to bed, Ellen sat up alone in the kitchen reluctant to join him. Instead, she nursed a cup of tea and went over the events of the last five months. How could what had begun as something so special have turned into this nightmare? He loves me, he loves me not . . . I love him, I love him not. If only she had Bea and Kate to ask for advice. But she had chosen to bust up their friendship because she had felt betrayed. There had been times during the days since the private view that she had almost picked up the phone to Kate but had stopped herself, just as she had deleted Kate's missed calls. She needed her two best friends and everything they gave her. But why on earth had Bea not talked to her before starting out on her ridiculous detective work?

Could she manage without the pair of them? She would have to. All she had to do was stick to her resolve and take charge of her own life. She had put a chain of events in motion that had ended in one of her children being hurt. That was her responsibility. This mess was hers and she had to sort it out and live with the consequences. But how? She sat there for ages, hardly aware of the time passing, but still a solution eluded her. Her last thought before she took herself upstairs was that perhaps she should get in touch with Kate after all.

34

They'd be here very soon. Ellen checked her watch – Simon's large Tissot that she'd worn since his death. She had ten minutes in which to pace around the kitchen, wondering what she would say when they arrived. Oliver had gone out earlier. She hadn't asked his plans. She was just relieved that she hadn't had to think of a pretext to get him out of the house. She didn't want him there when Bea and Kate arrived. Her eagerness to see her friends was matched by her apprehension about what they would say to one another. This was the longest she had ever gone without speaking to at least one or other of them.

It had been her mistake. Instead of shielding herself with voicemail, she had picked up the phone without thinking. It was Kate. She had been insistent that the three of them meet, refusing to take no for an answer. But although she was glad to hear her friend's voice, Ellen had stood her ground too. When Kate suggested meeting in a café, she refused. She recognised that on neutral ground the chances were that she would fall back into what she saw as her role in the group: to be the weakest and least confident. But she wasn't that person any more. She had changed and she wanted Kate and Bea to realise that. Being on her home turf would give her the confidence she needed for their first reunion. For the same reason she had refused to meet immediately. Kate had wanted them to get together 'as soon as we can, to sort this out once and for all', but Ellen was determined to be the one who chose when they met, as well as where. Small things, but they made her feel in control. Finally it was agreed they would meet the following Sunday morning at Ellen's when the children were out: Matt at football and Emma shopping with Freya.

Ellen was longing to roll back the weeks to the way things had been. She had so much to tell Kate and Bea. She had not entirely forgiven Bea's meddling but time and changed circumstances made her appreciate that Bea had acted out of friendship, not malice.

The few days since she'd asked Oliver to leave had been almost intolerable. He had been making enormous efforts to win the kids over to his side, to make her relent. The house was spotless. He cooked the children's favourite meals. He returned home with books or DVDs they might enjoy. He attempted to engage them in conversation about football, school, their friends. He behaved as if nothing had changed when, of course, everything had. Emma was implacable, studiously ignoring him and his presents. Matt was confused, unsure whose side to take, obviously wishing life would go back to how it had been before. Ellen seemed to be forever hovering, anxious in case Oliver lashed out again. But he had completely reverted to the charming man she had first known, which confused and tested her resolve to the limit. In bed, she couldn't refuse him. To her shame. That was her weakness and they both knew it. But every now and then she heard the crack of his hand across Emma's face, and her determination to make him leave was reconfirmed. But still there were no signs of him moving out and she knew she was reaching a point at which she would somehow have to force him to go.

At last the bell rang. She ran up the stairs to the door. Although they embraced like the old friends they were, there was a noticeable tension between them. Ellen sent them into the sitting room while she went downstairs to get coffee. By the time she returned, Kate and Bea were sitting in the chairs on either side of the fireplace, leaving the sofa between them for her.

'Why are you looking so serious? I thought you were here to clear the air.' She passed the mugs to them – skimmed milk, no sugar – before sitting down.

'We are,' Kate replied. 'But before we do, you've got to listen to what Bea has to say.'

Ellen tensed. 'I thought we'd been through all that.'

'We have. And I agree with you that Bea shouldn't have got so involved.' They both looked at Bea, who was concentrating on picking at the middle fingernail of her left hand. 'But I've heard her out and I think she was right. You have to listen to her too. Then perhaps you'll understand.'

'You do know Oliver's moved in?' She experienced a frisson of pleasure at their surprise.

Bea and Kate looked at one another, their expressions difficult to read: Bea's instant scowl made Ellen stop short of telling them what had happened. While she wanted nothing more than to be able to talk everything through with them, as she would have in the old days, she still didn't want to give them the satisfaction of knowing they had been right all along. She disliked the idea of them judging her, especially when she'd been so wrong.

'That doesn't make any difference,' said Kate, firmly. 'What you do with what she's found out is up to you. But you should at least know. Just hear her out.'

Ellen understood that if she wanted their friendship again, she had no alternative but to agree. She sighed and sat down on the sofa between them. 'Go on, then.'

Bea began to speak, hesitant at first, then gaining confidence as she went along. She explained how what had begun almost as an idle game had become much more. She tracked her route to Mary Keeting and on to Suzanne. As she related Suzanne's story, the abuse and the extortion, Ellen's eyes widened and she leaned forward in the sofa, picking up the photos that Bea held out to her.

'I know about Suzanne,' she interrupted. 'Oliver told me. But you've got it wrong. Oliver says he was the victim in this. He was the one who was hurt.' Despite everything that had happened between them, she still wanted to believe the best of him. He wouldn't have lied to her – would he?

'I'm sorry, but that's not true,' said Bea. 'I've met Suzanne.'

'She must be lying. No one would admit to what she did. Surely you understand that.'

'But I've met his wife too.'

'What?' Ellen gave a little cry. 'Don't be stupid. He's not married. He would have said.' But Bea's face told her it was the truth. However badly they fell out, Bea would never exaggerate or lie over something so important. She sat frozen, feeling completely numb.

Kate moved to sit beside her. 'I'm sorry,' she murmured. 'I really am.'

Ellen looked at Bea who was holding out a piece of paper. She was saying something but Ellen didn't understand. The words were rushing through her brain, confusing her. She took the paper, a photocopy of an article that Bea had found in the *Edinburgh Evening News*. As she began to read her face paled and she began quietly to cry. When she stopped, it was her turn to talk.

*

Half an hour later they heard Oliver let himself in. 'Ellen! Are you there? I've brought you some flowers.'

When he saw the three women sitting together, obviously deep in conversation that he had interrupted, he stopped. 'Hallo! What's going on?' He crossed the room to give the deep red tulips to Ellen. 'Aren't they gorgeous?'

When nobody spoke, he looked puzzled. 'Ellen? Are you all right?'

'I know about Suzanne . . .' Ellen began, not sure yet exactly what she was going to say, despite having talked it through with her friends. She had to do this her way, not theirs.

'Of course you do. I told you everything.'

'You lied to me. Don't!' Shaking off the hand that he tried to lay on her arm seemed to give her strength. 'I know about Marion and Natalie too.'

'You can't.' His composure cracked. He glanced at Bea, who stared directly at him but said nothing. He leaned against the mantelpiece for support, and unbuttoned his jacket as if giving himself time to think.

'Oliver, I do. I know everything now. Why didn't you tell me that you're married? That you have a daughter.' Still a little part of her wanted him to prove it was all a lie, even though she knew it wasn't.

'But that was over long ago. That's got nothing to do with us. The divorce is just a formality.' There was the familiar click of his thumb and middle-finger nails again.

'The fact you didn't tell me makes it everything to do with us.'

'We can't talk about this with Kate and Bea here.' He nodded towards the door, sounding desolate. 'Why don't you leave us alone so we can sort it out?'

They both looked towards Ellen, who shook her head.

'Oliver, there's nothing to sort out.' Ellen stood and faced him, her fists clenched so he wouldn't see her hands shaking. 'It's over. It was over when you slapped Em. I should never have let you stay then. Now you're leaving. Bea, Kate and I will go downstairs while you pack your things.'

'You're not thinking straight,' he blustered. 'You've got to listen to me. Please.'

She looked at him, as if for the first time. A handsome man, but his blue eyes were empty. There was no feeling for her in them any more. There was just panic. His first concern was how to save himself. 'I thought I loved you,' she said. 'I trusted you. But now I see you're not the sort of person I want near my children, or near me. You hit Em.

You assaulted your wife and Suzanne. That's enough. I don't want to hear any more.'

'But where am I going to go?' He bit his bottom lip, as he finally understood that she meant what she'd said, that there was no going back.

She shrugged, a feeling of liberation sweeping through her. 'I don't know. You'll find something. But you can't stay here. I'll come up to say goodbye when you're ready.' She turned and left the room, the other two behind her.

Downstairs, Ellen collapsed onto a kitchen chair, her legs feeling as if they'd never support her again. For a few minutes, they sat alone with their thoughts. Then Kate went over to put on the kettle. 'More coffee, anyone?' she asked.

Bea immediately leaped to her feet, crossed to the fridge and pulled out a bottle of white wine. 'To hell with more coffee. I don't know about you two but I definitely need something stronger. Ellen, you were fantastic. I didn't know you had it in you.' She found three glasses in the dishwasher and set about washing and drying them.

'Are you all right?' Kate asked Ellen, concerned. 'You're awfully pale.'

'I feel such a fool. What an idiot. How could I have been so completely taken in?' She felt exhausted.

'You'll be better prepared next time,' said Bea, wincing as Kate smacked her arm to silence her.

'You're probably in shock,' suggested Kate. 'I'm going to make that coffee for you anyway. With lots of sugar.'

'My God, Bea. You went to France and Edinburgh for me?' The enormity of the lengths to which Bea had gone on her behalf struck Ellen for the first time.

'I had to,' said Bea. 'I know I probably went too far, but at the time there didn't seem to be a choice. And, let's face it, I'm glad I did. It wasn't all bad, though.' She smiled, remembering the night she had spent with Mark in Edinburgh.

'How could I have done what I did to the children?'

'You made a mistake. Simple. And they don't need to know about Suzanne and Marion.' Kate joined her at the table while Bea gave them their glasses.

'And what would have I done without you both?'

'Got out of it a little slower, that's all.' Bea pulled the cork and poured. 'You'd already told him to go, remember? The cavalry – that's all we were.' She went over to the french windows and looked out. 'Hate that shed, by the way!'

Ellen began to giggle, her laughter growing louder as the tension of the last few weeks was released. Bea and Kate couldn't stop themselves joining in.

Eventually they calmed down, her two friends looking ashamed at behaving so inappropriately while Ellen was left utterly drained, her relief that Oliver was going tinged with sadness. She was aware that a tough emotional road lay ahead as she absorbed what had happened over the past months, but she was sure she was strong enough to weather whatever storms blew her way and face life alone again. And with friends like these . . . Then she remembered Oliver was still upstairs. 'Where's he going to go?'

'Not your problem,' said Bea. 'He's got this far in life without you. He'll sort himself out.'

'I'd better go up.' At least she should say goodbye.

'Are you sure? Wouldn't you like one of us to come with

you?' They both got up to accompany her. She stopped them.

'No. This is something I've got to do on my own.' As she climbed the stairs, she registered the silence that possessed the upper floors of the house. 'Oliver!' There was no reply. She ran up the stairs to her bedroom and pushed open the door. He wasn't in there. She pulled open the wardrobe doors. His side was empty. His case had gone from under the bed, his washbag from the side of the bath, the book he was reading from his side of the bed. She checked the other bathroom. Empty. He had gone – left without even a farewell. But what had she expected? As she went down to tell the others, she noticed a ghostly square on the hall wall that marked the spot where her Caroline Fowler print had hung. Surprised, she checked to see that it hadn't just fallen to the floor, the string broken. No. Not content with having sold *Starship*, Oliver had made off with her own memento from the exhibition where they had met.

'Kate! Bea!' She raced downstairs. 'He's gone! Without a goodbye and – I can't believe it – he's bloody well stolen a picture.'

'He can't have got far. I'll go after him.' Bea was slipping her shoes on, ready.

'No, no. Leave him.' Ellen was resigned. That part of her life was over. 'He's welcome to it. But I still can't help wondering where he's taken it.'

'Don't,' said Kate. 'He's gone and you've had a lucky escape. It'll be hard but you've got to put him out of your mind and concentrate on the children. Do you think they'll be all right?'

'All right? They might need a bit of time to readjust again but I'd say they'll be celebrating.' Ellen smiled, imagining their faces when they discovered Oliver had gone for good.

Just at that moment, the french windows opened and the three women turned as Jed came into the kitchen. His hair unbrushed, paint stains on his cheek and fingers, dressed in a faded paint-daubed blue boiler-suit with a couple of brushes in the breast pocket, he nodded at them. 'Good afternoon, ladies.' Realising that he was interrupting something private, he put his mug into the dishwasher and disappeared upstairs. They heard the front door open and shut.

Bea looked after him, open-mouthed. 'Well, Ellen Neill! I'll be damned. Who the hell was that?'

35

A vast grassy meadow sloped away to the valley floor where a white chalk track led through a five-bar gate towards a distant farmhouse. On the south side of the track, woodland rose away into the distance, circling round to encompass the meadow to its east and north sides. Above, just a few wisps of cloud drifted across the clear blue sky.

Over the brow of the meadow, smoke spiralled upwards from two small bonfires a hundred yards apart where two families had set up camp, one with a red motorhome and a canvas tent, the other with a gleaming 4x4 and two bright state-of-the-art dome tents. The barbecue eaten, the adults lay back in their deckchairs. The faint shouts of children playing hide-and-seek emerged from the trees. In the distance, the roar of a dirt bike broke the peace as a boy racer, oblivious to the disturbance he was creating, tore round and round a nearby field before disappearing into the woods. As he reappeared with a roar, just minutes later, the grazing sheep looked up with momentary curiosity, then lowered their heads again, ignoring the lambs frisking by their side or nuzzling for milk.

Into this landscape stepped two walkers. They emerged from a gap in the trees at the height of the meadow before climbing over a stile into the open. They turned round for a moment, as if waiting for someone, then carried on towards the shade offered by a lone oak tree. The one who took the lead was the slighter and fitter-looking of the two. Wearing black trousers, a green T-shirt and sturdy Mendl walking boots, carrying a badly folded Ordnance Survey map in one hand, she covered the distance with a brisk stride, then unknotted a light rain mac from her waist to spread it on the ground. Sitting down, she removed her backpack, unzipped it and pulled out a couple of big bottles of water, two battered bananas and four apples. She unscrewed the blue plastic top from one of the bottles, tipped her head back so her dark bob fell away from her face as she drank, revealing a neat profile. She wiped her mouth with the back of her hand before balancing the bottle upright on the grass.

Her friend was dressed almost identically except that a red and orange checked shirt replaced the T-shirt. She caught up, sinking onto the grass with no mac to untie and sit on. Her short grey hair gave the immediate impression of a rather older woman when, in fact, she was three years younger. They looked as though this was something they did often, comfortable in each other's company. She took a swig from the bottle, then started to pull out food from her own backpack: oatcakes, hummus, nuts and raisins, a packet of biscuits.

Finally out of the woods and over the stile came the third member of the party. Every step she took towards her friends spelled EXHAUSTED. Navy-blue shorts that had seen better, looser days and a mint green shirt flapping half open over a maroon T-shirt were further put to shame by the deep green suede walking boots, complete with tan leather trim. Strands of streaked blonde hair stuck to the sweat on her forehead. Her face, pink with exertion, had a determined set as she trudged across the grass to join the others.

'My feet are killing me,' Bea groaned, as she plumped herself down beside them. 'How much further have we got to go?' She took the map and turned it round, trying to work out where they were on their intended route. 'Oh, God. I can't see a bloody thing. I've left my reading glasses in the car. I give up.' She lay back with a great sigh.

'Mind the hummus, Bea!' Kate snatched the pot away. 'If you hadn't insisted on getting such fancy boots, instead of that pair I suggested, you'd probably be fine. Comfort over colour, every time. Would a Compeed help?' She rustled in one of the outside pockets of her backpack to produce a bright green packet of blister plasters.

'I know. I know. But I couldn't resist these. The colour's brilliant, you've got to admit.' Bea sat up, tugged off her right boot and started peeling off her sock. Then she took out a plaster to stick on her heel. 'Thanks. You're always so organised, Kate. Why can't I be like you?'

'Have an oatcake. Water?' offered Ellen.

'Is that what you call lunch? Oh, God.' Bea groaned again. 'I'd imagined some picturesque country pub with a Michelin-starred chef in the kitchen. It's the only thing that's kept me going. Haven't we even got a bottle of chilled white wine?'

'If we started drinking now,' Ellen reproved her, 'we'd never finish the walk. We've got another four or five miles to go and that's if we take the short-cut through the woods.'

'Can't we go back the way we came, then? I'm not sure my legs will hold up.'

'We're more than halfway now so we might just as well carry on,' said Kate. 'We'll find a pub next time. Promise. So, have an apple and some water and shut up!'

Knowing she was beaten, Bea did as she was told. The three ate their rations and lay back under the tree, watching the sunlight through the leaves, resting until they felt sufficiently recovered to continue. Ellen and Kate had walked together before and had established their own routine. Out of town, away from their families, they'd always enjoyed the countryside, rain or shine, relishing the physical exertion and the confirmation of their friendship that they found in walking and talking together for uninterrupted hours, going on until they were almost dropping. Bea, confirmed townie and fair-weather walker, only joined them when the weather forecast left her in no doubt.

'So when are you going back to Africa?' Ellen broke the silence.

'Going back? What's this?' Bea sat up. 'The two of you have only just come home.'

'I know,' said Kate. 'But I haven't had a chance to tell you. I've decided to take a sabbatical from the partnership so that Paul and I can join VSO as volunteers.' She laughed at Bea's incredulous expression and began to explain. 'You know how much we got out of our incredible trip to see Sam?'

'Judging from the number of photos – a lot.' Bea and Ellen had spent a late March evening poring over them and listening to travellers' tales straight after Kate and Paul had got home.

'You only got the edited highlights, pal. Anyway, that's not the point. We were so inspired by what Sam and his team are doing, we've decided that instead of stagnating in our child-free zone, we should do something and see the world at the same time. Not in the same place, of course, but wherever we can be sent in Africa. We're going to let the house for a year and see where we end up.'

'What about Jack?'

'He's moved out. Got himself a job with a TV production company and a flat in Brockwell Park. He comes home every now and then but he doesn't really need us any more. So we're off to see the world.'

'Good for you.' Bea clapped. 'Ellen and I will keep the home fires burning, won't we? In fact, she'll probably be masterminding a major gallery by the time you get back.'

'Steady on,' Ellen cautioned her. 'We've only just opened up into the top floor. There's a way to go yet.'

'From the woman who was never going to work with anyone else,' teased Bea. 'And within six months of meeting the guy . . .'

'I know.' Ellen sounded almost apologetic. 'But Jed has been fantastic. Having him on board as a partner in the gallery has meant that I've been able to expand. He doesn't get involved in the day-to-day running of the place but he's helped me out of a potentially nasty financial spot.'

'Is that all he's helping with?' Bea rolled onto her stomach so she could see Ellen's face.

'What are you implying?' She was definitely blushing.

'I just thought you might be dipping your toe in the old romance stakes again,' Bea teased.

'Oh, Bea, leave her alone.' But Kate was smiling.

'Well, he is a dear man and the children adore him.' Ellen was thoughtful as she pulled at a blade of grass.

'Well, that's half the battle won. What's stopping you?'

'I learned my lesson. And I'm still thanking God no lasting harm was done to any of us. We're taking things very slowly indeed. There's too much at stake. I'm happy with the way we are – good friends. He's been such a support since Oliver left.'

'You haven't heard from him, have you?'

'Not a word. And I haven't tried to find him. Why would I? No, I'm enjoying spending time with someone who likes me for who I am and who isn't in a hurry.' Ellen began to repack her backpack. 'Hadn't we better get going?'

'That's so like you to change the subject.' Bea laughed. 'But I'll be emailing you, Kate, with all the latest developments.'

'The poor woman won't dare make a move if you're keeping an eye on her. Come on, get your boots back on, Bea.' Kate was already on her feet, squinting into the sun as she looked about for a footpath sign.

'Don't worry,' said Ellen. 'I'll be careful, I promise. There's no way I'll make the same mistake again.' She looked pensive as she hoisted her pack onto her back. 'But I would like to find someone to share things with.

I know that now. And perhaps Jed *is* him. Although I made a terrible mistake, Oliver did show me that I could let someone else into my life. I can't be the grieving widow for ever. I've got a few good years left and I want to make the most of them.'

'Well said!' Bea grimaced with pain as she pushed her feet into her boots, tied the laces and, wincing, put her weight on them. 'I never thought I'd hear you say that.'

'Nor me.' Kate had turned to face down the hill, route sorted. 'But I think it's bloody fantastic. And if Jed's the one, then good luck to you.'

Ellen walked on to catch up with her, Bea going slower, gingerly testing out the blister plaster behind her.

'Now all we need to do is find someone for Bea.'

'No, thanks. I'm very happy with my arrangement with Mark, odd as it may seem to you. We're keeping our separate places. That works for us. Anyway, I need the other half of my bed for all the manuscripts – I'm never going to get to grips with my e-reader. It's just not the same.'

'Haven't you sorted out an office yet?' Ellen was only asking about what Bea had promised herself immediately she had negotiated her terms of leaving with Coldharbour. Knowing she was fighting a losing battle with Amanda, she had decided to take Adele's advice and forge a new path for herself.

'I haven't got round to that. Since I took myself out of office life, I've been inundated with freelance work – editing, rewriting, even a bit of journalism – so I've decided I'm going to set up my own editorial consultancy called Write On, and see how it goes. Thanks to Mum giving me that money when the house was finally sold, I can afford to do it properly and employ someone to help me.'

'How's she getting on anyway?' Kate asked, striding ahead.

'Happy as Larry. She loves the flat, being there with Janey and her new neighbours. It's worked out brilliantly.' Bea stopped, hands on hips, pink-faced. 'Do you have to walk so fast?'

'Come on. It's good for you.' Ellen and Kate turned and grinned at their friend.

'So you say,' she protested, before putting one foot in front of the other to match their pace. 'And there's one other thing. You know I went to that chocolate-tasting event I told you about the other night – which incidentally was amazing? Well, I'm going to take a chocolate-making course!'

'You're not!'

'I am. So who knows? Maybe one day I'll become one of the world's master *chocolatières*. Only joking,' she added, as she saw the surprise on Ellen and Kate's faces. 'But I am going to do the course. I'm pursuing my passion, that's what. How many more miles do we have to go? I honestly don't think I'll make it.'

'Of course you will. But if you're really worried we could take the short-cut through the woods . . . here.' Kate ran her finger over the map to show the new route. 'It seems quite easy.'

'Looks good to me. Let's do it.'

An hour later, they stood in a clearing where two paths crossed the one they were on. Beside them, a rack for fire beaters stood empty. Around them ranks of pine trees stretched away in every direction as far as the eye could see. Dried grass, fallen branches and pine cones littered the ground. The daylight couldn't penetrate the thick interlocking needles so, within a few feet of the trail, there was an eerie near-darkness. The only birdsong they could hear was the guttural squawk and clatter of an occasional pheasant. High above them, the earlier wisps of cloud had built up into greying cumuli that intermittently blew across the sun, stealing the warmth of the day. Bea was holding the map at arm's length, her left eye shut tight as she attempted to make sense of what she could read with the other.

'Kate. Where do you think we are?' She was doing her best not to let her impatience show.

'Look, we walked into the wood here, took this path straight up the hill, then the third main pathway to the left, so we should be here.' She pointed at a spot that even Bea could see was on the edge of a field.

'Well, we're not, are we? We're still in the middle of the trees. In fact there are so many paths running through this wretched wood that we could be on any of the crossways. God knows which dotted line we took off the main track.' She took a few steps up the path to the right of them. 'This looks more major than the rest. What if we take this?'

The other two agreed, Kate having abandoned the role of leader for the moment and Ellen knowing full well that, once Bea had the bit between her teeth, there was no stopping her. Nonetheless, Bea was surprised, not to say slightly alarmed, that she had so readily assumed responsibility for getting them home. For a moment, her aching thighs and burning heel were forgotten.

retched away in every direction as far as the eye could see. Dried grass, fallen branches and pine cones littered the ground. The daylight couldn't penetrate the thick interlocking needles so, within a few feet of the trail, there was an eerie near-darkness. The only birdsong they could hear was the guttural squawk and clatter of an occasional pheasant. High above them, the earlier wisps of cloud had built up into greying cumuli that intermittently blew across the sun, stealing the warmth of the day. Bea was holding the map at arm's length, her left eye shut tight as she attempted to make sense of what she could read with the other.

'Kate. Where do you think we are?' She was doing her best not to let her impatience show.

'Look, we walked into the wood here, took this path straight up the hill, then the third main pathway to the left, so we should be here.' She pointed at a spot that even Bea could see was on the edge of a field.

'Well, we're not, are we? We're still in the middle of the trees. In fact there are so many paths running through this wretched wood that we could be on any of the crossways. God knows which dotted line we took off the main track.' She took a few steps up the path to the right of them. 'This looks more major than the rest. What if we take this?'

The other two agreed, Kate having abandoned the role of leader for the moment and Ellen knowing full well that, once Bea had the bit between her teeth, there was no stopping her. Nonetheless, Bea was surprised, not to say slightly alarmed, that she had so readily assumed responsibility for getting them home. For a moment, her aching thighs and burning heel were forgotten.

'Is that all he's helping with?' Bea rolled onto her stomach so she could see Ellen's face.

'What are you implying?' She was definitely blushing.

'I just thought you might be dipping your toe in the old romance stakes again,' Bea teased.

'Oh, Bea, leave her alone.' But Kate was smiling.

'Well, he is a dear man and the children adore him.' Ellen was thoughtful as she pulled at a blade of grass.

'Well, that's half the battle won. What's stopping you?'

'I learned my lesson. And I'm still thanking God no lasting harm was done to any of us. We're taking things very slowly indeed. There's too much at stake. I'm happy with the way we are – good friends. He's been such a support since Oliver left.'

'You haven't heard from him, have you?'

'Not a word. And I haven't tried to find him. Why would I? No, I'm enjoying spending time with someone who likes me for who I am and who isn't in a hurry.' Ellen began to repack her backpack. 'Hadn't we better get going?'

'That's so like you to change the subject.' Bea laughed. 'But I'll be emailing you, Kate, with all the latest developments.'

'The poor woman won't dare make a move if you're keeping an eye on her. Come on, get your boots back on, Bea.' Kate was already on her feet, squinting into the sun as she looked about for a footpath sign.

'Don't worry,' said Ellen. 'I'll be careful, I promise. There's no way I'll make the same mistake again.' She looked pensive as she hoisted her pack onto her back. 'But I would like to find someone to share things with.

I know that now. And perhaps Jed *is* him. Although I made a terrible mistake, Oliver did show me that I could let someone else into my life. I can't be the grieving widow for ever. I've got a few good years left and I want to make the most of them.'

'Well said!' Bea grimaced with pain as she pushed her feet into her boots, tied the laces and, wincing, put her weight on them. 'I never thought I'd hear you say that.'

'Nor me.' Kate had turned to face down the hill, route sorted. 'But I think it's bloody fantastic. And if Jed's the one, then good luck to you.'

Ellen walked on to catch up with her, Bea going slower, gingerly testing out the blister plaster behind her.

'Now all we need to do is find someone for Bea.'

'No, thanks. I'm very happy with my arrangement with Mark, odd as it may seem to you. We're keeping our separate places. That works for us. Anyway, I need the other half of my bed for all the manuscripts – I'm never going to get to grips with my e-reader. It's just not the same.'

'Haven't you sorted out an office yet?' Ellen was only asking about what Bea had promised herself immediately she had negotiated her terms of leaving with Coldharbour. Knowing she was fighting a losing battle with Amanda, she had decided to take Adele's advice and forge a new path for herself.

'I haven't got round to that. Since I took myself out of office life, I've been inundated with freelance work – editing, rewriting, even a bit of journalism – so I've decided I'm going to set up my own editorial consultancy called Write On, and see how it goes. Thanks to Mum giving me that

money when the house was finally sold, I can a[f]   s
it properly and employ someone to help me.'

'How's she getting on anyway?' Kate asked, stridi[ng]

'Happy as Larry. She loves the flat, being there wi[th]
and her new neighbours. It's worked out brillian[t]
stopped, hands on hips, pink-faced. 'Do you have t[o]
so fast?'

'Come on. It's good for you.' Ellen and Kate turne[d]
grinned at their friend.

'So you say,' she protested, before putting one foo[t]
front of the other to match their pace. 'And there's o[ne]
other thing. You know I went to that chocolate-tasting ev[ent]
I told you about the other night – which incidentally wa[s]
amazing? Well, I'm going to take a chocolate-making
course!'

'You're not!'

'I am. So who knows? Maybe one day I'll become one of the world's master *chocolatières*. Only joking,' she added, as she saw the surprise on Ellen and Kate's faces. 'But I am going to do the course. I'm pursuing my passion, that's what. How many more miles do we have to go? I honestly don't think I'll make it.'

'Of course you will. But if you're really worried we cou[ld]
take the short-cut through the woods . . . here.' Kate r[an]
her finger over the map to show the new route. 'It se[ems]
quite easy.'

'Looks good to me. Let's do it.'

An hour later, they stood in a clearing where two[paths]
crossed the one they were on. Beside them, a rack f[or]
beaters stood empty. Around them ranks of pin[e]

Half an hour later, they were still walking, apparently no nearer the road than before. 'I can't understand it.' Bea stopped yet again to squint at the map. 'I could have sworn the last crossing must be this one, which means that if we followed that dotted line, we should be at the edge of the wood by now.'

'Let me have a look. You can't even see properly.' Ellen had had enough, aware they should never have entrusted Bea with navigating. 'For God's sake, Bea, that's not a track, it's a county boundary. Heaven knows where we are.' Hesitating on the edge of panic, she began attempting to retrace their steps from the point they'd entered the wood, knowing that it was impossible to remember every turn they'd taken. 'This is hopeless, we'll be wandering around for ever unless we take one direction and keep straight. We'd have to come to the edge of the wood then.'

'And what if we end up on the wrong bloody side of it? We'll be miles from the car park.' Bea's legs were protesting.

'We'll get a taxi or a bus or something back. I don't know.'

'Brilliant idea,' muttered Bea. 'Those lanes were humming with black cabs – not.'

'Well, you suggest something, then.'

'Stop it, you two.' Kate stepped in. 'Show me the map again. I'm going to work this out.' Ellen gladly handed it over. 'Right. We know the car park's to the east of the wood so if we walk keeping the sun behind us, we have to hit this road at some point and then it's only a short road walk to the car.'

'Why is it that this always happens?' Bea sat down by the path and rubbed her aching calves.

'What? Getting lost? It doesn't always happen, just sometimes.' Kate smiled down at her. 'We're not the best map-readers, that's all.' She stuffed the map into Ellen's backpack.

'Not the best? We're hopeless. Are you really abandoning the map altogether to follow the sun?' By this time, Bea was lying back and laughing. 'It's just like life, if you think about it.'

'Why not?' Kate began to laugh with her. 'We'll find our own way out. It's got to work. It's just a matter of common sense.'

Ellen sat down, laughing too. 'She's right. Takes longer but who cares? We've had a great day out.'

'Oh, I know,' said Bea, recovering herself, wincing again at the pain from her blister, then forcing herself to be first up. 'We'll get out of here somehow and get home safe in the end. We always do.'